D1552815

The Book of Whispers

The Book of Whispers

VARUJAN VOSGANIAN

TRANSLATED FROM THE ROMANIAN BY ALISTAIR IAN BLYTH

YALE UNIVERSITY PRESS ■ NEW HAVEN & LONDON

A MARGELLOS
WORLD REPUBLIC OF LETTERS BOOK

The Margellos World Republic of Letters is dedicated to making literary works from around the globe available in English through translation. It brings to the English-speaking world the work of leading poets, novelists, essayists, philosophers, and playwrights from Europe, Latin America, Africa, Asia, and the Middle East to stimulate international discourse and creative exchange.

Yale University Press books may be purchased in quantity for educational, business, or promotional use. For information, please e-mail sales.press@yale.edu (U.S. office) or sales@yaleup.co.uk (U.K. office).

Set in Electra and Nobel type by Tseng Information Systems, Inc.
Printed in the United States of America.

Library of Congress Control Number: 2017937447
ISBN 978-0-300-22346-0 (hardcover : alk. paper)

A catalogue record for this book is available from the British Library.

This paper meets the requirements of ANSI/NISO z39.48-1992 (Permanence of Paper).

10 9 8 7 6 5 4 3 2 1

CONTENTS

Photographs and Whispers

The Book of Whispers is both the title of a novel by Varujan Vosganian and the name of a book that exists prior to the novel, timelessly, outside and beyond the novel, in the memories of its protagonists, the old Armenians of the author's childhood, and in the minds of the living, within whom the voices of the dead make themselves heard in an endless susurrating lament. In this second sense, *The Book of Whispers* is the collective memory and unwritten chronicle of the tragic events that have shaped the modern history of the Armenian people: ethnic and religious persecution, genocide, exodus and exile, Communist totalitarianism: "In *The Book of Whispers*," as the author says, "are inscribed the names of the dead."

Varujan Vosganian is a Romanian-Armenian whose grandparents and great-uncles and aunts escaped from Anatolia in 1915 and settled in Romania, the first state in the world officially to grant asylum to those fleeing from the Armenian Genocide. It should be noted, however, that there was already a considerable Armenian community in Romania at the time; over the course of the previous thousand years, Armenians had settled in the principalities of Moldavia and Wallachia (the two historical regions that, together with Transylvania, make up modern Romania), having been displaced by the fall of medieval dynasties of Armenian kings, by wave after wave of invaders, and by historical upheavals and catastrophes seemingly without end.

But the Armenians who plied the trade routes between East and West also came, establishing themselves as merchants in Moldavian towns such as Focșani, where a large part of *The Book of Whispers* is set. In the novel, the colorful caravans of the Armenian merchants of olden days, who crossed the deserts bringing fruit and spices, throng the imagination of the author as a child. However, the merchant caravans are also a counterpoint to the convoys of Armenians marched to their deaths in the deserts of Mesopotamia, descending through the seven circles of hell to Deir-ez-Zor. As they traveled through the deserts, the Armenian merchants of old kept pomegranate seeds under their tongues to beguile their thirst. The pomegranate, says the author of *The Book of Whispers*, is the fruit of solitude and exodus, whose blood is like that of human suffering; it is

viii *Translator's Introduction*

a symbol of the Armenian people. And for the Armenians of the death marches, pomegranate seeds provided a last speck of enigmatic coolness before they perished in the burning sands of Mesopotamia.

Although *The Book of Whispers* exists in an Armenian version that the author has declared to be an original work of equal weight with the Romanian *Cartea șoaptelor*, first published in 2009, it was in Romanian that the book was first written. Armenians have played a large part in the cultural history of Romania. Notable Armenians born in Romania include Spiru Haret (1851–1912), who made important contributions to mathematics and physics and, as the country's minister of education, reformed the Romanian educational system; the literary critic and writer Garabet Ibrăileanu (1871–1936); the philologist and philosopher Aram Frenkian (1898–1964); Vazken Baljian (1908–1994), Catholicos of the Armenian Apostolic Church from 1953 until his death; and, more recently, the novelists Ștefan Agopian and Bedros Horasangian. Other notable Romanian-Armenians, such as the historian and orientalist Hagop Djololian Siruni (1890–1973), were born in the Ottoman Empire and arrived in Romania as refugees.

Both Hagop Djololian Siruni and Vazken Baljian can be found in the pages of *The Book of Whispers*, all of whose characters are real. Born in the Marmara region, Siruni was an intellectual and a member of the Dashnak Party, a nationalist organization that fought for the rights of Armenians. After the Armenian Genocide began in 1915, Siruni avoided arrest by living in hiding for four years. Three hundred Armenian intellectuals were rounded up by the Young Turks on April 24, 1915, and were the first to perish in the genocide. They included the great Armenian poet Daniel Varujan (1884–1915). As *The Book of Whispers* puts it, "Their enemies knew that in order to annihilate them as a people, they would, without fail, have to kill their poet. To an oppressed and threatened people, the Poet becomes the leader." In 1922, Siruni finally managed to make his way to Romania, where he was welcomed by none other than eminent Romanian historian and statesman Nicolae Iorga (1871–1940). Having escaped arrest by the Young Turks, Siruni was arrested two decades later, after the Red Army's invasion of Romania in 1944. Accused of being "hostile to the Soviet Union," he was deported to a Siberian labor camp and later held under house arrest in Yerevan. Frail and half blind, he was finally able to return to Romania in 1955. In *The Book of Whispers*, Hagop Djololian Siruni is one of the old Armenians of the author's childhood who talked to each other in a whisper.

The whisper is the most intimate form of speech. It is the speech most appropriate to the spiritual intimacy of the confessional: "*The Book of Whispers* is a chronicle not of things lived or imagined but of things confessed." But the whisper is also a sign of fear and wariness, the speech forced upon those who live under a totalitarian regime, where to speak out, to speak aloud, can bring imprisonment, deportation to a labor camp, or death.

The author of *The Book of Whispers* says that his book was perhaps born of another book written one thousand years earlier: *The Book of Lamentations*, by St. Gregory of Narek. (The ancient Armenian monastery of Narek, near Lake Van, was abandoned during the genocide and subsequently razed to the ground by the Turks, part of a "cultural genocide" that has destroyed centuries of Armenian material culture in Anatolia.) For the Armenian people, the passage of a thousand years has been a journey from lamentation to whispers. A thousand years ago, says the author of *The Book of Whispers*, "the people had not yet lost the freedom to weep and, as in Gregory of Narek's hymn to the divinity, . . . God was still close at hand." The journey from weeping to whispers "does not mean that one suffering takes the place of another. Rather, it is merely the difference between weeping and stifled weeping." In one of the most harrowing passages of *The Book of Whispers*, a "German traveler" witnesses the innermost circle of death in the deserts around Deir-ez-Zor and brings back the tale of the dying victims, who wept silently and without tears; theirs was an "uninterrupted groan, in a low voice, which, repeated by thousands of chests, made a droning sound. The weeping was not the streak of tears running down the cheeks but a sound. . . . The weeping did not ebb for an instant, until the convoys were taken from Deir-ez-Zor to the plateaus where the last deportees were killed. That dry weeping took the place of prayers, and of curses, and of silence, and of confession." The ceaseless drone of the dying, which even after death still thrummed in the stilled chests "like a note in an organ pipe," lived on in the whispers of the survivors: "I heard that weeping," says the author of *The Book of Whispers*, "when Grandfather Setrak used to rock back and forth on the chaise longue in the garden or when Grandfather Garabet used to lock himself up in his room and his violin fell silent."

While stationed with a German medical corps attached to the Ottoman Sixth Army in Syria and Mesopotamia, Armin T. Wegner (1886–1978), the "German traveler" of *The Book of Whispers*, witnessed at first hand the convoys of death and the deportation camps where tens of thousands of Armenians perished, and, defying orders aimed at suppressing information about the genocide, he took the photographs that today make up the core of the visual record of the genocide. From antiquity to Genghis Khan, from the conquistadors to colonial Africa, millions upon millions of human beings have been slaughtered and starved, but here, for the first time in history, images of the countless, nameless victims were captured, frozen in time, images that, as the twentieth century wore on, were to multiply. In *The Book of Whispers* photographs remind us that the dead, while countless, are not nameless. In photographs the dead live on: "In *The Book of Whispers*, photographs often take the place of living people. . . . When one of their number disappeared, standing in their dwindling circle, the Armenians put a photograph in his place so that the circle would not be broken. This is why, in their native lands, in the triangle among the three lakes (Van, Sevan, and Urmia), and wherever else they wandered, a photograph was a kind of harbinger of death for the Armenians." In 1915, as if gripped by collective foreboding, the Armenians queued to have their photographs taken by the itinerant photographers who went from town to town and from village to village throughout Anatolia: "It was their way of remaining together because shortly thereafter the families dwindled and were scattered. Even though many perished, in bewilderment and so timidly that to this day their graves have not been found, their faces thus remain imprinted on the sepia cardboard with the fading edges. Wishing at all costs to remind you that they once existed. Feeling a premonition of what was to become of them."

It is no accident that Garabet Vosganian, the author's grandfather and the central character of *The Book of Whispers*, is himself a photographer. He realizes that history, photography, and memory are intertwined and that the photographer cannot stand outside history. As a child, the author assists his grandfather as he attempts to photograph a mirror without capturing his own image: "How to photograph the mirror without seeing yourself in it? How to understand the world while placing yourself outside of it?" Unlike the photograph, the mirror, as Grandfather Garabet understands, has a "short memory"; the mirror is an image of forgetting and therefore of death.

Arshag Svagian, the protagonist of an important episode in *The Book of Whispers*, is regularly called upon by the prosecutor's office to photograph dead bodies but prefers to think of himself as a "photographer of souls" rather than a photographer of the dead. His photographs, Svagian believes, capture the souls of the dead, which reveal themselves as an "inexplicable blotch of light." Summoned by the police to photograph the dead body of Siruni's protector Nicolae Iorga, assassinated by the Iron Guard in 1940, Svagian is for years haunted by the photograph until he finally loses his mind. Death and memory merge in the photograph. Unlike the mirror, the photograph is the antithesis of oblivion.

During the Stalinist period, photographs also served as a means of coded communication between the Armenians who, like the author's uncle Simon, had been lured to emigrate to the supposedly paradisaical new Soviet Armenia and the Armenians who remained behind in the diaspora. As it would turn out, Stalin's object in encouraging the Armenians of the diaspora to come to

Soviet Armenia was in fact to eliminate them as a potential nationalist threat, since they were out of his reach as long as they remained scattered throughout the world. The Armenians who set off to the promised land of Soviet Armenia told those they left behind that they would send photographs; if the figure in the photograph was standing, then all was well; if he was leaning against something, then things were neither good nor bad; if he was sitting, things were bad. When they were finally able to write to their relatives in the diaspora, those who had survived the deportations to Siberia sent photographs in which they were shown lying on the ground.

Photographs stand in for the absent, whether living or dead. But it is hard to imagine a photograph of an absence; just a year or two after the Armenians of Anatolia had their photographs taken in 1915, if by magic their images could have vanished from the photographs when the people themselves died, then "those photographs would have shown a strange sight: empty chairs, walking sticks standing suspended without any support, children hovering in the laps of invisible mothers, mothers wrapping their arms around empty space; they would have looked like the fictions of exorcists in search of a nation of ghosts." The living pass away, but their photographs remain. So too the whispers of the dead live on in the minds and the memories of the living. And at the end of *The Book of Whispers* the late grandfather's voice becomes the living author's inner voice.

Ultimately, the whispers are the voice of the vanquished: "Of all these real-life characters, some of their names you will find in the history books; others you will find only in *The Book of Whispers*. Although more often than not it tells of the past, it is not a history book, for the history books tell of the victors. Rather, it is a collection of psalms; it tells of the vanquished." But as Grandfather Garabet used to say, "Don't be hasty. . . . The one who seems to have won is rarely the true victor. It is the vanquished rather than the victors who have made history. To be victorious is ultimately a way of being written out of history."

The Book of Whispers

"We differ from one another not by what we are but by the dead we each mourn,"
—said my grandfather Garabet

1.

More than anything else, I am what I have not been able to achieve.

Of all the lives I carry, like a bunch of snakes knotted at the tail, the most real is the life unlived. I am a man who has lived on this earth exceedingly. And equally I am a man who has not yet lived.

My parents are alive. This means I am not yet wholly born. Little by little, they are still smoothing my jagged shoulders. They are still pouring soul into my breast, whose outline shifts, like the amphorae of the ancient Greeks, which took the shape of the wine that thickened within them. They are still burnishing my coppery face.

Since I am not yet wholly born; death is still distant. I am young enough to be able to love death as if it were a beautiful woman.

My first teacher was an old angel. Anyone gazing at us from afar would have seen a child sitting beneath the huge walnut tree at the bottom of the garden. But in fact I was sitting at the feet of that aged angel, who was my teacher. His shade was redolent of iodine. And like clotted blood, his shadows stained my fingers as they wrote so that I no longer knew whose was the wound, mine or his.

From him I learned that names are of no use to you, even my own name, were I to write it without a capital letter, like the name of a tree or an animal. We talked to each other, and it was as good as when you run barefoot over grass. It leaves no footprints, which is why running over the grass is something sinless. I would kick off my sandals and run across the field at the edge of town. His shadow spread over me and we were happy.

One day, the old angel vanished. I gazed in puzzlement at the walnut tree, the thick trunk, the succulent leaves. Birds alighted amid the foliage. In autumn, the wind shook the branches, and the walnuts fell to the earth. I cracked open the shells and ate the kernels. They tasted good. I ate of his body. After that I stopped looking for the old angel. All that has remained is the scent of iodine, and sometimes I can still see greenish-black stains on my fingers. It is a sign that the flesh beneath has not yet healed.

The Focșani of my childhood was a town of wide streets and grand buildings. As I grew up, the streets narrowed and the houses shrank. In fact, they had always been like that, but my eye, a child's, lent them and the whole of the world dimensions that were enormous only to me. Foundations and porch posts ought to be made of living trunks rather than dead wood. In that way the houses would grow together with the people, the world would not shrink, and time would not be shortened.

Few things had changed since the Second World War. The roads in our district, in the eastern part of the town, were unsurfaced, as were the sidewalks, which were separated from the road proper by a stone curb a palm's width high. The fences were made of wood. Sometimes they were given a fresh coat of paint. But more often than not the pales were uneven, hammered together so that they overlapped, and they were either unpainted or whitewashed. Along the bottom of the fences grew chamomile. Toward autumn I used to pick the small, aromatic flowers. Grandmother laid them in the yard to dry, for use in herbal teas over winter. She did the same with apricot halves in summer and, a little later, with plums and slices of apple. Dried fruits quelled hunger because they required long chewing. And if you had the patience to chew them long enough, they took on the taste of flesh.

Our street was short. It had only ten houses, and at the corner was the wall of the ice factory, which we called "Frigorifer." The name of the street was March 6, 1945. The plaque gave the following explanation for the name: "The date when the first democratic government was established." After the 1989 Revolution, when the government of 1945 no longer seemed so democratic to the people from the town hall, the name of the street was changed to Jiliște, for reasons unknown to me. I sent a letter home at the time. It did not arrive until a few months later. The post office had found it more convenient first to deliver it to the village of Jiliște, which was also in Vrancea, the same county as Foc-șani. Blood flows more slowly than time, which is why it is hard to relinquish old habits. Another street name, a few corners away, proved to be more inspired: Revolution Street. After 1989 that name remained unchanged. Each thought of whichever revolution was most to his liking.

When it rained, brooklets formed on our street and drained into each other. I had found out the name of those streambeds, where the earth desiccated to a fine dust when the weather was scorching hot. Those streambeds were called *rigoles*. The walnut shells were argosies afloat on the swift brooklets that coursed along the *rigoles*. I would stuff each walnut shell with mud as warm as dough, into which I poked a turkey feather for a mast.

Motorcars seldom passed by. But carts carrying aluminum milk churns would come. Around the corner there was a milk collection and processing center. With its churns each cart would join the queue. We used to clamber onto the carts, riding perched on the axle heads. Sometimes a carter, in a foul mood at his milk sums not having come out right, would give us a flick of his whip on our backs. We jumped from the cart, and he urged on his horses with a yell.

In those days there were no apartment blocks in the town, and you could count on the fingers of one hand the houses with an upper story. The Jewish shops on the main street had had upper stories and mansards. But in the earthquake of 1940 the upper floors had caved in, and the shops had slumped into each other.

The people in our quarter were poor. Nor could we boast any great wealth, but my parents were educated; they were engineers. Newspapers arrived only seldom, and we kept abreast of current affairs from the cinema newsreel and the radio speaker, a yellow box on the wall from which droned news bulletins, folk ensembles, and patriotic choirs. When Mrs. Maria, our neighbor from over the road, bought a television set, it was a major event on our street. The Rubin-made television was Russian, like most things in those days. It had a screen as big as a saucer. On warm evenings, Mrs. Maria would bring it out into the yard, and the neighbors would each come with their own chairs. I would soon doze off, curled up on my chair, but I felt proud, like I was an adult. Given they were broadcast in the middle of the day, the two things I did watch from start to finish without falling asleep were the funeral of Leontin Sălăjan, the minister of the army, and later the funeral of Gheorghe Gheorghiu-Dej. For hours on end, more from curiosity than grief, the whole neighborhood watched the funeral corteges, drinking plum brandy and commenting on them as if they were a soccer match. Such funerals came too seldom for the taste of my grandfather Garabet and, even more so, for the taste of his brother-in-law, Sahag Sheitanian. Otherwise, nothing much happened in our quarter of town.

Fire has vanished since then. Thrumming, it has withdrawn into electrical cables hidden in the walls, buried in the earth. But in my childhood, fire was always coming out of hiding. The playful flame of the candle or the tranquil flame of the oil lamp. The ruddy flicker of the embers in the stove. The fire beneath the cauldron in which the plum jam bubbled. The fire beneath the blackened cauldron boiling the tar to caulk the cardboard roofing. The cauldron melting the tallow for laundry soap. The suffocating flame of the burning leaves in spring. In those days, the nights were longer and richer; the light was sparser and the shadows more alive. In the play of shadows on the walls, many phantasms seemed real. Fire was a living creature; it sat down with us at the table; its shadows licked around our shoulders; it elongated our faces, deepened our eyes. After I listened to them, many of the stories from those flickering walls retold themselves. That is why my childhood was freer and richer. Even for the dead it was better that way.

The other companions of my childhood were scents. Of all the senses, smell is the most laden with memories. It is enough to open a door; a familiar odor wafts out, and all the events caught up with that sensation return to your mind. An entire life might be described through its aromas. The story of my childhood might also be told in this way.

Above all else there was the scent of warm dough. Were I to reduce the whole of my childhood to a single material form, I would name it "dough"—the warm dough in Grandmother's basin. It rose from evening to morning, growing like a living thing. I was fascinated. So absorbed was I in the life growing in the basin that I felt each prod of the kneading hands hurt it. I was soothed only when I saw Grandmother Arshaluis (which means dawn) and her sister Armenuhi rolling it out and caressing it until it was transformed into thin leaves. The women then spread smooth sheets on the beds and tables, on which they laid the thin leaves of dough for the baklava.

On such nights, we slept huddled on the sofas. The leaves were not to be disturbed by any movement or sound. In their presence we moved warily and spoke in a whisper. From time to time, Grandmother would wake up, and by the light of the oil lamp she would grease the leaves with a mixture of oil and egg. In the morning, having dried like clay tablets, rustling like last year's straw, the leaves were laid one on top of the other. Ground walnuts were sprinkled between the leaves, and then warm syrup was poured on top. The edges were trimmed so that the leaves would fit inside the trays that had been slowly heating in the oven. On Sunday, at lunchtime, Grandfather Garabet cut the baklava with a long knife, and, sparingly, he gave each his share.

The same knife was used for slicing the dried beef, which we called by its Turkish name: *pastirma*. The meat was hung from the eaves of the house to dry in the wind and sweeten in the light. "Of all things," Grandfather used to say, "the taste of the wind is best. You have to know how to let it seep into the food." The dried meat was left to soak in a paste called *çemen*, sent all the way from Yerevan. Grandfather would take the knife and cut the first slice. We went out into the yard and peered through the reddish slice of meat. "I can't see the moon," I said. And Grandfather: "Then it is no good." He whetted the knife on a moistened stone and cut another slice. The thin meat, pierced by the rays of the moon, took on a yellowish hue. "Now I can see it," I said. "Then it is good," decided Grandfather. "Light and wind are the tastiest things, taken together. This is how the fruit comes to ripeness; this is how the meat slices just right."

The scent of fruit used to fill the whole house, especially on New Year's Eve, when Armenians are still keeping the fast that starts before Christmas and the *anush-abur* is boiling in the big pans. *Anush-abur* literally means "sweet soup." It is a kind of *kollyva*, but instead of being made from boiled wheat, it is a mixture of all kinds of fruit: figs, dates, raisins, walnuts, oranges. And on top it is sprinkled with powdered cinnamon.

Then there was the scent of the nooks. These were hidden places, tenebrous or bright, but rarely opened. And, most enticingly, they were forbidden places. Without nooks to explore, childhood is meaningless. The scent of nooks goes together with tranquility, which likewise has its own scents. First, there were the wardrobes, at the bottoms of which quilts and mattresses lay folded. In Grandmother's wardrobe were kept only the heavy clothes, the overcoats, smelling of mothballs, some of which had even belonged to my great-grandmother, Heghine Terzian. Of my great-grandfather's clothes, nothing remained, as all of them had been abandoned on a street in Constantinople, from where you could see the sun setting over the Bosphorus. They had fled one night with nothing but the clothes on their backs and some bundles in which they had thrown together a few things that might easily be sold. It was rumored that in the port at Pera a ship had landed and it was taking Armenian refugees. After boarding the ship, in the midst of the confused and fearful crowd on deck, my great-grandfather collapsed, falling headfirst, still holding his two daughters by the hand. They turned him onto his back, closed his eyelids, and unclenched his hands. They kept vigil over him, managing to procure a candle stump from somewhere. He was not the only one to give up the ghost amid the turmoil and terror. Before the ship reached Constanța, the captain gave the order to throw all the dead bodies into the sea. And so it was that the Black Sea became the shifting grave of my great-grandfather Baghdasar Terzian.

Then there was the bookcase. Grandfather Garabet knew all the alphabets it contained: the Latin, the Cyrillic, the Greek, and the Arabic. "So as not to make any mistake," he used to say. "The alphabet is the beginning. That's why it's called the alphabet. You can start off from anywhere, as long as you can unravel the beginning." My grandfather unraveled beginnings but tangled up endings. When he was on his deathbed, we children were taken in to see him. I did not understand what he was saying. He seemed tranquil and spoke with wisdom. But I could not understand. Finally, Father explained that Grandfather had been talking to us in a mixture of languages: Persian, Arabic, Turkish, Russian, and Armenian. All the lands he had known in his childhood and youth had come back to life within him. The same as when you are in a hurry to leave and you grab whatever things you can lay your hands on, he grabbed words at random as he spoke before departing from this world.

8

Then the books themselves: tomes in Turkish, written in the old oriental script; drawing textbooks in English; and old editions of the Larousse. My grandfather often leafed through a splendid book about carpets that was in German. "Our carpets are like the Bible," he used to say to me. "You can find everything in them, from the very beginning to the present day." The two of us would seek out the world's different guises. "Here is the eye of God," I would say, making a guess, and Grandfather Garabet would confirm it. "And this is an angel." "It is not an angel. He is old. He must be an archangel. Maybe it is Raphael. He is the oldest of all." I would have liked to tell him about the old angel in the yard who smelled of iodine in summer and who in winter laved his unshod feet in the snow. But I realized that those who had not been able to live a childhood free of fear had no way of meeting old angels. And then Grandfather would reach the page of which he was proudest: the carpet he himself had woven. That carpet used to be laid in our room, the children's room, and now it is in the room of my little girl, Armine. "It is important," Grandfather used to say, "to have a sturdy roof above your head and a thick carpet under your feet." Our Persian carpet was thick and hand-woven and had countless knots. "A carpet," explained Grandfather, "should be so thick that when you roll it up, it will weigh as much as a tree trunk of the same girth." Our carpet had come down through history and not just anyhow. In August 1944, Soviet troops entered the town of Focșani. Three officers were billeted at our house. They drank the whole night, until they were delirious. My grandfather and his brother-in-law, Sahag Sheitanian, my aunt Armenuhi's husband, sat up until dawn to keep watch over them, jumping up whenever one of the Russians dropped a lighted cigarette butt on the carpet. Despite being buffeted and cursed, Garabet and Sahag picked up all the cigarette butts. Today, no more than two or three singes are visible. Grandfather had a Kantian view of the world: a roof above your head, an altar before you, and a soft carpet beneath your feet.

I was unable to read all the books in the house. But I knew them by their different scents. It was Grandfather Garabet who taught me to recognize books that way. A good book has a certain kind of scent. Snugly encased in its leather binding, it smells almost human. In bookshops I sometimes find myself sniffing the books. "As if I were blind," I would say. "So what?" said grandfather Garabet, with a shrug of his shoulders. "Of all that you are, your eyes are yours the least. Light is like a bird that lays its eggs in another's nest."

I first came to understand books by touching and smelling them. I was not the only one. Between the pages I would sometimes find a reddish mite. "Don't kill it," my grandfather would say, staying my hand. "It's a book scorpion. Every world has to have its own living creatures. A book, too, is a world. Living creatures are fated to feed on the sins and errors of the world. It's the same with this scorpion: it corrects the errors in the book." For a long time I did not believe him. But now it is I who am the storyteller, a kind of scribe who wishes to rectify the old errors. I am therefore a book scorpion.

And then there was the other scent, which whisked my childhood far away, among the spices of the Orient: the aroma of coffee. My grandparents had brought that skill with them from their native Anatolia. Making coffee came naturally to them; they were like potters, who can tell by its taste whether or not the clay is good. They brewed it with fine discernment, scornful of those who drank coffee without knowing its meanings.

For a start, my grandparents did not buy roasted or (God forbid!) ground coffee. We had a copper pan, blackened from so much roasting. The lid had a special mechanism with a lever that allowed you to roast the beans evenly. Over a low flame, the whole process took about an hour. We children were given only the roasted beans. We sucked them like bonbons, and when the taste faded, we cracked them between our teeth and chewed them.

Then came the grinding. Nowadays, cylindrical coffee grinders with tapered caps, gilded and embossed with arabesques, can be found in the collections of snobs, alongside other objects that no longer have any use, such as samovars and coal-heated flat irons. In my childhood, the grinder was a member of the family. The grinding took a long time. The old folks gathered in the yard. My grandmother placed soft cushions on the wooden benches with the cast-iron arms. They took it in turns to grind, counting to a hundred in their heads. The person grinding did not take part in the conversation, so as not to lose count. But if he did join in, it meant the subject was serious. I can almost see them beneath the apricot tree in the garden: Grandfather Garabet Vosganian, who was calm and had a prodigal outlook on the world, and Sahag Sheitanian, his brother-in-law, who was restless and quarrelsome. And there was Anton Merzian the cobbler, who always told the same story about kidnapping his bride, Zaruhi, from her parents in the town of Panciu. When he told it, in his eyes the twelve-mile journey to Focşani, which he had made on horseback forty years before, attained the grandeur of the flight to Egypt. He embellished the tale with every telling because Zaruhi, who was as deaf as a post, was unable to contradict him. Then there was Krikor Minasian, the other cobbler from Main Street. Between him and Anton Merzian there was bitter rivalry. Finally, there were Ohannes Krikorian and Arshag, the redheaded bell-ringer from the Armenian church, the hunter of birds. And around them sat the women, plump, resting their hands in their laps, scented with eau de cologne: Parantsem, Zaruhi, Satenig, my grandmother Arshaluis, and her sister Armenuhi.

The grinding took one thousand five hundred turns of the handle. The grinder would heat up. It became so hot that you could barely hold it, my grandfather used to say. Before the coffee became as fine as sand, he would add. But he only said that when Sahag Sheitanian was not around. Sahag Sheitanian did not like sand.

Sometimes, they gave me the grinder so that I too could turn the handle. The brass heated up and through the joints seeped the scent of coffee. From time to time, Grandfather would sprinkle a little into the palm of his hand, sniffing it with the air of a detective gauging the quality of a haul of narcotics. More often than not, Grandfather would decree another round of grinding, and the old men would obey so that the wonderfully scented powder would be as fine as could be.

Then came the boiling of the coffee in the *ibrik*, which was a metal pot with a narrow spout, shaped like a truncated cone: "So that the steam will collect and whistle," said grandfather. "The more steam collects, the more aromatic the brew will be." From time to time, the contents of the *ibrik* were stirred. Here too there was a rule: the *ibrik* had to be kept over the flame until the liquid threatened to boil over. The froth was skimmed off with a spoon and poured into one of the cups, after which the *ibrik* was set over the flame once more. And then all over again, until the coffee had boiled to a froth as many times as there were cups. I liked to stand next to Grandfather when he was boiling the coffee. He was skillful and wise. It was at those times that he used to tell me the most amazing things. "When you are making coffee," he said, "you can say whatever comes into your head. Everything will be forgiven. Whoever gathers around the coffee is not allowed to quarrel. But in the end, it is his business what he does." It was his moment of freedom. At those times he resembled my old angel.

Now let me tell you about the cups. Like so many other forgotten customs, that of coffee drinking has also vanished. Nowadays, people drink from all kinds of cups, even from mugs meant for water. They drink instant coffee, which does not leave grounds, let alone produce any froth. "The froth is the coffee's blazon," explained my grandfather, stirring it with a spoon. Nowadays, the chairs are no longer soft, no longer arranged in a circle ready for people to chat. People drink their coffee first thing in the morning, when they are still half asleep and do not feel like talking. And for many people, coffee is just an excuse to have a cigarette.

The coffee cups were small, beautifully colored, and had matching saucers. In Turkish, the *ibrik* is called a *çezve* and the cups are called *fincanlar*. Every item had a Turkish name, and they sometimes even called the coffee *kahve*, the same as in Turkish. For my grandparents, who in the old days had seen the same objects in their old folks' houses on the banks of the Bosphorus or the Euphrates, the memories and the words had probably merged.

The old folk of my childhood drank their coffee at around six in the evening. By that time the ceremony of preparing the coffee would already have guided the conversation along a gentle path. The old folk settled themselves among the pillows. They drank their coffee without haste, making slurping sounds and smacking their lips in satisfaction. This was the moment when, despite exile and wandering, despite memories of bloodshed, despite the passage of time, the world seemed unchanged and tranquil and their souls were at peace.

Grandfather would pick up his violin and play until the coffee grounds settled in the cups, inventing all kinds of convoluted passages. Grandmother did not read the coffee grounds because Grandfather used to say that what is written must anyway come to pass. And misfortunes are bestowed on the world like grass or rain. If you try to avoid a misfortune foretold, it happens all the same, except that you cast it on another's shoulders. And so, in addition to all the other things you have to endure, why take yet another sin on your shoulders?

Now I should say a few words about my grandfather on my mother's side, Setrak Melikian. He was a good man, a cheerful man. May he be welcome to all that life gave him. May life be welcome to all it took from him. And if life took from him more than it gave him, who now can tally the score? He would shrug his shoulders, clap his hands, and laugh. Like Aeschylus at the Battle of Salamis. That was his philosophy, regardless of the times or people. Otherwise, faced with nothing but his own memories, he would have lost his mind.

My mother's family was originally from Persia. Their earliest identifiable ancestor was a kind of prince whose lands stretched from Lake Urmia in the east to what is now Tabriz. His name was Melik, which in Persian means "prince." Whence the name of my mother's family: Melikian, which is to say, "the line of Melik."

Prince Melik warred with the Turks, but finally, realizing the battle was lost, he took his family and his wealth and moved to the mountains of Karabakh in the north. Pushed out by invaders once more, he then settled in the mountain plateaus around Erzerum. The story is more than three hundred years old. Melik had seven sons. With their families, they founded a settlement named Zakar.

Grandfather Setrak used to play with me. We would tie knots in a piece of string and count. Sometimes, I used to imagine that the piece of string was a thick rope hanging from a bell set swaying by the wind or the hand of some lonely traveler. The bell would then ring. This is how I always imagined the bell:

as the voice best suited to my family. Each knot, clenched like a fist, was one of my ancestors. In fact, the rope was a necklace of clenched fists. With my grandfather Setrak I would write the chronicle. The first to be counted was Melik, the knot closest to the bell, so close that its chime sometimes sounded like his galloping horse. The next was my great-great-grandfather Khachadur, a proud and wealthy man, who arrived in Constantinople on horseback. The merchants knew him and invited him into their houses. Grandfather told the story of Khachadur's silver tea service with gilded handles, which had been passed down for three generations, and the story of a merchant's astonishment when he saw that one man could carry so much wealth about his person. Otherwise, great-great-grandfather Khachadur was a temperate man. Although they were of high lineage, the Melikians were content with the harsh life of a shepherd.

My great-grandfather David Melikian was a learned man. He studied at the Robert College in Constantinople. He wrote poetry and had such a beautiful calligraphic hand that people came to him from all the villages around; they came even from Erzerum that he might write their petitions. David Melikian was the overseer of the territory, what we would call a mayor today. When the Janissaries came in the spring of 1915, they threw him inside a building whose walls were only just beginning to rise and stoned him to death. This is how the Armenian leaders were put to death in other places too. Probably this is why my grandparents used to talk about not only the sky, but also the roof when they named the parts of the world. Nothing is worse than an unroofed house. Death can enter there.

Grandfather Setrak did not know the precise year of his birth. He knew only that he had been born in harvest time, and to him that seemed sufficient. Later, when the years began to take on a meaning for him, he was to say that he had been born at the same time as the new century. It made it easier to keep a tally.

There were five siblings: two sons and three daughters. Makruhi, the eldest daughter, had married in Erzerum. Then there was Harutiun, Maro, Grandfather, and the youngest daughter, Satenig. Makruhi died during the massacres. The Turkish soldiers withdrew one night, leaving bands of Kurds to plunder the convoy of deportees that was on its way to Aleppo. Makruhi and her husband had been slaughtered. Nothing is known of what happened to their baby.

The Melikians refused to join the convoys that were setting off to Deir-ez-Zor, and when the soldiers surrounded the village, Maro was taken along with some other girls. One night she managed to escape, and before her guards knew what was happening, she threw herself off the rocks into the waters of the Euphrates. In her memory, Grandfather baptized his eldest daughter Maro.

Grandfather was in Erzerum, staying with some relatives, with his grandmother, the wife of his grandfather Khachadur. When they came back, they saw the village in flames. Harutiun, the eldest brother, met them on the way, recounting the atrocities that had taken place there. Their grandmother urged them to flee, but she was too elderly to go with them. They hid in the forest. But not having craft enough to live in the forest, they were captured. Grandfather told this part of the tale only once in his life. We know the story from cousin Khoren, who discovered it on a certain occasion and passed it on. The captain of the Janissaries had them brought before him and ordered them to kneel. He drew his sword and killed Harutiun, the eldest brother. In Armenian, Harutiun means resurrection. Perhaps someday, who knows?

Then the captain went up to him who was to become my grandfather. The boy was weeping, with his eyes turned to the ground. The captain yanked his hair until the boy was forced to look him in the face. "Look well!" said the captain, turning his head toward the burning village at the foot of the hill and the corpse of the boy's brother. "Do you know my name?" With his eyes clouded with tears, my grandfather shook his head. The captain uttered his name and made him repeat it. Then he added, "You will live! You are old enough to understand, to tell your people who I am and what I did to you, to you and your kin!" My grandfather could not believe that he was going to escape with his life. Only after the captain kicked him a few times, as if he were a stray dog, did he go away, mistrustful at first, and then bolting, running as fast as his trembling legs could carry him. He avenged himself on that captain in the only way he could: he did not forget him, but he forever remained silent in regard to his name.

No one else was known to have escaped from his village, apart from his younger sister, Satenig, whom he sought for years, after he became a merchant in Craiova and was able to afford to pay to have enquiries made at the orphanages run by foreign congregations. Many years later he received an answer from an orphanage for girls in Aleppo no less. He sent money to provide for her and to pay somebody to accompany her. In the port at Constanța, in order to convince himself that my grandfather was really the girl's brother, the chaperone took him aside and made him recite the names of his grandparents, parents, and siblings. It was like a memorial list. They had all died, in a place in the mountains, near Erzerum. Once he had proved that he mourned the same dead as his sister, the chaperone handed her over to him. Satenig later married a merchant from Brăila. After the war, she emigrated to America, which is where she died. I know her only from photographs.

Grandfather hid wherever he could. Some friendly Turks who had known his father sheltered him in a stable with the animals and cured him of typhus. He had fallen sick on the road, eating whatever he could find, like a wild animal, and sleeping huddled against the cold. When he regained his strength, the Turks gave him victuals for the journey and a fez to wear on his head to avert suspicious eyes. Grandfather headed north, toward the mountain of Moses, the Musa Dagh, as it is called in Turkish. He had heard that French ships had arrived there to rescue fleeing Armenians. He traveled by night, avoiding the roads. He eluded the galloping bands of Kurds and shunned the routes of the convoys of deportees making their way into the deserts of Mesopotamia. And again, cousin Khoren recounted how Grandfather would sit down and weep, with the fez in his lap, gazing at the waters of the Euphrates, down which the bodies floated. The waters were sluggish and red, tangled and braided like tails, the same as the waters of Babylon must have been in ancient times. "Didn't you throw away your fez?" I asked him, after my grandmother Sofia told me the story of his weeping by the waters of the Euphrates. "Why?" asked my grandfather. "I had it from some kind-hearted Turks, and in any event it shaded me from the sun. I put it on my head and carried on. What do you know? I had to live." Finally, my grandfather pricked his finger and showed me the bead of blood. "Let's see; can you do the same?" I was afraid to but also ashamed of being afraid. With my eyes closed, I let him prick me and held my finger tightly so it would not hurt. Then my own bead of blood showed itself. "I am an old man, and you are a child. But look: your blood is as alive as mine. That is love of life." Grandfather sometimes wished to sweeten his memories and that is why he spoke about blood in a strange way. He was a philosopher of blood. "The blood is unrulier than the flesh," he used to say. "That's why they say 'the voice of the blood' and 'the curse of the blood.'" Or he would say, "When the blood grows weary, you get yourself a staff to lean on. In any case, the blood is like an inner staff. Each man leans on his own blood." Sometimes he would say, "The blood always returns like a beast with a wet maw to bite you. It is never sated. God forbid it be sated." Or he would encourage me, saying, "Don't forget, your blood is like a sword thrust in the ground." Probably a part of him had remained forever on the banks of the Euphrates, talking to the bloody waters. People often talk to their thoughts. My grandfather Setrak used to talk to his blood.

He arrived at the bottom of Mount Musa too late. The fighting had ceased, and the ships that rescued the last of the fighters from the mountainside had long since departed. And then my grandfather turned his face from the sea and made his way north once more, toward Russia. A long journey: Yerevan, Tiflis, Rostov on Don.

He was going to Europe. It was the family custom that young men should travel like Peter the Great, learn a trade, learn how to comport themselves and to talk in a European way. They then returned home and married. This was how some of the elder cousins from the Melikian family managed to avoid the slaughter: Oskian, Artur, Melkon, Kalust, Nshan, and Khoren. From the letters, which in more peaceful times used to be read out in the village church at Zakar, my grandfather learned that his cousins had gone to Romania. He was now on his way there too, heading westward. Meanwhile, the world around him had changed. He saw crippled soldiers without epaulettes, limping along, and motley bands that scattered at the sound of the galloping horses of the imperial police. The Russian Revolution was drawing nigh.

Mingling with convoys of soldiers, townsfolk's carts, and bands of beggars, Grandfather Setrak reached Odessa. There, an Armenian barber hired him as his apprentice, intending to leave him his shop and give him his daughter's hand in marriage. Grandfather swept up the shorn hair and washed the towels. One day, a young man arrived on horseback, tethered his horse outside the shop, and entered. As grandfather was placing the towel around his neck, their eyes met in the mirror. Sometimes, life arranges things in such a way that even life itself is astonished. That young man was cousin Khoren, whom the other cousins had sent out to trace their kinfolk. Khoren did not wait to be shaved. He tossed the towel aside, embraced my grandfather, and said, "A Melikian is not allowed to be any man's servant!" My grandfather mounted the horse behind Khoren, and they set off back to Craiova. Amid tears and sobs, Grandfather had told him that there was no point in continuing his journey eastward because all the other Melikians were dead, including Satenig, he said, without suspecting that he would meet her years later in the port of Constanța. That was the only time in his life when he told the story of the death of his older brother Harutiun.

The cousins all chipped in and helped him to open his own shop, which sold colonial wares. Through hard work, Grandfather then developed the business into a chain of shops. He built himself two houses. In photographs he is smartly dressed, wearing a straw hat, a pocket watch, and a bow tie. He faced up to all history's vicissitudes with the same serenity. Because he was stateless, the holder of a Nansen passport, the Liberals only grudgingly granted him a trader's license. During the rebellion, the Iron Guard thought he was a Jew and almost burned down his shop. The Communists took everything away from him, and he barely escaped being thrown into prison. It was his good fortune that during the German occupation he had sent free bread to the Soviet prisoners, among whom there were also a few Armenians. When the Red Army occupied Craiova, an officer who had been held prisoner by the Germans remembered him, and that was how he avoided jail. He eked out a living until he retired, working as a night watchman at the Buzești Brothers Lyceum and then at other similar jobs that barely kept you from starving to death. He never held a grudge against anybody and was always reconciled to his lot. He was a cheerful and wise old man. He never wronged anybody, and he forgave all those who had caused him suffering.

In his final years, in Craiova, he led a simple life. In the morning, I would accompany him to the park surrounding the St. Demetrios Church. Four of them played cards there. One was the Colonel, whose given name I never knew. The Colonel was always elegantly dressed and had a cane with a silver ferrule. He had spent many years in prison, having been a member of the Iron Guard. The other two were jowly and wore clothes that were too tight for them: comrades Botrîncă and Butnaru. Botrîncă was retired, but he had worked for the People's Council and was one of those who had arranged to have my grandfather arrested all those years ago. Now, all four of them—the Communist, the former Iron Guard member, the former shopkeeper, and the proletarian—played cards together and talked about medicaments and the weather. It was their way of reconciling themselves to history after all that time. Playing cards was their Potsdam Treaty.

Apart from that and especially on cold winter days, my maternal grandfather Setrak Melikian communicated with the world. At six o'clock in the morning, he listened to the news on Radio Bucharest. At eleven o'clock he listened to the Radio Moscow Romanian service. Before lunch he listened to Radio Tirana when he could pick up a signal. At half past two he listened to the Voice of America in Romanian and then Radio Freedom in Armenian. In the afternoon he listened to Emil Georgescu on Radio Free Europe's *Romanian News*. Finally, at seven in the evening, he listened to the Voice of America again and, a little bit later, to the BBC news. After ten o'clock, sipping linden tea, with his eyes half closed, he listened to *A Day in One Hour* on Radio Bucharest. Then, he would turn to me and say, "You see? All lies!" The next day he would start all over again. And he would laugh, clapping his hands. Above a blood-drenched, tortured, inimical history, he would laugh.

He was a very healthy man. He never bothered anybody even when he was ill. He died of cold in the cruel winter of 1985. The gas fire was barely a flicker. Probably because of the cold, his blood, his good friend, no longer had the strength to flow. I arrived in time to take his olive-stone rosary beads from his pocket, and ever since then I have kept them in my breast pocket. When we put him in his coffin, he was as light as a bird.

ALEATORY SONG. My grandfathers, Garabet Vosganian and Setrak Melikian, learned from their century only how hard it is to die in the same land as the one that gave birth to you. The old Armenians of my childhood never had any graves at which they could weep for their parents. They carried their graves with them wherever they wandered, and like the Jews, who laid down their ark and built their temple around it when they sojourned in a place, they unloaded the graves from their shoulders, and there they built their houses.

I often sense them, up there, in the heavens: my grandfather Garabet Vosganian, calm and measured in his words; my grandfather Setrak Melikian, smiling and sliding his rosary beads between his fingers. They play *gyulbahar.* "You have to give the dice a good shake inside your fist, to let them know what you want from them," says Grandfather Garabet. "That's if you yourself know what you want. Look at that!" he says, in delight. "Double one!" Grandfather Setrak does not get annoyed; he laughs, leans to look down from the eaves. "If you've thrown a double one, there'll be another war. Look over there in the distance." It is true; from somewhere down below, plumes of dark smoke can be seen rising. Grandfather Setrak blows on his fist and throws, squinting his eyes at the dice. "Double six!" he laughs, and claps his hands. "You see," he says, looking down once more. "The mists have cleared. There is peace." "You're cheating," frowns Grandfather Garabet. "Next time, I'll make you shake the dice in a cup." "That's nothing much," laughs Grandfather Setrak. "Five-four! There won't be any deluge. Look, here!" And he pulls a face. "Three-two. Now nothing bad is going to happen. Nothing new!" "God forbid that there be anything new," says Grandfather Garabet. Setrak stares at the dice. "But what's this? Look, it's my face, and yours!" "You've mixed them up," says Garabet, the wise one. "These are the old dice; they're somebody else's. Give them back." "Back to whom? There's only the two of us here!" Grandfather Garabet shrugs his shoulders. "That's how it is! When the cast dice show our faces, it doesn't count as a throw. It's your turn." And on they play, ordering the world with their dice, ordaining wars, births, miracles, and, above all, suffering.

I was protected among the guises of fire, the scents of childhood, the trees, and the phantasms.

But nonetheless the times were troubled. Sometimes Grandfather Garabet and Sahag Sheitanian, the neighbor with whom we shared our yard, used to speak in a whisper. One day, an old man whom we did not know turned up in the yard across the road: Carol Spiegel. For a time, the old man went no farther than his yard; he would sit on a couch, staring into space. Once, through the pales of the fence, I saw him go to the gate and look down the street. One morning, he came out to sweep the dead leaves from the pavement. And a few days later, but in the evening, he ventured to knock on our door.

I did not know what prison was. It was not until much later that I understood the explanation my grandfather gave me but which at the time had sounded like a game: "Prison is where everybody else's world is as wide as can be, but your world is as narrow as can be."

Carol Spiegel had been what is known as a collaborator. During the war he worked at the town hall. Being German, he had a job as a translator. The German occupation of the town had been orderly. The German troops left the populace in peace. They did not get drunk or cause a commotion. It was completely different when the Red Army arrived. The women bolted themselves inside their houses, and the tavern keepers locked up their liquor.

But when it came to the bombing raids, it was the other way around. The Russian ones were easier to bear. Of all the misfortunes that befell the town during the war, my grandparents said the earthquake of 1940 was the worst. They mentioned it more often than the bombing. "What point is there in hiding?" my grandfather Garabet asked. "When the American bombers flew overhead, we could rest easy. They were looking for the German barracks on the highways. They bombed each side of the highway so accurately that everything else was flattened, but the road remained intact. As for the Russians, again you had nothing to fear: whatever they aimed at, they always missed. Apart from the one evening when two bombs fell on our neighborhood, although neither of them went off. The first landed in somebody's vegetable patch; the other fell on somebody's house and made a hole in the roof. The man buried the bomb so that it wouldn't frighten the children and repaired the tiles on his roof."

Grandfather lived through both world wars. He did not fight, but he watched. Those who fought understood less of what happened.

This is why Grandfather Garabet used to tell stories about the wars. In his stories, the victors were not always the ones we knew from the history books. "Don't be hasty," he used to say. "The one who seems to have won is rarely the true victor. It is the vanquished rather than the victors who have made history. To be victorious is ultimately a way of being written out of history." He fetched the big book. "This is Vardan Mamikonian. And this is the battle between the Armenians and the Persians, in the year 451, on the field of Avarayr. Our army was defeated to the last man. Satisfied, the Persians said that that was enough for one day, and they went away thinking they would come back and conquer the whole of the Armenians' kingdom. And what happened in the end? The Persians never came back. They were forced to relinquish their religion, and instead of continuing to worship the sun, they converted to Islam. But we have remained Christians to this day. In other words, Vardan Mamikonian and his slaughtered army were the victors."

And Grandfather Setrak, my mother's father, the philosopher of blood, used to say, "The blood is unrulier than the flesh. Victory is not the power of shedding others' blood; that power is rather contempt or hatred. Victory is the power to shed your own blood." And Grandfather Setrak, who measured history and its victors by the power of the blood, sat down with his hands in his lap so that the blood could flow in a circle and take its ease.

This was why Grandfather Garabet believed that those who really made history were not the generals but the poets, and the true battlefields were not to be sought beneath the horses' hooves. But even my grandfather remained puzzled and was forced to accept that the laws of war were not entirely known to us. For he was not the only one who knew the story of the bomb buried in the yard. Some children also learned of the story and secretly set about unearthing the bomb. There exist two realities: the one we know and another, which is the reality of seeds. Without realizing it, the children had caused the two realities to merge. And the seeds of war, buried for so long, burst forth, high into the sky. Sergiu, my friend, a boy older than me, was killed instantly by the explosion, and little Tofan barely escaped with his life, bearing to this day the scars of a war that had not been his. "And so," decided Grandfather, "the war has not ended." "Which war?" I asked. "Well, there is only one. But it keeps breaking out in different places, like a rash. The harder you scratch, the more inflamed it gets. In the end, history is nothing but one long bout of scratching."

One day a man wearing a leather coat arrived and asked Grandfather about Carol Spiegel. Grandfather spoke sparingly and mostly just shrugged his shoulders. That evening, Carol Spiegel came and asked about the man in the leather coat. Grandfather shrugged his shoulders once more. In doing so, he convinced neither of them. But even so, neither of them dwelt on it. The stranger never came back, and Carol Spiegel died a few days later. Besides Mrs. Spiegel, the only people at the funeral were my grandfather Garabet and his brother-in-law Sahag. None of the others even noticed that for a brief interval Mrs. Spiegel had worn flowered dresses instead of the black clothes they had been accustomed to seeing her wear ever since the war. As far as they were concerned, Carol Spiegel had vanished from this world many years before he died. He was like a rain that streams down your face before it begins to fall from the sky.

In childhood, I lived in a world of whispers. Those whispers expressed wariness. It was not until later that I found out that a whisper could also have other meanings, such as affection or prayerfulness.

There were also things that were said unguardedly, even over the garden fence—for example, that the van had arrived with the bread ration. Other things were said only behind closed windows or on the bench in the middle of the yard, if nobody was passing on the street. Even then, such things were said in a low voice, as if there were windows that you could not close and passersby that you could not see.

It would have been simpler if people had sat with their heads bowed close to one another so that they would not have had to listen so hard, lest they miss a word. "From afar, everything has to look natural," explained Grandfather. "They have to think you're making small talk, that you don't care. As if to say: let them overhear." And they used to sit talking on the wooden benches, holding their backs straight, their heads high. They did not lean toward one another when they lowered their voices. All of them were extraordinarily skilled at hearing each other's whispers, even Arshag, who was hard of hearing because of his bell; when he was unable to read your lips, he would ask you to repeat yourself, but never when you whispered. Miraculously, he always heard the whispers. They thrummed through the air, and he could sense them through his skin, like a bat.

There were many things we were not allowed to talk about. Above all, under threat of the direst aftermath, we were not allowed to tell anybody, either the nursery school teachers or any stranger, that at home our family spoke in a whisper. "What are you saying in a whisper?" I used to ask. "I'm reading," Grandfather Garabet would reply. "How are you reading? Where is the book?" "I don't need the book. I know it by heart." "All right, but what is the book called? Who wrote it?" "Perhaps you, one fine day." And that is what I am doing now. And that is what I have named it: *The Book of Whispers.*

One visitor to our house who used to talk in a whisper was Hagop Djololian Siruni. He was a short man, with two tufts of hair carefully combed over his ears. His eyelids crinkled up higher than the upper rim of his thick spectacles as he tried to focus on the faces that he could descry only with difficulty. The effort of doing so lent him an air of agitation, which was augmented by his hands, which he fluttered to the rhythm of his speech. When he read, he leaned close to the letters, almost gluing his eyes to the page. Above all, he liked old books written in Arabic script, a few of which Grandfather kept.

Siruni had returned from Siberia a few years earlier. Grandfather explained that Siberia was a place of great whiteness, where even the animals were white because of the cold and the snow. I went up to Siruni holding my book, *Fram the Polar Bear,* and showing him the pictures, I asked him whether the place where he had been was as beautiful. "Even more beautiful," said Siruni. But I was surprised when he told me that he had seen hunters but never any bears.

Otherwise, Siruni and his story were subjects that my family strictly avoided. A long time afterward, at the suggestion of writer Bedros Horasangian, I began to piece together all those things in my mind and to understand them, including the fact that the hunters Siruni told me about had been hunters of men.

My grandfathers Garabet and Setrak were very good storytellers. But they themselves did not appear in the stories they told. It was as if they had never existed in this world. Stories without a storyteller, their words were set down on old and anonymous scrolls, discovered in earthenware vessels. Neither of them told stories about themselves. Each became a character in the other's stories, and you always had to go seeking back and forth, from one to the other, in order to find out what happened next. For that reason, the story of the Armenians of my childhood is a story without an ending.

But nonetheless they did tell stories about themselves. And this is how it went: at dusk, my Grandfather Setrak would seat himself on the chaise longue beneath the vine arbor in the yard of the house in Craiova. He would count his rosary beads and rock backward and forward on his heels. He would murmur. The murmur might have been anything, a prayer or a prophecy.

My grandfather Garabet would shut himself up in his room and sing. They were foreign songs, in Turkish or Arabic, of the kind the Dervishes sing in the desert even today. Grandfather Setrak's murmuring and Grandfather Garabet's incantations were seamless. They breathed in a different kind of way; they breathed a different air. It was pointless calling to them at such times or knocking on their doors. They would not answer; they would not open the door.

The war had ended. During the disorderly dividing of the spoils a few Armenians managed to go over to the victors' side. You cannot be a victor unless you find yourself someone to vanquish. And so they presented themselves at the door of the newly established embassy of the Soviet Union and handed over a list of "collaborators," which included, as was inevitable, all the cream of Bucharest's Armenian intelligentsia. As it was not difficult to find anti-Communists in the autumn of 1944, after handing over their first list, the new collaborators brought another and yet another, until even the Soviets felt they had gone too far. Faced with those never-ending lists, Sava Dongulov—the embassy consul and an Armenian to boot—declared, to his credit, "Stop! At this rate, we're going to wipe out the whole community!"

The first batch of ten, including Siruni, was arrested on December 28, 1944. From the frontier, they were taken in a sealed railroad car to Moscow and thence by truck to the Lubyanka, where they were sorted. Without trial, Siruni was sent to a labor camp in Maryinsk. He was made to collect pine resin. Which is to say that you had to raise your eyes to the treetops when the wind and snow would sooner have forced you to shield your face. When the survivors of that ordeal, Siruni and lawyer Vahan Gemijian, formerly the president of the Association of Armenian Students, came back from Siberia, their eyesight was very dim. When they read, they held the book so close that it looked as if they were burying their faces in the pages.

I am not sure whether anything existed in this world before my birth, even whether the world itself existed. But I shall tell you the story as if it had existed. It is the autumn of 1952. The prisoners are assembled in the mess hall. Behind the cook towers a stack of frozen fish, brought by truck and dumped there years ago, when the camp was built. Twice a week, the prisoners who are unfit for labor hack at the block of fish with picks and toss the glassy shards into cauldrons, where the fish boils until the flesh falls off the bones and the ice turns to soup. For prisoners whose teeth chatter in bleeding gums, it is suitable food. The steam from the fish has frozen to the plaster of the mess hall like festive glitter. A female comrade who has come all the way from Moscow speaks to them of the lofty achievements that followed the Great Patriotic War. Many of them do not speak Russian, but they pretend they understand. The comrade asks them something about the history of the Communist Party of the Soviet Union. The prisoners' eyes bulge in terror; the eyes of those who speak Russian bulge because they do not know the answer, and the eyes of those who do not know the language bulge because they do not know why the woman has suddenly stopped talking. Siruni stood up and answered her. The woman looked at him in puzzlement, detecting his harsh Caucasus accent, and asked him another question. And Siruni spoke at length about the situation in the Caucasus of ancient times, listing names, dates, wars, and treaties with a precision that only the gulag and solitude could give you. Returning to Moscow, the woman told Evgeny Tarlé— she was his assistant—about the unusual knowledge displayed by the prisoner from Maryinsk who, to cap it all, knew Armenian, Turkish, Persian, and Arabic, including the forms spoken in the Middle Ages, which were preserved only as languages of worship. At Tarlé's insistence, the Academy of Sciences in Moscow had Siruni transferred from the labor camp to the Museum of History in Yerevan, where his task was to decipher old manuscripts.

Every man lives in the world, but more than anything else he lives in an image of the world. In those days, and in who knows how many other ages, this used to be explained as follows: your name is spoken, on the one hand, and written, on the other. And the written name sits on the cover of a file. You have to live your life cautiously. You wake up, wash your face, shave, comb your hair. When you catch sight of yourself in a mirror or a shop window, you lift your head and smooth the creases in your coat. Life is a ceremony. The file is also life but a life captured unawares. It is a house in which each room has only three walls. You can lean against them, but you have nowhere to hide.

This was why a file had to be compiled on Siruni. Searching his life, a life captured unawares, the drudges discovered an article published in the *Araz* newspaper in Bucharest in 1944 in which Siruni deplored the death of a friend ignobly slain in the Soviet Union years previously. His eulogy to his late friend, Aghasi Khanjian by name, turned into an indictment of Lavrenti Beria, whom he accused of murder. Not only that particular murder, but many others. Unlike other people, Siruni knew what was happening in the Soviet Union. And he poured out all his bitterness in that obituary. It was an accusation you could easily make in those days in a Romania allied with the Germans, but not in a Soviet Union ruled by the NKVD. Consequently, Siruni, already sick and half blind, was sent to another labor camp, this time in Potma, a place of extermination. Escape was impossible. When a given number of dead bodies accumulated, they were stacked on an uncovered cart, taken outside the camp, and dumped in a mass grave. There was no hurry; because of the cold, the bodies did not decompose. Lest any prisoner try to escape by pretending to be dead or lest any of them not be fully lifeless, at the gate the guards smashed each head with a hammer. Potma was too far away for the prisoners to hear the news of Stalin's death. Endlessly multiplied in his portraits, Stalin died an infinitely multiplied death. One day, his portrait vanished from the mess hall. A few months later, Beria's photograph vanished from the commandant's office. The accusing article published in *Araz* in 1944 now became providential. Voroshilov himself signed the order for his release, and Siruni was taken to Yerevan with honors. And from there, in 1955, he was taken home to Romania, where everything had changed. His family had been scattered, his archives and manuscripts confiscated. Most of his friends had disappeared. One of them, Garabet Vosganian, was waiting for him on the wooden bench in the yard, gazing over the fence at history's carts, laden with gun carriages, bogged down, pushed by tattered, straining figures.

In *The Book of Whispers* are inscribed the names of the dead. Siruni and Grandfather Garabet spoke of them but in hushed voices. After the first batch was arrested in December 1944, there followed a second, on April 24, 1945. The youngest of those arrested was Levon Harutiunian, and he was the last of them to die, in Los Angeles in 1999. It is from him that I know the story. It would have been hard for Grandfather to tell me about how Armenians ended up betraying one another. In any event, Grandfather was coy about recounting those times since it was then that he had felt one of his rare urges to fight. Apart from that, he kept aloof as much as he was able, watching wide-eyed and seeking to understand. But to do that you also need courage. "Think about it," he would say; "to be prepared to confront the reality, no matter what might happen. To be able to face all four winds at once." And he also said, "Being a hero is a form of cowardice. You cannot endure the suffering and so you try to put a stop to it, recklessly and at any price." Nevertheless, us children he raised to worship heroes. He used to tell us the stories of the legendary Haig, Ara the Fair, and Tigran the Great. He philosophized in his own way, sooner talking to himself, his eyes gazing out of the window: "The only thing people have in common is stories. When you say that two people are of the same nation, it means that they have listened to the same stories. All kinds of stories are told about heroes because such stories always have a beginning and an end. You cannot tell the story of those who endure and, even less so, the story of those who endure and understand, because their suffering is endless. And who will tell stories that have no end, and above all who will listen to them? For that, there is not even any need to listen; it is enough to look out of the window, or to gaze over the battlements, as they used to do in the olden days . . ." But like houses, even castles fall into ruin, windows and all. "That has nothing to do with it," objected Grandfather. "You can always find a window to look out of. And there is always at least one unconquered castle."

Without knowing it at the time, I knew only the ending of the story—namely, the unpaired shoes we wore around the yard when it rained. So that we would not trample mud inside the house and so that it would be easy for us to take them off on the threshold, Grandfather had had a cobbler cut off the backs of the shoes, turning them into lace-up slippers.

That, then, is the end of the story. And I have only just begun to narrate the beginning. Among the second batch of those arrested and taken away were Levon Harutiunian, our uncle Yervant Hovnanian, and his brother Vagharshag. It was in Passion Week. The Armenian church in Focşani had a large yard, surrounded by huge chestnut trees. In those days, the Armenians were numerous, and the church was full on holy days. So the man who tugged my grandfather by the sleeve, after peering through the crowd for a long time until he found him, had to push his way past the other people and put up with their admonishing glances. When Grandfather followed him outside into the yard, this time the parishioners humbly stood aside to let them pass. Grandfather looked imposing in his deacon's robes, and the people thought it was part of the service. The stranger handed him a crumpled-up piece of paper that somebody had tossed from a truck on the corner of the street. It was a military truck, covered with a tarpaulin. The man was afraid, but he had fulfilled the request hastily written on the scrap of paper: "To the verger at the Armenian church." It was Good Friday, and he had decided to do a good deed without making his name known. He did not ask what was written inside the folded scrap. He did not wish to know anything more than he did. It was better that way.

The note contained something written in Armenian, simply: "We are alive."

Grandfather went back inside the church, and beneath the puzzled gaze of Father Aslanian, he drew Sahag Sheitanian, the other verger, to one side. Still wearing their cassocks, they made their way down Main Street, past the Jewish shops, which had leaned crookedly ever since the earthquake, and arrived at their own shop, where there was a telephone. They called Bucharest, and their suspicion was confirmed. Aunt Nvart, Yervant Hovnanian's wife, answered, sobbing. The Soviet soldiers had burst into their house and pushed them with their faces up against the wall. They had ransacked everything, piling papers, books, and insignia pell-mell into a suitcase. They had taken Yervant away, along with his brother Vagharshag and another eight "collaborators." Some said they had been stood up against the wall of Văcăreşti Monastery and shot, others that they languished in the cellars of Jilava Prison. They had run to the monastery, but the walls seemed tranquil, and nobody in the neighborhood had heard shots. "It means they're taking them to Siberia," said Grandfather, this being the only substitute for death. "Siberia! Oh, Lord!" sobbed Aunt Nvart over the telephone. "He was wearing his slippers when they took him away; his feet will freeze . . ."

Grandfather and Uncle Sahag returned to the church, where the service was almost over. They conferred with Father Aslanian and the men from the parochial council. The priest kept the church open so that each could return with whatever shoes he found at home. Ohannes Krikorian took off the shoes he was wearing and left them in the large box. They collected around a dozen pairs. Or rather, there were some twenty-odd shoes because some brought only one shoe without its pair. Even that was good. Grandfather matched them up by size, left with right, and formed another seven pairs. It was good even if the shoes in the pair were of different colors. What was important was that they should have a lining and a sound sole. Anton Merzian, the cobbler from the Main Street, fetched his shoetree and reinforced the soles, hammering in small wooden studs. In front of the prefecture he had seen a truck that looked like the one the stranger had described.

In his memoirs Levon Harutiunian tells the story of how the arrested were taken off the truck and bundled into a cramped room, with an armed guard standing in the doorway. The guard was changed at intervals and forced the men inside to remain standing all the time. The more tired they became, the easier they were to guard. They had to prop up the weaker ones, such as Vagharshag Hovnanian; otherwise, if they fell, the soldiers kicked them with their boots until they stood up again.

Grandfather, who spoke not only Romanian fluently, but also Russian, went to the walls of the prefecture and tried to look through the windows. Appearing from around a corner, a sentinel shouted at him in Russian and grabbed him by his overcoat, trying to bundle him inside. Grandfather wrested himself free and the soldier let him go, pointing down the street with his gun.

Nobody can say he really knows what silence is unless he has heard the click of a gun being cocked behind him. Grandfather started to walk away, with hesitant steps, and he kept looking behind him. It was then that the Russian cocked his machine gun. And silence fell. Grandfather Garabet probably then broke into a run, keeping close to the walls, ready to throw himself to the cobbles at the slightest sound and make himself one with his own tracks.

Levon Harutiunian takes up the story where it left off. Early in the morning, with the old and exhausted leaning on the young, they were loaded onto trucks. They were thirsty. The truck came to a stop on the highway, near the River Milcov. They drank water from the river, kneeling on the riverbank, and they washed their faces. From the border, their journey was the same as that taken by the first batch, arrested four months previously: the Lubyanka, sorting, and then Lefortovo Prison, with its thick walls that dated from the reign of the Empress Ekaterina, where not even the most primal freedom, the freedom to choose to die, was permitted. The prisoners slept with the lights burning, and they had to keep their arms above their blankets, lest one of them, having got hold of some sharp object or quite simply using his teeth, severed his veins and thereby cheated the jailers, dying in secret. A metal net on the first-floor landing prevented them from taking their lives by throwing themselves onto the concrete below. The prisoners were more useful alive than dead because through their confessions any of them might drag others down after them. It was there that they were isolated. They were locked in separate cubicles, they were stripped, their every cavity was searched, and they were forced to bend over twenty times, after which they were clothed in prison shirts and trousers. "I left my cigarettes with Sarkis Saruni," answered Harutiunian when the first interrogator asked him whether he smoked. "We don't have anyone by that name," came the blunt reply. "But we have only just parted," insisted the then young Harutiunian. "I told you that no such person exists!" shouted the interrogator, banging his fist on the sheet-metal tabletop. He soon discovered that nor did any such person as Levon Harutiunian exist. He was now called 7–35. "What is your name?" he was asked as he climbed out of the railroad car on numb legs, having reached the camp at Krivoshchyokovo, an outlying district of Novosibirsk, on the banks of the Ob. "7–35!" shouted Harutiunian to make himself heard above the din of the guards' barking dogs. "What's the rest of your name?" asked the officer seated in the gatehouse of the camp, above whose arch was written, "Onward to Freedom through Labor." Which is to say, that is your first name, but what is your surname? "58!" shouted Harutiunian, which meant "Enemy of the people." He was now a member of a numerous, swarming, freezing family, scattered throughout Siberia, a family of dangerous social elements, enemies of the people, thus named by an article of the Penal Code.

Harutiunian was released after eleven years of imprisonment. The People's Republic of Romania welcomed him in a number of different ways. Seeing him dressed in the garb typical of the labor camps, a man in Bucharest's Northern Station bought him a bagel. Another man went up to him and asked him about a missing relative. As he emerged from the station, he was met by a military patrol, and a truck took him to the Securitate Tribunal on Rahova Avenue. There he was handed a certificate from the Embassy of the Soviet Union, a kind of diploma granted to Stakhanovites.

> CERTIFICATE. Issued to citizen Levon Harutiunovich Harutiunian, born in 1913, this certificate attests that he was in the USSR from May 8, 1945, to September 24, 1955. During the time in which he was in the USSR, Harutiunian, L. H., was employed in various types of work. Most recently he worked as the chief accountant of a timber production sector. His comportment was conscientious.

Indeed. When he was arrested, he weighed 180 pounds. By the time of his release from prison his weight had fallen to 110. When boredom made them soft-hearted betimes, the guards used to call him *tonki-zvonki*, or "scrawny-tinkler," as if his bones clinked against one another. His hair had almost completely fallen out, and what remained looked like two silver horseshoes hanging above each ear. His left hand had a slight tremor, and for that reason, when he smoked, he had to keep his cigarette under the table, out of sight. And his teeth had fallen out. Let me say this to the friendly stranger in the Northern Station who gave that bagel to the man wearing labor camp clothes: your kindness surpassed what he was able to receive. But Harutiunian had learned not to hurry. He sucked the hard crust between his gums at leisure until it softened.

His home, which had been reduced to a low, cramped mansard, welcomed him joyously. His released friends were also waiting for him: Siruni, Arshavir Acterian, and Vahan Gemijian. The photograph has been preserved. On the back, Arshavir wrote, "Four prison inmates." In other words, prison does not come and go; it is like damp, which, once it has seeped into your bones, you carry around with you. What Arshavir meant to say was that there are prisons from which you are never released, no matter how many bolts might be drawn back, no matter how many doors might be unlocked. There always remains a door you can never open. And nobody can help you; nobody can lend his shoulder to help you budge it because only you can see it.

And the four prison inmates went to see the fifth, Hovhannes Babikian. He greeted them standing up, leaning on a staff. Vahan, who knew how ill Babikian was, wanted to help him lie down. "Piffle," replied Babikian. "A bed is for sleeping on. You greet death standing up." As they went downstairs, they could still hear him singing *My Cilicia*; they could hear his yearning for the native land. He finished his song, although according to his daughter-in-law, to judge from the glaze of his eyes, he died after the first verse. What is more, although the song was still audible, his lips were no longer moving. They went back upstairs; they went to the bed of the dead man, who had remained standing, and leaning him backward, as rigid as a post, they managed to lay him supine. This they did so that the few who came to the wake would not take fright at seeing him still standing up. Likewise, they had to dig him a grave as deep and as round as a well.

Levon Harutiunian brought us all these things, inscribed in a legible hand and with few crossings out. I promised him that we would not be in a hurry to print his manuscript. "Let it be after my death," he said. I told him of the joy every author feels when he holds his freshly printed book in his hands and leafs through it. "I might even be tempted to read it, mightn't I?" said Harutiunian, laughing. Then, seriously: "Writing liberates. I wrote these things down, and now I can forget them. But reading also burdens. Let others read these things and not forget them. I have remembered them long enough."

I think that what he said was not entirely true. He was not in any way able to forget, especially given that he was the last survivor and it was left to him to take the memories to others. Memories die later than people. As Grandfather Garabet used to say, no man dies all at once, but little by little, gradually, first his body, then his name, then others' memories of him.

I used to play under the table in the yard while the old men told stories in a whisper or crooned beautiful songs with sad meanings, songs they themselves had heard during childhoods spent on the plateaus of Anatolia. "Send that child away," one of the plump women who smelled of eau de cologne would say, be it Parantsem or Aunt Armenuhi. "Leave him be," Grandfather used to say. "Somebody always remains to tell the story. I shouldn't wonder if he himself is going to be the storyteller."

He put a pen in my hand from an early age and surrounded me with blank sheets of paper, just like they surround other children with sweets or toys. This is how I came to be the storyteller of the stages of my grandfather Garabet's life. And in this way he will endure until he loses his memories of this world.

When it rained and I had to cross the yard, I would put on the old shoes. They left deep prints in the mud, prints that looked unnaturally deep to a child. My footprints were alien to me. I was afraid of them. Water sloshed in them.

They were like the prints left by a horse's hooves. When the earth dried, they remained there, stern, deep, like a soldier's heavy tread. It was as if something weighed on my shoulders, using my footsteps greedily to bite the earth as I walked. That was why I did not recognize them. The footprints left in the mud or stamped in the dry earth were not mine. I did not yet have the right to my own footprints since too many painful things had happened before my birth. Those footprints could have belonged to any one of them: Harutiun Atanasian, Vartan Arakelian, Yervant and Vagharshag Hovnanian, Kevork Kestanian, Ruben Israelian, Kevork Hazarian, Hapet Kasparian, Khosrov Bedrosian, Hovhannes Sahagian, or Mkhitar Harutiunian, who all perished in the tracts of Siberia. Or to Jhirayr Karakashian, Hovhannes Babikian, Zaven Saruni, and Serop Surian, who died shortly after their return home, having become inured in the camps to the thought that the world would outlive them but unprepared to confront the new reality, in which they had outlived a world that had been theirs but which now had vanished.

Even if the box of shoes had been able to reach them, my uncle Vagharshag Hovnanian would not have had the opportunity to wear his. Exhausted by the journey, he was the first to die, in the Lubyanka, without ever reaching Siberia. He died barefoot, which means that even in a place like that he received death with humility.

2.

To the child I was then, the cemetery was like a big garden, where the trees and flowers blossomed a minute earlier than anywhere else. I did not know whence came the power of the trees and flowers. Back then death held no meaning for me. I sensed its silence, I sensed it blooming, and to me that was enough. Death was like an early spring. The first dead man I saw was Grandfather Garabet. He had taught me all kinds of things that are in earth and heaven, showing them to me. He also wished to be the one to show me death. Later I told myself that it happened that way because the world was too small to hold the both of us and all our fantasies at the same time.

Just as no two lives ever resemble each other, no two graves are alike. Perhaps one fine day the dead will come to resemble one another, as Ecclesiastes says. But memories of the dead differ. The grave is a kind of memory, a kind of dying on the inside that leaves a name on the outside, like when you swim sucking air through a reed. Likewise, to develop the idea further, you will never find two cemeteries that are the same. The Armenian cemetery in Focşani was different from the others. In the first place because it was mine and because without my knowing it, it was there that I met death. It revealed itself to me in the form of a flowering apricot tree. In the second place, it was because there were no wooden crosses. I get the impression that in a world of orderliness, where people erect all kinds of walls between themselves and death so that they might protect themselves, the planting of a wooden cross means death has come too quickly.

The Armenians of my childhood were orderly in their dying. They had crosses of stone or marble made for themselves; they chose lovely photographs of themselves to have imprinted on the glossy ceramic plaques. At Paupers' Easter, they would come and sit on stools in front of the crosses, looking at their own names and faces on the stone. Until one day when, having looked and looked, they no longer knew which was which, which was the living person and which the one in the picture. Death was a way of mixing things up, a way of forgetting to go home. The Armenians of my childhood lived long, and they all died in their old age. I used to think it was impossible any other way. In them they had a kind of weariness that prevented them from resting, let alone dying. They felt bewilderment at all the cruel things they had seen in their childhoods, without being able to understand them. Death has an illumining wisdom all of its own. Wonderment prevented them from dying.

Nevertheless, for each of my grandfathers a wooden cross was erected in the beginning. They, Garabet Vosganian and Setrak Melikian, believed that as long as you were alive, you were immortal. They were impassive as they made their way through the world, giving the impression that there would always be time to set a thing right. At any rate, that is what all the men in my family were like, nor do I appear to be any different.

One photograph in particular was dearest to Grandfather Garabet. It showed him with a hat on his head and wearing a raincoat with an upturned collar. When I replaced his wooden cross with one made of stone so that he too might join the ranks of all the other dead, above his name I placed that photograph, imprinted on ceramic. But Grandfather played a trick on us. We say: let's go and visit Grandfather at the cemetery! When we get to the cemetery and look, it is a strange feeling. Wearing his hat and his raincoat with the upturned collar, Grandfather looks like he is the one who is coming to visit us. He continues to roam, smiling waggishly; we are left behind in this world, and he drops in on us every now and then. Life did not succeed in taming him, nor did death. He vanquished them with his hat and his checked raincoat, and the upturned collar is an affectation because he does not look like he is cold in the next world, just as he was not cold in this world.

Grandfather Garabet had a camera with a tripod. Through it we viewed the world. And ourselves. In the old days Grandfather had been a skilled photographer. At a time when color film did not exist, he used to tint his photographs with pastels. But more than anything else he liked to take photographs of himself. Here is Grandfather with a moustache painted under his nose and a lock of hair combed across his forehead, mimicking Hitler. Here he is with a narrow-brimmed hat, cocked to one side, smiling like Charlie Chaplin. Doctor Jekyll and Mister Hyde. Laughing, crying, crouching, leaping. *"Seconde!"* he would cry. You pick the spot. You make a chalk mark. You press the button, run as fast as you can, teeter on tiptoes where the chalk marks the spot. You have exactly three seconds to do that. Then the button automatically clicks. Grandfather took photographs of himself only up until the start of the war. For a while he no longer felt like taking photographs, and after that he was no longer fleet enough to jump inside the frame within three seconds.

We have a lot of photographs. The oldest are also the most beautiful: my great-grandmothers Mariam and Heghine; my great-grandfather, with his harsh face and round-lensed, black-framed spectacles; Grandfather as an adolescent, playing the mandolin. Mixed in with the others are photographs of my grand-father on my mother's side: Setrak. Look, this photograph is from 1915. In the background you can see white walls scorched by the Anatolian sun. The family is gathered around paterfamilias David, who is seated in a high-backed chair. The boys, Setrak and Harutiun, crouch by his feet. The women are behind him: the two little girls, Maro and Satenig, in festive garb, wearing bows in their hair and dresses with white-lace collars. The photographer used to send word ahead a few days beforehand. He traveled from village to village. The wealthiest folk received him at home, and together they would look for the most suitable spot for the high-backed chair, in which the paterfamilias would sit and around which all the others would stand. Other people, the poorer folk, would come to the village square and queue, perspiring in their stiff collars, in their long pleated dresses and shawls. After a while, the photographer would return, going from village to village to deliver the framed photographs. Perched on a stool in front of the crowd, he held up the cardboard sepia prints. Those who recognized themselves raised their hands and received the photograph they had paid for and for the sake of which they had sweated so long.

In almost all the old Armenians' houses I found such photographs. Families gathered around their elders. Unsmiling, rigid, more like exhibits than human beings. In those days the Armenians were dead set on having their photographs taken. It was their way of remaining together because shortly thereafter the families dwindled and were scattered. Even though many perished, in bewilder-ment and so timidly that to this day their graves have not been found, their faces thus remain imprinted on the sepia cardboard with the fading edges. Wishing at all costs to remind you that they once existed. Feeling a premonition of what was to become of them.

Grandfather Garabet and I used to play. He would prime the mechanism and shout, "Run!" And then, "Stop!" He would smile and shrug. "The seconds are up! You didn't get very far!" He would make me listen. "*Seconde*, lad! You can't have any idea who you are unless within three seconds you're ready to be where you have to be. Or else it means you're too old already, like me." He taught me to measure the seconds, without my having to resort to any external mechanism. That is, he taught me quickly to recite in my mind the Prayer of the Heart: "Lord Jesus Christ, Son of God, have mercy on me, a sinner." And with that, the brief time would be up.

The chronicle of my family is like the rope of the big bell. Each turning page is one chime of the bell. And so too were the lives of those in my family: monks, princes, merchants, bookmen, and shepherds, wandering exhausted, faces made gaunt by the wind blowing from the times that they breasted.

For them, history was not to be an orderly stack of graves, each laid on top of the last. You imagine people full of hope, following a diviner with a hazel twig. "Dig here," says the diviner. "You will find water." The news of the diviner's arrival is cause for celebration. Where there is flowing water, sooner or later a well will be dug nearby. Where there is a well, one fine day there will also be a house.

Our diviner was not received joyfully, however. He did not wear townsman's clothes. He looked more like a monk. He went barefoot, and his cassock seemed never to have known the needle's prick. His feet glided over the stones without bleeding. The people left behind their homes and their chattels and followed him in silence, with their babes in arms, leading by the hand the children old enough to walk. "Dig here," said the guide. "In this place there will be a grave." The convoy thinned out, like an unraveling string of beads. In the meantime, the infants absorbed a little strength from their mothers' teats, they descended from their mothers' arms, and others took their place. They had been walking for so long, without knowing where, that they now unwittingly climbed to heaven, up the unseen rope of a bell whose round, undented lip merged with the horizon. And this is why within me many things have neither come to birth nor died; they merely come down from heaven.

Once, my grandfather took me to the circus, a large, dark-hued tent in the field that had previously been the cattle corral. The lion tamer set fire to the hoop he was holding, and wavering briefly, the lioness leapt through. Then she obediently went and sat back down in her place. "Wait," cries my aunt Maro. She wipes her wet hands on her apron and then joins the others in the photograph. Like in a game of pick-up sticks, each is lifted out of the photograph. An unknown hand lifts the sticks one by one, trying not to disturb the others. In the photograph Maro smiles, her palms pressed to her skirt so that their wetness will not gleam. The entry into time. Then the egress. Maro, pursued by Janissaries, casts herself off the rocks into the roiling, ruddy waters of the Euphrates. The hoop remains behind her, burning still. Other women, brides or mothers, get ready to leap after her. An endless convoy. Pietà. The women approach silently, and for a moment each rests in the arms of the Virgin. I do not know what comes afterward.

The only photograph of the whole family is in my stamp album. You will be amazed, but instead of Armenian faces, with thick eyebrows and swarthy eyes, you will find there the powdered wig of George Washington, the crown of Queen Elizabeth, and the cedars of Lebanon.

My grandfather taught me how to unglue stamps from envelopes without spoiling them. Place moistened cotton wool on the corner with the stamp. When the paper dampens, the corner curls up, and once the adhesive has dissolved, the stamp peels off easily. Then lay out the stamps to dry on the little shelf above the stove. And so here they are. The new history of my family, all that remained of them after the convoys unraveled. Having set out from Adana, Van, Afion Karahisar, Constantinople. Having crossed the deserts of Mesopotamia, where the corpses littered the roadside or bobbed water-bloated; having passed through the dark bowels of the ships and over the greasy decks, through orphanages; having stood amid the hurriedly packed baggage. The bodies had to grow lean before they could leap through the next ring of fire.

The Statue of Liberty is my aunt Hayguhi, the sister of Sahag Sheitanian. She came to Romania in 1919, and after the Second World War she emigrated to the United States via Lebanon. The envelopes with the stamps of the Statue of Liberty show her neat handwriting; they were posted from Hartford, on the East Coast. George Washington arrives from the West Coast, and below him the address is written in the hurried hand of Uncle Kevork Kiulahian, Father's cousin, or in the painstaking hand of Aunt Anahid, the sister of Uncle Kevork. Here is the American eagle, wings spread, moistened by the lips of Aunt Satenig, the sister of Grandfather Setrak. Simón Bolívar, wearing epaulettes, his rigid hand grasping his sword hilt, is the face beneath which lies hidden Haig, the brother of Dikran Bedrosian the watchmaker, in Venezuela. The exotic birds come all the way from Argentina, posted by Zaruhi, the sister of Grandfather Garabet. The small stamps, with Slavonic script, tell of Ovannes, the younger brother of Grandfather Garabet, who ekes out his days in an old people's home in Silistra; the stamps are attached crookedly; his eyesight is dim; and even the writing, thinks Grandfather, is not his. He dictates his missives to someone else. Beneath the swarthy features of Gamal Abdel Nasser I divine the delicate face of Luisa, the daughter of Ovannes, who married in Cairo. In their shade the cedars of Lebanon shelter our other cousins, who remained in the Orient, reckoning that Europe, so indifferent to their sufferings, would not provide them with a good home. But even so, here is the face of Napoleon, here a painting by Delacroix, from the midst of which a woman wearing a Phrygian bonnet gives the battle cry; they were posted by Berj, the son of Yervant Hovnanian, who died in Siberia.

I arrange them in meticulous order. I decide to put the closest blood relatives at the front, behind them the relatives by marriage, with whom my grandparents shared only surnames, and then those with whom they were akin in suffering above all else. I start over. This time in order of the distance separating them. First, those who took a different road as long ago as the time of the massacres, crossing into Syria, Lebanon, or Egypt, remaining there or crossing the Mediterranean to Marseille or not stopping even there but crossing the Atlantic all the way to New York. Then the others, who came to Europe at the outset, waiting for the gates of the Black Sea to open and bearing a name that never before in history had been given to any people: the stateless. Which is to say, not deprived of a homeland to love but deprived of a state to protect them. And so that they would still have a name in the dictionaries and a country beneath which, on a scrap of paper, their identity might be inscribed, a new country was invented that lay everywhere and nowhere. They were the wandering sons and servants of this new and strange homeland, invented by Fridtjof Nansen, the League of Nations commissioner for refugees. If you have a stateless person's passport, it means that of all the rights you formerly possessed you preserve only those bestowed by God: a name originating from a nation, which is to say, a surname, and the mark of baptism, which is to say, a Christian name. Birth and baptism. Most Armenian family names end in "-ian," denoting membership in a family, principally via the paternal line. Kevorkian, for example. That is, "of Kevork," which in the Armenian language means George. Thanks to this new father, blue-eyed, white-skinned, snowy-haired, wholly untypical of a swarthy, dusky-eyed folk, the Armenians called themselves Nansenian, which is to say, "of no man." In our house we have a photograph of Nansen, with his feathery moustache and gentle gaze. No one else, not even the Norwegians, mentioned the name of this intrepid explorer more than the Armenians. "We did not gain Romanian citizenship until 1948," Grandfather Garabet wrote in the papers I found after his death. "Up until then they didn't let us join the army; we couldn't start a business under our own names; and although we could leave and travel wherever the eye could see, no one else would take us. We were Nansenians." This new species, the Nansenians, disembarked in the port of Constanța with the permission of the Brătianu government, the first government in the world willing to recognize that there could exist citizens of a state not to be found on any map. The Nansenians, hardworking and taciturn, dispersed among the nearby towns: Galați, Brăila, Babadag, Silistra, Balcic. Then, emboldened, they fanned out to Focșani, Buzău, Ploiești, Bucharest, Pitești, and Craiova. They filled the streets with the aromas of the oriental spices they sold in shops whose round signs were inscribed with strange names. They spoke an ancient language, one harsh and at the same time mournful; they spoke crisp words, which, around the time of my birth, gradually faded to whispers. After the war, many of them, swayed by the Communist propaganda, sold everything they had, gathered their bundles once more, and set off to Soviet Armenia. Others, taking advantage of the fact that their new land, having tried in vain to persuade them of its virtues, deemed it better to let them leave, scattered in every direction. Most of them headed for America. These were the last wave to find their place in my stamp album, even if, who knows, one fine day it might turn out that this shore was not the one they had been seeking after all, and they will set off yet again.

Then I decided to arrange them according to the only border of which I could be sure: that of my birth. First, I arranged those whom I had known, the fewer in number, and then those whom I had not known, the many. The younger I placed before the older, the living before the dead, those who had not wandered before those worn out by wandering. To judge by the state of things at my birth, history no longer had any logic. In other words, none of the things that had previously happened could have foretold me. I was an accident, and looking through the narrow window that was my life, barely wide enough for an eye to peek or the barrel of a rifle to poke, the meanings of history blurred. History itself became random.

I arranged them in order of birth. But this is not how people are told apart; all people are born, and each starts the count afresh. Then I came to an understanding with Grandfather Garabet, and I arranged them in order of death. People are told apart not by how they are born but by how they die. First came Lenin, surrounded by red flags. Lenin was the messenger of old man Hrant from Constanța, who wrote us that he had been released from prison camp, but because he possessed neither papers nor the strength to make the return journey all the way from the Taimyr Peninsula, he had decided to end his days in the Soviet Union. Then Simón Bolívar, who kept vigil over the spent body of Grandfather Garabet's sister, buried in Buenos Aires not far from the monument erected to the glory of Hovhannes Tsetsian, Kossuth's general, who after the defeat of 1849 went from Transylvania all the way to Argentina, where he founded the Military Academy. In the time that followed upon their deaths, it was easy to place my family members in sequence. But what of the living? With the intransigence and candor of a child, I decided their fates. And so this is their group photograph, after a whole century of wandering, after two world wars, after so many exoduses. They pass from the random pages of history into the thick leaves of the stamp album, which are like the sepia plates of a daguerreotype. The postmarks of my nation, for which the earth has always been round, boundless. Wearing strange faces, to match the strange roads that stretched away beneath the soles of their feet, like thick Isfahan carpets.

It is in the middle that George Washington always takes his place, with his round face and curly wig, leaning haughtily on his sword. Flanking him are Napoleon Bonaparte, Simón Bolívar, and Gamal Abdel Nasser. They draw back a pace, beckoning to Queen Elizabeth II, who, enlivened by the presence of so many heroic figures, takes off her crown and dons the Phrygian bonnet, becoming the new wife of my uncle Berj Hovnanian in Paris. In the background can be glimpsed thick cedar branches in which the shed ages rustle like leaves. To one side, with slanting, suspicious eyes, stand Lenin and Dimitrov. "Smile!" I tell them. They obey the child's command. Solemn and awkward, they stand rigidly. Of all the things to which history might inure them, for them the hardest of all is to learn how to smile.

What do they all have in common, these postage-stamp queens, emperors, and generals, whether on horseback or planting their spurs in freshly conquered and therefore blood-soaked earth? How is it that they can coalesce to form my family photograph? What is it that connects all the powdered faces and crowned heads, stern and satisfied, on these stamps? What is the mark that the photographer of long ago—the one who took a picture of my family in the village of Zakar in Anatolia, a few days before the massacre and the dispersal— perhaps retouched in puzzlement? That mark is the postmark.

Smile. My ancestors, then my uncles and aunts, withdraw behind curtains, pleats, frock coats, and sweating saddles. Straining to fit inside my stamp album, emperors, kings, queens, generals, monseigneurs pell-mell force themselves to smile. The things that bring to mind my Armenian people, among the pleats of regal trains, amid the uniforms and frock coats, and in the gleam of swords and the darkness of the canon's mouth, are nothing but postage stamps.

This is the new photograph of my family. A postmarked history.

I did not like mirrors. They sensed this and punished me for it. A huge creature watched me, dozing, lazily lifting one eyelid, a ravenous creature that wielded mirrors or anything capable of reflection so that it could steal my soul.

It was from my grandmother Arshaluis that I learned the following. The daughter of Ionescu the cobbler from the corner of our street died young. She had not been suffering from any illness, in any event not from any earthly illness. She had grown gaunt, her eyes sinking into her head, until unawares, she vanished from this world. No one recalled her funeral or whether it ever took place. The cobbler kept her photograph on a shelf in his workshop, among the jars of shoemaker's paste and the shoetrees. The photograph was faded, and the features of the face were no longer distinguishable. She slowly trickled off the silvered surfaces in the same way as she had slid out of this world. Grandmother Arshaluis had discovered the cause of death: "Her sleep was reflected in the mirror." Which is to say, the girl's bed stood in front of a mirror. People can look at themselves in the mirror as long as they want, but not so dreams. Once reflected, dreams remain riveted there. Rather than dissolving with the coming of dawn, they collect like hoarfrost or like beads of cold sweat on the brow. And indeed this had been the first sign of the girl's illness. "Her dreams used to collect in cold beads on her brow." Dr. Zilbermann, who after the war changed his name to Argintaru, "silversmith" in Romanian, stubbornly refused to believe a word of it, but even he agreed that it was unusual for a brow so cold, without any trace of a fever, to be beaded with sweat like that. Ionescu the cobbler's daughter died because she had been unable to disentangle herself from her own dreams. Submerged ever deeper in the visions of her dreams, she had gradually frayed apart.

Grandfather Garabet, on the other hand, was fascinated by the short memory of mirrors. "Not a trace," he used to say, stroking the bright surface. Not a quiver, not an echo. Viewed in a mirror, history is equal to naught.

My grandfather suggested that we should vanquish the mirrors. Together we began to wage war against them. "The direst weapon against mirrors is memory," decided grandfather. "Therefore, let us imbue the mirrors with memory."

Our most fearsome foe proved to be the largest mirror. We could only vanquish it by cunning. We began by taking advantage of the treachery of mirrors. A second mirror, placed in front of the large one, multiplied the images endlessly. But we accomplished nothing. The mirror's moment in time proved to be infinite in appearance but equally devoid of traces. The moment had depth, but it did not have duration.

We had to seek another way. Grandfather placed the camera tripod in front of the mirror. "If it so flatly refuses, we'll just have to shove memory down its throat." Photographing it seemed the easiest thing in the world. You don't need to lie in wait for it, as it remains motionless anyhow. But what must you do to lure the memory into approaching without noticing the cunning trick? The photographer and his apparatus had to capture the image while remaining outside of it. The mirror proved to be exceedingly rapacious. It would cast a net of light at us, capturing us every time. Struggle was futile. It was a different kind of fishing, where the net was flung from water to dry land. We decided to photograph it from one side so that it would not see us. But then the mirror would turn into a knife blade. There were no longer any images within it but only glints of light. And without images, memory slips through our fingers.

How to photograph the mirror without seeing yourself in it? How to understand the world while placing yourself outside of it?

The problem is ultimately trigonometric in nature. Your position inside or outside the world is expressed as the sine and cosine. Grandfather set about making calculations. The best angle proved to be one of twenty-three degrees. "We are too high up," reckoned Grandfather. "We need to view the core of the earth from the tropics. It is the best place from which to view the world while remaining outside it. The higher you climb toward the North Pole, the more quickly life engulfs you." Our room, with its pendulum clock, its large mirror, its mysterious bookcase, its photographic equipment and pots of paint, seemed to me wider than the world. And therefore we had to believe that the largest and greediest mirror was the very core of the earth, that our room might have its own tropics. I measured the floor with my paces. "Stop!" Grandfather marked the spot with chalk and set up the tripod. We had to be careful lest the mirror pounce and swallow Grandfather, tripod and all. "Let's lure it somehow. Let's divert its attention. You will be the mirror's bait." I sat down in front of it. I spread my arms out so that the mirror would have more to work on. The image was beautiful. Had it not been for the thick black wooden frame, with its arched top, the image would have looked like the real me. Out of the corner of my eye I saw the reflection of the tripod in the mirror. I realized that our battle was in vain. We were battling not against the mirror but against light itself and all the more so given that viewed that way, the problem was solved. Even if it treads only over mirrors, light has a memory.

The largest mirror knew, and it wreaked its vengeance. Grandfather took great pains to seek fresh angles, to creep furtively with the tripod. We even tried after dusk, but the mirror never slept. Grandfather gave up. He sat down in front of the mirror and talked to it, to his image, which had no means of answering him. Or perhaps it answered in some way because Grandfather, after a few moments of silence, went on talking. Again he jumbled together the different languages he spoke.

Until one day. The largest mirror was old. Sometimes the reflections would coalesce crookedly, as if underwater. He called me over to him. My corner of the mirror was limpid, my image smooth and clear. His part of the mirror was murky, the image blurred. "You see," said my grandfather Garabet. "Even the mirrors have tired of me. It is time to die."

My grandparents were merchants. All the travelers in my family were merchants of one kind or another. They brought to Europe the melancholy waft of spices. They were enveloped in the steam of coffee and in the aroma of blocks of *lokum* and halva. They went all the way to the western ports, to Amsterdam and Marseille. From there the more intrepid ones went to America, mixing rice into the coffee beans or chickpeas so that its grains would entice the moist ocean air, so greedy for dryness, and leave the coffee untouched. The journeys of the caravans were long. The merchants awaited their goods in the ports; they marshaled them in the warehouses of Aleppo, Tabriz, and Tiflis; and then they set off by more sheltered routes, via Odessa and Lvov. Some went down to Suczawa, where there were cattle markets, and thence over the mountains, making their way to Vienna. Others traveled as far as the misty lands by the North Sea. In those days, peppercorns were scarce and costly. Sprinkled on meat left to dry, they helped it keep over summer, and with their sharpness they invigorated the body. In return the Armenian merchants received handsome sums in coins, which they tested by biting on them or by scratching the metal with a needle. Or else they grasped the coins in their fist, closing their eyes, in silence; the blood could sense the gold, which throbbed, warming their fingers.

They would buy tools, bolts of cloth, wine, and honey, goods hard to come by in the dry, mountainous lands of Anatolia. But the journey did not end there. In Karabakh or in Bukhara, the merchants converted their coin into carpets, which in those regions were thick and soft, so that they might substitute for grass beneath the soles of the feet. Once finished, the carpet was spread in front of the shop to let the passersby feel its softness and so that its colors would catch their eye. The carpets' journey led to the far ends of the earth, to Bombay, Calcutta, and farther still, to Macao and Shanghai. There, by the yellow seas, the carpets completed their journey, and the merchants returned by way of the Silk Road. The merchants never stopped. When a translucent streak could be seen glimmering on the horizon, it was said that some had not stopped for centuries, and now they haunted the desert roads and caravanserais, mingling coin and the passing centuries.

When the servants and the pack animals, the donkeys and the camels, demanded their rightful rest, the merchants would go round and round in a smaller but just as bounteous circle. They would fill their carts with fruit from Yerevan or Baku: pomegranates, red-fleshed melons, honey-fleshed melons from Turkestan, apricots as big as your fist, small fresh seedless grapes in summer, and raisins in winter. The journey of the fruit was shorter, as far as Rostov or Simferopol, where it was exchanged for salt fish or cheeses preserved in barrels of saltwater. The trade in foodstuffs was over shorter distances; it depended on the season and had nothing of the lonely grandeur that dominated the spice routes, linking oceans and auroras. The swarthy merchants, with their peppercorn-colored eyes, drove their caravans, sleeping in the saddle, their chins resting on their chests; like wild beasts they sniffed the open sky for signs of a storm; the sharpness of the wind-driven sand and snows from the high plateaus furrowed their cheeks. When the waters dwindled and hid during the drought, like snakes inside the earth, the Armenian merchants kept a pomegranate seed under their tongues, filling their mouths with coolness and beguiling their thirst.

Together we followed the passage of the caravans. I mingled with the horses after their burdens were unloaded for the night; I stood by the fires around which the men danced, leaping over the flames to the rhythm of the drums and the flutes; I walked beside the creatures that drowsed as they went, sometimes starting but never falling asleep. Then I sought the merchants in the town of my childhood, on the narrow cobbled streets with their wooden fences. I looked at them through the dusty windows and went inside, seeking in the darkness of the hemp sacks the aroma of coffee and spices. Focşani, a city in the plain, at a cross-roads, had sprung up as a way station. Later, the way station, like any other place of rest on the banks of a river, had mellowed, had worn in. It was here that the *voivodes* set up customs posts between Moldavia and Wallachia. The merchants who happened to have grown weary in that very spot tethered their horses and built houses. As they grow, the largest trees, like the cedars of Lebanon, drag the earth up after them; they raise it and fix it in place. This is how towns arose, an-chored to the largest tree, which was the church. After the first altar was erected, booths sprang up around the church. They extended farther and farther along the road, as each new booth vied to be the first the customers would come to. That street was called the High Street (what else?), and after the Commission of the Principalities was established in Focşani, it gained the name by which it is known to this day: Unification High Street. The merchants were mixed: Arme-nians who had come down by the Lvov road from Botoşani, Jassy, or Suczawa; Greeks who brought goods from the Danube ports; Albanians who sold sweets; and craftsmen from Vrancea, who in that town in the plain continued to ply their Wallachian trades: weaving and woodcarving. At the end of the nineteenth century, driven from the east and encouraged by more hospitable laws, Jewish merchants arrived too, dotting the High Street. They began to sell a ware that was wholly out of the ordinary and that nobody had ever thought of laying out on his stall before then: time. The purveyors of time had no shelves; their win-dows were unwelcoming, half-shuttered. Their shops were dark and their coun-ters narrow. But they were wide enough to hold stacks of that imaginary ware. In a town that had thitherto existed outside time, that ware found countless customers. Those merchants had piercing eyes, which bored into you. They sat hunched up, their shoulders bent over palms that rubbed together endlessly, like rolling mills. They had no use for scales or weights. Each merchant's time was inscribed on the yellowing pages of ledgers. The man who came to buy time found out the price later. As he consumed what he had purchased—that is, leisure—the seeming calm was transformed into disquiet, carefreeness into care. This was the first price he paid. Time always proved to be a ware dearer than it had seemed at first sight. In his mind, the customer cursed the trader, he cursed the covenant he had made, realizing too late that the time he had purchased remained too short, that it was useless, unlived. And because time as such does not belong to people and because you cannot sell time, the same as you cannot sell the night or the wind or the light, the merchants gave it a dif-ferent name: interest. The longer the time you needed, the greater the interest.

Time flows at the same speed as blood. A world devoid of blood is a world devoid of time. The customers had pallid faces; their blood had been thinned by the too short time at their disposal. The merchants weighed them up with a glance. Then, on the sly, in the dark, their eyes glinting, they produced the shiny coins. The man took the fistful of money; he gained a little time, but what he had to give back was always more, always too much. That is why the purveyors of time were held in enmity. The priests anathematized the usurers. By day, people crossed to the other side of the street. But in the evening, the bankrupt debtors, the card players, the fallen women, and the impoverished shopkeepers knocked at their doors and slipped inside, fearfully casting their eyes up and down the street. As such a trade could not go on for long without the enmity becoming perilous to them, the Jews gradually gave it up. They became grocers, tavern keepers, and sometimes craftsmen. They built shops with an upper story, and the High Street, with its cobbled road, its broad pavements and shady chestnut trees, became a place where it was a joy to stroll in the evening and greet people, giving them a bow so that you could receive a bow in return. The High Street was closed to motorcars and carts. On May 10, the anniversary of the dynasty, the regiment would march down the High Street with cadenced step, past the people crowding the pavements, followed by the military brass band and a gaggle of children. On a number of occasions the king himself passed by, in a carriage drawn by horses adorned with tassels, on his way to Czernowitz. When war came, the Jewish shops began to close. The earthquake of 1940 destroyed the upper stories. Unsold time leaked from the padlocked chests and rose into the sky above the town. The dust floated above the ruins for many hours.

After the war, during the famine, commerce moved to the outskirts, where grain brought on trains from Oltenia was sold. And with the coming of the Communists, when private trade was no longer allowed, the merchants of former days were replaced by the managers of state commerce. The more stubborn merchants and craftsmen—Armenians among them—moved their businesses and their trades to their own homes, where they worked after nightfall. By daylight they were managers or cooperative workers; they received goods to sell for ration-book points or at the prices published in the newspaper and pasted on the wall. On the May Day and August 23 holidays, those prices were reduced by five bani as a way of demonstrating the superiority of the new Communist times, compared with rotten capitalism. Grandfather Garabet and his brother-in-law Sahag closed their shop on the High Street. During the war Grandmother Arshaluis made dolls to sell. Grandfather, with his tripod slung over his back, roamed the streets. Sometimes, a German soldier would stop him to have his photograph taken so that he could prove to his folks back home that he was still alive in that war against the Russians. Later, he photographed the Russians, who wanted to prove to their folks back home that they were still alive in that war against the Germans. And finally, he photographed the returning Romanians, who, not having anybody to whom they could send the photographs, wanted to prove to themselves that they were still alive.

From the monks in my family I received the strength to say the Prayer of the Heart without needing any words. To make the sign of the cross, about which Grandfather Garabet told me the following story: "The trees make the sign of the cross where their branches intersect. When they spread their wings to fly, the birds make the sign of the cross against the sky. Of all things that exist, only man does not incorporate the sign in his body. This is why our Lord Jesus Christ was crucified for us."

From the warriors in my family I received the strength to be vanquished, for only the vanquished truly die for their ideas, but to carry myself like a victor for precisely that reason. I learned to read history differently, by the tracks left by the horses' hooves. In the silence after the battle, those tracks say that there is still an arrow that has not struck home, a wound that has not bled its fill; a neigh can still be heard that the foaming bit has not choked. In my mouth I taste mingled flavors. The mounted warriors of my family kept a straight path no matter how much the times rose and fell. In this way, my family intersected with history, just as you cannot cross from one bank to the other without intersecting with the waters.

From the shepherds of my family I received the strength to honor the seasons. And I have never ceased to seek the merchants. As a child I felt a fascination for shop counters. I would sit huddled on the stone steps, looking through the window or lingering within. The wood was dark, greasy, dotted with crumbs; across it hands reached to grasp wads of money, and the goods were smoothed down, handled, weighed up. It was a frontier that could not be found on any map, across which could pass hankerings and phantasms but never living people. Like the banks of the Acheron.

I lived among poor people. The victuals were in keeping with the poverty. The sugar and flour were sold straight from the sack. We gleaned the chaff from the rice spread over a newspaper. Marmalade was cut with a knife from a block, and the cheese, of a single variety, was sold from barrels in which the brine strained to disguise the lack of freshness. The floorboards were doused with diesel so that the tread of feet would not wear them thin, and from the ceilings hung a kind of ventilator, like a rotor blade, to drive away the flies and preserve a smattering of coolness on the meats, whose blood coagulated into blackened ridges. There were many other things that we made at home. Sweetmeats were made using fruit from our backyard, picked from the tree or gathered from the ground. Cabbages and green tomatoes were crammed into pickling barrels that were broached on the eve of the festive season. Rancid fat was kept in the larder, and having seethed for a whole day, it was left to set, congealing into soap. Linden and chamomile flowers, mint leaves, and rose hips were dried for tisanes. At the bottom of the backyards henhouses were knocked together and sometimes pigsties. The meat was stored in jars, preserved in grease. During the war, many people had learned how to bake their own bread, and an evening before they would leave the dough to leaven, watching the yeast raise it as if by miracle. We would look mindfully at the few foodstuffs that could be bought. Like guests, we would eat them awkwardly, after every mouthful weighing with our eyes the part remaining.

And that was precisely why the shop was such a wonder! I would slip inside on my own or hand in hand with my grandfather, and I would rejoice. The hemp sacks of flour, maize, sugar, and rice in Bobîrcă's grocery shop looked to me like bags of gold coins in a treasury. All that could be found on the other side of the counter acquired the devouring dazzle and aroma of a forbidden world. The counter was a threshold too high for my height as a child.

Bobîrcă, the gatekeeper who guarded things forbidden and enticing, was swarthy and wore long-sleeved overalls. He wore a broad knife in his waistband, and when he raised it above the blocks of marmalade and halva, his hand would trace circles, as if the gleaming blade demanded a sacrifice. The olives were shriveled, and Grandfather would pour oil over them. He would leave them for a while so that the tegument around the stone would swell enough to allow you to bite into it. The salt fish was fearsome, and the brown paper bags leaked trails of gray flour from their corners. But how wonderful everything became within the shop! The flour looked like powdered silver, and the grains of salt glinted like crystals in a cave. The open mouths of the hemp sacks watched like the eyes of marine creatures, the packets were nacreous, and the hanks of meat and salamis hanging from hooks spun like birds with outspread wings. "And this, and some of this," Grandfather would say. Bobîrcă would float above his wares, jerking his arms. There seemed too many things for just one man, but for each he had a tool with which to cut, mince, bind. "And something for the lad here," Grandfather would add. We went outside, and it was daylight again. I had to accustom myself to the light outside, shading my eyes with my hand.

I never crossed to the other side of Bobîrcă's counter. And I do not remember him ever crossing to this side of it. Bobîrcă would gaze out of the windows. He would sit on a stool, leaning his elbow on the counter, with his eyes on the street. He did not look happy when he saw us come in. Speaking to him about the world outside, we stole away from him something of his image of that world.

I do not even know when he vanished. He seeped away between his sacks. In the shady air, he added to the damp, absorbed by the greedy powder of the flour, the maize, the grains of rice.

In the other shop, Angheluță's candy store, the light was refracted; it unraveled among the candied sugar; it filled the jars, as thick as honey. I dipped my hands in it and anointed my face with it. In Bobîrcă's world, the things were only half visible and sometimes frightened me: the fish with split bellies, rolled in salt; the pipes; the funnels; the thick-bladed knife; the bones, like petrified horse heads with gaping muzzles. But in Angheluță's candy store it was always nice. Not much light came through the windows, but inside it was augmented. It enveloped things in such a way that you did not know whether they received light or were a source of light.

Angheluță was a stooped old man. His face was withered, and so were his hands. His body was the only form that did not partake in the enveloping light. He had been appointed guardian of the light, and he was not allowed to keep any of it for himself. But with his dark eyes he craved it. He spoke softly and moved to the rhythm of his speech. Bobîrcă's footsteps bashed the stone flags, as if he were wearing soldier's boots, but Angheluță's gait was inaudible. I think he walked barefoot. Angheluță and Bobîrcă were the same in one respect. They both spent long periods looking out of the window at the street. They yearned. Bobîrcă yearned for the light on the street, which was more copious than in his shop, where the light sprang mainly from the salt glinting on the dried meats. Angheluță yearned for the light on the street, which was less copious than in his shop but warmer.

Then there were the candies in Angheluță's store. The sugar candies looked like the crystals in the big chandelier of the Armenian church. The colors of the blocks of Turkish delight—green, yellow, pink—were blurred beneath white powder, which melted on the tongue, as cool as snow. The packets of wafer biscuits rustled between the fingers like dry leaves. In the tall glass jars, the sugared almonds, the fruit drops, the caramels gradually grew sticky. I used to roll them from one side of my mouth to the other, trying to preserve their taste for as long as possible. The fruit jellies crunched between the teeth, releasing their scent of mingled seasons.

Conversely, Mercan's establishment seemed not to have any trace of mystery. He did not ply his trade in a shop, and he did not look out of a window, yearning for the light. Mercan's shop was in the open air. In his yard, stacks of bottles and squarer stacks of jars formed a kind of pen, whose entrance was like the portal of a higgledy-piggledy fortress. "The time has come!" announced Grandfather, looking at the crammed shelves. It was the signal for us boys to wash the bottles. The green and yellow cooking-oil bottles, the *zakouska* jars, the milk bottles. Sometimes there was even a champagne bottle, which was the most precious of all. Using a whisk, we raked the innards of the bottles, removing droplets of oil or sticky sauce and flecks of mold. To be accepted, the bottles had to have an inscription embossed on the bottom, in large letters. Without that inscription, Mercan would reject them: STAS. That is, State Standard. The ones that were not STAS were no good, even if they were the most beautiful, being foreign or old, with strange shapes and designs. In my childhood there was room only for things that were State Standard, for things that looked like everything else, things that you could judge solely by their likeness to each other. The bottles and jars stood in a row on the shelf. Grandfather examined them one by one. These were good: no chips, cracks, oil stains, or glue from labels. The others were no good. And if the ones that were not STAS or that were chipped did not have a neck wide enough to allow them to be used for compote or tomato broth, we took them to a sinister place called the CAD, the collections and acquisitions depot. That was where mounds of broken glass, threadbare clothes, and yellowing books were collected, alongside the rusting hulks of old motorcars. The Gypsies came there to load their carts, and they grazed their horses on the surrounding fields. From time to time, the large, flat bones of beasts of burden emerged from the useless mounds. Once, I saw a horse's skull, bleached by the sun. Nonetheless, the horses grazed peacefully nearby. As long as there was grass, they felt secure. Either grass or death. On that field of dismal heaps eternally raked by the carters' pitchforks, the grass grew stringy and undisturbed.

Mercan bought bottles and jars. He lived among his stacks, which grew ceaselessly and which, when the wind whipped up, chimed like a forest of silver. In town he was the first to sense it when the winds rose. I do not know whether he was short or tall because I only ever saw him sitting down. I suspect he was short, however; otherwise his head would not have felt it needed to be so big and pointy. He had wide nostrils and jug ears, which were like that deliberately so that he could gobble up air and sounds. Lord of a nation of breaths, he detected the slightest rustle with those huge fleshy funnels that hung where his nose and ears should have been. "Tell your grandfather that spring is on the way," he would say. I would run back home as fast as I could. "Spring is on the way," I would pant. "Mercan said so." "Finally! Thank the Lord!" Grandfather rejoiced. And he set about planting seeds in the garden. Or else Mercan would say, "That's an Arctic wind. It will snow tomorrow or the day after." Grandfather did not wait to be told twice, even though it was only the middle of November. He quickly wrapped the stumps of the rose bushes in foil.

When the air was as soft on the one side as it was on the other and there was calm in the sky, Mercan would carefully examine every bottle, every jar. He ran his finger over the lips of the bottles, raised them to the light, sniffed them with greedy nostrils. Two or three he would give back to me. The others he would place on the stacks. "Why?" I complained, knowing how upset Grandfather would be at every rejected bottle; he waged a muffled battle with Mercan. But Mercan had his own customs regulations, and he never changed his mind. "Even this one?" I asked in desperation. He looked up and placed his finger on his lips. "Shush!" And a few moments later: "A bird is flying past." To mollify him, I used to help him arrange the bottles in crates. "Put that one with the butterflies," he said, pointing at the stacks. "Put that other one with the birds." I looked at the empty bottle in puzzlement. Where was the butterfly? With closed eyes, he sniffed the opening of the jar, like a wine taster. "A butterfly has flown in this air," he said, unperturbed. "And so do like I told you." "How do you know?" "The traces are left in the air," he said. "There's no grass to cover them over." I obeyed. Some bottles and jars went with the butterflies, some with the leaves, some with the birds. Once he paused and sniffed again for a long moment. He then pointed at a heap of bottles in one corner. "Put this one with the angels."

At Mercan's I felt in my element. There was no counter. Or if there was one, it floated above our heads.

On the other hand, the stall of the halva seller was everywhere. At every step there is a tollbooth you have to pass. He would arrive from the west of town, at the crack of dawn, from the other side of the railway barrier on the road to the village of Cîmpineanca. But others would swear that in the morning he came from the other side of the Brăila barrier, in the east of town. During the day, I encountered him where I least expected, always in a different place. His stall was an oblong box in which he kept the halva. The box had two wheels and two long handles. The halva seller held the two handles and pushed the cart. He walked slowly, swaying, along the edge of the road, turning his head at the passing cars. More often than not, he stood at a crossroads, in the places where passersby lingered, having to decide which way to go next. He wore two white sleeves over his shirt; he tied them with elastic around his elbows. He brought out the block of halva and carved it with a long knife. A slice cost one leu. When the leu began to fall in value, the halva seller did not raise his price but rather cut thinner slices so that he could go on receiving the same coin for each slice.

We used to run to buy halva. But the stall was no longer there. We gave up. Carried away with our games, we forgot about the stall, and it was then that it would appear at the crossroads. You had to have a coin ready at any moment. The halva seller's stall was a tollbooth different from the others. You sought it but did not find it. It arrived unexpectedly. It was the tollbooth for which you had to be ready at any moment.

Bobîrcă kept an ink pencil behind his ear. He moistened it between his lips and wrote sums in a notebook. You counted out the money, and he gave you the change, sometimes with inky fingerprints on the banknotes. Angheluță did not do his sums with a pencil. He moistened his finger in his mouth and did his sums in powdered sugar spread over the countertop. You had to take him at his word; you couldn't check because the white powder recoalesced, ready for a new sum.

The halva seller did not have to do sums. For him things were simple. Each customer had to do his own sums and to know how many coins he was prepared to give him, how many equal slices he wanted.

We spread out and stood on street corners to keep a lookout for him. Toward dusk, at the crossroads he had chosen for that evening, he gathered up the slices that were left over because people had not been ready for him. He took off his white sleeves, rubbed his knife on the hem of his coat, and set off slowly. It was easy to keep up with him; he did not quicken his steps, and he did not glance to either side. He walked past the cinema and went down Tanners Street. He was heading westward, we thought. All of a sudden we saw him stop and turn toward us. We huddled together, expecting him to stand in front of us and scold us. But as he approached, it was as if he were receding into the distance. He was coming toward us, and yet he grew smaller and smaller until he vanished completely. Watching him, we could not tell whether he was drawing nearer or moving farther away.

A web of fine threads connected the town to stop it disintegrating: the traders. Arriving by the same road as the caravans, they continued to weave their web even in the scanty times of the Communist period. Mr. Romaşcanu, the soda water seller. Old man Ardeleanu, who sold cheese pies at the Merry Invalid. Auntie Azoiții from the State Grocery Store. Then there were the Armenians. Dikran Bedrosian, the fountain pen seller. Vrej Papazian, the watchmaker. And Arusica, his wife, stooped over a lamp, plying a trade that no longer exists: the repair of ladies' stockings. Anton Merzian and Krikor Minasian, the cobblers. My godfather Sahag Sheitanian, with his cake booth at the train station, which he opened for business at the crack of dawn for the travelers taking the Bucharest train first thing in the morning. The last of the Jews, Mr. Weissmann, who traded in trade, running a commission shop in the market. And there was also a throng of street vendors who sold all manner of things, from fish and cow bellies, which they plunked in the basin of the Covered Market, to wooden spoons carved by the monks from Sihla.

In an adverse world, which had got into the habit of making the least amount of movement possible, a world where clothes and bread were rationed, where most of the thriving shops of yesteryear had had to adopt new methods—state managers and inspectors, trade union meetings, workplace safety posters, fire regulations, inventories, overalls—in that world genuine trade still put forth tendrils and flowed like little rivulets beneath the snow.

Blood is alive only if it flows into blood. This is why the traders sometimes sought each other out. Angheluță closed the shutters on his store of wonders and set off for the town's western barrier. Mercan released his wafts of air to gather like a cloud above the town and followed Angheluță. The hardest to persuade was Bobîrcă. He, who in the darkness of his shop could not see his face in any mirror, was fearful of meeting other people. It was dark in there, although the air cast an unearthly light. But up above there is a different kind of light that never descends to earth. And so without having to draw the shutters since his shop windows were dark anyway, Bobîrcă timidly went outside and slowly picked his way across the cobbles. The other traders emerged from the darkness of their shops, they peeled away from the walls like paint, they slipped through their doorways, they glided under their warped shutters. They turned up their patched collars, they thrust their hands in their darned and redarned pockets, they greeted each other silently, as if they had met by chance, but nonetheless they walked huddled together, shoulder to shoulder, in step, a closely packed, unbroken procession of pilgrims. One like all the rest raised his abacus and slid the black and white beads back and forth, as if playing a harp. Another whistled, his nostrils too narrow for the hunger of his blood. Nobody looked at the sky since there was sky everywhere. They did not look at the cobbles underfoot, at the miry gutters, at the roots poking through the soil, for thence they themselves had come. Fingers felt for gold pieces sewn inside seams. They were where they were supposed to be. Or else they were not. The fingers continued to search in the hiding places of the clothes or the body. The gold pieces, the cockerels, the Napoleons, the thalers, the doubloons jingled. Thank the Lord, the world is not wholly lost; its outlines are not wholly blurred. Thank the Lord, the world still has coin. The procession advanced, to the accompaniment of pockets jingling like spurs. The traders slid along the streets in silence, like a gastropod. The baggy clothes glided over fences, through thorn bushes, through the cracks in doors, without snagging. Perfect gliding. The murmur, the jingle, the rustle of sightless counting in the bottoms of pockets, but a counting no less exact for all that. They moved in the same way, but nonetheless they were very different. Sheep dealers with shaggy sheepskin coats and caps pulled down as far as their eyebrows. Market stallholders. Vegetable and fruit sellers. Melon-heap guards. Butchers and fishmongers, with fingernails blackened by dried blood. Jews with keen eyes, broad beards, hunched shoulders, moist hands. Greeks with trousers tucked into their boots, bringing cheeses, olives, and smoked fish from Brăila and Galați. Albanians with lollipops and ladles of kvass. Armenians with thick eyebrows and hooked noses, emanating a subtle scent of spices, sometimes sweet, sometimes sharp.

At a signal they come to a stop. At our gate there is silence. We still have a fence of pales nailed higgledy-piggledy, depending on where the rains have rotted them or the winds have dried them. The sky is lit up, flickering like an oil lamp. The earth is dark and in motion, like a river. Nothing is the same as it was. It is a moment in which to remember the future rather than the past. Angheluță draws the latch and opens the gate. They enter one by one and fill the yard. They timidly go up to the window. They see what they knew they would see. But still they look, crowding together as closely as they can, as if the window were a huge eye and they wanted to be in its field of view. The first of them steps inside. The others follow. The room is narrow. They do not jostle each other, but still they are all able to fit inside. Some of them will later say that I watched with the eyes of an old man, just as my mother says that when I was born I did not cry but laughed. Most of them will say that I was a quiet baby, even in that moment. My eyes were closed, most of them will say, and so I was either asleep or afraid.

The first to approach is Angheluță. His gift is whiter than the powdered sugar on his fingers and more luminous. It is a ball of light that is motionless but rustles, pulsates, spins. Angheluță moves back in line with the others. The second is Bobîrcă. He steps forward timidly, not in a straight line, but tracing the circle of light made by the candy seller's glowing coal. He places next to it his ball of umbrage. It casts no shadow on the light. Each of the two gifts sparkles in its own way. Then comes Mercan, in silence. He will place his gift above the other two. He blows into his cupped palms. The wings spread, fill the corners of the room; then they settle but without covering the glowing coals of light and darkness. They watch, stooped, their hands folded across their chests in reverence, the same as in the paintings I was to see much later. Gaspar, Melchior, and Balthazar. The circle parts to make room for the halva seller, Taor, with his swaying walk, who simultaneously draws nearer and farther away. Taor's dance is the dance of time.

In Focșani there were two Armenian churches. There was barely a town in Moldavia where the Armenians had not built their churches. In the days when there were no other meeting places, the church was proof that the community existed. When twenty or so families gathered together, their heads formed a parochial council and chose a site for the church. In Suczawa, Bacău, and Bucharest, the shops and houses sprang up around the church, and even today, the street where the church stands is called Armenian Street. In the narthex, which often had a lateral entrance, according to Moldavian rather than Armenian custom, there was an inscription listing the church's first benefactors. The Armenian names with which they had arrived from afar changed over time. Either they acquired Russian or Polish endings or the endings vanished completely. They are old names; many now remain only as inscriptions on the walls of churches or on tombstones: Missir, Alach, Trancu, Buicliu, Pruncu, Ciuntu, Ciomac, Ferhat, Aburel, Asvadurov, Asakievich, Simonovich, Yakobovich.

They even built monasteries. One evening, the Donavak brothers, traveling westward with their herds, spent the night on a road outside Suczawa. There they had the same dream, in which the Mother of God revealed to them that place. They sold their cattle at the market in Leipzig, and on their return they built a monastery that they dedicated to Her. It was around the year 1512. It was one of the first Armenian monasteries to be built in Europe. It still exists today and is called in Armenian Hagigadar—that is, "Fulfillment of Desires." On the feast of the Dormition of the Mother of God, the women set out early in the morning and climb the hill on their knees. They circle the church on top of the hill three times, and in the cracks between the stones they insert pieces of paper on which they have written down their wishes.

At the other end of Suczawa, also at the end of the sixteenth century, the Armenians built another monastery, called Zamka, which is surrounded by fortress walls. It too still exists today. The monks are no more, however. People of various ethnic groups gather at Zamka to commemorate their dead. It is a different sort of meeting place. When the depths of the earth become too heavy, the dead rise through the cracks in its crust, taking the form of grass or steam or roots, and they collect the crumbs of the living commemorations.

And so too in Botoșani, Jassy, Roman, Tîrgu Neamț, Gura Humorului, Tîrgu Ocna, Bacău, Brăila, Galați. Arriving by the trade routes, enticed there by the princes of Moldavia, by Alexander the Good and by Stephen the Great, the Armenians spread their commerce, their customs, their churches.

Our church was built in 1780. Two streets away there is another Armenian church, now abandoned, its spire in ruins, surrounded by waste ground. There were many Armenians in the old days. As the churches were too small for the congregations, they were surrounded by large yards so that there would be room for all to gather at Easter.

In time, the Armenians dwindled in number. Those who arrived later, driven from their native lands by poverty and then by the enmity of others, brought with them fresh Armenian names and wounds just as fresh. Some were driven farther by the same roads that had brought them here, others died, and others forgot.

It was decided that our church should be repaired. I shall present all of them to you in silence. The parochial committee. And so: my grandfather, Garabet Vosganian. His brother-in-law, Sahag Sheitanian. Arshag, the bell ringer. Krikor Minasian, the cobbler. Anton Merzian, the other cobbler, and his sons, Krikor and Dikran. Agop Aslanian, who kept the keys to the office. Then the clock-makers: Vrej Papazian, Dikran Bedrosian, Mgrditch Tcheslov. Anton Grigoriu, the factotum. Ştefănucă Ibrăileanu, smoking cigarette after cigarette. Dikran Khatchadurian, with his big nose. Ohannes Krikorian, with his cheeks ruddy from drink. Minas Ohanesian, the blind man. And my father, Berj Vosganian, the last of them and who still stubbornly preserves things as they were.

We light the candles in a circle, one for the place where each sat. Back then you could still find large silver candlesticks, for the living and for the dead. The dead wax in numbers, while the living dwindle, relegated to a little corner.

Each person covers himself with the world in which he was born, pulling it over his head like a quilt. This is how it goes; when you are born, your world is as large as can be. Anything is possible. As you grow up, your world shrinks. You keep growing; in the beginning your bones grow, then your memories, and all the while your bones become yellower. After a time the world around you becomes so small that you have no more room to grow.

Grandfather Garabet: "I belong to your world, *manch'as*,"—that is, young nipper—"but you do not belong to mine. What is more, you add to my memories without adding to my world. In a way, you hasten my death. You push me from behind." I was sad. But he laughed. "Whichever way you might look at it, life doesn't really have a purpose. If death at least has some meaning, you can count yourself lucky. Which is to say, *manch'as*, you give my death a meaning."

It was true: I did not belong to his world. The photographs looked strange to me. Great-grandfather Kevork Vosganian wears a fez. Next to him in the photograph, Grandfather Garabet, not yet an adolescent, plays the mandolin. He wears an embroidered waistcoat and baggy pantaloons. Behind them can be seen the white roofs and rounded tiles of a Mediterranean port, perhaps Adana. The sky seems serene. As the date at the bottom of the photograph shows, two years had passed since the massacres that had taken place in the town in 1909. Tens of thousands of Armenians had been killed in the town and the surrounding area. In another photograph, my great-grandmother Mariam Vosganian sits cross-legged, wearing *shalwars* and a wrap blouse, as was the fashion in Constantinople at the end of the century. So that had been the world of my grandfather Garabet. "With a fez and *shalwars*?" I ask. "In those days we didn't know that *shalwars* were *shalwars* and that a fez was a fez. They were just clothes like any others."

Now Grandfather and the others stand in a circle under the chestnut trees in the large yard of Focşani's Armenian church. Behind them are the stones of the old graveyard, from the time before the dead were moved to the new cemetery on the outskirts of town; the stones are leaning or have fallen over so that they look up at the sky and lie like coverlets on top of the old dead. The men stand with their legs slightly apart and their hands on their hips, as if they are about to quarrel. Old man Minas leans on his stick but has the same tense posture as the others. In the middle is a fire. The dry wood of years past makes a lively, orange fire; the wood cracks, baring its innards. There is also new wood, which resists with all its might, spewing thick smoke. The men stand facing the fire, but I do not know whether they look at the fire. Their faces are hidden behind masks. The first to move is Grandfather. He stamps his right foot and then his left. It is as if he plants himself in the earth. The others do likewise. They seem to wheel around the fire, but in fact they are standing still. Their feet, stamping on earth thickened by the taut skin of the old dead, create a rhythm that sounds like the beating of a drum. The voice of my grandfather is harsh, like a commandment. "Man-tree." And again: "Man-tree. Why does the sun rise and set?" They answer one by one. Behind their masks I cannot guess which is which. Their trader's clothes, their craftsman's clothes, their worn, patched waistcoats are no longer discernible. They are like tunics, smoothed and thickened by the shadows. At Grandfather's signal, they stop. The sky dilates. They remain motionless for a few moments. First of all the younger ones run to the fire and without hesitation leap over it to crouch on the other side. Bewildered, the fire dwindles; its tongues sway like ruffled bushes. Now it is the turn of the older ones. The fire rebels, clutches at their sleeves, the hems of their coats. The leapers tear themselves loose, sparks cling to their clothes, their faces glow. Now it is the blind man's turn. He sees the fire better than any of them since he feels its glow from afar. Another man tries to help him, but Grandfather stops him. Each must do battle alone. The blind man makes the leap; first he plants his cane in the earth and then his feet. And then suddenly he reverts to his faltering walk. The last to leap is Ohannes Krikorian. The fire regains its strength and grasps the soles of his feet. Ohannes rolls on the ground to smother the flames that beset him. He manages it and then looks around him, waiting for a word of encouragement. But the others know, and so they avert their eyes. It is true: shortly after that Ohannes Krikorian died. Now they sit down next to each other. The masks grin at the fire. The fire grins back at them. For the time being, the reckoning is complete. At dawn, when a new sun rises, the questions will be asked again. Here in the land of Vrancea, the world begins anew every day. The masks change. Grandfather Garabet has taken off his masks, and he signals to me that we might enter the church.

In the narthex the candles are burning. In Armenian churches the candles for the living and for the dead are not lit in separate niches. Living or dead, each takes as much as he requires. Large paintings adorn the walls. They were brought from Vienna at the beginning of the nineteenth century, from the studios of the Mekhitarists. The canvases glint darkly; the figures of the saints have been blackened by candle smoke. The halos on their heads are barely visible. But naturally, the Annunciation's ray of light is unusually white and clean. The church has been emptied for repairs. All that remains is the large chandelier of Bohemian crystal, a gift from the landowner Simonovich at the beginning of the century.

In Focşani, the same as in the other towns of Moldavia, there once lived many rich Armenian families. Like all Armenians, they liked to have their photographs taken: with their twirled moustaches, with their bellies almost bursting their waistcoats, with their stern gazes, achieved thanks to the skillful photographer bidding them to look upward and a little to one side. They sat on round-backed chairs, and the women stood behind, wearing dresses of heavy fabric, their waists constricted by corsets so tight they caused them to faint. War swept away worlds, and communism leveled them with a harsh hand. Baying mobs burst into their houses on Station Road; their boots ripped the carpets. Into the houses from which they were evicted moved departments of the town hall and various museums, where we would later be taken on school trips, led by the hand. Station Road changed its name to Karl Marx Street, a name that Simonovich, Ferhat, Missir, and Alach had never even heard of. Many of them retreated into the brown world of daguerreotypes, and there they vanished even before the Russians arrived. Others, who were smaller and able to slip through the times unnoticed, withdrew to mansards or damp rooms in semi-basements, where, their hearts shrinking to the size of a flea, they listened to Russian boots tramping around the guest rooms above. And in storerooms they crammed as best they could boxes of goods from the shops they had hurriedly emptied, and they concealed their gold coins in the chinks between the tiles of their stoves or buried them under the dog kennel.

Simonovich's chandelier illumined the passing of time evenly, whether there was peace or war, whether there was famine or plenty. I liked to look at it. In the morning, Arshag the bell ringer would take me by the hand, and we would both enter the church. "Come," he said; "let's listen to the chandelier." He lit it, and then, treading as softly as we could, we sat down on a wooden pew. We sat in silence, holding our breath. After a while, Arshag slapped his knees in satisfaction. We were safe for another day. The big chandelier foretold earthquakes. In Vrancea, the place where the mountains made a turn, rising toward the higher peaks of the Bucegi, the lands had been laid one on top of the other in a rather slipshod way. From time to time, they shifted. The earthquakes could be felt all the way to Bucharest. That was what happened in 1940, for example, when the Carlton Building collapsed. The aftershocks could still be felt for a few days afterward, and my old folks made themselves a shelter in the storeroom, not daring to go back inside the house until a week later. It happened later, too, in 1977, but that is within my living memory. Arshag said that on days when there was going to be an earthquake, the chandelier rustled like a forest of silver.

This time, however, the chandelier was motionless. We had sat down, each in his own place. Grandfather sat in the middle and I in front of him. It smelled of raw plaster; the walls had not yet dried. The air was damp, and it was as if it were drizzling. The walls were greedily absorbing dryness and warmth. We sensed how they craved the warmth of our bodies. "The time has come," Grandfather told me. And he laid the case on his knees and opened it without haste. He took out the violin and checked the strings. He had carefully tuned it at home. "Lest any dissonance sneak in," he had explained. He placed the violin beneath his chin, positioned his fingers, grasped the bow. When he closed his eyes, I knew he was about to play *Dle Yaman*, the song of exile. It was a slow melody, with notes held for the entire length of the bow. And it soared above us, away into wider and wider skies, as if raining from earth upward into the heavens. Then it soaked into the walls.

Finally, we both listened. There was no echo. The walls, with their raw plaster, were so greedy that they had absorbed everything. Grandfather nodded and bent forward to put the violin back inside its case. And then, still leaning forward, with his open palms resting on his knees, he sang. The song of the crane. "Krrunk." The plaster absorbed the sounds, and it yellowed a little. Once again the walls had imbibed, without missing a single word. The walls were no longer so pale; they had taken on life.

We both sat by the fire. Grandfather listened again, and the silence seemed to satisfy him. The candles had gone out; all that remained was the votive lamp with its grain of light. Grandfather locked the wooden door of the church and hid the key in the place known only to him and the bell ringer. Then we sat down. "From now on it will sound nice," he explained. "It was the best moment to help the song seep into the plaster. Now the echoes will sound right." It was an old story. The sounds bound the plaster together. In such a way that even the silence sang. That was what the troubadours of old used to do; they were called not only to feasts, but also to accompany the church builders. "True silence," said Grandfather, laying his mask and his violin aside and raking the fire, "is the silence that sings."

Sometimes I accompanied Minas the blind man to church. He rested his hand on my shoulder and walked half a pace behind me. I was proud of what I did, although it was not much at all since the blind man, in the clear light of his habits, knew the way by heart.

I only ever knew him as an old man. Most of the men around whom I spent my childhood were old. "What is that child doing here among us?" Arshag the bell ringer would ask with a laugh. "Leave him be," Grandfather Garabet would say. "He's no ordinary child. He's a child old in years." Grandfather took me by the hand, and we entered the church on a weekday morning. First we sat down, and, following Arshag's example, we listened to the big chandelier. The forest of silver was silent, a sign that the earth was resting peacefully. Then we looked at the big icon in the altar. The Mother of God shed no tears, a sign that the heavens were resting peacefully. "Jesus is no ordinary child. Do you see?" "All I see is a child with a small body and a big head," I said. "That's precisely it. He is a wise child, and he is sad most of the time. He is a child without a childhood, born an adult, with a body too small for him. That's why they say that Jesus was a child old in years." By making such a comparison, Grandfather Garabet was certainly poking fun at me. "In fact," he added, "it's not quite the same thing. He is old in his own years. You are old in our years. The years we haven't lived are heaped onto yours. Whole haystacks of years . . ."

Grandfather would tell me, "Go and see how Minas is." He lived in one of the two buildings in the churchyard that had been built a hundred years ago to serve as Armenian schools, one for girls and one for boys. Now, the other building was the church trustees' office, smelling of old furniture, with worn floorboards, peeling walls, and huge paintings that depicted heroes or saints. There was also a portrait of Komitas there, drawn in pencil with amazing skill by Haig, the brother of Vrej Papazian who died of tuberculosis at the age of sixteen. In the evenings, the old men still sang the songs of Komitas, while Grandfather accompanied them on the violin and the women wept. "Did he really die insane?" I once asked, and silence suddenly fell all around. "Who told you that?" snapped my godfather Sahag Sheitanian. "I read it . . ." I mumbled. Then Grandfather began to play his violin again, and the others sang. I was right. Overwhelmed by the tragedy of his people, Komitas had gone out of his mind with grief. He died in Paris in a sanatorium, two decades later, insane. But the old men were right too. The age was more insane than any that had gone before.

Similarly, you were not supposed to tell Minas that he was blind. "Do you see I'm right?" Grandfather would ask him. Or "Did you see that the weather has warmed up?" Or "As you see . . ." And Minas would nod, as if to say yes, he saw all those things. The things that others understood, heard, or felt. I climbed the steps and opened the big door with its iron handle. "Armaveni?" I heard him call. And then, "Luisa?" The names of his daughters. I did not answer, and then he knew it was I. "Come in, lad." Another time, when he was growing frailer and frailer, he called out names of people I did not know. I was afraid. I had found out they were the names of his dead, who were waiting for him.

His eyes had turned white. He kept them open, looking greedily. He spun around when he heard a sound so that I thought he could hear with his eyes. I led him to the church, where he had his own place on the front pew. He listened to the service motionless. Then we went into the churchyard, where he sat down on the bench beneath the chestnut trees. When the shadow reached him, he held out his palm, as if feeling for fine droplets of rain. He could tell light and shade apart, the same as you can tell dry from wet. When darkness fell, he no longer needed a guide. In the dark, he was the one who showed the way.

THE STORY OF MINAS THE BLIND MAN. In the beginning was the light. Later the light fell asleep. It dreamed, and thus from its dream, shadow was born. "When I was your age," said Minas, "I dreamed I was blind. In the dream it was nice. Now I dream that I see . . ."

On dark nights he lit the lamp and went out into the street with it. Minas had a lamp the likes of which I had never seen before. It had a thick glass mantle that augmented the light and protected the flame from the wind. In our town, because of the economy drive, they did not light the street lamps at night. The headlights of a truck would sweep the streets at rare intervals. "Look," the people would say, "the blind man has come out, holding his lamp."

And so Minas the blind man, lamp in hand, was the best and most useful of people. The others followed him until one after another they came to a stop, each in front of his own house, thanking him. He would continue alone, holding his lamp, roaming the streets, until he sensed the darkness thinning. On moonless nights Minas was master of the town. At dawn he returned to his room, lifted the glass mantle, and placed the palm of his hand over the flame until it went out. In the middle of his palm he bore the round, black sign of the stifled flame. At daybreak he became the blind man once more.

THE STORY OF MINAS READING. Minas was a blind man who read. He had a wall full of old books. When he sat on his bed for a long space and did not hold his staff, he would pick up a book. He caressed the thick covers, speaking the while or else gazing into space. From time to time he would turn the pages of the book. Then he would smile. When he stood up, a yellowish powder remained around his feet, sifted from the crumbling old pages.

Grandfather used to send me to him with a book. "Armaveni?" he would ask. "Luisa?" It was his moment of weakness. At such times he was completely blind, and his eyes glittered white and dry. One day he called, "Kevork? Is that you?" When I asked Grandfather who Kevork was, he was saddened. "Hey," he called over his shoulder to his brother-in-law, my godfather Sahag Sheitanian. "Poor Minas has been calling after Kevork Chavush."

I would open the book at random. Minas would nod. I would read. He would be amazed, indignant, amused. Sometimes he would ask, "Does it really say that?" He could not believe it. "Give it here; let me see." He took the book and felt it. "Where?" I would put my finger on the place and hold it there until his hand touched mine. He ran his fingers over the corner of the page. Then, suddenly, he was enlightened. "That's right!" In secret, I tried feeling the page, but I could not understand anything. I suspected that Minas could not understand either but was pretending. But sometimes he took the book, turned the pages, felt them, and his finger stopped somewhere. "Read it again!" And they really were the words that had puzzled him a moment before. "How can you read a smooth page with your fingers?" "You can't," laughed Minas.

Sometimes, the old men gathered to read. The Bible had been printed in the mid-nineteenth century in Constantinople, the city the old folk called Bolis for short. The ones who, like Grandmother Arshaluis, had been born on the banks of the Bosphorus, called themselves *bolisians*, or city-dwellers. Constantinople was the City, the center of the world. The genocide was commemorated on April 24, the day when the massacres began in the City, in Constantinople.

The pages of the Bible were not entirely smooth. The letters at the beginning of the chapters were depicted as animals, birds, or floral motifs, like in old Armenian manuscripts. The layered inks made them thicker than the other letters. A saint leaning forward and spreading his arms was the letter *pen*. A leaping tiger was *re*. A stork with folded wings and outstretched neck was *t'o*. Most of all I liked the letter *vo*: two swans with entwined necks. Broken love: this was the first letter of my family surname. Usually, Minas's fingers lingered on the page. He turned the pages without haste and ran his palm over them lightly, as you might stroke the cheek of a child. "He really does read!" my grandfather assured me. "Does he read in his mind?" I asked. "Not in his mind. He reads." "But he can't hear anything!" "How could he hear anything? You read aloud; he reads by feeling, which is a different kind of seeing. When you don't want to be heard, you speak in a whisper. He sees in a whisper."

But another time, he really did seem to read. On Sunday, before the service, the men sat on the pews with their arms crossed over their chests, and the women sat with their hands folded in their laps. Minas announced the chapter from the Gospels, from which the verse to be interpreted in the sermon would be taken. Then he read in an even voice, accentuating and lengthening the vowels when he repeated the words of the Savior. "He's reading!" I whispered in Grandfather's ear. "He's not reading. He's remembering . . ." "But he's holding the book in his hands . . ." "The book is the most important thing. Without it he would give the impression that they are his own memories." He was right. I have never met anybody who read the Gospels more clearly and more beautifully than the blind man.

HOW MINAS THE BLIND MAN DIED. I swear I heard him call out my name for the first time, and I was overjoyed. Of all those who no longer lived and whom Minas seemed to be waiting for, I remember the name Kevork best of all. He was his cousin on his father's side. Kevork Chavush had fought in the mountains, alongside General Andranik. Grandfather had shown me a photograph of him in an old magazine, with his sheepskin cap and his banderole of cartridges, striking a martial pose, with one foot planted higher up the slope of the mountain and the stock of his rifle resting on the bent knee of that leg. When he had almost reached the end of this world's darkness, Minas glimpsed the light of the next world. The first man he saw was probably Kevork Chavush, and that is why he called out his name.

Now, Minas was calling out my name. I hurried up the steps but came to a stop in front of Armaveni, his youngest daughter. She was weeping. The blind man was dead. As he gazed back from the other side, I was probably the first he glimpsed. But I did not tell anybody that. Just as I was puzzled when I heard him calling out the name of Kevork Chavush, probably Kevork Chavush was puzzled on the other side when he heard Minas call out my name.

Rather than an icon, between his joined hands I placed the old Bible, whose sole reader he had been in the final years. I wanted to close his eyelids, according to the custom. "Leave them open," said my grandfather Garabet. "He has kept them closed long enough."

At the wake, the old folk kept their distance from Minas's deathbed. They were afraid of the dead man with the open eyes, eyes that were white and that glinted like two pebbles.

3.

"It is a great responsibility to live on this earth longer than Jesus Christ," said Grandfather. "You have to have solid arguments to be bold enough to do that." "And what if you don't?" "It remains to be seen . . . It is all too plain that many people live in the world longer than Jesus without having any good reason to."

I thought that that was why Kennedy was shot. If it was true, then I was the only person in the world who knew the truth.

For me, that was how the cinema came into being. In fact, we had gone to see a Laurel and Hardy film. The difference among the three protagonists—Laurel, Hardy, and Kennedy—was none too clear to me. Back in those days, people did not have televisions. At the cinema, before the main feature, they showed a newsreel on speckled film, with rasping voices. It would invariably begin with a view of Băneasa Airport and the smiling face of Gheorghe Gheorghiu-Dej, who would either himself be alighting from an airplane, waving at the people there to greet him, or be standing next to an airplane, waving at the foreign dignitaries alighting. At the end of the reel would come the foreign news: antiwar protests or workers' strikes in the capitalist countries. Whereas in our country, everything was good. On August 23, National Day, butter was five bani cheaper. What did it matter that you did not have anywhere to buy butter?

Manuk Derderian was a lively man with a hurried gait. "How are you, Manuk?" He would not stop to answer; with splayed fingers he would jiggle his hands, meaning "so-so," and continue on his way. He always seemed to be occupied. He had an unhappy old age and a hard family life, with three sons who resembled him, always in just as much of a hurry. Of the three, two died, one by drowning and the other in a car accident. Manuk almost lost his mind.

Manuk did not come to the Armenian church very often. His parents had brought him into the world in a French-run refugee camp in Syria, and for that reason he had been baptized into the Catholic Church. He came to the Armenian church once every few years, when Orthodox Easter fell on the same date as Catholic Easter. Manuk was the director of the Union Cinema. In our town, there was also another cinema, the Flame, a rather dilapidated building, where they showed Russian war films. The only people who went to see those films were those who, in exchange for one leu and fifty bani, wanted a warm place to snooze for a couple of hours.

Manuk invited us to come and see a film. So one morning, after Grandmother Arshaluis wrapped us up warmly, hand in hand with my brother Melik,
who was by now in his first year at school, we bravely walked down Tanners
Street, at the end of which stood the cinema, at the crossroads, opposite the
Armenian church. We came back full of enthusiasm. "Then the man with the
moustache broke their window. Then Laurel and Hardy broke his car window.
The man glared at them and broke their door with an axe. Then they smashed
the door of his car." We were mimicking the action, and Grandfather Garabet and his brother-in-law Sahag were laughing at us. "Everything was getting
smashed up. In the end they broke the car, demolished the house, and shot
Kennedy." Grandfather stopped laughing. We were giggling and telling the story
as if it were all part of the same Laurel and Hardy film. Grandfather told me
to tell it again from the beginning. I started it over again, corroborated by my
brother, saying that the car in the film had some people in it at first, and then
one of them fell backward, and the woman next to him wanted to jump out of
the car. But we were afraid to laugh any more. Grandfather turned to Sahag
and said, "Summon the parochial council. Two hours from now, in Seferian's
funeral vault." He wrote something down on a scrap of paper and told me, "Run
to Arshag, the bell ringer. Don't show anybody the note."

I kept a lookout on the cemetery path. It was late autumn. The ground was
covered with dry leaves. I looked for walnuts and chestnuts under the leaves.
I rolled them at each other. You won if you could hit one with another. I was
not afraid there, among the tombs. The cemetery, with its trees, its grass, and
its flowers, was so alive that if the walnuts had rolled down a crack and fallen
deep inside the earth, I would not have been surprised if somebody had tossed
them back up.

In the cemetery, the crosses were sparse. There was more space than the new
dead were able to occupy. Some had erected crosses for the dead they had left
behind in the villages whence they had fled, but even so, the crosses were still
spread widely apart. Accustomed since their own childhoods to seeing so much
death, the Armenians of my childhood had enlarged the cemetery to the very
outskirts of town. But it was obvious that they had overestimated the community's capacity to die. "We have dwindled in numbers," reckoned Arshag, pacing
the paths of the cemetery. "We no longer have the strength to die sufficiently."
The exodus to America that immediately followed the war had left the cemetery looking even more awkward. The very rich left straightaway, even before
the Communists took full control, in the period when nationalization had not
yet begun. The Israelian, Vartbaronian, Diarbekirian, Varteresian, and Seferian
families went all the way to Argentina, which they thought was far enough away
for Bolshevism not to catch up with them. The rich who remained—Alach,

Missir, Goylav, Frenkian, and many more—were evicted from their houses. The luckier ones did not go to prison and were not thrown into the street; they were allowed at least to live in the attics and basements of their own houses. But the Communists demolished their terracotta stoves and carefully sifted the rubble, in case any gold coins had been secreted between the tiles or concealed in the ashes of the grate. Cockerels, as they called such gold coins. I have never seen a gold cockerel. From *The Book of Whispers* I discovered that Grandfather had saved a few before the war, from his trade in colonial goods. When the madness began, on the very corner of our street, at the Romanoaie family's, the cars sped up one night and men in leather coats kicked the door down; hauled everybody outside into the snow; and then ransacked the house, searching everything from the ash of the stoves and the down of the mattresses to the books in the bookcase, which they tore apart page by page. On the grounds that Romanoaie had traded in grain, they screamed at the terrified family, ordering them to bring out the money from its hiding place. Grandfather decided that the best thing to do with his cockerels was to make them disappear. One night he buried them in the securest spot in the yard: under the dog's kennel. The dog's name was Fidel, and he was white and shaggy. He was still alive when I was little. In the meantime, the kennel had been moved a few times, so Grandfather could no longer remember where the original burial place had been. But it was definitely on the side of the garden where the vegetable patch was later in my childhood. And the best time to search was in spring, when people passing on the street would not wonder why we were digging in the yard. When I was big enough to wield a spade, I turned over every clod and crumbled it in search of treasure. I never found anything. I was never able to plant the spade as deep as my grandfather did when he dug from fear.

So the first to leave took their bundles with them, they converted everything they could into gold, and via the port of Constanța they managed to flee in every direction. They left behind them empty houses, emptied drawers, Viennese pianos with dented keyboards, and empty picture frames, the paintings having been carefully rolled up and concealed inside their bundles of clothes. Also left behind were the family tombstones on which they had inscribed their names, but nobody knew what year of death to carve for them after that. A cemetery for the half dead. Such was the Seferian family vault, in which nobody was interred. Old man Seferian, the merchant of colonial wares, with warehouses in the port of Brăila, went to Buenos Aires before the day fated for his death arrived. Eduardo, his grandson, augmented the money his grandfather had taken with him when he left and became the most eminent member of Argentina's Armenian community. What with one thing and another, the niches of the vault had remained empty. It was a good place to meet when nobody else had to see or hear.

They arrived one by one. First came Arshag the bell ringer, who sniffed around. Then Father Varjabedian, short, white-haired, with a chin beard so round it was as if it had been sculpted by hand. They went from grave to grave, reciting prayers and swinging the censer. Then the others arrived: my grandfather Garabet, my godfather Sahag, Anton Merzian, Krikor Minasian, Ohannes Krikorian, and the younger men: Vrej Papazian, Dikran Bedrosian, Agop Aslanian, and Mgrditch Tcheslov.

"What is the priest doing?" asked Mgrditch in puzzlement.

"Nothing," explained Grandfather. "He's pretending. He's pretending to say requiems for the dead."

"Requiems? On a Tuesday?"

"Who knows? Maybe it's some Armenian custom of ours. Because if today is not a day for requiems and there's certainly no funeral being held, what are we doing here in the cemetery?"

They stole into the vault one by one.

Agop Aslanian: "I've brought candles for old man Seferian. They'll also shed some light."

The flames of the candles lengthened the men's faces, and shadows began to dance. Their eyebrows thickened and their noses, large enough as they were, seemed to jerk up and down on their faces. Father Varjabedian shook the censer and sat down, making room for Minas.

"Have you heard?" asked Grandfather.

Each had heard something. Each was afraid to be the first to say what he had heard.

"Kennedy is dead," continued Grandfather, breaking silence made thicker by the smoke of the incense.

They met in the vault only when extraordinary events were afoot. The things they could talk about only in the vault were bad things. The first time had been when the news of the repatriations arrived. The second time had been when the King abdicated. The third time had been when Grandfather brought the news that in Bucharest Bishop Vazken and his mother had been evicted from the bishopric in the middle of the night, and the offices of the bishopric had been turned into a store for old lumber. The fourth time had been during the Hungarian uprising. Many years had passed since they last met, although that did not mean the times were any better, rather that now they were even more lacking in hope.

"What is to be done?" asked Anton Merzian.

It was natural that he should be the one to ask. Anton Merzian spoke only in questions. He never said, "The weather is nice today," but rather: "It's nice weather today, isn't it?" He would say, "I don't feel very well today, what do you say?" And when everything was clear and there was no room for any question, he would conclude: "It's clear, isn't it?" Now, as if his first question had come too quickly, he asked another: "Who is to blame?"

Each had his own answer to that blunt question. As follows:

Sahag Sheitanian: The Russians are to blame.

Father Varjabedian: The Cubans are to blame.

Arshag the bell ringer: The Turks are to blame.

Anton Merzian: The Kurds are to blame.

Krikor Minasian: The Mafia is to blame.

Ohannes Krikorian: The Albanians are to blame.

That part about the Albanians was completely out of the blue.

"I've been listening to Radio Tirana," added Ohannes Krikorian, sure of himself. "They've sworn revenge against Kennedy."

"Revenge for what?" asked Mgrditch Tcheslov.

"How should I know? Just revenge."

"The Albanians are always threatening everybody," said Mgrditch dismissively.

"There, you see . . ."

But the hypotheses had not yet been exhausted:

Vrej Papazian: The Vietnamese are to blame.

Mgrditch Tcheslov: The Mexicans are to blame.

Dikran Bedrosian: The Americans are to blame. Imperialism. Kennedy was a Democrat.

"No offense," said Sahag Sheitanian, "but the real imperialists are on the other side, where the sun rises."

"The Bolsheviks fight for peace," said Dikran Bedrosian defensively.

"Couldn't they fight a little less?" said Sahag, annoyed. "They'll finish us off completely with all their fighting for peace. Have you forgotten what they did to you? Didn't that teach you a lesson?"

Dikran Bedrosian turned red. In '44 he had been the only one among them to rejoice when the Russians came. He had been the first to go to the town barrier to welcome them. He had rushed up to the first Soviet soldier he met and kissed him on both cheeks. The soldier had allowed himself to be kissed, somewhat taken aback, but then, all of a sudden enlightened, he had jabbed the barrel of his gun under Dikran Bedrosian's chin and pointed to his wrist. At first, Dikran Bedrosian could not believe it, but the snap of the gun being cocked brought him to his senses. He took off his wristwatch and handed it over. The Soviet soldier had reasons to be satisfied. Dikran Bedrosian was a clockmaker; he was discerning when it came to wristwatches. The soldier snatched the watch from him and with the butt of his rifle shoved him in the ditch. Sprawling in the mud, rubbing first his wrist, then the bruise under his chin, cowering, trembling, Dikran Bedrosian, the fervent admirer of Bolshevism, had thus been the first to review the ranks of the glorious Red Army, albeit from a rather inconvenient position.

"Learn a lesson, him?" growled Krikor the cobbler. "Give them the church clock while you're at it. Let them hang it on the tower of the Kremlin."

"So who is to blame?" repeated Anton Merzian.

This time the answer came in many voices all at once but formed a single and therefore enlightening word:

"Bolshe-turki-cuba-mex-alb-namese."

Grandfather raised his hand. Silence fell.

"The war will heat up," he said.

"How can it heat up?" asked Arshag. "There isn't any war at the moment."

"Mankind is on a knife edge," said Grandfather. "It's a hidden knife edge. Words wage war in our place. And we die in their place."

"We were waiting for the Americans to come," complained Mgrditch. "And in the end it's they who are dying . . ."

"Keep it down," interrupted Sahag. "Father, go outside and do another round with the censer."

Father Varjabedian reached for the censer and appeared in the doorway. I quickly moved away, with my chestnuts, lest he see that I had been eavesdropping. The priest called me to him and gave me a communion wafer. He went back inside and hung up the censer.

"Is there anybody in the cemetery?" asked Grandfather.

"Only the Good Lord and those He has already forgiven."

"Could you put less incense in that censer?" complained Vrej Papazian. "We'll suffocate in here . . ."

"That's the way it has to be at a requiem," explained Arshag. "The smoke has to be thick."

"In that case," said Anton Merzian, scratching himself, "may the what-do-you-call-it? the soil, rest lightly on him. But weren't we talking about what we are to do?"

"What do the Jews say?" asked Agop Aslanian. "Let's ask Dr. Argintaru. If something is up, they're the first to find out . . . If the Jews start leaving, we need to be on the move too. It means it's starting again . . ."

"Well I'm not going anywhere!" said Anton Merzian curtly. "Have I got a

66

pension? Yes, I have. A burial plot in the cemetery? Praise the Lord! I've got one, as well as ones for all the children yet to be born. Do I make enough from cobbling to get by? And isn't my wife Zarhui as deaf as a post? Where am I supposed to go?"

"I wouldn't leave either," said Arshag. "Tot it all up: from Shabin-Karahisar to Aleppo, from Aleppo to Odessa, Kishinev, Brăila, Silistra, and now, since the war, here in Focşani. In my whole life I haven't accumulated enough even to fill a cart."

"It's easy for you to talk then, isn't it?" said Anton Merzian. "What about me? Haven't I built myself a house? What am I supposed to do? Take it with me on my back, like a snail?"

"Not to mention the burial plot here in the cemetery, isn't that so?" said Krikor, mimicking him.

There was a long-standing rivalry between them. Their parents had been shoemakers in Malatya, with shops on the same street, each scowling at the other's sign and trying to steal the other's customers. In those days, cobbling was held in high esteem, and it was no mean feat to learn the craft of stitching leather and shaping footwear on a wooden boot tree. Their workshops were razed to the ground, looted by the Turks and the Kurds, while the Armenians were rounded up in convoys at the edge of town. Having learned the craft from their fathers, the boys were saved from starvation. And each making his own journey, they both ended up at the same crossroads, six hundred miles away, on the Main Street of Focşani, among the Jewish shops. The Jews either left or gave up trading, but their shops remained. In fact their customers remained because the workshops now operated clandestinely, without shop signs or permits. The rivalry between them smoldered as fiercely as ever. Lately, Anton Merzian had gained an advantage. His sons, Kokor and Dikran, now worked at the Crafts Cooperative, and at nightfall they brought leather, glue, soles, and nails back home to the workshop. Krikor had threatened to denounce them to the police, to the Securitate, to the tax authorities, everywhere. "Are you stupid?" snorted Anton. "Before they come for me, won't they come to arrest you? Where's your own shop sign?" Krikor gulped. He did not have sons to help him, and in the evening he and his wife Parantsem enviously counted the customers who knocked on Merzian's door with bags full of shoes to be repaired.

"Maybe there'll be a war . . . ," began Vrej Papazian pensively.

"If there's a war," interjected Ohannes, "they'll be too busy fighting each other to have time for us."

"War's the worst thing," concluded Dikran, who since the incident with the Soviet soldier had minded his own business and no longer wore a wristwatch. "If they don't kill you deliberately, they kill you by accident."

"If the Russians go to war with the Americans, maybe the Americans will finally come," said Sahag, whose dream had still not come true.

"Only to ring our bells," growled Ohannes. "I've spent my whole life waiting for the Americans to come. The first time, I was just a kid. That was in 1909, in Adana. When the massacres began, Father said, "Let's flee to the port because the Americans will definitely come to rescue us." After that, I waited for them to rescue us from the Turks in 1918 and from the Russians at the same time. Not to mention in 1944 . . . Do you remember, Sahag, how you waited in the church tower for a whole week, among the bats and death's head moths, so that you would be the first to see the Americans arrive? And what came of it? The Russians came, with their trousers fit to burst, so women-starved were they, and with their parched throats craving vodka. And that good-for-nothing Dikran Bedrosian went out like a chucklehead to greet them. They let you off lightly, just taking your watch. They should have taken your trousers while they were at it and made you walk home bare-assed. They didn't go far enough because it still didn't knock any sense into your head."

"When I die," said Mgrditch dolefully, "fetch an American to ring the bells for me. At least then I'll know they came . . ."

And that is what happened in the end. The Americans did not come to him; he went to the Americans; he emigrated with his whole family in the 1970s. But he could not adjust to life there, and he died soon afterward. And from the man who rang the bells to the rope, the clappers, and the hamburgers at the funeral repast, everything could not have been more American.

"You've gone completely soft in the head," said Arshag. "The only thing that is going to come our way is sorrow. That's what it was like in Sarajevo and when the Iron Guard assassinated Armand Călinescu. I remember it even now: they pasted cardboard targets over their hearts when they put them in front of the firing squad."

"We need to organize ourselves," interrupted Grandfather.

"Let's hide the big chandelier and the silverware," said Father Varjabedian.

"Let's hide in the cellar," said Vrej Papazian.

"Let's hide out in the mountains," added Agop Aslanian. "Until things settle down."

Silence fell. They looked at each other awkwardly.

"Swing the censer, Father," murmured Anton Merzian, forgetting for the first time to phrase it as a question.

They waited in silence. Father Varjabedian returned from outside and hung the censer from the nail for the icon.

"Nothing out there," he said. "Apart from the crows. From time to time you can hear the walnuts and chestnuts falling."

"General Dro's arms are no more," said Grandfather in a whisper.

"They must be somewhere," Krikor contradicted. "You know very well he fled in '44; he couldn't have not taken his guns."

"What would you do with guns?" asked Anton Merzian. "Take to the streets with them? Or do you want to play the resistance fighter? Why not hang necklaces of gold cockerels round your neck and do a dance while you're at it?"

"You don't know what you're talking about," Sahag interrupted. He was the only one who had been in the army, during the war. "It would have been a good thing if we'd had a few guns."

"You wouldn't even get a chance to use them because they'd stuff them down your throat before the Americans ever got here," said Agop Aslanian dismissively. "And anyway, before they get around to fighting our Communists, the Americans are busy enough with their own Communists. Besides, they're tied up with the blacks and the Vietnamese . . ."

"Who are these Vietnamese you keep talking about?" asked Vrej Papazian.

"They're like the blacks," explained Agop, "except yellow."

"What time is it?" asked Garabet, my grandfather, now speaking measuredly.

Who else would reply but Dikran Bedrosian? Even though Vrej and Mgrditch were clockmakers too, Dikran was regarded as the true clockmaker and was the only man Grandfather allowed to oil the mechanisms of the church clock, twice a year, in the fasts before Easter and Christmas.

"Five to four," he answered, consulting his pocket watch.

As I said, he no longer wore a wristwatch, just a leather bracelet that was from Jerusalem, or rather he imagined it had been brought from Jerusalem.

"Moscow time," teased Sahag.

Dikran was about to answer back, but Grandfather cut him short.

"We don't have time for nonsense. Mgrditch, fetch the Telefunken. Father, please go and swing the censer."

Father Varjabedian took the censer and went outside to look around. Mgrditch moved aside the lid of the tomb, pulled out the sack, and untied it. He placed the radio in the middle of the vault. There was no need for batteries. When they had installed electricity in the cemetery chapel, they had laid the cable as far as the vault. Vrej moved aside the wreaths of moldering flowers that hid the plug socket. The two men stooped over the apparatus. The box began to whistle. Father Varjabedian returned.

"What's outside?" asked Grandfather.

"Nobody but Vartuhi, Kalustian's wife, at her parents' grave. She's a good woman. But unlucky."

"And what did she say when she saw you swinging the censer all alone?"

"'Poor Seferian,'" she said. What else could she say? "'It's nice of you, Father, because otherwise he wouldn't have anybody to light a candle for him.'"

"That's right, Father; it's nice of you. But it would be even nicer if you didn't swing that censer in here because the air is so thick it will make our noses even longer."

Agop did indeed have an impressive nose. His mother, Mariam, the wife of the late Father Dajad, used to say that when he was little and did not know the meaning of repulsiveness, he used to wipe his nose with his tongue in secret.

"Quiet!" said Vrej.

"How wonderful it sounds," said Mgrditch, in ecstasy on hearing Big Ben from the tower of the Houses of Parliament in London.

"That's a bell and no joke," said Arshag, wiping away a soft, old man's tear and pointing at his chest: "I can feel the chime right here . . ."

The first words were familiar. It was the same newsreader as during the war, whom they had listened to under their beds, in cellars, in woodsheds. But then things got complicated.

"Translate, Arshag!" said Grandfather.

He used to say that if you want to understand the soul of a people, you have to understand the chimes of their bells. Bell clappers, although they look similar, differ from nation to nation. The same as the sky. When they look up, people see the same sky, but each finds different gods and saints up there. In the places where he had worked as a sexton and bell ringer, Arshag had learned all the languages. From the Catholics he had learned Italian. From the Protestants, English, and from the Lutherans, German. He understood those languages, but he did not speak them. When he spoke, he would say in different rhythms and tones, "Bang-ba-bang-ang-a-bang." That was German. Or "Banga-anga-anga-banga." That was Italian. He spoke the language of each nation according to the sound of its bells.

"Don't move!" he said.

That was his way of saying, "Don't talk!" In order to hear, Arshag required not silence but motionlessness. Deaf as he was and naturally not being able to read the newsreader's lips, he knelt down and pressed his ear to the wooden top of the radio so that he might hear the vibrations.

"What is he saying?" said the cobblers Anton and Krikor, craning their necks.

Arshag raised his index finger, a signal that he was beginning to understand.

"A man. Johnson. The new president. Says they'll overcome. Hard. Death. Justice. You'll see. God bless America. That was Johnson. Now the newsreader. Strikes and mourning. Murderer found. Lee Oswald killed Kennedy. Jack Ruby killed Lee. Nobody has killed Ruby yet."

Arshag listened for a minute in silence. Anton nudged him impatiently. Arshag stood up.

"That was all. More news in an hour."

"We won't be here that long," said Agop. "Requiems in the dark; who's ever heard the like? They'll think we're vampires."

"It's clear," said Sahag. "The Communists are to blame."

"They didn't say that," Arshag pointed out.

"What, are they so stupid as to say it openly? Whoever is intelligent enough will understand. Let's recapitulate. This Lee, you say he killed Kennedy?"

"That's what he said. That he shot him twice."

"Right," continued Sahag. "Lee is a Chinese name. Right?"

"Only the Chinese have such short names," agreed Krikor.

"Are the Chinese Communists? Yes, they are. Who killed Lee? Ruby. They might as well have come out and said Rubinstein. Who brought in Bolshevism if not the Jews? Lenin, Zinoviev, Kamenev, and Trotsky were hardly what you'd call Orthodox Christians. There you have it. It's a quarrel among Communists."

"The Communists don't quarrel among themselves," said Dikran Bedrosian. "Proletarian internationalism . . ."

"Pfui, the devil!" exclaimed Father Varjabedian.

"So here's the way of it," continued my godfather Sahag, emboldened. "The world is all topsy-turvy. The Americans are at odds with the Russians, the Russians are at odds with the Chinese, the Chinese are at odds with the Vietnamese, the Vietnamese are at odds with each other in Indochina, Indochina is at odds with the French, and the French, with De Gaulle and all the rest, are at odds with the Americans. Full circle. It's no longer a world war; it's universal war."

"We've been through two wars; wasn't that enough?" moaned Anton Merzian.

"Looks like it wasn't," answered Agop Aslanian. "Mankind has gone insane."

"The Apocalypse," said Father Varjabedian, making three signs of the cross.

"We're not going to let them push us around," decided Krikor Minasian. "I've been through too many wars already, and I'm tired of them. If we also take into account the Iron Guard and the Communists, it's way too much."

"The arms of General Dro," repeated Sahag Sheitanian. "Let's look for them."

It was getting dark. Grandfather decided that it was enough.

"Turn off the radio," he said to Arshag, who still had his ear pressed to the wooden casing and was listening, unable to make head or tail of it. Maybe there would be a war, maybe not. The Russians had left the country, maybe just so that they would have somewhere to come back to.

"When we find out something, we'll meet again. What is to be done? God knows. Now, each of you go back to your homes."

They went out silently, each going to meet his fate. First, Ohannes Krikorian. Then Arshag the bell ringer. Father Varjabedian. My grandfather, Garabet.
Anton and Krikor, the cobblers, and Sahag Sheitanian. And finally the youngest: Dikran Bedrosian, Agop Aslanian, and Vrej Papazian. Mgrditch went to die
in a different land, although first he reserved a place for himself in the Armenian cemetery, next to his mother, Makruhi, and his aunt Aghavni, a name that
means "dove."

Grandfather did not send me to summon them again. The chestnut trees
went on flowering in the town, and on the outskirts the chestnuts and walnuts
mingled together on the paths and in my childhood games. The door of old
man Seferian's vault remained ajar for them. From time to time the thin, sweet
smell of incense wafted out. Arshag hangs from the thick ropes of Big Ben, tugs,
swings, whoops. Grandfather watches the others quarrel, mixing steadfastness
with aloofness, and the powerlessness of empty palms with the legendary arms
of General Dro. He raises his hand for silence. The name is always different.
Martin Luther King, Kennedy, Aldo Moro, Anwar Sadat, Olof Palme, Indira
Gandhi, Yitzhak Rabin, Anna Lindt, Benazir Bhutto. And many other lesser-
known names but which they nonetheless know. "Don't move!" cries Arshag,
spelling out the whistling words of the Telefunken, but now there is no longer
any need because in the world down below, among the roots, they know all the
languages of the earth. "Who is to blame?" asks one. "The world is topsy-turvy,"
says another. At rare intervals, when there is peace on earth, they can be heard
whispering. You might think they had nothing else to fear, but it is not like that
at all. They want to protect the living, and they need the living the same as they
did before. Because only a world that is alive has a right to its dead.

When from afar they heard the sound of Mantu's tuba, people swarmed outside into their yards. And by the time the moans of the trumpet and flugelhorns
could be made out above the low rumble of the tuba, the people were already
lining the sidewalks of Tanners Street to see the funeral procession.

Tanners Street ran between the center of town and the Cîmpineanca railway
crossing. Beyond the barrier was the cemetery. It was the only road along which
corteges traveled. The deceased was collected from home or from the church.
The person in question, thitherto ill and mostly ignored or else in his prime and
struck down by a swift and unexpected death, all of a sudden became the center
of attention. They would talk about him with interest, sometimes with tenderness; he would be washed, dressed in his best clothes, carried back and forth,
everywhere accompanied by a retinue, like a bride.

In our quarter, there were a number of elderly women, mostly widows, who
took care of such things. They appeared out of the blue, sometimes even be-

72

fore the sick man gave up the ghost. Those women gave rise to fear, and people watched them out of the corner of their eye, from behind their fences. The women had a honed instinct; they could sniff out the sweet scent of death even before death itself arrived; they were never caught unprepared. We breathed to the rhythms of the seasons and sniffed the raw scent of spring flowers; the dry, heavy aromas of summer; the steam from the cauldrons of jam, schnapps, and tomato broth; the metallic scent of the snow. But for them, the world had but one season, one of mingled, stifling scents. A rumor would arrive: "Madam Stavarache came by our street today. Poor Temelie, the carpenter; it means he hasn't got much longer." And it was true. The old man, who polished our wooden swords so that we could play *haidouks* and who on Heroes Day put on his best clothes, pinned his medals to his chest, and went to the Heroes Statue in front of the courthouse to lay a flower, passed away shortly after that. Another time, the neighbors on our street grieved for Mițu, as old Mrs. Rădulescu was called. Widow Nistor had been to the old St. Demetrios Church. The Rădulescu family lived in the churchyard. Widow Nistor was right: she had scented thinning blood. Mițu lived for another ten years, however, smoking her Carpathians brand cigarettes, coughing and hacking as she sat on the couch under the lindens. The one who died was her son, Mr. Rădulescu, whom I used to see every day cycling to work, wearing clips on the bottom of his trousers so that they would not get caught on the pedals.

People wept even when the invalid had languished and suffered for a long time or when he was very, very old. When death was not sudden, when the man was not in his prime, the mourners wept sooner for themselves.

Everybody was afraid of Mitică the madman, who lived in a mud-brick hovel on Petru Maior Street. He had a wrinkled face, as if furrowed by claws, after which the wounds had never fully healed. His eyes were watery. The irises dissolved into the whites; he was not blind but rather saw with the whole eyeball, like an ancient Greek statue. He always wore the same khaki trousers, and in winter he also wore a tunic. He had had them since the war, he had been wearing them when he was demobilized, and he would probably be buried in them. His hands were callused from woodcutting, which he did for a living. The neighbors were afraid when they saw him holding his axe. They bargained with him, and when he came to chop their wood, they kept their children in the house, behind locked doors. They left food for him on a stump; he ate what he was given; he never asked for anything extra, not even salt if the beans were insipid, not even onion if they were too sweet, not even water if they were too salty. When he was thirsty, he drank straight from the barrel placed under the roof gutter to collect rainwater for washing clothes. In winter, he gathered snow in his fist and bit it like an apple. He walked with his right shoulder lowered, his laughing head hanging below the hump formed by his other shoulder, which he found puzzling. He was always laughing, a low, rattling, joyless laugh, as if he were clearing his throat. He had been like that ever since Stalingrad, according to Temelie. He had been run over by a Russian tank; running away, he had fallen into a hole in the snow, and the tank tracks had rumbled over the top, crushing him only with their roar and the fear of death. He had lain hidden for a long time; they had thought him dead and made a parcel of his effects, intending to send them home. That was when he got into the habit of eating snow—not licking it, like the wild animals do, but gobbling it up, munching it, crunching it between his teeth, like slender bones. The two of them used to go to the statue in front of the courthouse together on Heroes Day: Temelie dressed smartly, wearing a pressed white shirt and a black tie, his medals pinned to his chest, and behind him, hopping and cackling, Mitică, wearing his frayed soldier's uniform. The carpenter and the woodcutter, heroes of Stalingrad. Temelie laid a flower at the base of the statue and stood motionless, looking at the ground. His cackling laugh chopping up the words, Mitică shouted out the inscription on the statue's plinth, which commemorated those fallen on the battlefield. But he did not stop there; he went on to read the words that the Communists had in the meantime plastered over and that he, his soul crushed by the Russian tanks, knew by heart. "Fallen in holy war," cackled Mitică, "during the glorious reigns of King Carol I, the Founder, and of King Ferdinand, the Unifier of the Land." When the policemen tried to make him shut up, he struggled in their grip, and, dragged across the square, he roared and cackled so loudly that in the end they preferred to let him recite the whole thing, both the visible and the invisible inscription. Mitică would then take his bottle of plum brandy from the Tanners bodega and sit leaning against a fence, drinking long, chest-scorching draughts to melt the snows within him. He would get up and walk away, hiccoughing and cackling. He would plant himself in front of passersby, poking his forefinger in their chests and leaning his weight against them, and he would roar, "You're going to die!" Then he would find another and roar, "You're going to die! You're going to die!" I told Grandfather about it. "He's right," he replied. "Of all of us, Mitică the madman is the one who is right all the way." That is how I discovered people were afraid of death because death is the one thing that is true.

When death came, those elderly women suddenly became useful. They knew everything. They knew how to hang the black cloth on the front door. They knew how to draw the curtains so that the sun would not cast its rays on the face of the deceased and make him spoil. They knew how to cover the mirrors with black veils because they knew that if a relative of the deceased looked in the mirror, death would drag him into the unsealed grave before seven years had elapsed. They knew that you should not wash your hands or face, that the women should not comb their hair and the men should not shave, that death should leave no crumbs behind on earth. They knew that the body should be rubbed with cloths dipped in holy water and oil of spikenard under the armpits, on the temples and forehead, and on the belly, in order to de-baptize what had been baptized so that the grave could fully and truly be shut and the soul would not roam abroad. They knew how to place the penny between the deceased's fingers so that he could pay his toll, and they knew that his hands should rest on top of an icon to show his humility at the Last Judgment. They knew how to bind his legs so that the body would lie straight during the service, and they knew that afterward his legs should be unbound so that nothing would hold him back in this world, so that he would have no regrets, and so that he would be unfettered in the next world. They knew how to arrange the candles at the wake and that the wicks should be trimmed with a pair of scissors so that the candles would cast neither too much light nor too much shadow so that the flame would not be too clear nor give off too much smoke. They knew how to cover the grave, as if with a sheet, how to cast the clods of earth onto the coffin, how to sprinkle wine over the grave, how to share out the boiled wheat and honey. They knew that the deceased's things should be given away as gifts, along with clean towels that had pennies knotted in one corner. They knew how to wail but also how to make wishes for the best, even in such circumstances: "May God grant you his days!" In other words, the days the deceased had not managed to live.

There was a meaning in the whole affair. The ceremonies and traditions were designed to mollify grief. You are carried away with the task, your mind is on making things come off well, on what others are saying, and you cease to notice your own grief. At such times, the widows who sniffed out death were useful, for they knew what was appropriate for everyone—for a man, for a woman, for him who died a sudden death, for an unmarried man, for an unmarried woman. The lifeless man, having led an insignificant, unnoticed life up until then, now had his moment of glory. In some cases, the widows made the funeral the most important thing in the deceased's life, albeit the last thing: borne in a hearse, if he had plenty of money, or on a flatbed truck, with a thick, brightly colored carpet neatly laid over the coffin, followed by a procession of people who, seeing the onlookers gathered on the sidewalk, believed themselves at least as important as the deceased and who in turn were followed by the gawpers, the beggars, and the poor, who received the knotted towels and portions of boiled wheat and honey on pieces of card. At the head of the procession, solemn harbingers, walked Mantu's brass band, their instruments gleaming brightly, deafening and doleful at the same time, abruptly falling silent when the cortege came to a stop in front of a church and the priest swung his censer to the four winds.

Mantu was short and scrawny. He carried his tuba in slow motion, clinging to it like a snail clings to its shell. As he walked, he would turn, and by moving his eyebrows up and down, he would conduct the trumpets, flugelhorns, and saxophone: his brother, Mantu junior; Budișteanu; Frunză; the Cîlțea brothers; and Fofoc. In summer, they wore black trousers and white shirts, and in winter, sheepskin coats and sheepskin caps crammed down over their ears. In winter, they left in their wake a bluish cloud of breath thickened by puffed cheeks and lips straining against mouthpieces.

Funerals were held at around noon. Mantu's tuba could be heard from the farthest away, first as a pressure in the ears, as if the air had suddenly become heavier and was pressing on the eardrums. Then the sound came like a distant thunderclap, fading somewhere over the Milcov River. People would then gaze out of their rattling windows. If the weather was fine, they knew it was Mantu's tuba. If it was cloudy, they waited for the next signal—namely, the moan of the trombone and the cry of the trumpets.

When he passed our house, the air forced through Mantu's tuba throbbed against your temples, against every brittle, translucent surface. In winter, it eddied the smoke from the chimneys. At Christmas the carolers passed with the big drum. To the beat of the drum the carolers, wearing bear and goat heads, danced on the street. I never saw the head of the huge creature that danced above the town to the rhythm of Mantu's tuba. But although invisible, it did exist because when it passed, the smoke from the chimneys struggled in vain to rise. It flopped down over yards and houses, fumbling, seeking some crevice through which it might escape and rise. Death held the chimney smoke fettered on the ground. When Mantu's tuba receded into the distance, the traces of death, dancing above the town, receded too, and the smoke began to rise into the sky again. The air took on the clarity that always follows death.

I would see him in the afternoon at our gate, mopping his brow with the towel he had been given at the funeral, which he then stuffed in his pocket, letting the knotted end dangle outside. He leaned his tuba against the wall—it was tired too, the poor thing—and then he sat down, blue and spent from all that blowing. He lit a cigarette and took a deep drag so as to befriend once more the smoke he had kept shackled. He slowly drank a glass of wine, licked his lips with his bluish tongue, and looked at Grandfather with frightened impatience.

"The trombone," said Grandfather Garabet.

Other times he would say, "The trumpets."

"What's wrong with the trumpets?" asked Mantu in a hoarse, faint voice, like air wafting through the funnel of his tuba in his sleep.

"They came in too early during Chopin's funeral march. They should have left the flugelhorns for another bar."

"They left them long enough. It was me who gave them the signal."

Grandfather poured him another glass, and then he went inside the house. Mantu knew that the hardest moment came next. He shrank in his chair, to the size of a cat. He knew what was going to happen, and had he been able, he would have run away. But he could not. He was never parted from his tuba, and he would not have been able to run while lugging it. He had started playing the tuba at the age of fourteen, when old man Mantu had decided that since his son's chest was already two palms wide, his lungs were ready for blowing. When he was not playing it, he kept his tuba alongside him, polishing it with his sleeve until it shone like a mirror. They went everywhere together, man and tuba, with slow steps and stooped shoulders. In fact, from the day when his father measured him with his palm and decided he was able to blow an instrument, Mantu had never run again.

Now, however, he felt like breaking into a run, but too much time had passed, and he would not have known how to without tripping up. The inevitable occurred: Grandfather returned with the score and spread it on the table. Then, he pointed with his finger.

"Here!"

Mantu leaned over the score and looked at the place where the finger pointed. All he could see were tangled black squiggles.

"That must be right," he whispered. "If you say so . . ."

Another time, it would be the trombone that made a mistake or the flugelhorns. Grandfather laid the sheets of music one on top of another, like leaves of pastry. He moved his finger along the staves of Berlioz's *Symphonie fantastique*, Fauré's *Requiem*, Handel's *Messiah*. Mantu screwed up his eyes, gazed at the pages dotted with beetles.

"Which is the tuba?" he asked.

"The one at the bottom," replied Grandfather, pointing at the stave with the least number of dancing beetles. At intervals there was a circle without a tail or arrowhead at its top or bottom.

"How about that!" he marveled. "Is that me?" And then, looking at his shining tuba, he went on: "It looks so easy! In the end, you've got to roll your soul up into a ball, stuff it in the funnel, if you're going to make a sound . . ."

But Grandfather was still annoyed with the trumpets. Mantu summoned them all: the Cîlțea brothers, who were the trumpeters, and then Mantu junior, Budișteanu, Frunză, and Fofoc. They sat down on stools in the yard, each sucking his sherbet spoon with blue lips, each holding his spoon with fingers pink on the inside and blue on the outside. Grandfather turned the ebonite gramophone disk on both sides, rubbed it lightly with the sleeve of his jacket, and then placed it on the turntable. He lifted the arm of the pickup, held up his finger to signal silence, and lowered the needle. The Gypsies craned their necks. Over the Dixieland rhythms Louis Armstrong's trumpet burst forth, splitting the air. Grandfather nodded his head and tapped his hand in time to the music. They all listened in fascination. When the music ended, the craning necks retracted in embarrassment.

"Did you hear the high notes?" asked Grandfather Garabet.

They had heard them, naturally.

Grandfather continued, relentless: "No matter how high the sound, it's full and open. Why can he do it and you can't?"

"If they is well fed . . ." ventured Cîlțea senior.

"Aren't you well fed? Look at the belly on you."

"That's from grief," wailed the Gypsy. "And from swallowing bread without chewing. That's how you get a belly . . . from bread and grief. But from what I can see, with that music, you need balls, not a belly."

"I think what you need is brains," Grandfather contradicted him.

"Even worse then," insisted the Gypsy. "Bread makes you stupid."

"Eat polenta instead," said Budișteanu, turning it back on him.

"But polenta doesn't fill you up," said Cîlțea, despondent that nobody was taking his side.

Another time I see them on the hill, on Homeland Street, in the Gypsy quarter. They are seated in a circle, with towels around their sweating necks, each with his own individual belly, hollow or bulging, depending on his luck. Mantu alone is standing, leaning on his tuba and propping it up at the same time, puffing on a cigarette. In front of them, Grandfather sits at a table and explains. Pages of sheet music are scattered over the table, causing the Gypsies to perspire all the more.

"Beethoven's Ninth Symphony," announces Grandfather. "Third movement. Andante."

"Is it more stuff by them black men?" asks Cîlțea fearfully.

"Shut up, stupid," Budișteanu hisses at him from behind. Budișteanu studied a little music at the People's Art School, and he is the only one who knows how to read the notes. He reads them one by one, the same as he spells out the words in the newspaper letter by letter.

"If it's not stuff by them black men," says Cîlțea, "then maybe we can do it . . ."

"The tuba will play the bass and big drum parts. The trombone will play the cellos and horns, the flugelhorns, the wind section. And the trumpets will play the violin melody."

"What's that?" cried the Cîlțea brothers indignantly. "Violins is for wedding fiddlers. We ain't no fiddlers . . ."

"What are we then?" asked Fofoc.

"Fiddlers play at weddings," explained Budișteanu. "We play at funerals. That means we is musicians."

"Shut that mouth of yours, musician!" barked Mantu, lighting another cigarette. And then, to Grandfather, "Go on, boss!"

Mantu spoke little. From blowing into his tuba with bulging cheeks, his lips formed the words with difficulty, as if always having to get used to speaking anew. He did not have enough breath to say a long sentence from beginning to end. He would break into a cough, turning purple or even black.

"If you don't give up smoking," Grandfather advised him, "you'll end up burning out, exactly like that cigarette you're tossing away. That's if you don't lose your strength and die with it glued to your lips."

Mantu shrugged. His breath whistled, as though he were blowing into a mouthpiece. He was not accustomed to exhaling into thin air.

"It's been long enough for me," he said. "I've blown enough for three lifetimes."

Mantu spoke about death with indifference. For thirty years he had seen death in every guise, at every age in a man's life and enveloped in every possible kind of funerary lament and custom. "During the war," he recalled, "it was a bit quieter. Death struck far away." But otherwise, he was unafraid. For him, for whom life and blowing from the bottom of your lungs were one and the same thing, to breathe was a duty and death was a release.

"I've had enough blowing," he concluded. "Let me inhale every now and then."

"Well then!"

Grandfather beat time with his left hand and turned the pages, humming. Then, one by one, the trumpets, flugelhorns, and trombone followed their different melodies, learning them by heart. From time to time Grandfather spoke strange words: flat, sharp, tremolo . . . The Gypsies could not understand with their minds what they could not understand with their ears. And so when Grandfather said "sharp," he would jab his thumb upward; when he said "flat," he would jab it down, as if he were signaling someone to fill his glass. The sign for "tremolo" was a slight flutter of the fingers. When he was unable to reach a high note with his voice, he would take out his violin. Then he would make them play, like a choir for seven voices. Or rather six voices since Mantu filled his cheeks only at intervals, when Grandfather bunched his fingers into a fist, at which Mantu would puff: boom-boom, stamping his foot for added emphasis. The choir mumbled rather than sang. "Master it with your voice first," said Grandfather, "and then with your fingers . . . Play it from the inside so that it will sound good on the outside." Then he would say, "Louder on the trumpets!" And the Cîlțea brothers mewled: *tee-teee-taaaah. Ba-da-bam*, thumped Budișteanu on the trombone. And below them came the *boom, boom* of Mantu's tuba.

"Tell me what you're going to do!" demanded Grandfather.

"When you die, boss . . ." mumbled Mantu.

Invariably the Gypsy would weep, inhaling through his nose, contrary to his usual habit.

"Cut it out," said Grandfather. "Be a man. Aren't you ashamed in front of that tuba you lug around on your back? Say it!"

"Bay-toe-ven."

"That's right!" approved Grandfather.

He had made Mantu repeat the syllables *bay-toe-ven* until he had them off by heart.

"Beethoven! And what else?"

"Andante . . . Soft, in other words . . ."

"Moderately. Sometimes soft, sometimes loud. But moderately . . ."

"Yes, boss!"

"And without mistakes . . ."

"On my mother's life . . ."

"Otherwise I'll wake from the dead."

"May you wake, boss!"

"As this lad is my witness," said Grandfather. "Come over here." He signaled to me.

I stopped playing with my chestnuts and went over.

"Look me in the eye and say it so that he can hear too."

"Bay-toe-ven . . . Ninth . . . Moderate . . . Without mistakes . . ."

It was already too much for Mantu. He was suffocating from all that talking. And to smother his cough, he put his tuba to his lips. The cough was transformed into stuttering notes from the tuba. Grandfather pretended to be fooled, and taking me by the hand, we went away, followed by the sounds of the tuba, which struggled in vain to disguise the holes in Mantu's ravaged lungs.

Homeland Street was the Gypsy quarter. It joined Tanners Street at the railway barrier on the road to the village of Cîmpineanca, where Angheluță kept his shop. On the other side of the barrier was the cemetery, and a little farther away, at the very outskirts of town, the Armenian cemetery. Homeland Street

---

was long and straight, unpaved, ploughed by the heavy carts of the tinkers who collected old iron. The fences were crooked, askew, propped up or quite simply absent since "Gypsies don't need fences 'cause they don't steal from their neighbors," as Mantu proudly pointed out. The houses were made from mud bricks and had crooked windows so that the heat would not enter in summer or escape in winter. They were in a deplorable state, some without panes in the windows, some with blankets in place of doors. Instead of chimneys they had stovepipes poking through the windows that soured air already reeking from the miasmas that wafted from the patchwork of gardens at the back of the houses. Those with carts had built lean-to sheds for their animals, for the horses. In winter, the animals heated the wall of the house with their breath, and the people huddled on the other side of the mud bricks. "We didn't want to live in the town," Mantu explained, "but the town came to us!" Otherwise, it was merry there. The women chattered endlessly, calling to each other over the road; the numberless children played in the mud, alongside the geese; the stray dogs dozed, electing to ensconce themselves next to the dilapidated houses of people whom poverty had made generous. In summer, the mud dried and cracked, the cartwheels creaked, and the children raced each other, chasing bicycle wheels with shredded tires. In autumn, the mud grew deeper, climbing houses and fences like ivy. It was the same in spring, when the thaw softened the mud. In winter, on the other hand, it was as beautiful as anywhere else in the snow. There were fewer fires, and the snow melted later there. When the children's ice slide on Homeland Street melted, you could be sure there were no other slides left anywhere in town.

The Gypsy brass band players were the heralds of death, but they also took it away with them; they led it like a chained bear, and the air filled the space it left behind. The sky descended to the grass below, and the smoke from the chimneys rose up into the sky.

Grandfather loved books with a passion. And that is why it happened. Thus: THE DAY THEY BURNED THE BOOKS. The postman brought the list of banned books. The trailer stood at the corner of the street for three days. The people brought the books in sacks. They did not know whether or not it was a good idea to show they had banned books. Books twist minds and create enemies of the people. The list of books was so long that even school textbooks were included, so it was impossible for somebody not to have at least one banned book in the house. Embarrassed, the people stuffed their books in sacks and breathed a sigh of relief after they surrendered them to the man in overalls on the steps of the trailer at the corner of the street. "It's better this way. Instead of them coming and making a search, it's better we take them ourselves." "All very well, but we don't have any of the books on this list. Or else we've got just one or two. What will we fill our sack with?" "What does it matter?" shrugged the head of the family. "We'll fill it with whatever we've got in the house . . . In the end, they'll ban them all anyway. Better we get rid of them all at once. What use are yesterday's books to you now? It does you more harm than good to remember."

Nobody examined the books. They remained in the sacks tied at the necks with clothesline. It made them easier to unload. Mechanical diggers pushed the contents of the emptied sacks into a heap in front of the Pastia Theater, in front of which, as if by miracle, a bust of Mitiţă Filipescu still survived. They collected so many books that they filled the square; stray pages floated like white birds on the breeze. Feet trampled the books, which tried to escape; they sensed that something was amiss, that people had not previously treated them like that. The boots kicked the books back onto the heap. The books leapt through the air, pages fluttering; then they cowered, waiting for a hand to leaf through them rather than a boot to kick them. The mechanical diggers shoveled the sacks, ripping them. Pages and covers streamed through the ripped sacks, smelling of old bookcases. Then the sharp smell of gasoline. The fire. I had not been born at the time, and my father was a young man of twenty, slim, with a moustache. He watched, unable even to shed a tear since the heat of the fire scorched his cheeks and dried out his tear ducts.

The fire blazed the whole night. The men guarding the bonfire were like giants, elongated by the light of the flames, casting enormous shadows over the people who watched in silence, over the houses and windows, over the whole town. Early in the morning, smoke mingled with sparks rose from the smoldering heaps. From the street on the hill that only later was to be given a name, Mantu's brass band broke the silence hanging over the town. The Gypsies played all day, until nightfall, in a circle, with Grandfather Garabet in the middle, turning the pages of the score. And so the smoke was unable to rise; it hung thick and gray, like the cover of an old book. Only when the news reached them that armed soldiers were looking for them did the Gypsies disperse to their ramshackle houses. The people looked in bewilderment at the thick smoke, which hung from the sky as if in punishment. Only after nightfall did the sky clear, and the stars came out. On the day when the books burned, the transition from one night to the next took place without a sunrise and without a sunset, traversing a suffocating dusk. Such was the power of Mantu's tuba and the brass instruments of the other Gypsies, a power that they themselves did not understand and that they feared.

They also feared the relentless gaze of Grandfather Garabet, as he turned the pages of the score. They sweated as they played. The cortege came down Tanners Street on the way to the cemetery, and Mantu knocked at our gate, asking for a cup of wine and for mercy, which grandfather did not dispense. "The saxophone!" he said sternly. "What's with the saxophone?" asked the Gypsy, in a faint voice. "He was playing a semitone too high . . ." "Budișteanu has got a cold . . . ," Mantu essayed. "His ears is blocked up." "No mistakes—I've told you!" said Grandfather, and the Gypsy gulped.

In the end, there were indeed no mistakes. But the man who led the sparse cortege was my grandfather Garabet, and the music was not heard along Tanners Street but began on Homeland Street. Mantu did not languish. He stumbled and died coughing. To hide his dry cough, with the last of his strength he raised the tuba to his mouth, both of them leaning against a wall. From the funnel issued jerky notes, to the rhythm of the dying lungs. When the rhythmic sound became one continuous note, like an apparatus signaling that the patient's heart has stopped beating, the others knew that it was over. The note was still audible. Fofoc bent down and removed the mouthpiece from his lips so that Mantu's breath could rest. Then, the sky began to lower, like a bird that, after wheeling and wheeling, finally sinks to earth. And the smoke from the chimneys could rise once more, like blades of grass springing back after the horses' hooves have passed.

In our yard, there were three adjoining houses. The first my family had built in the 1930s, on a vacant lot near the St. Demetrios Church. In my childhood, after the priest died, the church was abandoned. We children had a terrific soccer field in the churchyard, and we held matches between streets. It would be March 6 Street against Snowdrops Street or Tanners Street against Gheorghe Asaki Street. All the children joined in, big and little. On the other side was the Frigorifer ice factory and then Tanners Road, which ran from the center of town to the western railroad crossing and the cemeteries. Other than that, there were houses large and small, each according to the skill, patience, and means of the owner. There were rain-washed fences behind which dogs barked. There were sidewalks of bare earth or asphalt, dust in dry weather, and wheel-churned mud and dark rivulets flowing along the *rigoles* when it rained. It was there that Grandfather Garabet and his brother-in-law Sahag Sheitanian built their homes. Later, Father built another, adjoining house for himself and us children. The yard was large, full of flowers, fruit trees, shade, nooks, and crannies. In those days, people were not in such a hurry. Time was approximate. "Come by in the evening and we'll drink coffee and play backgammon," Grandfather Garabet would say to his old friends. In other words, not at such-and-such a time, not at six or at seven. Or he would say, "I'll see you on Main Street in the morning. We'll have coffee at Dikran Bedrosian's clock shop." In that way, they waited calmly and were never late. And they always managed to meet up. Even the meals were longer. They began at lunchtime, in a leisurely way, and just as they were about to finish, as evening fell, they would sit down again for cheese and *pastirma* and *sujuk*, dishes you ate a little bit at a time but had to spend a long time chewing.

When places are new and you have yet to become used to them, time flows more quickly. But among long-familiar furniture, rummaging among the same shelves, wrapping yourself in the same quilt, and lolling on the same armchair, you find the hours longer. "Clocks were invented because people were unable to master time," old man Simon used to say, sinking into the soft cushions of the sofa in the yard and closing his eyes in contentment. "The same as weapons, which are a sign of powerlessness rather than power." He would sit for hours on end, gazing at the yard. He spoke seldom and with a certain dissatisfaction. There was a weariness in him that he could not shake off, even on the afternoons he spent motionless, sipping coffee, his eyelids drooping.

Old man Simon was the elder brother of Uncle Sahag. He had gone to Armenia in 1946, along with the first consignment of repatriates. You will not find the story of the repatriates anywhere because nobody wanted to tell it, let alone write it down, in all its horror. Nor would it have found a place even in *The Book of Whispers* if old man Simon had not been such a heavy smoker. I had never seen such cigarettes. Half of the cigarette was filled with acrid-smelling tobacco, which gave off a smoke that was yellowish, like withered leaves. The other half was an empty cardboard tube, which the smoke turned yellow.

Daidai Simon, or Uncle Simon, as we children called him in Armenian, smoked constantly, and when he was not silent, he said strange things. Like all the old men of my childhood, Grandfather Garabet was fascinated by ethereal things: "What a pity," he would say; "people are not capable of seeing the light as it really is or of listening to the air with all its melodies without having to unravel them, speed them up, or throttle them. If the air sings when blown through a tuba, through a funnel or an aperture, it doesn't mean that a sound has been invented but that the sounds are audible more thinly and more loudly. Unfortunately, people don't have the patience to understand the air in its quiet form." Grandfather listened to the sounds that are inaudible. Uncle Sahag was drawn to things that either happened or did not happen. He liked to play dice. He played backgammon or *gyulbahar*; he invented sophisticated ways of shaking the dice in his cupped palms, in coffee cups covered with the flat of his hand, or by tossing them up in the air first so that they would be unaffected by any human influence. This is why Uncle Sahag was fidgety and prone to dream up or believe in any fantasy, in any plot, in hidden, tangled threads. For him, anything was possible. Every man was a rolling die. The world was made up of millions and millions of rolling dice, which jumbled together and then tumbled onto the board, showing numbers high or low, odd or even.

On the other hand, *daidai* Simon felt no attraction to ethereal or doubtful things. He spoke of settled matters that were beyond all doubt. Namely, he spoke of the earth and stones. The earth was the living part, the stones the dead part, at least in outward appearance, like the bones in the body. Grandfather used to gaze up at the uppermost expanses of the sky, and he would laugh at Arshag the bell ringer, who, when he looked up, saw only as high as the birds. But *daidai* Simon looked down at the ground. "Last night I had a vision," he once said. "I gazed into the center of the earth. It was light there, like in the sky."

When he was a child, *daidai* Simon had been a seeker of water. In Anatolia, the lands were arid and it rained seldom, with large, swift raindrops. The rain barely quenched the earth's thirst, let alone the people's. This is why the people, when they sought a cure, looked not to the sky but to the earth. The seekers of hidden treasures were in fact the seekers of water. Some were magicians and did all kinds of strange things in order to detect springs in the depths of the earth. They buried burning sulfur, they beat taut drum skins, they mumbled ancient words, a mixture of Aramaic and Egyptian. Others were charlatans. They allowed themselves to be feasted royally, then they revealed the spot, and when the villagers began to dig, they made a run for it, leaving behind them the sharp noise of picks clashing against stone. There were also readers of signs. They interpreted the way the grass grew and what kind of grass, the way the earth cracked or bound together, the color of the soil, the gait of the donkeys or camels. Sometimes they found water, sometimes not. Sometimes the water was fresh; sometimes it was briny, good only for lye.

Uncle Simon was guided by the taste of the earth. He walked slowly, with his head lowered, peering at the ground as if through water. Then he would press his ear to the ground and listen. Finally, when his senses of sight and hearing prompted him, he scrabbled with his fingers. When he struck soft earth, he put it on the tip of his tongue and rolled it all around his mouth, with his eyes closed. In the beginning, people regarded with disbelief that strange child, who sniffed the earth like an animal, caressed it, talked to it, chewed it like a cake of wheat. Then they saw that he seldom failed, and they came from far and wide to ask his parents to send him to show them the way to the water.

"There are good places and bad places," said *daidai* Simon. "The same as the world, the same as people, the earth is not the same everywhere you go. It is either fertile or barren, moist or dry, alive or dead. Some earth is sticky, good for pots or bells. Some earth is useless; it crumbles between the fingers and will not bind. There is earth for houses, earth for plowing, earth for flowers, earth for roads, and earth for burial. Where the earth has no rest, where it is worked, the place above it is quiet. That's what happens in cemeteries, for example; where the earth labors, the air above it is peaceful."

In 1946, *daidai* Simon, together with his wife and two daughters, Arpine and Hermine, was repatriated to Soviet Armenia. He sighed, "There is too much stone there." Here in Romania, he yearned for the homeland, but he loved the earth of this country. In the homeland, he longed for the earth of Romania, with which he was wont to talk.

THE STORY OF SIMON'S REPATRIATION. Each pays for his desires in his own way. The place where you settle is not big enough for all that you wish to keep. In any event, what is yours also belongs to the place. You change place, you therefore give up some things and gain others. You fulfill a yearning, but you open the door to another. Every open wound is the beginning of a journey or a journey abandoned. In healing yourself, you harm yourself.

In the autumn of 1945, the heads of all the Armenian communities in Romania were summoned to Bucharest. For decades, the Armenian émigrés, bearers of nebulous Nansen passports, able only with difficulty to obtain permits to open their shops, had preferred to be forgotten by the authorities, and for that reason they had been fearful of the laws and obeyed them, but now they assembled in momentous circumstances. The Soviet Union was preparing to invade Kars and Ardahan, Armenian lands that, like many others, had remained Turkish territories. Romania's Armenians were to organize a demonstration of solidarity with the Soviet Union. "A Bolshevik trick," growled Sahag Sheitanian, the man who was to be my godfather, but he had no choice. With the members of the parochial council and a few others, he boarded the morning train to Bucharest. He was to board the same train a year later, crowded between wooden suitcases and broad-chested bodies swathed in greasy military capes without epaulettes, on his way to Craiova, where, in the Old Square, by Purcicarul Fountain, he bought two sacks of grain and one sack of corn, returning with them two days later to a Focșani ravaged by famine, weakened by starvation, scorched by torrid heat.

Now, however, the time is autumn 1945. The people have other concerns. Some mourn their dead; others rejoice in the peace. But there are also those who mourn and rejoice at the same time, torn between the son who died and the son who returned. The dead had moved into the photographs on the shelf; their clothes had been folded up and stuffed into trunks or passed down to younger brothers, who wore them with the overly long sleeves flapping. The last of the troops, those forgotten in garrisons or returning after being held as prisoners of war on the western front, were returning. The trains were filled with a motley crowd: soldiers with unbuttoned tunics, old widows wearing black, young widows with glittering eyes, people fleeing, people returning after the war had scattered them to the winds. It was such a train that my old folk, then men in their prime, boarded, staying close to Grandfather Garabet, who kept the tickets in the black painter's bag slung over his shoulder. Sahag Sheitanian had been right: it had nothing to do with Armenian lands; it was sooner a pro-Soviet demonstration. Romania's Armenian anti-Communist parties, the Dashnaks and the Ramgavars, had been disbanded; only the members of the pro-Communist Hunchakian party were still active. The leaders of the community, who were all Dashnaks, had already been deported to Siberia, and nothing more was known about them. The pro-Communists had founded the Armenian Front, which they named after Shahmunian, an Armenian revolutionary killed during the tsarist period. Marshaled, to their amazement, into a column, the Armenians marched from the headquarters of the front, on Armenian Street, along King Carol I Boulevard; they paused for a moment in University Square to "group," and then they headed right, to the Embassy of the Soviet Union. They were invited into the main hall, where a representative who had come from Soviet Armenia mentioned the word "repatriation" to them for the first time. Grandfather remembered his name because it was wholly unusual in a place like that. The man was called Astvadzadurian, which would translate as "Gift of God." He spoke to the Armenians about the unbelievable plenty of Soviet Armenia; about the new residential districts; about the broad, illuminated boulevards; about the fraternal joy of their fellow Armenians, who awaited them in Yerevan, in Leninakan, and in all the other cities and villages of Armenia. They listened wide-eyed, trying to make sense of that awkward, barking Armenian idiom peppered with Russian words.

"All lies," snorted Sahag Sheitanian, but not there since at the embassy they had all been as quiet as mice, with their eyes on the armed soldiers. Rather, he said it after they returned, in the square meeting room of the parochial council.

In the yard of the Armenian church on Station Road in Focşani, the buildings had served as Armenian schools until the beginning of the century, but now they had other uses. In the Boys' School now lived Minas the blind man and two or three other paupers from the community, those who gathered at funerals to receive alms wrapped in cloth and who, to keep warm during the service, huddled around the Godin stove, in which was burned sawdust. The Girls' School was now the church office, smelling of unaired, stuffy rooms; a place of long, heavy tables of dark wood, with portraits on the walls depicting saints, generals, and emperors, all mixed up together. Since time is best concealed in locked chests and among books, in the offices and the rooms at the back there were to be found both the one and the other. After more than twenty years, when everything was moved to Bucharest, to the Ecclesiastical Museum, we discovered the secret of the locked chests. They contained religious items and vestments collected over more than two centuries, since the building of the St. Mary Church. The books, handsomely bound in leather, smelled of animal sweat, and the pages were yellowed with time, incense smoke, and the fingers that had turned their pages. They were written in old Armenian, now spoken only in church services. Grandfather had made an inventory of them: numerous Bibles, Moses of Khoren's *History*, David the Invincible's philosophy, Gregory of Narek's *Book of Lamentations*, and the poems of Sayat Nova. Those books lived only once a year. On the feast day of the Holy Translators, Mesrop Mashtots and Sahak Partev, the monk and the patriarch who had translated the Bible into Armenian in the fifth century, we children took the books down from the shelves and dusted them with soft cloths. We were not allowed to open them. Their pages were often as dry as withered leaves, and they would have crumbled in our hands. Grandfather placed them back on the shelves, each in its proper place, and there they would slumber for another year. For books, the centuries pass more quickly.

"They're all lies," repeated Sahag, sitting at the head of the table, close to the books, as if taking them for his witnesses. "Ask Temelie, who was at Stalingrad. Ask him to tell you what he saw in Russia."

"That was in the war," said Dikran Bedrosian.

"People are coming from all over the world," Astvadzadurian had continued in a harsh voice, gazing down on the people's heads from up on the podium.

The ones in the front rows had nodded, looking from the corners of their eyes at the end of the row, from where they would be given the signal to applaud. It would not do to be left behind. The speaker had carried on, spreading his arms: "From France, Greece, Syria, Lebanon, from all over. Armenia is becoming the center of the world. The convoys of repatriates are returning home."

"First of all," said Sahag Sheitanian, taking up the thread, "I don't like that word: convoy. A free people does not line up in convoys. Only refugees and deportees . . . driven from behind."

The councilors looked at their feet. Nor did they like the word.

"The convoys set off from a given place, but nobody knows where they are going."

"Or if they will ever arrive," whispered to himself old man Nshan Maganian, the teacher, who had come all the way from Ploiești and who had listened in silence to both the one and the other.

If he had voiced his thoughts aloud, he would have said exactly the same thing as Sahag Sheitanian. He had been in the convoys that had set out from Zeitun, with his wife Azniv, carrying his one-year-old daughter in his arms. They had headed into the deserts of Mesopotamia. The little girl had been unable to withstand the burning heat. They kept watch over her, they tried to revive her, clutching her to their breast, but in vain. The little girl no longer breathed. They had done the only thing they could to protect her, this time from the wild animals of the desert: they buried her deep in the sand. After a long while, Azniv gave voice to their fear, asking, or rather wondering aloud, "What if she was not dead? What if we buried her alive? We should have pricked her with a needle to check . . ." That is why old man Maganian had said nothing in Bucharest when there was talk of the convoys of repatriates. And that is why Sahag Sheitanian had not remained silent.

But the times appeared to bear out the words of Astvadzadurian, the gift of another kind of god. The new authorities provoked fear. Astvadzadurian also came to Focșani. Grandfather proposed that the meeting take place in the church, but the envoys from Bucharest refused. Furthermore, Father Dajad Aslanian had been advised not to show his face if he knew what was good for him. The auditorium of the Pastia Theater was decked out in red drapes, against which backdrop was hung the face of Lenin, with portraits of Generalissimo Stalin and the young King Mihai to his left and right. On the stage sat a presidium made up of representatives from Soviet Armenia: Papken Astvadzadurian, the chairman of the Repatriation Committee; his deputy, Eduard Fabrikov; and Sava (Sahag) Dongulov, the envoy of the Embassy of the USSR, also an Armenian. Representing the Romanian Repatriation Committee in Bucharest, Harutiun Baboian was also present on the stage. The members of the Armenian community sat in the front rows of the theater. The seats at the back were filled with unfamiliar, scowling faces. Grandfather and the others looked with foreboding at the representatives of the new authorities, who so little resembled the solemn, gold-embroidered old authorities. On each side of the stage, men in leather coats kept a close watch on the audience.

From the back, somebody went up to the first rows and started giving out little red flags; the Armenians did not know what to do with them. Sahag was about to throw his away when Grandfather raised one eyebrow and made a sign for him to wait. They laid their little red flags in their laps and looked in bewilderment at the people on the stage and then over their shoulders at the grim-faced strangers in the back rows.

"Read it!" says Grandfather in the chancellery, handing the bell ringer a copy of *Bahag*, the only Armenian-language newspaper authorized to be published in Romania since the Soviet occupation.

"Sunday morning. In Focşani, groups of Armenians hurry to the Pastia Theater. The delegation arrives at the appointed hour; the audience gives a standing ovation . . ."

Arshag the bell ringer pauses, frowns, shows the page of the newspaper to the others, as if wishing to prove that this is really what it says.

"Read the rest," says Grandfather Garabet, tapping the newspaper on the table with his index finger.

Arshag looks around him, gulps, continues, reading syllable by syllable, as if trying to make his own ears believe it.

"A rustle of excitement passes around the theater. A continuous murmur. Hushed respect. All of a sudden the audience falls silent; the Armenians' hearts give a leap. Their friend Dr. Astvadzadurian mounts the podium. On his chest gleams a red flag. Impassioned enthusiasm grips the audience. The entire auditorium erupts in applause, cheers, ovations."

The men crane their necks. Arshag puts down the newspaper again.

"That was us?" asks Anton Merzian finally.

"You heard it," replies Krikor Minasian, the other cobbler.

Arshag folds up the newspaper and places it on the corner of the table. Grandfather does not urge him to continue reading. Nevertheless, the hectoring voice of Astvadzadurian makes itself heard. It swells, climbing the walls, blotting out the portraits of saints, emperors, and generals. The walls blanch, the paintings flinch, the faces melt, like a chunk of salt immersed in water.

The steady, booming voice of Astvadzadurian makes itself heard. Nothing is more important, nothing less important; everything is very important.

"Today we develop in conditions of freedom because everything is in the hands of the state and supported by the state. Let us not forget that if we have the opportunity to live and work freely and if the whole world has been released from slavery, it is thanks to the Soviet Union and the Red Army, with Generalissimo Stalin at their head."

From the back rows comes frenzied applause. The men in the front rows jump. Some of them timidly press their palms together as if about to clap. They look as if they are at prayer.

"Collaborate with and support the Romanian democratic organizations, and in that way you will serve the Soviet Homeland. The fate of the Armenian people is closely bound to the great Russian people, who have supported us and defended us with fatherly care. Let us unmask the perfidious Dashnak Armenians, who have betrayed the Homeland, debasing themselves like Hitler's lackeys!"

Indignation erupts from the back rows, voicing itself in cries of "Down with them!" Astvadzadurian is speaking in Armenian. He does not understand what the people in the back rows are shouting in Romanian. The people shouting in the back rows cannot understand a word of Armenian; all they understand are the proper names and even then not all of them. They have never even heard of Dashnak. But they see an arm up on the balcony. When the arm points up, they know they have to stand and applaud. When the arm points down, they know they have to be indignant. And the most convenient thing to shout in such a situation is "Down with them!" It never misses the mark, even when it is not at all clear to whom "them" refers.

The speaker does not understand the shouts from the audience. The shouters understand nothing of his speech. But even so, they are satisfied with each other. My grandfather Garabet, Sahag Sheitanian, Krikor Minasian, Anton Merzian, Arshag the bell ringer, and the others feel as if they have less and less room between the red-flag-draped stage, which is descending lower and lower, and the shouters at the back, who are stomping, crowding them, jostling them. Grandfather Garabet must be thinking of his friends who were arrested and deported to Siberia. He does not yet know that the shouts are accurate. "Down with them!" It is the beginning of November 1945, and the Hovnanian brothers are already dead and have been dumped in the mass graves. For a long time, the peasants did not plow the fields around the camps, so fearful were they of the mass graves. Farther down than that you cannot go. "Down with" the others too. And Astvadzadurian does not stop there:

"Maintaining the determined step of the triumphal march to progress, the Soviet People of Armenia walk shoulder to shoulder with the other fraternal nations of the USSR onward to the peaks of human civilization. A huge effort. A titanic labor. A heroic odyssey that surpasses all imagination. Armenians scattered to the four winds now demand to return to the homeland. Their place is in Soviet Armenia. They want to be Soviet citizens and to bring their tribute of labor and creation to the Soviet Armenian State."

At the signal, the audience rises to its feet, applauding. Those in the front rows, who did not understand the signal from the balcony, stand up one by one, in slow motion. Their silence is inaudible.

Grandfather Garabet is the only one who remains standing. He lays the flat of his hand on the newspaper, as if to muffle the rhythmic applause that still rings in his ears. He fixes his gaze above the others' heads.

"Sahag?" he asks.

Sahag Sheitanian is silent.

"Anton?"

Anton Merzian is silent too. He lowers his eyes.

"Krikor?"

The cobbler rubs together his calloused hands. Grandfather pronounces the name of each in turn. Like applause, silence has its own rhythm.

"Simon?"

He answers in his own way:

"The land . . . Our land."

It was then that Sahag Sheitanian understood his brother was going to leave. For Simon, who viewed the world downward, toward the core of the earth, the others' arguments counted for little. To him all that happened above the soil seemed as insignificant as blades of grass. In the air above, my uncle Simon felt as if he were buried alive.

He gathered his things together and he left, taking with him his wife and two daughters, Arpine and Hermine. Grandfather Garabet and Uncle Sahag went with him on the train as far as Constanța. In the port, the *Rossiya* was waiting, huge, noisy, overbearing. It was now the spring of 1946. After embracing him, Grandfather Garabet did not say to him, "Write us!" since Uncle Simon was not gifted at writing. His fingers, so gifted at crumbling the soil, were clumsy when confronted with a sheet of paper. Instead, he told him, "Send us a photograph!" Uncle Simon, the son of a treasure hunter, now a man in his prime, said the following: "I'll send you a photograph that will contain a message. If the photograph shows me standing, then all is well. If I am leaning on something, the corner of a wall, the back of a chair, then things are so-so. If you see me sitting, then it is bad." Others too had conceived of the same trick in order to explain a situation simply but indirectly. For years and years, no photographs from Soviet Armenia arrived. It was not until 1949 that the first came. The Andonian family from Bucharest received it. In church, the photograph passed from hand to hand until all had seen it. The family had crowded together in front of the camera lens. But the head of the family, Nerses Andonian, was neither standing nor leaning nor even sitting. He was lying on the grass. But it was too late. The repatriations had stopped in 1948. By 1949 the deportations had already begun.

But the time is still 1946. The repatriates crowd the deck of the *Rossiya*, each wishing to be the first to spy land on the other side of the sea. The weather was calm, fortunately, because otherwise they would have had to take shelter in the cabins and there was not enough room for everybody. At night they slept wrapped in thick, rough blankets. When they ate, they spread sheets of newspaper on the deck or the lids of the wooden trunks, placing the food on them.

On the other coast of the Black Sea, Grandfather Garabet scours the Armenian and the Romanian newspapers and correspondence from Soviet Armenia. Somewhat more accustomed to the Latin alphabet and bored with Arshag's syllable-by-syllable reading, Grandfather takes the newspaper from the bell ringer's hands and continues:

"Before the *Rossiya* entered the port of Batumi, a motorboat set out from the quay to greet the ship carrying the repatriates. A few minutes later an Armenian general boarded, accompanied by Dr. P. Astvadzadurian, holding in his arms a six-year-old child. All the while, an orchestra of repatriates was playing on board. To the applause and cheers of the crowd assembled on the quay, streams of repatriates began to flow toward the town. The new arrivals were everywhere greeted with great warmth. An eyewitness describes the touching scenes that took place in the port of Batumi. Embraces, kisses, sobs. Delirious excitement. The repatriates are then led to the special accommodation where they will be living as long as they are in Batumi before traveling on to Yerevan."

"Is this how it is to be?" asks Anton Merzian.

This was how it was. For it was not until the morning of the next day, after another night spent on deck, that they saw the port in the distance. Thitherto some of them had lived their lives in the intervals between ports, with one port receding and another approaching. The ports that receded: Constantinople, Izmir, Trebizond, Antakiya. Or else nameless shores but open to ships, such as the shore at the base of Mount Musa, where French vessels landed to pick up the Armenian refugees who had held out for so long on the slopes. The ports that approached: places with houses different from those left behind, with the white, sunbaked walls and flat roofs of lands where it does not rain: Marseille, the Piraeus, Constanța, but also places farther flung: New York, Montevideo, Mar del Plata. For some, Constanța now receded and Batumi approached, where the buildings were squat and black, with windows whose panes were broken, like eyes gouged from their sockets or that were patched with crooked boards. The approach of a port is always an unsettling experience. This time, the feeling was accompanied by bewilderment.

THE MULTIPLICATION OF THE BREAD. Instead of sailing into the port, the huge ship *Rossiya* slowed down and cast anchor while still slantwise to the shore. The captain ordered everybody onto the deck, although there was no need since all the passengers were there already. A number of sailors, carrying a rolled-up tarpaulin, picked their way through the crowd and came to a stop in the midst of the passengers. They signaled the people to make a space. The passengers crushed up against each other even more closely. Those with small children lifted them onto their shoulders, lest they be trampled or get lost.

"Russian!" came the captain's voice as he tried to string together the few words in Romanian that he knew. "Who knows Russian?"

Garabet Daglarian, from Constanța, came to the front. The captain called him over to the raised platform on which he was standing. Then he started yelling. The sky was quite clear for a spring morning at sea. The captain's voice issued forth loudly, unintelligibly, in a rush. The people looked fearfully at Garabet Daglarian, who, naturally having understood what the captain said, now looked at him in bewilderment. The captain stopped yelling as abruptly as he had started. He made a sign for Daglarian to translate. He started to translate but then suddenly stopped on receiving a nudge that he should speak more loudly.

"The captain asks," resumed Daglarian, shouting out each word, "if you have any bread or flour about your persons."

The survivors of massacres, refugees who bore the seal of statelessness and who were accustomed to not drawing attention to themselves, to speaking in a whisper and eking out their days quietly, the Armenians had fallen out of the habit of shouting. They became enraged only rarely. The less attention others paid to them the better. There was little room for them in this world. They had learned to live pent up.

This is why it was torture for Daglarian to shout; he was listening to his own voice for the first time. This is why the others were surprised to hear one of their own shouting, and they were all the more surprised when they heard what he had been told to say:

"The captain says that if you have bread or flour about your persons, you are to put them on the tarpaulin in the middle. Whoever fails to do what he says will be punished."

After a few moments of bewilderment, someone took out a crust of bread. He was embarrassed to throw it; he laid it slowly, like a flower on a grave. Another placed a whole loaf on the tarpaulin, looking for a spot that was reasonably clean, either because he hoped to get his bread back or out of an innate sense of what is proper. A round loaf and a crust. The people looked in silence, huddling up against one another. The captain gave a signal, and one of the sailors grabbed a knotted cloth at random. Without bothering to untie it, he slashed it with a knife. He rummaged through the jumble of things and took out a piece of bread, which he laid on his broad palm, as if on a salver, and raised it in the air, showing it first to the captain, then to the crowd, like the head of St. John the Baptist. He tossed it onto the tarpaulin and turned to the owner of the bag. The man thought he was required to say something and started to stammer. But the sailor, who had not asked him any questions, did not appear to be satisfied with the man's answer, whatever it might have been. He dealt him two brutal slaps, which sent the man tottering to one side and then sprawling to the other side. He fell to the deck, covering his burning cheeks with his hands. With a triumphant smile, the captain made a sign to show that he was waiting. The passengers began to open their luggage, with slow movements, taking out their bread and bags of flour. They went to the front one by one since they did not dare to pass it from hand to hand and carefully laid down their bread. They stumbled and fell, tripping over each other. A number of bags of flour burst. A warm, bluish, caressing steam rose but quickly dissolved, scattered by the blare of the siren, which announced that the business there on the ship had been concluded.

A motor launch approached from shore. A thin man wearing a Soviet officer's uniform, with a chest full of medals, climbed onto the deck. From the way in which his thick black eyebrows joined together at the top of his hooked nose, he appeared to be Armenian. Looking at the heap of bread and white powder, he said in Armenian:

"Henceforward you will no longer be forced to eat the bread of exile!"

The loaves were of every variety, according to the means and the skill of each: round and long, smooth and plaited, leavened and unleavened. In Armenian, unleavened bread is called *lavash*, and in autumn it is stacked in the larder; sprinkled with water, it is then freshened on the hob. Dusted with flour, glinting in the sunlight, the heap of loaves looked like the preparation for a wedding. It required eight sailors to lift the tarpaulin by its edges. The passengers did not venture to help them; they stood aside, allowing them to go to the gunwale. There, the sailors swung that unusual load back and forth, to gather momentum and then, with a final heave, cast it into the sea.

The ship set in motion. The bread bobbed in the wake left by the propeller. The gangplank was lowered and the people, tripping over their luggage, disembarked, looking back at the expanse of water, which, with its power to swell, break, and consume, had swallowed up the bread.

Simon then recounted the wretched aspect of the docks, the black buildings without doors and windows, the suspicious eyes, and the barked questions. When you move from one place to another with your wife, your children, your chattels; when you need a roof over your head and a job, regardless of what you are called—an exile, a stateless person, a refugee, a repatriate, or whatever—people are loath to make way for you, and an uninvited guest you remain. The procedures were extremely long and complicated. In turn, they all had to stand in front of a table at which sat three men in military uniforms, of whom only one spoke Armenian; the ones who asked the questions and wrote down the answers, sometimes even writing more than they were told, were Russians. First they called the men of the family, like Simon. He handed over the identity papers of all the family members, which were sequestered and carefully copied. The papers were to be returned only when the family presented themselves to the authorities in the town to which they had been allocated. In fact, only the certificate of repatriation counted for anything, and the Nansen passports were never returned. Then came the questions about their birthplace, and if this was Anatolia, as it most frequently was, they then demanded details of how the person had ended up in Romania, what he had done for a living there, what his profession was, what his politics were, whether he had known General Dro. After that, the man was asked to point to his wife and his children in the crowd and to fetch his luggage. The wife was asked the same questions; the trunks were opened and searched. Those who had answered the questions were sent to a hut whose door was guarded by armed soldiers. This was so they could not speak to the people who were still waiting and tell them about the questions, preventing them from agreeing on their answers with each other beforehand.

The interrogation lasted until dusk. Then, by candlelight, they were finally told they could eat. They were given nothing but bread, as it was thought that they must still have food from home. The bread was black and crumbly. You could not break it. You had to bite straight from the loaf because otherwise it crumbled like sand between your fingers. It also crunched like sand between your teeth. "That's why they made us throw away the bread we'd brought with us," said Simon, concluding his tale. "So that we wouldn't see the difference between the bread we'd left behind and the bread we were going to receive from then on."

The journey to Yerevan lasted more than a day, although the distance was not great. In the goods train, they sat on the bare floor as best as they were able, and the only difference between deportees and repatriates, crowded among their luggage, sweating, sleepless, was that the repatriates' wagons were not sealed, and when the train was in motion, the doors remained open a crack to let in air and light, whereas the deportees could breathe only through the cracks in the walls of the wagons. From time to time the train stopped in the plain so that those who felt an urgent need could get off, ignoring the embarrassment they had brought with them from home.

Let us say that Simon was lucky. He was allocated to Yerevan. His family, along with another two families, fifteen people in total, was given temporary accommodations in a three-room house. The house was dilapidated and had remained unheated too long for the spring sun to be able to take the edge off its chill. For a period Simon was unable to find work. He sold everything he had brought with him: clothes, material . . . One fine day they were given a plot of land, a thousand square feet, on which to build themselves a house. It took them more than a year because building materials were scarce and there was barely enough money for food. After that, life slowly, slowly got under way. The repatriates were viewed with mistrust; they stuck together, wherever they were from:

Bulgaria, Romania, Greece, Lebanon, France. They met in the park and talked about the world they had left behind, about parties and churches, about the bread that had not ended up being cast in the sea. That park, which still exists, near Republic Square in Yerevan and the spot where the huge statue of Lenin stood, was for a long time known as Lats'i Partez, or the Garden of Lamentation. Sometimes, nostalgia cropped up where and when you least expected it. In the autumn of 1951, when the first round of deportations to Siberia ended and people still did not know what would happen next—whether the repatriates would return or whether those who remained would be deported—Johnny Răducanu was invited to perform in the Philharmonic Concert Hall in Yerevan. A swarthy young man at the time, his voice not yet made hoarse by tobacco, he did not know that the audience was mainly made up of Armenians who had lived in Romania for a long time, but he found out in a way that placed him in a quandary. After the first round of polite applause died away and Johnny was about to twang his double bass, a man's voice called out in Romanian from the balcony. The voice was reedy but sounded deeper because the man cupped his palms around his mouth to form a funnel: "Hey, Johnny my lad, do the whores still hang out at the Marna?" The murmur from the audience showed that most of the people understood what the man had shouted, but Johnny Răducanu gulped and started to play, not knowing what else to do in a country where such things could have unpredictable consequences. Pondering it now, more than half a century after the fact, Johnny and I reached the following two conclusions, although his input was decisive, given the period and the topic. First of all, the repatriates selected to go to Soviet Armenia were mainly poor Armenians since the whores from the hotels around Bucharest's Northern Station, such as the Marna, were hardly high-class. And second, just as the Armenians who remained in Romania didn't know anything about those who had gone to Armenia, so too those who left did not know very much about what was happening in Romania. In any event, the question was superfluous since the hapless women had long since been kicked out of the hotels. In the end, after soldiers returning from the front and the prisoner-of-war camps dwindled away on the platforms of the Northern Station, the whores decided to give up a losing game. And in the new world of communism and ration books, there was no place for them anyway since not even in the most equal of all possible worlds, as the Communist world claimed to be, has prostitution ever been rationed.

INCENTIVES TO STAY PUT, OR THE TALE OF GOOD OLD "MR. STAYPUTIAN." Perhaps things were not really like that, and the cattle trucks, the houses that were like cattle stalls, the poverty, and the cold existed only in the imagination of Simon Sheitanian. Or else perhaps it was only a part of the reality, the inner

reality. Because the outward reality looked completely different. My grandfather Garabet recounted it in the meeting room of the Armenian church in
Focşani, reading the letters from Soviet Armenia:

"Headline," announced Grandfather: "The first letters from Armenian repatriates from Romania have arrived." And then: "The letters received up to
now demonstrate that those who left Romania received a good welcome in the
Homeland, and good accommodation was quickly provided. The authors of the
letters emphasize in particular the plentiful food and reasonable prices, adding
that the prices are constantly going down. The homes where the repatriates live
are very comfortable, and the treatment they have received from the authorities is beyond reproach. The public parks, the restaurants, theaters, cinemas,
and all places of entertainment in general are swarming with repatriates, who
are entitled to free entry everywhere. Special shows are put on daily in honor
of the repatriates."

"What can you say?" asked Anton Merzian, as puzzled as ever. And he turned
to Sahag Sheitanian, who had tried with all his might to persuade his brother
Simon not to leave. Sahag ignored the question, picked up the newspaper, and
read it over carefully once again.

"There's something strange here," he said. "If they're letters sent home, why
does it say it's correspondence from the Soviet Union?"

"Has anyone here received a letter? Have you heard of anybody who's received one?" insisted Anton Merzian.

"I haven't heard of anybody who has, it's true," admitted Arshag the bell
ringer. "What's with that?"

"It means somebody reads the letters before they get here. Who's ever heard
of letters that arrive in the pages of a newspaper instead of in the mailbox?"

"Well, over there, in the Soviet Union . . ."

Other than in the pages of the newspaper, letters had not arrived for a long
time. For more than a year, it was the Soviet Union that wrote letters to those
who remained in Romania. And the letters were not read except on the correspondence page. The anonymous sender could not be happier, everything was
going up when it was good to go up—which is to say, wages, production, the
mountains of food in the shops—and everything was going down when it had
to go down—which is to say, prices and taxes; everything was going forward if
its duty was to go forward—which is to say, the soviets, labor, and enthusiasm—
and everything was on the retreat where appropriate—namely, imperialism and
Coca-Cola. In the letters that the Soviet Union assiduously wrote to Grandfather Garabet, there were no names, no faces, no feelings. A man's name is his
primary flaw; it distinguishes him from other people. The people who wrote to

Grandfather, Sahag Sheitanian, and all the others who listened to news about the repatriates were the Soviet People.

In the end, the Soviet Union stopped bothering to write letters and contented itself with carefully reading other people's, and it was then that the first real letters began to arrive. It would appear that those who wrote the letters knew their readers well and provided each with a different opportunity to understand. Just as there are choirs of singers with different voices, so too there are choirs of readers. The letters were written in Armenian, for the sake of the Soviet reader, and the envelopes were only loosely sealed, so as not to annoy him too much when he opened them. Every now and then, the letter writers slipped in a word or two in Romanian so that the reader back home would understand what was to be understood. Simon wrote as follows to his successive readers, first the Soviet, then the Romanian: "It is very good here. We have everything. Lots of people come to visit us. For example, Mr. Carne ["meat" in Romanian, for the benefit of the reader back home] comes about once a month. Mr. Brînză ["cheese"] comes about once a week. You really should come to visit too. Find a nice girl for Anton Merzian's son Dikranig and after they get married, you should really come over here so that we can all celebrate."

Anton Merzian's son Dikranig was a babe in arms at the time. The Soviet reader, in his uniform with the worn elbows, who did not know and did not understand, will have rejoiced, but the Romanian reader, who knew, will have despaired. Sometimes the letter would be less indirect: "Often, in the evening, we remember the people back home. Please pass on our best regards to Mr. Stayputian."

The more plentiful the food, the lower the prices; the more beautiful the houses, the more irrepressible the enthusiasm; and the more splendid the concerts in honor of the repatriates, the more numerous were the inducements addressed to Mr. Stayputian, until he was overwhelmed.

But then one fine day, the letters, whether sent directly by the Soviet Union or on its behalf by newly made Soviet citizens, stopped arriving. It happened in 1949. It was then that the repatriates began to be deported. And it was only then that the repatriates fully understood what had happened to them. The Soviet Union had not needed them. But a diaspora meant those on the outside posed a permanent threat, and it presented a permanent temptation for those on the inside. The diaspora had to be uprooted. There was plenty of room for them in Siberia and no temptation for the others. Many of the repatriates were sent to Siberia, as were the locals who had been foolish enough to intermarry with them. They used to whisper to each other at home: "They've taken so-and-so." The defenseless person in question was taken, taken off, taken away. "They've got him." Only the object of the verb was precise: the fleeting individuality of a person. The subject, the "they," was mysterious, omnipresent but invisible.

In the beginning was the pronoun.

Like a register that reads itself, its pages blowing in the wind. When each hears his name, he rises in silence, with slumped shoulders, and leaves the room. "Him" is not an object that reads itself; the verb requires a subject. Other convoys, other trains, this time with padlocked doors. Into the desert once more, not a desert of sand this time but a desert of snow. Only the wind remains the same. And Mr. Stayputian has been left behind; he has stayed put, all alone.

The deportations of 1949 bypassed Simon Sheitanian. They stopped and did not resume until the spring of 1953. The repatriates were assigned temporary, unimportant jobs. Everybody knew that the ones who remained would be deported eventually. Of all things, waiting is the hardest to bear. Some tried to escape once more, traveling to Odessa and attempting to stow away on ships, among the bales. Or else they tried to reach the border with Romania, in the places where it was thinnest, along the River Prut or in the forests of Bukovina. They were to be caught every time, without fail.

Simon had a family; he could not leave. He bought himself a saw and learned how to cut wood. He knew it would be useful to him in Siberia. Fortunately, however, in the spring of 1953 Stalin died. And on his death, the deportations ceased too.

For Uncle Simon, the earth was not round. Nor was it flat, like a plate, as it seemed on the plains that spread from the foot of Mount Ararat. For him, the earth was a line that stretched from the spot on which the soles of his shoes rested to the core of the earth, to the point where nothing can go any deeper. That is why all he needed was to have the soles of his shoes on the ground in order to understand, and nothing came between the soles of his shoes and the soles of his feet, the same as nothing comes between the knife and the bread.

For Stalin, the earth did not have depths or crannies. It was like a tabletop, any of whose edges he could touch with his index finger. His fantasies did not have depths but edges, borders. And when the index finger came to a stop at a point on the tabletop, if the frontiers could not be pushed further than that point, then the people had to be brought inside the frontiers. A diaspora is mobile; it is hard to clasp it in your arms; it is too weary of wandering for you to lure it, and nonetheless its wounds are too fresh for it to stay still. With its nostalgias, with its dream of rebuilding the historic Armenia, prepared to make any alliance to that end (as happened during the war, when General Dro and his battalion allied themselves with Germany against the Bolsheviks), the diaspora was a source of disquiet for the Soviet Union. On that earth spread out like a piece of oilcloth, the diaspora streamed in every direction, like droplets, as far as the edges, to Australia, Argentina, Ethiopia, Canada. And since they could not be brushed from the table like crumbs into a cupped palm and then cast away, those points that freckled the cheeks of the earth's two hemispheres had to be lured into coalescing. It was then that Stalin proposed the repatriation of the Armenians. Shortly after Japan surrendered, the Supreme Soviet of the USSR, acting on the "wishes of Armenians all over the world and the requests of the Armenian SSR," authorized the repatriation, providing incentives, land for houses, financial aid from the state, and tax exemptions—benefits that were late in coming and were delivered only in small part. The Soviet propaganda put forward the figure of three hundred thousand repatriates, but the real number may have been just half that. It was then that Stalin decided as follows: the Armenians were to be summoned to their country. The process was to be worldwide and to be completed quickly so that those who wished to be repatriated would not have time to find out from those already repatriated what terror and poverty awaited them. But even so, the repatriation lasted two years, during which time letters were intercepted at the border, read and reread by industrious operatives, who then rewrote them and mailed them in the same envelopes, preserving from the original text only the proper names. It was only when the compliments directed at Mr. Stayputian multiplied that the people back home began to be worried and then to realize the truth. Beloved, flattered, famous, Mr. Stayputian did not, however, arouse the curiosity of the official scribes, who took their duties seriously and regarded Mr. Stayputian as an honorable person who had to be complimented at every possible opportunity. He was a highly respected person, to the point of pious reverence, since nobody ventured to address him directly but only obliquely, the way a sinner addresses a confessor, with eyes lowered and head averted. And when the repatriations ceased, when the mist above the sea, at Batumi and Poti, was no longer thick with the white dust of flour dumped overboard, the deportations began. Slowly, without haste, like a delicacy to be savored. The first to be taken away were the repatriates, so Stalin had decided, and then locals began to be mixed in among them. Until the population of the Soviet Socialist Republic of Armenia had been reduced to less than a million. And what had begun with Nakhichevan and Nagorno Karabakh would now be finished. With a population of less than a million, Armenia would have lost its status as a republic, and its territory could be divided between Georgia and Azerbaijan.

When Stalin died, there were plenty of people in Soviet Armenia who mourned him. There were probably plenty in Siberia too, although only among the locals. Most people did not shed a tear. They included Simon Sheitanian, naturally. Above all else, what distinguished Stalin from Uncle Simon was his mistaken view of the earth. In any event, the earth did not rest until it had proved it to him: Stalin's body, emptied of guts, macerated in chemicals, brushed with paint and cosmetics, remained unburied for a long time. Whereas for Simon the earth opened up to him at his very first invocation.

It was the autumn of 1960. Now sheltered from the danger of deportation, the repatriates had begun to marry and have children. Simon Shcitanian became a grandfather after his daughters Arpine and Hermine married. After 1958, when the insurrections that followed the Hungarian Revolution finally died down, repatriates from Romania were allowed to visit their relatives. And so here is Simon Sheitanian, almost fifteen years later, sitting on the couch in the middle of the yard, beneath the apricot tree, talking and smoking cigarette after cigarette. All of a sudden:

"Armenia deserves your love. Everywhere you look there is nothing but stone. In the mountains the stones grow tall, like trees. I'm afraid to die there and have them throw stones on top of me. Here the earth is good; it's worth dying here."

The earth heeded him and opened up to him. That very night Uncle Simon was wracked by a fit of coughing, brought on by his smoking. He coughed until his heart burst. They buried him in Focșani. Thus did he return to the larger body from which he had never fully emerged when he came into the world. In the Armenian cemetery in Focșani, Simon Sheitanian was the first of our dead. Shortly thereafter he was followed by my great-grandmother Heghine Terzian, born on the banks of the Bosphorus and crossing to the other world at the age of almost ninety.

Every morning Grandfather Garabet picked a few tubes of pigment at random, mixed them together, and spread them on a canvas. He looked at the colors, gauging their intensity; he studied the flexion of the lines and their termini. Then he would conclude: "How peaceful we are this morning!" Or: "We woke up in a bit of a bad mood today . . ." Sometimes he would stop talking in the middle of a conversation and abruptly vanish into his workshop. He would come back holding a brush or a knife, his fingers smeared with oils. He would invite his interlocutor into the workshop and show him the canvas on the tripod. "Look at how strident the green is, compared with the whiteness of the canvas. And how out of place it is, with that red stripe underneath. And the lines end abruptly, as if the painter had suddenly vanished." In bewilderment, the guest would look at the intersecting lines on the canvas. "What does it mean?" he would ask. "What it means," Grandfather would snap, "is that you really annoyed me." Or contrariwise: "This combination of blue and orange seems to come off well. Especially since the colors are soft, blurred on either side. And the lines are slightly curved, as if they were stretching over the surface of the earth. What that means is that no matter how hard you tried, with all the stupid things you said, you weren't able to annoy me."

This greatly simplifies an understanding of the world. Everything is a combination of lines and colors. Including the soul. In every moment the soul expresses itself through the color most appropriate to it. It would be a mistake to understand the world through its shapes. Wine poured into a cup or an amphora or through a funnel into a narrow-necked bottle has the same taste. The harsher, the more strident the taste of the color, the angrier the soul. When colors are strong but pure, it means cheerfulness. Blurred colors: tranquility. Clashing colors: suspicion, foreboding, annoyance.

Grandfather kept notes in a journal. In the top right-hand corner he wrote the date, but apart from that there were just colored lines. He sometimes leafed through the journal: "Lately I haven't been feeling well," he would say. "Maybe I'm getting old." "Change the colors . . . ," Sahag Sheitanian, his brother-in-law, would say, sipping his coffee. "It's not me who chooses the colors; they choose me. It's not something where you can get away with tricks. What would be the point of deceiving yourself?"

Grandfather painted landscapes. Sometimes he slung his tripod over his back and we went to the edge of town, on the other side of the railway tracks. Most of the time he copied old postcards. He divided the postcard into squares, tracing thin lines with a pencil. Then he expanded them, square by square. Sometimes he placed a few objects on a shelf: jugs, fruit, headscarves. He studied them for a long while and then drew them. He mixed the colors on a palette. I liked the palette best of all. I thought it the most successful of his paintings. Its shape was beautiful, rounded like a violin. The colors were various and differed in technique. You could see the brushstrokes, sometimes heavy, sometimes soft, like a lock of woman's hair. The knife spread the colors like thin slices of fruit, raw or ripe. Then there were the traces of the fingernail, when the colors were mixed using the finger. But most of all I liked the fact that the palette was an endless painting. Grandfather painted, but to me the painting was the palette. The surplus colors formed paintings on canvas. Grandfather agreed with me. "It's more useful to view things back-to-front," he said.

First we arranged the cloth, more often than not with one corner falling over the edge of the shelf. Then the jug, always filled with water, so as to look useful, and placed so that its handle was visible. Around it we placed seasonal fruits. Grandfather gazed at them for long minutes. He closed one eye, gauged the proportions holding up his pencil, moving the tip of his thumb up and down.

From time to time he would call me so that we could look at what he was painting together, especially when he was satisfied with it. I would look first at the objects, then at the canvas. More often than not he would paint something completely different. Instead of the jug, for example, on the canvas there would be a samovar; instead of the apples, grapes. "It's unimportant," said Grandfather. "Every choice is random." "But why did we put the objects on the shelf? What's the point of looking at them?" "It's good to interrupt yourself from time to time. If you keep looking at a thing, at the same thing, you stop seeing it. In the end, this samovar is not nowhere, nor are the grapes. It's the still life I arranged here a month ago." "That's right," I admitted. "When you painted the wine bottle and peaches." "It's only now that the time for the samovar came," he said.

When he was not painting grapes instead of apples and peaches instead of grapes, Grandfather painted photographs and postcards, as I said. He skillfully enlarged them and meticulously reproduced the details. In the old days, he used to add pastel colors to the photographs. We had albums of colored photographs from the 1920s. "In the days when your grandmother was young and beautiful and deserved all those colors." The charm of it is to place yourself slantwise to the flow of time. In the days before color photographs were invented, it was something special to color them yourself. Nowadays, when you can make your own color photographs, it is nicer to discover the hues of black and white behind the colors.

I was a child, and it was hard for me to understand such things. But I listened and understood as much as I could of what they said as they studied a photograph, calculating the angles, unraveling the light, and searching for new techniques. Behind the cupboard we had negatives on glass. But Grandfather had adapted. He had found an enlarging device with a hood, in which he placed the celluloid film. He fixed a panel with a variable frame inside the beam of light and then inserted the photosensitive paper. He adjusted the ray of light until the outlines came into focus. Which is to say, until the pupil of the person in the photograph became a black point. Then, depending on the quality of the negative, he counted. Sometimes he counted for a whole minute. After that he placed the paper in plastic trays in which he had dissolved developing and fixative substances. Finally, after checking it in red light, he hung up the wet photograph on a line stretched from one end of the room to the other. We would stand in the miraculous red darkness, leaning over the trays that reeked of chemicals, isolated from the rest of the world by the black-painted cardboard with which Grandfather occluded the windows.

That is why I did not like it when Arshag Svagian came to our house. I would retreat into a corner. They covered the chemicals trays and sent me off to Grandmother, closing the door behind me. Then I knew they were looking at that one particular photograph again.

The Armenians raised on the high, sunburned plateaus within the triangle formed by Lake Van, Lake Sevan, and Lake Urmia had swarthy faces and, like other mountain folk, were small in stature. God placed his finger on a particular spot on the bodies of each people, and in that spot are gathered all that people's traits. In the same way, when she finishes sewing, a woman makes a knot in the thread so that the coat will not unravel. This is what I remember above all else when the old folk of my childhood pass before my mind's eye: the eyebrows. Whether arched or straight, they were always thick, often joined in the middle, and thus easy to knit into a frown. And what is more, they were black and therefore stubborn, full of life. If there were a world of nothing but eyebrows, the Armenians of my childhood would have reigned supreme. So, on an Armenian's face, God's mark is the place at the top of the nose where the eyebrows meet. From that spot the strongly outlined eyebrows spread to either side of the hooked, powerful nose. The eyes are piercing, and your gaze fixes on that point from which the face seems to spread and to gather at the same time.

Arshag Svagian did not look like the others. He was blond, and because his hair had turned gray, he looked even blonder. He had white skin, a straight nose, and blue eyes. And in addition, he was tall and still preserved an elegant gait that years of imprisonment had been unable to impede. He seemed aloof from everything around him, and this, along with his other qualities, lent him a special charm. Arshag Svagian had been a man of the world. He had spent his youth in Constantinople, and it was there that he had acquired the art of lively conversation that made him well liked around the cafés. He had come to Romania after the war of 1922, when the greater parts of the Greeks, Italians, and what was left of the Armenians after the massacres of 1915 were driven out of Constantinople. With the skills he had acquired on the banks of the Bosphorus, it was not at all difficult for Arshag to become acquainted with the upper crust of Ploiești: the American engineers from the refineries, the rich merchants, and the intellectuals who wore scarves and tight clothes, but also the city's underbelly, the swindlers, the horse dealers, the go-betweens, the pimps, and the knife fighters. Jumbled up among them were anarchists, outlaws, Communists, legionnaires, Germanophiles, and Russophiles. "In that way," reckoned Arshag, "whoever comes to power, I'll remain standing." He was wrong, naturally. No matter who might have come to power, they would still have thrown him in jail.

Arshag did a little bit of everything, but above all he was a watchmaker and photographer. He earned his living from watchmaking. When there were not enough watches to cover his expenses, which were minimal, beneath his counter he polished the diamonds stolen by one of the nondescript men who knocked on his window after nightfall. And if nobody knocked, he would arrange his photographs and look at them for a long while. He was an occasional photographer, and the occasions were among the least expected. They were provided mainly by the prosecutor's office, which called on him when it required a photographer but no press. Although Svagian loved to converse with café habitués and passing faces, the prosecutor did not have any worries on his account: the permit for Svagian's watch repair shop had been granted to him as a gesture of goodwill, although the law did not allow a stateless person with a Nansen passport to hold such a permit. As for the diamonds that passed through his hands, no matter how well he secreted them under the counter, their glimmer could still be seen through the window. That was why Arshag Svagian did not really have a choice; he performed that eerie, morbid task, a task completely out of keeping with his usual character.

"Smile!" he would say to the grooms, sweating in their black suits, and to the brides, suffocating in their tight corsets. He would wave to the people at the edges to move closer so that they would all fit in the photograph. He positioned them so that the light would shine on them from the front and so that there would be no trace of shadow on their faces. But lately and with increasing frequency Arshag Svagian was required to take photographs of faces that did not smile. Death is just another way of belonging to the light. It is a way of belonging to the light from which there is no turning back. The eyes are empty; the face is pale. A dead body is a well; no matter how much light you pour into it, it is never full. Arshag had two kinds of flashbulbs, ordinary ones, for photographing the living, and more powerful ones, to compensate for the pallor of the dead. That pallor was more obvious in those for whom death had come not from inside but from outside, rendered by a bullet, a knife, poison, a garrote. Sometimes, when the smell of death was fresh, a smell that was sweet rather than sour or bitter, Arshag's photographs revealed an inexplicable blotch of light above the forehead, which he reckoned to be the soul. For that reason, in order to be rid of the inner burden of the occupation he was forced to perform, he said to himself, "I, Arshag Svagian, am not a photographer of the dead but a photographer of souls."

The photographer arrived. This time, it was at the edge of a wood. Things seemed different than usual. The prosecutor, with a solemn air about him, had been accompanied by two soldiers when he picked him up from his house. In the past, he used to talk with Arshag on the way to the scene. They chatted; the words laved them like a balm, protecting them against the closeness of death. But this time, in the car, when Arshag tried to chat, the prosecutor had looked out of the window, pretending not to hear. Arshag had felt as if he were guilty, as if they were taking him to the scene of the crime that he might confess. The prosecutor walked on ahead. It was so dark that Arshag, recollecting the event, thought he would have tripped over the corpse if he had not come to a stop in time. In all there were three investigators from the prosecutor's office. They were standing with their hands behind their backs. They pointed out the angles from which he was to take photographs. The light erupted like a stone shattering a mirror. Jagged images flew from every side. Arshag had the feeling that he could see blood everywhere. Like on the face of the corpse, a trickle of blood ran down his temple, from the spot where two painful states coalesced: the slow darkness and the silence.

He did not look at the body attentively. He was content to do what the men told him to do. An abrupt, powerful glare lighting a lifeless body enveloped in darkness is indecent, like snatching the covering from a face. On the way back in the car, the cadaver had taken on life. The body found it difficult to get to its feet, it had to lean against a tree, it brushed the dried mud off its clothes, it picked the dry leaves out of its straggly beard. The dead man was tall and balding, with a slightly hunched back. It was not until he had wiped the blood from his face and looked into the camera lens once more that Arshag Svagian recognized him. The old man made a signal for him to take the photograph, lifting his right hand in that familiar way of his. Arshag wanted to say, "Smile!" but all of a sudden he felt embarrassed. The old man sensed it, stopped pretending, let his arms fall helplessly, and from the corner of his right eye ran a trickle of blood. Arshag took out his handkerchief and went to wipe it away, but the prosecutor's voice halted him: "Careful! Don't make any mistakes . . ." To help him, the old man went back inside his body, which lay like a tree trunk, face upward, with the trickle of blood congealed between eye and temple.

They had arrived in front of the workshop. Arshag suddenly came to his senses. The prosecutor followed him inside. Arshag opened the door to the darkroom and slammed it shut behind him, drawing the bolt. From the other side came knocking, surprised at first and then angry. Fists and boots hammered on the door. Arshag Svagian was panting, soaked in sweat, glued to the door. "Have you gone mad? Open this door right now!" He could not. First he needed to convince himself that the old man was really he. With slow movements, the old man continued to pick the leaves out of his blood-caked beard. He was still alive; he still possessed light. "I've opened up the camera," Arshag shouted at the men trying to batter the door off its hinges. "I can't open the door. It'll ruin the negative." He managed to unfasten the back of the camera, although his normally deft fingers were trembling. The battering ceased amid a flood of curses. It was not until much later that Arshag realized he had not lit the red bulb.

He groped, his fingers trembling, sweat pouring down his face. "I was afraid to turn on the light. Because it was red. I didn't want to see red before my eyes." "You're talking nonsense," said Grandfather, trying to reassure him. "Light is light; blood is blood." Nevertheless, when Arshag developed the photograph from the negative, the light and the blood merged before his eyes. He no longer had any doubt. The old man's eyes were closed once more, the head lolled to one side, and a trickle of blood ran from his eye to his temple. It was indeed Nicolae Iorga. Arshag stood there, gazing vacantly at the photograph. They had started knocking on the door again. He quickly made a copy. He hid it, still wet, under a pile of old photographs, and opened the door. The prosecutor snatched the photographs and the negatives from him.

Arshag Svagian did not want to take any more photographs after that. He shut up his studio and locked his equipment away in boxes, along with the old photographs. He kept just two, at which he looked every night. One he had taken the summer before, in Văleni. In it Nicolae Iorga, wearing a straw hat, is smiling alongside Siruni and a group of Armenians from Ploieşti who had come to visit him. Behind him can be glimpsed the heads of two children. I published the photograph in *Ararat* magazine, almost seventy years later, asking whether anybody had any information about the two children peeping from behind Nicolae Iorga's massive shoulder. The answer came all the way from Paris: Anoush Kirmizian, who was born in Ploieşti and emigrated to France after the war, where he went into the textiles business, recognized himself as one of the children; the other was Zadik Muradian, who also lived in Paris and had become a famous astronomer. They described to us the event that had taken place so many decades ago, remembering Arshag Svagian's camera and tripod and how the photographer had raised his hand.

Arshag Svagian, face to face first with Nicolae Iorga—huge, smiling, his eyes wide open, surrounded by people—and then moving on to the other Nicolae Iorga, just as huge but as still as a log and with congealed blood on his face. Arshag did not want to take any more photographs, nor did anybody ask him to. To photograph the dead during the war would have been the most pointless thing possible. Death spread over the earth, taking on countless faces, like the facets of a bee's eye. After the war, gazing vacantly at his photographs, Arshag Svagian, in whose drawers diamonds no longer glinted and whose warm voice, made hoarse by tobacco and alcohol, no longer rang out around the cafés, waited to find out what price he would be asked to pay. One night, different men in different uniforms arrived, but their boots kicked the door in the same way as before. Arshag Svagian did not open the door this time either, but unlike then, the men did not seem surprised. They put their shoulders to the door and broke it down. Arshag, who had done nothing more than to secrete his photographs in a crack between the floor and the wall, was not even surprised at the way in which they had entered. He sat patiently until they had finished searching through his boxes of old photographs, tearing down the curtains, riffling through every page of the books on the shelves, rolling up the carpet, and tapping the floorboards to see if they sounded hollow. Arshag strove to keep his eyes fixed on the window, lest he be tempted to look at the corner in which he had hidden the photographs, in the slender sheath between woodwork and plaster. The grounds for his guilt were simple: his name was undoubtedly on the lists of those who had collaborated with the pre-Communist prosecutors. He did not have to explain himself because nobody asked him to, not even later, when he was taken to the prison in Aiud and then to Poarta Albă on the Danube–Black Sea Canal. There, nobody wondered or asked what he was doing inside. The question was more likely how anybody still remained on the other side of the barbed wire.

When, many years later, the gates of the prison opened to release him, Arshag Svagian stood on the threshold, confused and alone. He took his first steps outside, looking behind him at the gray walls. The new world received him with neither friendliness nor hostility but rather with indifference. The same as in the cinema, when the show has begun and all the seats are taken and you fumble along the rows in vain since everybody is paying attention to what is happening on the big screen. Arshag Svagian, wandering through this world that had long since closed its doors behind him, trod fearfully. Between him and photography there were no longer walls to guard him. He dozed in chilly trains; countless times he took his release papers from his pocket to quell the nudges of the ticket inspectors; he gazed at the endless plain; he alighted unobserved in Ploieşti Station; he set out on his own trail, the trail of the man about town he had once been, a trail too narrow for the soles of the clod-hopping boots he now wore. On Station Road, the once fresh and beautiful houses were now gray. Only the chestnut trees, which human hands had been unable to harm, were unchanged. He wanted not to find his house and workshop, but it was there, waiting for him, with a rusty padlock that came undone no sooner had he touched it. The photographs were also waiting for him, hidden between the wall and floorboards. He trod over the shards of broken glass; he sat down on the heap of books thrown on the floor, whose pages were curling from the damp; he sat on the mattresses shredded and hollowed by mice, on the mounds of clothes. The old man with the blood-caked beard and the gentle eyes remained his only link to the world he had left behind. In fact no, there was another link: sixty miles away, another old man was traveling across snowy fields, dozing in other frozen trains, shivering as he walked down another Station Road, this time in Focşani, where likewise only the chestnut trees remained unchanged except by the passing seasons. The other old man, my grandfather Garabet Vosganian, from whom Arshag Svagian had learned the art of photography, was the only man on whose door he knocked.

My grandfather placed the photograph on the table and took a photograph of it. Then he enlarged the negative. "It needed more light," said Grandfather. "It was too dark," said Arshag Svagian in his own defense. "There was not so much as a moonbeam." "You ought to have been prepared." "I wasn't. I haven't succeeded even to this day." "Don't cry," said Grandfather. "I'm not crying," said Arshag Svagian, taking umbrage. "I've been like this since prison, from the wind."

In fact, enlarging the photograph, as if entering into its light, Arshag Svagian caused himself pain; he picked at the scab to prevent the wound from healing. "Why?" Grandfather asked. "After all, you took photographs of so many dead people, of every kind." "I don't know," said Arshag, shivering from a chill that never left him. "I think about it all the time. I think he reminds me of my father. He looked exactly like that when I found him among the dead, in Pera, when they burned down the Armenian quarter. I remember all our dead. When they're covered in blood, the dead look alike, don't they?"

Kept beneath his shirt, the photograph had yellowed, and the corners were curling. Arshag Svagian would look at it until, with weird slowness, the outlines again began to move. The old man stood up, and steadying himself against the tree trunks, he came toward him, picking the dead leaves from his beard. One morning, Arshag found some dead leaves among the heaps of things scattered around his room. Horrified, he slept only fitfully at night. But the dead leaves kept multiplying. In order to explain them somehow, Arshag Svagian started collecting leaves from the pavement, taking them home, spreading them on the floor. That was how they found him one morning, not anybody who had been looking for him in particular, but some wanderers like him who had come in through the unlocked door in search of a little warmth. He was sitting with his eyes wide open, looking at the photograph and through it, beyond it. On his chest and arms were scattered dry leaves, shed by the chestnut trees on Station Road or the birches in Strejnicu Forest, leaves that were yellowed, that, like the photograph, were reddened by all the bodily humors that can run down the temples in a slender trickle: sweat, blood, and fear.

Despite appearances, the Seferian family vault, where the parochial council met in secret, was not completely empty. On the morning of Easter Saturday, after we had all passed beneath a coffer festooned with flowers in the churchyard the night before, on the Easter of the dead—the coffer was supposed to represent the tomb of Jesus Christ—on that morning we went to the cemetery to commemorate our dead. Each family went to their burial plot and waited for the priest to come and say the prayer for their dead by the grave. They shared out *halva*, made from a fried mixture of walnuts and semolina and sprinkled with powdered cinnamon, and they poured a few drops of wine onto the earth around the cross, earth still not dry after the departure of winter. The people, who dwindled year after year, sobbed quietly. We children were unmoved by such things. Death was nothing but a wisp of smoke; it was the scent of fried walnuts and semolina, of ground cinnamon mingled with orange zest. We did not think of death in the interval between one religious holiday and the next. We ran along the cemetery paths, looking at the ceramic portraits on the crosses, as if at the photographs in an album, and we played with the chestnuts and walnuts we found that had nestled among the moldering leaves through the winter. We watched in puzzlement as the priest and Arshag the bell ringer recited the prayer in front of the empty Seferian vault. I still did not know why at the time, but I sensed that those who approached the vault did so with a certain amount of awkwardness. But even so, the men formed a semicircle behind the priest and listened in silence. Nobody shared out halva; nobody poured red wine on the moldering leaves or, if Easter fell early, on the snow. Nobody spoke, nobody wept, and at the end of the prayer they merely made the sign of the cross and went away. But in the long letters he wrote to his sister in Buenos Aires and that he let me fold inside the envelope, Grandfather always added the following words at the end, words that were always the same: "Tell Eduard and his parents that we were there this year too. God rest his soul."

After the priest left and the others dispersed, Arshag the bell ringer remained behind. He entered the vault, stayed there for a while, and then came out, peering all around.

I knew that nobody was buried in the vault. Old man Seferian had long since gone to Argentina with the rest of his family. Arshag was not nimble. When he walked, his legs were slow and splayed, and so were his arms, held close to his body. It was as if they were tied by the ropes of a bell. So when he closed the door of the vault behind him, I had time to glimpse one of the ropes that bound his limbs and slowed them down; that rope was a glimmer of light.

The light gave me courage. I went inside and looked. The air was cold and still. Clumped shadows flickered across the wall. I ought to have been afraid. But the face in the photograph, even if solemn, was gentle: a tall, erect man in a white uniform with epaulettes and all kinds of braids. The photograph was not very large, and from the not entirely crisp outlines it was obvious it had been chosen in haste, more for what it meant than what it showed.

In *The Book of Whispers*, photographs often take the place of living people. Because the twentieth century mowed down so many lives prematurely, people did not manage to match up the dead with the dead and the living with the living. In that century, death took mankind by surprise, more than any century before. When one of their number disappeared, standing in their dwindling circle, the Armenians put a photograph in his place so that the circle would not be broken. This is why, in their native lands, in the triangle among the three lakes (Van, Sevan, and Urmia), and wherever else they wandered, a photograph was a kind of harbinger of death for the Armenians.

For the Armenians of those days photographs were like a last will and testament or like a life insurance policy. If the person came back from the convoys of deportees, the orphanages, the voyages in the holds of ships, the photograph was once more put away for safekeeping, and the person resumed his place among the living. If he did not return, then the photograph brought the deceased back to the midst of his family when they opened the old, handsomely carved boxes on feast days. In that too hurried century, the photograph became the excuse of those who had departed without managing to say farewell.

The Armenians of my childhood lived among photographs more than they did among people.

Those photographs included the one in Focșani's Armenian cemetery, which, strangely enough, took the place of not only a living man, but also a dead man. Arshag the bell ringer displayed far more care toward that photograph than toward any other of the dead he commemorated. Whereas at any other grave, it was mainly the members of the family who gathered around the priest to say the prayer for the dead, around that nonexistent resting place gathered all the men who came to the cemetery on the Saturday after Good Friday.

In our box of photographs I found the same photograph, except smaller. I then realized that Grandfather had enlarged the photograph in the cemetery from this smaller one, in which the facial features were crisper. On the back was a legible signature: Onik Tokatlian. And beneath it: "En route to Odessa, April 10, 1944."

But in order to tell the story of the man whose photograph was placed in a funerary niche above which burned an unsleeping lamp tended by Arshag or whoever else, I must first tell the story of another man whom you will not find in any of the boxes of photographs kept by the old Armenians of my childhood: Mesia Khacherian.

Not even later was I able to find any photograph of Mesia Khacherian from the 1940s, although I searched stubbornly since he cannot be omitted from *The Book of Whispers*. It was because of him and others like him that this book lived before it came to be written. And above all, it was because of those like him that it was read in a whisper.

Rarely is a name more beautiful. In Armenian it means what it means in Romanian or any other Christian language for whoever is prepared to understand. In Armenian, *khach* means cross. It would therefore be appropriate to call Mesia Khacherian the Messiah of the Cross. This is a tragic irony, in fact, since Mesia leagued himself with the Antichrist when he was still a young man.

I recently found an earlier photograph of him. He is sitting at the corner of a table, next to baritone David Ohanesian and graphic artist Chik Damadian, looking sidelong at Martiros Sarian, the great painter who was then visiting Romania. Mesia is sly and watchful, his lips pressed tightly together. He is already old, you will say to yourself, since his hair is completely white.

"So what?" Grandfather Garabet would have said, shrugging disdainfully and uttering his name out of the corner of his mouth. "Because of the whiteness of his hair," others would have said, who avoided crossing his path, "you can't tell whether he is young or old. Mesia has had hair like that ever since we've known him. He turned white in prison, waiting to be executed. Death did not come for him in the end, but it fell in love with him and took its vengeance on others instead."

This story, about what linked Onik Tokatlian and Mesia Khacherian, about why a votive lamp was lit above the photograph of the one while every last trace of the other vanished from the photograph boxes of the old Armenians, is a story without which *The Book of Whispers* cannot be understood. The silent prayer of the men in the Armenian cemetery in Focşani; the letters to Argentina, with their laconic conclusion; Arshag's circumspection when he came out of the Seferian vault, dragging behind him a streak of light, like a bell rope—all these are incomprehensible without the splendid image of Onik Tokatlian, the captain of a seagoing vessel, a man bedecked with medals and braids, nor without the white hair of Mesia Khacherian.

Each of them chose his death in his own way, and death chose between them, loving each of them in its own way.

They met only once, on the cobbled lane that climbs from the Constanța Port Authorities to Ovid Square. Even if they had never seen each other before, they recognized each other immediately, Mesia Khacherian because he had been hunting Onik Tokatlian and had hated him for a very long time, and Onik Tokatlian because he had been avoiding Mesia Khacherian for a very long time. They walked up to each other, Onik bearing himself erect, Mesia clomping along on his lame leg. They exchanged only a few words and then walked away from each other without looking back. I shall record those words since, spoken in a whisper, they have their purpose in *The Book of Whispers*.

Onik Tokatlian was born in Brăila. His parents had come to Romania after the massacres of 1895, during the time of Sultan Abdul Hamid. He had a select but harsh education. He studied at the German Lyceum and at the Marine Officers School. Armenians are a people of the land. Since ancient times they have viewed the peoples of the sea with mistrust, and they have not ventured to confront the sea except to bridge two shores. With the exception of a short period in the Middle Ages, during the Kingdom of Cilicia, when they built wooden ships on which they crossed the Mediterranean, the Armenians have viewed the sea as a desperate path of last resort.

Onik Tokatlian was a man of the sea. He crossed the Mediterranean, following in the path of his Cilician ancestors. He delivered cargoes to Constanța and there took on cargoes for Constantinople, the Piraeus, Trieste, and Marseille. But when the sea once again became a path of last resort, Tokatlian abandoned merchant voyages and captained a ship taking military transports to the eastern front. The captain of the *Transylvania* took part in the operation known as the Sixty Thousand: the evacuation of Romanian soldiers encircled in the Crimea. He received numerous Romanian medals, as well as the Iron Cross, as a token of Germany's gratitude.

Mesia Khacherian, on the other hand, received no schooling. He was the child of poor Armenians who could afford to provide him with only two or three years of primary education in Constanța's Romanian and Armenian schools. He then became an apprentice cobbler. And that was what Mesia remained, no matter what other titles history puffed him up with: a cobbler. But in the lively, motley port of Constanța he had felt mocked by the merchants, the officers, the lawyers, the accountants and their big ledgers inscribed in red and blue ink, the teachers from the Mircea Old Lycée, and the café intellectuals. They had mocked him with their banknote-lined pockets, with the jingle of gold coins in their pouches, with their cigar smoke, and with those sweeping gestures they made when they raised their hats on their evening strolls along the seafront, as they acknowledged other wearers of frock coats and possessors of banknote-lined pockets. Yes, all of them mocked the frail cobbler every second of his life as he lugged his sack of freshly cobbled footwear to customers who did not even bother to look up and thank him.

Mesia did not imagine a better world. He imagined a vengeful world. This is why he joined the Communist Party. During the underground period, when the party was outlawed, he was one of its most industrious activists. When the Communists came to power, they made Mesia Khacherian head of secret police cadres in Constanța County. He was then able to slake his thirst for revenge against a world that had mocked him, albeit unwittingly, but whose punishment was therefore all the more richly deserved. Even more than the mockery that had stung him when he sat watching the promenade, hunched on the steps of Manisalian's house on the seafront, what hurt Mesia was the indifference of a world that set his worth at less than a crinkle that at least warranted the effort of smoothing. He avenged himself methodically on the uniforms and frock coats, he scattered the banknotes and the treasury bonds to the winds, he ripped up floorboards, he tore the tiles off stoves and walls, he rifled drawers and bookcases, he had laborers dig up yards and clear out woodsheds in search of gold pieces, he ransacked the biggest houses, throwing the owners into the street. The evictions, the arrests, the interrogations, the torture took place only at night, when fear, combined with confusion and darkness, turns to terror. And when they saw that man—that lame man with the white hair that otherwise would have lent him an air of piousness but which in the given circumstances became yet another cause of fear—when they saw Mesia, they knew that there was no escape. He looked at them in turn; he rejoiced in their horror, allowing them to kneel before him and not interrupting them, no matter how long, groveling, and (it goes without saying) useless their pleas might be. What he enjoyed more than anything else was the sweat of fear, which, like mother-of-pearl, had a gleam of its own since it shone no matter how dark it might be. Mesia watched the sweat collecting in beads on their brows, on their temples; he watched it trickle; he watched as the people, clutching their children to their breasts or hurriedly gathering up a few belongings, tried to wipe the sweat with the sleeves of their coats, not knowing from how deep it welled. Some even tried to look back at him, to feign indifference to their ransacked rooms, tangled bedclothes, torn-up floorboards. But the sweat welled up from the crevices of their minds, and sometimes Mesia felt like dipping his fingertip in it and tasting it. It would have tasted as sweet as honey to him, of that there can be no doubt. There was still time for that, however, since sweating people differ from one another, but sweat is always the same.

Manisalian's house, on whose steps Mesia once sat hunched, watching the parade of frock coats and flounced dresses along the seafront, had been demolished. In any event, he would no longer have had any use for those steps. Now, he himself strolled along the seafront, followed by two men in leather coats. Revenge pranced before him, like a flautist before a king. Some knew him by sight; others merely suspected him on seeing his limping gait and his white hair, which was like an undeserved halo. "It's Mesia," they would whisper, thereby adding fresh fear to *The Book of Whispers*, which is so full of fears. Mesia: the harbinger of a darkened world.

Unlike Mesia, Dinar Markarian had attended the lycée, taking night classes, and was the secretary of Constanța's Armenian school. He had a gentle face and a soft voice. Although he later became a general in the Securitate and for a time represented Communist Romania at the United Nations in Geneva, he maintained the same unusual gentleness toward the people around him. In *The Book of Whispers* you will find all kinds of characters. Some are nameless and faceless, anonymous collective characters, hobbling under the weight of their bundles or weapons, characters seemingly without beginning or end, exuding a resigned sadness precisely for this reason. The collective characters bore the seal of the twentieth century. Because of wars, dictatorships, deportations, and massacres, what was common to individual biographies outweighed the differences. There are also characters that stood out, people who gave more orders than they received and consequently experienced less suffering than they spread around them. But if we are to speak only of the Armenians in *The Book of Whispers*, then Dinar Markarian is unusual in at least two respects. First of all, after becoming an officer in the Securitate, he changed his name, to Ion Moraru—something that not many Armenians did—and second, he managed to live beyond his own century, into the new millennium, half blind and living in reclusion in a house at the edge of Bucharest, in the Pantelimon district, but still finding the strength, before he died, to revert to his Armenian name, which was carved on his tombstone.

But the time is now April 1943. Mesia Khacherian and Dinar Markarian have just been arrested by State Security. Behind the Armenian school, where Dinar works as a secretary, there is a German munitions warehouse. Dinar has studied the plans of the warehouse and calculated where best to plant a bomb so that the whole place will blow up. Mesia goes to Bucharest to get hold of some explosives. All that I have been able to find out, following in the footsteps of Mesia (who at the time still had black hair, sound legs, and a brisk gait) is that he met with a character called Dusha, who gave him a bag containing everything he needed in order to make a bomb. Later, they found out that everything went wrong because of Dusha, who was arrested in Bucharest. Dinar confessed and was sent to prison. In Mesia, hatred was stronger than pain. He endured torture without confessing. Because of the torture, his hair turned completely white and he was left lame for the rest of his life. Little did it matter to him because at the time, the rest of his life looked set to be short. Mesia Khacherian was found guilty of sabotage and sentenced to death, along with Ardash Torosian, Khachig Kazangian, and Garabet Daglarian, whom we will find a few years later among the repatriates on the deck of the *Rossiya*. But shortly before the executions were to take place, the Romanian Army changed sides, turning against its former German allies on August 23, 1944, and the Red Army became a liberator, at least for Mesia Khacherian. Mesia went back into the world with that new and easily recognizable appearance of his. Now he was inexorable, inescapable. He took part in creating the Communist secret police in Dobrudja, recruiting men like himself, men who would hate and nourish themselves on the fear they spread around them.

In the same period, Onik Tokatlian unpinned the Iron Cross he wore on his chest, which he had received shortly before the Russians entered the country, and put it in a drawer, alongside the Crown of Romania and Military Valor medals he had been awarded on the eastern front, to which he had transported arms and from whence, in the spring of 1944, he had evacuated throngs of Romanian, Slovak, and German soldiers and officers, as well as war materials, rescuing them from encirclement by the Red Army. After the war, Onik Tokatlian had returned to the merchant fleet, plying the Mediterranean route between Constanța and Marseille. But the same as for many others, the war had not ended for him, and he continued to save people from encirclement. The war among nations and armies was indeed over. But it had been too short, given the many reasons that had caused it to break out. Now that the nations no longer warred among themselves and were catching their breath, people within the same nation started to war among themselves. Now it was words rather than shells that killed. Cold and ruthless, a new war settled over Europe in which the biggest killer was the word.

The world of the merchants and traders was left devastated. Goods became harder and harder to find. The stock exchanges hobbled. Gold coins began to vanish, hidden in the soil, in the plasterwork, under floorboards, secreted at night and under oath. Banknotes became larger and larger and more colorful but also increasingly worthless. In Constanța, Mesia Khacherian's men were a constant menace. They could be recognized by their leather coats, by the bulges of the holsters on their right hips, and by their shadows, which were longer than other people's. With the port more and more deserted; with the cranes motionless as they waited for ships that never came; with goods requisitioned; with shop windows gray, as if with the ashes of another war, a war waged according to different rules, the town's stores glimmered more and more faintly until their stocks dwindled away to nothing. Within the space of a few years, the stores closed, they were struck from the official records, and in their place appeared a different kind of store, depressing, impoverished stores without names or else plainly called "Bread," "Tobacco," "Food," "Textiles," or, so as not to create any obligation on the part of the seller or any hope on the part of the buyer, simply "Store." What a difference between those names and the lively, exuberant, pompous, exotic names of the stores they replaced, stores with colorful windows and gleaming pavements outside, often covered with thick carpets imported from Karabakh or Bukhara. The shop signs were like a Noah's Ark: Zadig Tatzikian's "The Turkey"; Agop Kazazian's "The Tiger"; Puzant Sahabian's "The Elephant," with its sign that was as big as an entire shop front; Krikor Siropian's "The Golden Lion"; Hovhannes Daglarian's "The Ant"; Maria Grigorian's "The Parrot"; Krikor Selian's "The Dove"; Levon Horasangian's "The Stork"; Pilibbos Kevorkian's "The Camel"; Manuk Ovanesian's "The Cockerel"; Agop Apkarian's "The Deer"; Maria Levonian's "The Eagle"; and Onik Kazazian's "The Bison." The shop signs of the Armenian traders were an endless journey along the roads of the Orient. At Yervant Krikor's "India" you were invited to sample colonial goods, and Mikael Arikian's "Egypt" likewise enticed you with wares from the colonies. Krikor Diarbekirian called to your mind "The Bosphorus"; Aram Mariginian, "The Caucasus." Then there were Nshan Ovanesian's "Arabia," Nubar Papazian's "Bukhara," and Dikran Balian's "Ceylon." The journey followed not only the roads of the Orient, but also its night sky: Mardiros Zakarian's "The Moon"; Nazaret Aramian's "Venus"; and, farthest of all, Mihran Dobagian's "The Planet Jupiter." Other shop signs were boastful, with enveloping aromas and slippery smiles: Hapet Kasparian's "Ideal," Sarkis Boghosian's "Swiss Clocks," Suren Abramian's "Élite Coiffure," Armenak Silvian's "Chic Cavalier," Victor Kardashian's "Golden Horseshoe," Haygazun Pilibbosian's "Modern Lamp," Yesayi Yeramian's "Bon Marché," and Arshag Mardiros's "Everything Cheap." And then there were "American Watches," "Competitive Bazaar," "International Hairdressing," "Special Clocks," "The Special Crown," "The Royal Crown," "The Romanian Railways Chronometer," "Special Bread," "Deep Shade," "Modern Chic," Mrs. Araxi's "Miss Romania," "The Triumph Bakery," "The Million," and "Original"—shop sign after shop sign along Stephen the Great Boulevard, King Carol Boulevard, Ovid Square, and the city's straight, sunbaked streets, bleached by the salt winds, shop signs like variegated, raucous birds. And in that Noah's Ark, the last to remain was the rainbow itself, a sign that the waters had receded and that gray but rainless clouds were gathering again. The final shop to close, in 1948, was Agop and Garabet Kumbetlian's shoe and dye shop, "The Rainbow." For stubbornly trying to keep the store alive and raising its shutters morning after morning, Agop was sent to the labor camp at Poarta Albă.

All these traders had a small store, a factory, or a workshop with a few apprentices. The house where they lived was often behind their store. They invested their money in goods, and the decision to close down could not be brought into effect overnight but only after they had gradually reduced their stocks.

However, there were traders who had managed to put money aside, converting it into gold and jewels. These were the first to leave. Of the others, some ventured to leave only fifteen years later, going to America via Lebanon, in an operation involving the whole of the Armenian diaspora. But in 1945, the times were uncertain, the same as buildings, the same as people. You did not know whom you could trust. Those who wished to leave did not tell anybody. They even left pointless but reassuring word that they would meet their friends for coffee or sherbet the next day; they lent money; they ordered goods and paid in advance so that nobody would suspect they were planning to leave. Then they stuffed their jewels into little pouches, which they then secreted at the bottoms of chests, and at the crack of dawn they drove to Constanța from Galați, from Brăila, from Sulina, from Bucharest. Trying to blend in among the hubbub of Constanța during the day, at night they went down to the port, where one of Onik Tokatlian's trusted men was waiting to hide them in the dark, damp belly of a ship, behind the bales of merchandise. In Marseille, blessing Onik Tokatlian and trying in vain to persuade him to accept some jewel in a token of thanks, they would seek shelter among the port's large colony of Armenians, or else they would board a ship for a more distant and therefore safer destination. This is how the wealthy families of Armenian merchants—the Israelians, the Varteresians, the Diarbekirians, the Seferians—traveled, among sacks of rice, bales of cloth, crates of olives, and bins of wheat, arriving in Buenos Aires. And so the Seferian family vault remained empty, lit only by the lamp that burned beside the photograph of seagoing captain Onik Tokatlian.

The time is still the beginning of January 1946. Onik Tokatlian has, the same as always, supervised the unloading of his vessel; he has handed out money to his crew; and having made sure everything is shipshape, he goes into the port, up the cobbled lane that runs between the Port Authorities and Ovid Square. There were more trees along the lane in those days. Onik recognized him even before he emerged from behind a tree in the darkness. He recognized him by the sound of his uneven gait. There was a frost, but Mesia Khacherian did not wear a fur hat, and his white hair shone.

Since nobody overheard what they said, we can recount it without fear of error, especially given that the gist of their conversation can be divined from its outcome.

Mesia said, "I know everything, Onik Tokatlian."

The captain asked him nothing; he neither denied nor admitted it. Quite simply, it had to happen.

Mesia continued, with a voice as dry as a snapping twig: "On your next voyage, disembark in Marseille and vanish. It's all I can do for you. If you return, I'll arrest you for high treason."

Then they moved toward each other. It would have been just a monologue had not Onik Tokatlian said, as they drew alongside each other, "God forgive you, Mesia," and had not Mesia replied, "God forgive you, Onik."

In that new world, where the new things were the most dangerous, the words of Communist cobbler Mesia Khacherian had become the norm, rather than anything Onik Tokatlian, hero of the war against Bolshevism, might have said. Without a doubt, Onik, decorated with the Iron Cross, rescuer of the Romanian troops that had fought in the east, would have been arrested in the end, as were many other officers of the Romanian Army who were incapable of showing the same respect for overalls as for uniforms, for desertion as for heroism, for Red Army tanks as for returning prisoners of war.

Likewise, we would not be mistaken if we imagined that that short conversation was in Armenian. Mesia loved his mother. She had been a woman who suffered greatly, and, like all the other women who on Sundays gathered at the Armenian school by the seashore (which was converted into a church after the fire of 1942), she was convinced that nothing, not even her own suffering, could exist without God. Mesia might have uttered the word "God" in memory of his mother or because often the words learned from your parents come not from understanding, but from habit.

They walked away from each other in silence, Mesia Khacherian on his way to one of his nocturnal raids, Onik Tokatlian on his way to the station, to take the Bucharest train home. As ever, Mesia Khacherian inspected his men. They were men who knew how to search, who could pick up the scent of gold and find gold coins where you would least expect them. Mesia himself never searched; he merely watched.

Onik Tokatlian, on the other hand, never met anybody ever again since nobody can remember having seen him. He went home, to the solitude of his seagoing captain's room. He took from his trunk his white dress uniform with the gold braids, the same uniform he wears in the photograph in the Seferian vault. He shaved. Probably by then he was no longer in control of himself since later they noticed he had nicked himself under the ear with his razor. He carefully put on his uniform, socks, belt. He pinned all his medals to his chest, probably even his German Iron Cross, although it was not found afterward. Probably one of the people who broke into the room a few days later, no doubt one of his friends, unfastened the medal and disposed of it, reckoning, stupidly but wholly understandably in such times, that Onik Tokatlian still needed to be protected and that the new inquisitors might do him some harm, even in the condition they found him in.

What is strange is the fact that Onik Tokatlian felt the need in those moments to look in the mirror. He refused to be blindfolded, as it were; he looked death in the face. And so, wearing his dress uniform, Onik Tokatlian looked at himself in the mirror, bade himself farewell, and put a bullet in his temple.

The Armenian cemetery was full of people: the relatives of those who had managed to leave, crammed into the bellies of ships and protected by Captain Tokatlian; those who would have liked to leave but were unable; and many others. Among them were strangers with keen-eyed faces who had not come to mourn and did not even bother to pretend. But even so, the other people, knowing full well they were being watched, wept. In the face of all the multifarious constraints of the times, tears refused to obey.

4.

The year 1958 began on a Wednesday, and on the same day the European Common Market was born. And, as is always the case except in leap years, 1958 ended on the same day of the week, the Wednesday when Fulgencio Batista fled Cuba, driven out by Fidel Castro's revolutionaries. Exchanging one dictator for another, the year 1958 bowed out defeated and helpless, leaving it up to future times to untangle good from evil.

The Earth revolved around the Sun with the same accuracy as ever but also cautiously, on tiptoes, as it were, preserving the things on its surface and mollifying the things beneath; 1958 was not a year of natural catastrophes. Even when the Earth could not restrain a twitch, it quaked in faraway places, such as Alaska, where it deemed its twitches would be more easily borne, even if they did clock up an eight on the Richter scale. While the Earth proved temperate and cautious, the same cannot be said of its inhabitants. They could not have been more restless, bellicose even. The old wars had still not ended by 1958, and new wars were breaking out.

In France, war hero Charles de Gaulle had come to power once more, this time as president of the Fifth Republic, having previously won parliamentary elections and served as prime minister. Whereas in France a man can only be prime minister and head of state consecutively, in the Soviet Union there was no need for such niceties. Nikita Khrushchev, first secretary of the Communist Party of the Soviet Union, sacked Nikolai Bulganin and took over his job as prime minister, although not even this could persuade him to get his teeth fixed; unabashed, between making threats of nuclear destruction, he showed off his gap-toothed grin. Not to be outdone but more attentive to his appearance and in particular his collar buttons, Mao Zedong unleashed the Great Leap Forward, pulverizing tens of thousands of Chinese villages, where villagers now poured molten steel from buckets and worked on the shells of tanks using screwdrivers. They were cast into slavery, as in the times of the Great Wall, the difference for the worse being that ideologies had sprung up in the meantime so that the squandered labor of the Chinese people merely transformed the Great Leap Forward into a great leap backward to the time of the famine and civil war. The Middle East continued to broil. Egypt, Syria, and later Yemen formed the United Arab Republic, deposing Gamal Abdel Nasser.

Israel armed. But Europe was busy at home. The Cold War had entered a new and dramatic phase, and the conflict over West Berlin was in danger of plunging the continent into war. To prove that they were not joking—although the nations of Eastern Europe in particular were by then very clear as to just how serious they were—the Soviets decided to execute the leader of the 1956 Hungarian Revolution, Imre Nagy, with the willing cooperation of the Romanian authorities holding him captive.

When they no longer have internal enemies, nations begin to fight among themselves. China and Taiwan continued their civil war. Lebanon embarked on its own war. Triumphant in Europe and sharing in the glory of Konrad Adenauer's Germany, France lost territory after territory in Africa: Chad, the Sudan, Congo Brazzaville, the Gabon, and the Central African Republic. Algeria continued to break away and remained French only in the writings of Albert Camus. Fidel Castro laid siege to Havana. Faisal became prime minister of Saudi Arabia, a belated echo of British policy from the time of Lawrence of Arabia. Another Faisal, the young king of Iraq, was assassinated. Following the example of the United Arab Republic, Iraq and Jordan merged but then diverged more quickly even than the new state ruled by Nasser.

The Cold War on Earth set the sky in turmoil. The USSR continued its Sputnik program, while the USA launched its Explorer series of satellites and established NASA. Rent to its bowels by the commotion of the satellites, the vengeful sky lashed out at random. Two-thirds of the players of the Manchester United soccer team were killed in an air crash. The airplane came down over Munich, on its way back from Belgrade, where the team had qualified in the semifinal of the European Champions Cup, after a draw with Red Star. Eight players, including the captain, Roger Byrne, met their end. Legendary trainer Matt Busby survived, as did one of my childhood heroes, striker Bobby Charlton, who went on to be the hero of the 1966 World Cup.

As always when He senses that people are losing their religion, the Good Lord decided to call His Pope to His bosom, in this case Pope Pius XII, after a pontifical reign of almost two decades. During that reign he had run the Vatican skillfully, according to some, but with inadmissible concessions, according to others, as is always the case when a pastor is forced to lead his flock through wars cold and hot. The Pope himself, having doubts as to the meaning of his existence, issued the encyclical *Meminisse Juvat* before his death, in which he urged a return to Christian values so that the world might finally be redeemed. A year later, his successor, John XXIII, listed those values in his first encyclical, *Ad Petri Cathedram*: truth, unity, and peace. If we think of the years that ensued, such principles were to be found only in the splendid libraries of the

Vatican and in the pages of the pontifical biographies. The revolutions and wars continued apace, providing inexhaustible material for future encyclicals, and the intervals of peace were punctuated by terrorist attacks.

If the wounds of war had healed to the rhythm of jazz and their ache had been soothed by the rhythm of the blues, the cold and hot wars of 1958 were waged to the rhythm of the cha-cha: the war between Eastern and Western Europe, each tugging West Berlin like two looters of the dead squabbling over a rag on an abandoned battlefield; the war between a China taking great leaps forward and a still hobbling Taiwan; the war between France and north African rebels; the war between the CIA and General Sukarno's Indonesian rebels; the civil wars in Lebanon and Iraq; the wars between satellites up in the sky; the revolutions that replaced old, exhausted dictators with fresh new ones. Three quick steps, cha, cha, and another cha, then another step back, as if things had pranced forward too quickly. The other half of the world, the half not embroiled in war, witnessed African children with bellies distended and arms withered by famine; it sensed the chill of the black clouds released from the bowels of the earth, rising above the Bikini Atoll and Christmas Island atomic bomb test sites; the other half of the world still lay dreaming.

Dmitri Shostakovich was in Paris, the soloist and composer of two concertos for piano. On the same side of the wall, Truman Capote and Jack Kerouac wrote of sleepless suffering and being lost. On the other side of the wall, Boris Pasternak was writing *Doctor Zhivago*, a kind of *Gulag Archipelago* of people still at liberty, in which the pangs of love combined with all the pains of the Gulag. The Soviet authorities forced Boris Pasternak to refuse the Nobel Prize, but even so, down at the bottom of the wall, he remained the great victor of 1958. At the top of the wall, on the battlements, unable to find a place for himself on either the western or the eastern side, Albert Camus stood smoking cigarette after cigarette.

Three years previously, Vladimir Nabokov had written *Lolita*, and in 1958 a tragic Lolita by the name of Marilyn Van Debur won the title of Miss America. Many years later, she was to reveal how her father had raped her throughout her childhood, and she was to fight for the silent victims of incestuous abuse.

Dissatisfied with kings produced by dynasties, ensconced in palaces, and concocted by triumphant yet ruinous revolutions, the people created their own kings, the kings of easily accessible pastimes, whose venues were the more welcoming spaces of sports stadiums and concert halls. The new kings were young, and their reign was to be endless. One of them, Elvis Presley, became the King of Rock and Roll. Whereas the cha-cha, the salon dance of 1958, came from Latin America, born from the mambo and giving birth to salsa, rock 'n' roll came from nowhere; for centuries it had stayed in the same place, the outskirts of Memphis, blending the rhythm of Robert Johnson and John Lee Hooker's blues with the gospel sung in Negro churches. In 1958, Elvis was conscripted and sent to Germany, an opportunity for his female admirers to miss him and for the makers of legends to plant him more solidly on the foundations of his absence.

The other king of 1958, begotten, not made, was Pelé, the King of Soccer. That year Brazil became world champion, with a team that included Gilmar, the two Santos, Garrincha (who had one leg shorter than the other), Zagalo, and the others, whose names were like the pattering of raindrops: Didi, Vava, Zito, and Pelé. Behold the young eighteen-year-old, crying for joy after scoring three goals against Kopa and Fontaine's French team in the semifinal and two goals against host country Sweden in the final; behold him weeping as only kings crowned with laurel wreaths know how and as kings crowned with precious jewels will never know how.

The year 1958 was one of confusion and lucidity. As for the first mood, the year 1958 described itself in Alfred Hitchcock's *Vertigo*, starring James Stewart and Kim Novak. The mood of lucidity was described by the discovery of the laser beam. Confusion and precision, like a rifle with a telescopic sight moving slowly across a crowd before firing at random. The mixed inventions of the year 1958 heralded the genocide of the second half of the century—namely, RANDOM KILLING—aimed at the silent and bewildered masses of those slain or threatened unawares. A combination in which only the first can be victorious: one provides the aim, the other the blood.

And those who conjoined the aim and the blood gradually withdrew into the deserts and the mountains. In 1958 Romania was the only country where the anti-Communist resistance still held out. It held out until 1962, when the Securitate killed the last hero of the resistance in the mountains of the Banat, a peasant by the name of Ion Banda.

In 1958, Petru Groza died. A splendid funeral was held for him. Ion Gheorghe Maurer succeeded him as chairman of the Grand Presidium of the National Assembly. As for foreign affairs, Romania signed all kinds of treaties, while repression redoubled internally, to show the Russians that the government was on top of the situation and that the Red Army could leave Romanian soil without having to fret. The most convenient form of repression was that directed against intellectuals. The students arrested and interrogated against the backdrop of the uprising in neighboring Hungary were expelled from their universities. Constantin Noica, Arshavir Acterian, and other writers and philosophers were imprisoned. So too were the founders of the Burning Bush theological discussion group; Father Daniel Tudor died shortly after being sent to prison, and poet Vasile Voiculescu died just a few months after his release. Arsene Papacioc, the great monastic spiritual teacher, was imprisoned, and so too was theologian Dumitru Stăniloae. "You wanted to set fire to communism with your burning Bush!" yelled the prosecutor. Nevertheless, the fire was still smoldering thirty years later.

The old executioners of bodies and minds were deposed: party ideologues Iosif Chișinevschi and Mihail Roller (who, inexplicably for such a man, committed suicide. Which is to say, it was not just another staged suicide; he genuinely did commit suicide). Before long, the new executioners redoubled the oppression, extending it to the wealthier peasants and small traders. A tortured drive to industrialize the country commenced. The same as in China, the more the economy grew, the deeper the poverty became. "What are we to do?" Gheorghe Gheorghiu-Dej asked Nikita Khrushchev. With the same gap-toothed grin that he gave when he bashed his shoe on the podium of the United Nations, Khrushchev imparted some wise advice in the Soviet mold: "Sell your Yids!" Which is what happened. They set a price per Jew to be sold to Israel. It was not until later that Ceaușescu adapted the prices to market demand, even if differential prices were out of keeping with the values of a dictatorship of the proletariat; in other words, an exit visa for an intellectual cost more dollars than one for a laborer. Since there were a lot of Jewish intellectuals, the Communists did a roaring trade.

Life went on. After Securitate rifles cleared the forests of Hațeg of every last trace of the anti-Communist resistance, aurochs returned to the mountains after more than two centuries. The first pair was brought from Poland, and in their honor a special stamp was issued. Television came to Romania and a handful of new films: *Two Neighbors*, with Geo Saizescu, and *Hello? Wrong Number*, comedies starring handsome young actors: Iurie Darie, Ștefan Tapalagă, Rodica Tapalagă, Stella Popescu. Three years after the great composer's death, the first George Enescu Festival was held. The new nomenclature applauded Yehudi Menuhin and David Oistrakh in Bach's double concerto for violin, conducted by George Georgescu, whose past philo-German sentiments were overlooked for the sake of the occasion. David Ohanesian was given a standing ovation in the first Romanian production of Enescu's opera *Œdipe*, conducted by Constantin Silvestri. Iolanda Balaș won her first European high-jump medal, and Petrol Ploiești, captained by Pahonțu, won the national soccer championship.

In our yard in Focșani, beneath the apricot tree, the old folk meet in the afternoons for coffee and stories of sunsets on the banks of the Bosphorus and the taste of the grapes of childhood. The young folk have exceeded the annual plan and look set to exceed the five-year plan. They adopt a haughty gait, in the style of jazz drummer Sergiu Malagamba, and on Saturdays go for outings on the factory bus. Carol Spiegel is released from prison and returns to our street, but three months later he is arrested again. When he leaves prison for good in 1964, he does so only out of a stubborn insistence on dying elsewhere than under the indifferent eyes of his jailers.

Temelie the carpenter and Mitică the mad woodcutter, each with his own style of dress, each with his own walk, go to the Heroes Statue on May 10. They are the only ones who still honor the heroes on Dynasty Day since the speakers hanging from the walls of buildings buzz Russian-sounding patriotic songs the day before, on May 9, the anniversary of the Soviet victory against Nazi Germany, a holiday that obliges the war dead to march in line behind Russian tanks and stamps Red Stars on their livid brows.

A sad year that, overcome with remorse and trying to sweeten the times to come, gave birth to Madonna, Sharon Stone, and the blonde-haired Barbie doll.

As for myself, my mother remembers that in the moment when I was born, she heard a funeral procession passing beneath the window to the sound of a brass band. It was around noon. The nurses rushed to look out of the window, and Mother cried out in an exhausted, frightened voice, "The baby's falling!" I did not fall. Instead, I released an arching jet of wee-wee, marking the beginning of my relations with the world in the most natural way possible. This was how my mother found out I was a boy without having to ask anybody. I have never found out who died to make way for me in this world and was being carried on his last journey to the accompaniment of cracked brass instruments and under the curious rather than grieving eyes of the nurses.

Also in the moment of my birth, Gheorghiu-Dej was holding a reception to mark the departure from Romania of the last detachment of Soviet troops. I encountered death and history from my very first moment, and my birth was thus held in a balance. With my birth, the number of all those who had ever lived exceeded the number of the dead in all the ages up to then.

The old Armenians of my childhood experienced three kinds of events: events they avoided, events they waited for, and events that took them completely by surprise. Properly speaking, all the events they experienced may ultimately be ascribed to the third category since the things they avoided ended up happening anyway and the things they waited for never came to pass. Viewed like this, the lives of my grandparents are a chronicle of the unexpected.

Thus, to speak of the unexpected is also a way of writing *The Book of Whis-*

pers. To list the things they wished to avoid would mean writing *The Book of Whispers* inside out. And as for the things they waited for, the old folk of my childhood, even in the times when they were not so old, were divided into two camps: those who waited for the Russians to come and those who waited for the Americans to come. Ultimately, both camps merged to form a single camp because after the Russians really did come, the Red Army soldiers abandoned themselves to drunkenness, stealing wristwatches, and dragging young girls off to patches of waste ground; they put illiterate laborers and vegetable market porters in charge of the country. So those who had been waiting for the Russians to come meekly moved to the other camp and waited for the Americans to come instead. The pro-Russian camp was in fact made up of a single man: Dikran Bedrosian. Meekly, but still under suspicion, given the argument that Bolshevism is an illness that sometimes goes into remission but of which you are never cured, Dikran Bedrosian was received into the parochial council and the pro-American camp and even attended the secret meetings held in the Seferian vault.

All the others were in the other camp. Some of them had waited for the Americans previously too, and still they had not been cured of their waiting. They waited not only for the Americans, but also for the French and the British. They remembered how their parents, in the time of the "red sultan," Abdul Hamid, terrified by accounts of the massacres of 1895, waited for American ships to pour into the straits and save them. From their parents they also knew that a British ship had saved Armen Garo and the members of the Armenian Revolutionary Federation who had occupied the Imperial Ottoman Bank Headquarters in 1896. Among those still alive since that time there were even some who, like my grandfather Setrak, then a lad of fifteen, on hearing that French ships had come to save the fighters on Mount Musa, had wandered south to the shores of the Mediterranean, sleeping huddled like wild beasts by day and wandering by night, at the edges of forests, skirting the villages, avoiding the roads, dressed in Turkish garb. But no more British and French ships came. And after the battle of the straits, at Gallipoli, won in 1916 by the captain from Thessaloniki, Kemal Pasha, later known as Atatürk, nor did the Americans show themselves again. What is more, as Anton Merzian the cobbler from Union Street pointed out, the Americans had also abandoned the small Armenian Republic, rejecting the protectorate suggested by the Treaty of Sèvres. "They won't abandon us," said my godfather Sahag Sheitanian, who stubbornly repeated those words even after Arshag the bell ringer relayed the BBC news bulletin from the Yalta Conference, with his ear pressed to the wooden casing of the radio in the Seferian vault. Meanwhile, the Russians had entered Focşani. Armenian

intellectuals had been arrested in Bucharest and Constanța and sent to the Lubyanka, to be sorted like vegetables and then deported to Siberia. In Bucharest,
the Armenian Front had been founded, and as its first order of business, it began
to wage war against the books in the Ovsep and Victoria Dudian Armenian
Library and the photographs on the walls, piling into cardboard boxes the ones
they reckoned to be dangerous to the new times and then burning them in the
courtyard of the Armenian cathedral. In the parochial offices of the Armenian
church in Focșani, they removed first Roosevelt's and then Churchill's photographs. Finally, with bitterness, they also removed the portrait of the king, whose
abdication statement they had heard over the radio, unable to believe their ears.
Sahag Sheitanian adamantly refused to hide the photograph of General Andranik, who fought against both Ottoman and Bolshevik occupation, or that of his
comrade-in-arms Kevork Chavush, arguing, and rightly so, that since the photographs showed them in uniform, with bandoliers and lambskin caps, they could
be presented to any visitor to the parochial office as Suren Spandarian, Lenin's
collaborator, and Stepan Shahumian, the fighter from Baku, both of whom had
died too soon for their photographs to be included in the panoply of Bolshevik
leaders. As the books on the shelves thinned out and the photographs vanished
from the walls, hopes too dwindled. One hope alone remained, to which fewer
and fewer people gave voice more and more seldom, and even then in the form
of an opinion rather than as a sign of lucidity. The story of this hope may be said
to be one of the most silent in *The Book of Whispers*.

THE ARMS OF GENERAL DRO. I have already told the story of the meeting in
the Seferian vault, the final meeting, convened after the assassination of President Kennedy. None of the old folk of my childhood, hemmed in by all kinds
of imaginary threats, knew how to answer the question, "What is to be done?"
Nevertheless, my uncle Sahag Sheitanian did answer it, in a soft voice, as if
fearful he might be overheard: "Let's look for the arms of General Dro." All the
others abruptly fell silent, and Father Varjabedian made the sign of the cross,
not because he was trying to banish some evil thought, but because the arms
of General Dro were the last thing you would search for; it was a desperate
and heroic gesture, of which some of them would have been incapable even in
1945, let alone in 1963, not so much because of how greatly they had aged in the
meantime, but because of the events that had overtaken them.

Grandfather Garabet never told me the story of General Dro's arms. He told
me many stories: about Thaddeus and Bartholomew, the apostles who brought
Christianity to the Armenians; about St. Gayane and St. Hripsime the martyrs; about King Drtad and the visions of St. Gregory the Illuminator; about
Vardan Mamikonian and David Beg; about Kevork Chavush and General An-

dranik—true stories or ones that had become true in the telling. But nobody knew whether the story of the arms of General Dro was true or not. Those who might have known had either died or fled. Any who did know the truth would not have told it to others, knowing that they would only trouble minds and deepen despair. One of those who stubbornly believed in the reality or rather the illusion of the story was Sahag Sheitanian, and he told me it shortly before he died. In fact, he told it in snatches. *The Book of Whispers* is a story that nobody can tell in its entirety, as if each teller feared to understand the whole, thereby trying to save his life from meaninglessness.

The beginning of the story is a photograph. The end of the story is a short sentence that Sahag Sheitanian whispered to me shortly before he died, as much of the story as he deemed necessary to tell me: "The arms of General Dro are hidden in a forest." Such stories, consisting of a single sentence, like the story of the arms of General Dro, reveal that in fact they are short precisely because they are endless. Such stories will exist for as long as people stubbornly believe that behind what happens to them, above their heads, something else might take place, something that, in the depths of despair, might be achieved. They do not know what exactly, they do not know how, but it is in this vagueness that the invincibility of their final hope resides.

The photograph at the beginning of the story shows General Dro astride a white horse in a clearing with a stand of young trees in the background. General Dro is wearing his campaign uniform, with an officer's bandolier and belt, from which hang all the necessary instruments of war. He wears a white sheepskin cap, pulled down over his ears, almost as far as his thick, slanting eyebrows. He has a black chin beard, which, after it began to show white hairs, he later shaved. His proud gaze and studied, straight-backed pose, with one hand resting on his leg, show that it is a photograph taken for others rather than for himself. It is a photograph of the victor of Sardarabad. His 1918 victory over Turkish troops allowed the ephemeral existence of the small Armenian Republic. Drastamat Kanayan, or General Dro, his *nom de guerre*, became the republic's minister of defense and made strenuous efforts to preserve its fragile independence, unable to decide between aggressive pan-Turkishness and Russian Bolshevism when it came to which side to fight and which side to make concessions to. In the end, it was history that decided. The Armenians made concessions to both the one and the other, and Turkey and Russia carved up Armenian lands between them. As for General Dro, during his tumultuous life, he decided to fight both the one and the other. Arrested by the Russians and kept under surveillance for three years, the general was allowed to go to Romania in 1924, where he remained until 1944.

The second photograph tells of a General Dro who is now corpulent and white-haired but who has the same black, arched eyebrows and the same dark glower. Grandfather sought the most advantageous angle. In the background can be seen the apartment blocks on Strada Armenească and a willow that still stands today. To the left can be glimpsed the top of a fir tree. The photograph was taken in the yard of the Armenian cathedral in Bucharest, at the unveiling of the bust of General Andranik. The statue is garlanded by flowers, from which hang ribbons. The steps of the plinth are covered with the multicolored carpets of which the Armenians know no lack and with other wreaths and ribbons. A man of the narrow mountain trails and a life simple and harsh, General Andranik would surely not have approved. With his grave mien, a chest full of medals, and the unhappy air typical of armless busts, General Andranik looks up at the other general, alongside whom he had fought. General Dro is wearing a Sunday suit, hat in hand, beard neatly trimmed; he has a rather bourgeois air about him. The other guest of honor at the unveiling is barely visible in the background. It is Grigore Trancu-Iași, a scion of one of Moldavia's great Armenian families, formerly a minister in the Averescu government, formerly president of the Union of Armenians, and author of Romania's first code of labor legislation. Trancu-Iași will have spoken first, in Romanian. General Dro spoke next, in Armenian, urging the crowd to take up the fight. Barely having managed to cobble together businesses and start families in Romania or, if they were lucky, to reunite families scattered by massacres and exoduses, those in the crowd were ready to admire the general's eloquence and enthusiasm but seemed reluctant to follow him. As was his wont, Grandfather has written the date on the back in ink pencil: April 13, 1936.

The name "General Dro" was very rarely mentioned in Romania after the war. Those who knew him well had either fled the country or were arrested and, at best, deported to Siberia. Those who did not know him well, although they had heard of him, preferred to keep their silence, lest they fall under suspicion. Regarding Dro's exploits during the Second World War, the silence was total. And as for his arms, if they ever existed, the silence buried them much deeper than could spades under the leaf mold in a forest, as my godfather Sahag Sheitanian told me with his dying breath. The rifles and pistols and bullets lay buried like seeds. The vagueness as to the spot allowed a legend to be born. Thus, for all eternity, the arms of General Dro will never be found.

Drastamat Kanayan, or General Dro, erstwhile resistance fighter in the mountains, erstwhile minister of defense in the short-lived Armenian Republic, and one of the heroes of the Battle of Sardarabad, received permission to leave the Soviet Union in 1924, having been held under house arrest in Moscow up until then. He was to live in Bucharest and Ploiești. The exact reason why the NKVD decided to release General Dro remains unknown to this day. Those who believe that the general was spared in order not to provoke rebellion in Armenia ascribe to the NKVD fears that it never had. It may be that in their boundless pride and at the same time holding members of the general's family hostage, the Russians believed they could exploit Dro. But they were bitterly mistaken and would come to regret it, although as in other similar situations, Bolshevik regret did not manifest itself as humility or sadness but as bloody repression, claiming thousands of victims, from Ploiești to Odessa and Rostov on Don. Among the victims were the general's wife and one of his sons, who met their deaths in the Siberian taiga. What is for sure is that the general did not return to Armenia until May 24, 2000, exactly eighty-two years after the Battle of Sardarabad and forty-four years after his death. He was reburied with military honors in Bash-Abaran at a ceremony attended by a huge crowd. Also in attendance was his second wife, Gayane, whom he married in Romania in 1935. As is the case with women more often than men, Gayane was one of the few people who managed to outlive the century, without even having had to take up arms against it. Born in 1900 in the village of Nukhi in Karabakh, later living in Cetatea Albă in Bessarabia after its reunification with Greater Romania, Gayane Kanayan died in Boston at the age of 105 on April 24, when the Armenian community commemorated the ninetieth anniversary of the 1915 genocide.

The story of General Dro's arms begins in 1915, when the general, aged forty-one, arrived on Romanian soil. His house in Bucharest, at 55 Strada Popa Soare, still stands today. It is built in the style of the time, but today, on its wall, with its stylized moldings, the general's nom de guerre is inscribed in Armenian letters. Dro became the manager of an oil company, assisted by his friends from the Armenian Revolutionary Federation, the party founded in 1890 by Christapor Mikaelian, Rostom Zarian, and Simon Zavarian, known as the Federation for short, or Dashnaktsutyun in Armenian. Whence Dashnak, a name uttered with opprobrium by the new, postwar leaders of the Armenian community at meetings in the House of Culture, at 43 King Carol I Boulevard, by then a kind of second Soviet Embassy, at assemblies in the Miorița Cinema on Moșilor Avenue, and even in the Soviet Embassy itself. Under the vigilant eyes of the secret police, it was the name that an audience of stooges who did not even speak Armenian promptly and raucously booed.

For more than a decade, Dro led a bourgeois life, working in the oil industry, organizing the small Armenian community in Ploiești, uniting the former members of the Armenian government who had taken refuge in Romania, and from time to time attending meetings of the Central Bureau of the Armenian

Revolutionary Federation in Paris, serving as the organization's Balkan representative. The murder of his family in Omsk, in the Siberian taiga, rekindled his hatred of the Bolsheviks. General Dro thus became one of the most active militants for the liberation of Armenia from Soviet occupation.

My grandfathers, Garabet Vosganian and Setrak Melikian, did not tell me anything about all these things. Grandfather Garabet awakened in me the joy of writing, hoping that one day I would be the storyteller, but without ever urging me to be and without ever revealing the thread of the story. It would have been too simple, I thought. It would have been a mistake, thought my grandfathers. And when I was already a grown man, Setrak Melikian, my maternal grandfather, confessed to me one evening while we played *gyulbahar* under the vine arbor in Craiova: "He who has suffered cannot tell the story as it was, but only his own story. He who has suffered cannot understand. Nor can he who harbors enmity understand." My grandfathers were guides who walk in front of you but who do not turn their heads to see whether you follow them.

In the end, I picked up the thread of the legend of General Dro's arms, or at least one end of the thread: the forest beneath whose undergrowth the arms were supposed to lie buried. But what legend can survive if it be told from beginning to end . . . ?

The group around Dro was mainly made up of friends who had shared the same fate as he had and who had also settled in Romania. Among them were members of the former governments of Armenia: Hovhannes Katchaznouni, the first prime minister; Sarkis Araradian, the former minister of finance and trade; Kevork Hazarian, the minister of education; Hovhannes Devedjian, the first secretary of the Council; Abraham Gyulkhandanyan, the minister of communications and justice; and others. In fact, from the prime minister to the chancellor, a genuine Armenian government in exile could have been formed in the Romania of those days. But perhaps because Dro believed—and rightly so, after the English had reneged on the Treaty of Sèvres, which had created the illusion of a Greater Armenia—that their homeland would not be liberated except through armed struggle, he gathered to his side all the members of the Nemesis group who had taken refuge in Romania: Misak Torlakian, his right-hand man; Yervant Fundukian; Aram Yerganian; Mgrditch Mgrian.

I was taught to distinguish good from evil and encouraged, naturally, to choose the good over the evil, without it being very clear what line separated them. I was later to discover that more often than not you have to choose between two evils and that more important than choosing is the power to choose. It has often been thus in the history of the Armenians, surrounded on all sides by enemies who coveted their lands, from the Assyrians, Babylonians, Medes,

Persians, Parthians, and Romans to the Arabs, Tartars, Turks, Kurds, and Russians. And so the Armenians have been made to choose not between friends and enemies but between which enemy to accept as an ally and against which enemy to fight.

In the end, it turns out that the better evil did not exist, and the choice between two evils does not leave you with any chance. So it was with General Dro at the end of that decade, when war broke out once more. He chose to collaborate with Nazi Germany against Bolshevik Russia, believing that he would achieve two things simultaneously: protect the Armenians of German-occupied Europe and liberate Bolshevik-occupied Armenia. He achieved neither the one nor the other.

Recruiting began for the Armenian Legion but not from among the Armenians of German-occupied Europe since for the most part they were stateless and had not been called up. Because of this situation, for which the Armenians were the least responsible, things very nearly took an unpleasant turn in Romania. Less than half a year after the invasion of the Soviet Union, when General Dro's fantasies still rippled over the whole of Europe and the armies of Germany and its allies had not yet become bogged down in the fierce resistance at Stalingrad or fallen into the trap of the Don Bend, therefore believing that everything was still permitted to them, Marshal Antonescu's advisers viewed with mistrust the Nansenians, the stateless Armenians who had not been enlisted, for the simple reason that they did not exist in any record of the Romanian population. Feeling themselves defied by those immigrants who, if truth be told, had experienced ordeals far bloodier, the advisers tried to persuade the marshal to deport the Armenians to Transnistria. And it almost happened. After much tergiversation, a delegation appeared before the marshal, consisting of as many members as was allowed, which is to say, two, chosen with the express aim of softening his resolve: a man and a woman. The man was Archbishop Husig Zohrabian, the head of the Armenian Apostolic Church in Romania. He spoke to the marshal of the centuries-long presence of the Armenians on Romanian soil, presenting him with a copy of the golden bull issued by Alexander the Good in 1401, which, with the blessing of the patriarch of Constantinople, had permitted an Armenian bishopric to be established in Suczawa. The second member of the delegation did not have to say very much since she already wielded a certain amount of influence over the marshal. She was the graceful Mrs. Sofia Cihoski, née Ferhat, the wife of a general of Polish origin, formerly minister of the army, and a valiant commander of the Romanian Army during the First World War. A few years later, General Cihoski was to die in Sighet Jail, having been imprisoned by the Communists. In return for permanent abandonment of any plan to deport the Nansenians to Transnistria, the Armenians were to be subject to military conscription. Some met a tragic end, and their names are included in the lists of those to be commemorated, which are read out on Heroes Day in the Armenian cemetery on Chaussée Pantelimon in Bucharest. Others, like the old Armenians of my childhood, were conscripted toward the end of the war, and the only fright they experienced was when the Allies bombed Bucharest's Northern Station. Since nobody had time for them in the given situation, they went back home, despite the increasing rumors about the front nearing the Galați-Focșani line. But by then, the Armenian Legion, which had formed in 1941–42 and reached the Don Bend via the Crimea, had long since been annihilated. Some of the legion's soldiers, the best trained among them, were parachuted behind enemy lines, but they were betrayed, machine-gunned in midair, tumbling down on the steppe in a hail of bodies. Others were hunted like wild animals through the forests. What is sure is that the Armenian Legion never achieved the purpose for which it had been created; the legion never even reached Armenian soil, let alone liberated it.

But in 1940, such events were still far off. Germany was unvanquished; a year later, German troops invaded Russia, gobbling up hundreds of miles a day, and nobody had yet heard of Stalingrad. General Dro scoured the German prisoner-of-war camps in search of Soviet soldiers of Armenian origin. Such men seemed to have no escape. When the war began, the officers of the Red Army had warned them that they could choose either to fight or to die; better they commit suicide than fall prisoner. Every Soviet soldier who was captured would be regarded as a traitor. If you cannot fight for the victory of the Soviets, then you are a dead man. You must keep the last bullet in your magazine for yourself. Given the threat of being exterminated in the German camps, on the one hand, and the threat of being shot as traitors by the Red Army, on the other, the prisoners of war were easily swayed by Drastamat Kanayan, who in any event was gifted with great powers of rhetorical persuasion.

By the autumn of 1941, the Armenian Legion had amassed almost eight thousand volunteers. There were Armenian prisoners of war scattered around Romania who, in the absence of a concentration camp, had been made to perform various kinds of labor; they too were sent to Germany to begin training and swelled the ranks of the Legion.

The Legion was mustered in Germany, and the officers were mainly recruited from the ranks of the Wehrmacht, with the object of instilling discipline in that ragtag army, whose ranks contained a mixture of grimly determined volunteers and Soviet ex-prisoners in fear of their lives; experienced fighters and untrained greenhorns; patriots and cowards. Each member of that army was seeking salvation in his own way, and each hoped to avoid death. General Dro, the organizer of the Armenian Legion—or, as those unnerved by the word "legion" preferred to call it, the Armenian Battalion—traveled the length and breadth of the continent to recruit willing and not-so-willing volunteers, returning at intervals to Ploieşti, where a different kind of command center of the Armenian Legion was based, an illusory command, given that most of the officers were from the Wehrmacht. But that did not prevent the imagined command from dreaming up resounding and uninterrupted victories, from the steppes of the Crimea to the plain at the foot of Mount Ararat, where some of the current soldiers of the Legion had fought in the victorious Battle of Sardarabad.

THE TALE OF HARUTIUN KHNTIRIAN'S OBSTINACY. Having arrived in Bucharest, loyal son of his homeland that he was, General Drastamat Kanayan went first to the Consulate of the Republic of Armenia. For me, the storyteller, it is quite hard to keep to the thread of the story. It is intermittent, like a book read in the flare of lightning bolts. Perhaps instead of *The Book of Whispers*, this story could be called *The Book of Healing*. For it tells of people who went through unimaginable suffering, which each in his own fashion tried to heal. And since reality is seldom the cure for reality, my grandfathers and the grandfathers of my grandfathers seemed to go round in a circle, always encountering the same pains and the same apparitions. Leaving real things behind them, my grandfathers' people let themselves be guided by imaginary things and by imagined things, which is to say, by things that did not exist and things that, although they existed, my grandfathers stubbornly viewed as different than what they really were.

The consulate was established in 1918, thanks to general enthusiasm on the part of Bucharest's Armenians, who opened it as soon as the republic was declared on May 28. The Romanian authorities recognized it, in the belief that a new country, rising from an unraveling empire, would set a good example to the peoples and provinces of the Austro-Hungarian Empire. The man appointed general consul was Harutiun Khntirian, one of the founders of the Union of Armenians in Romania and its first chairman.

In December 1920, the Bolshevik armies of Anastas Mikoyan and Alexander Miasnikian occupied an Armenia ravaged by famine and typhus, an Armenia of terrified people, huddling up against each other, the tenants of a house with two doors, one to the east and one to the west, at which two different enemies were battering simultaneously: the Turks to the west and the Bolsheviks to the east. The first door to open, or rather to be battered from its hinges, was the one to the east. Armenia was occupied by a motley army, commanded by Armenians but made up of Russians, Georgians, Azeris, and Tartars. A stirring of revolt on the part of the population of Yerevan, led by the remnants of the last independent government, was quashed in a bloodbath in February 1921.

Meanwhile, Harutiun Khntirian was torn in different directions. Troubled, he kept reading wire cables about the fate of governments that succeeded each other, merged with each other, were at odds with each other. Untroubled, he went on opening the consular office, in premises provided by the Union of Armenians in Romania, and beneath the red, blue, and orange Armenian flag he sat straight-backed with his chin raised.

In 1922, Armenia became part of the Trans-Caucasian Soviet Republic. The last fugitives—members of the government, various other dignitaries, generals, and partisans—had arrived in Romania or traveled to the West. Khntirian received them and learned the news without being able to offer them anything in exchange, not even a rubber stamp on their travel documents. Unfortunately, after 1921, the Romanian authorities no longer recognized the existence of the consulate. No matter how pedantic Mr. Khntirian may have been, with his checked jacket, with his bow tie knotted beneath wing collars, with his thick eyebrows beneath the black frames of his spectacles; no matter how praiseworthy his conscientiousness may have been; and no matter how many diplomatic qualities he may have possessed, he lacked the one vital quality for a consul: that of having a country to represent. As for Harutiun Khntirian's relations with Soviet Armenia, things could not have been plainer: Khntirian did not have the slightest intention of representing Bolshevism or the Soviet Union in Romania, nor did the vaguely independent government of Armenia have any desire to be represented by the small, sprightly, but too restive Harutiun Khntirian. Not to mention the fact that, mutual scorn aside, the situation was unequivocal: Bolshevik Armenia could not be represented in Romania anyway since neither the Averescu government nor the Brătianu government recognized the Soviet Union.

Despite all this, Khntirian held on to his rubber stamp, for the simple reason that nobody had asked for it back. In any event, there was nobody to whom he could return it. Likewise, he kept the official envelopes and letterhead paper, which began to yellow with the passing years. The flag that had once flown from the window was moved inside and spread over the wall, next to a portrait of the final prime minister, Simon Vratsian. This was subsequently replaced with a portrait of Vardan Mamikonian; the commander of an Armenian army of almost one and a half millennia ago, he was appropriate to any Armenian wall. Aram Vdarantsi, Khntirian's faithful secretary, after cleaning the offices and drawing the blinds, was able to immerse himself undisturbed in his translation from Persian to Armenian of Omar Khayyam's *Rubaiyat*, an occupation that perhaps explains the obstinacy with which Aram continued to hold on to the position of functionary in a consulate that represented melancholia rather than reality. As practical as any port inhabitants, who otherwise like to cultivate their nostalgias, the Armenians of Constanța closed their vice consulate, run by Givan Altunian, and so too did the Armenians of Galați, paying the appropriate honors to vice consuls Simion Kehyayan and Harutiun Sbengian.

In Bucharest, Khntirian assiduously signed various wire cables, which he sent to Yerevan, relaying information about the way things were going in Romania, a country now recovering its senses after the war. He received wire cables in return—fewer than he sent, it was true—about the Armenian government's solemn and then increasingly desperate appeals for the Treaty of Sèvres to be respected. After the war, he continued to send wire cables about Armenian refugees, about the glory and then the fall of the Averescu government, about Brătianu, about the refugees who swelled the ranks of the Armenian community, about General Dro. The wire cables that came back dwindled, until finally he received nothing from the homeland and only one or two snore-inducing letters from various governments in exile, which the fleeing ministers cobbled together overnight where you least expected: Paris, New York, Beirut. Khntirian ceased to classify such missives, keeping them under seal in files trussed with ribbons and locked away in massive filing cabinets since they no longer contained anything in the slightest bit secret. They were depressing at most, and in any event the same information appeared soon enough in the newspapers that arrived from abroad. Although he could see that nobody answered his dispatches, Harutiun Khntirian continued to write them nonetheless. His secretary Aram still copied them in his fine calligraphic hand, except now he filed them away without dispatching them anywhere. Once a month, there would be a familiar knock on the door. It was the only knock ever heard at the consulate and was awaited with a mixture of joy and shame. The knock in question signaled the arrival of the envelope containing money for the following month. It was accompanied by a letter stating that the Union of Armenians had done its duty in collecting the money and that it saluted the distinguished functionaries of the consulate in their capacity as representatives of the homeland. The text was always the same; only the signature changed, depending on who happened to be chairman at the time: Grigore Trancu-Iași, Armenag Manisalian, Terenig Danelian.

During its short existence, the Armenian Republic had nonetheless had the opportunity to be included on maps of the world, but the small country itself had long since been erased, its governments in exile had ceased to issue their bombastic proclamations, and the stateless emigrants from Anatolia had found refuge in the four corners of the world, reuniting the remnants of their families and starting to knock together small businesses so that they could make a living. All that remained was the consulate in Bucharest, with Harutiun Khntirian and his secretary Aram, with its drawn blinds; its red, blue, and orange flag pinned to the wall; and its filing cabinets accreting dispatches to nowhere, the last vestige of a republic that now existed only in Armenians' nostalgias and on the official rubber stamp. On October 7, 1929, the knock on the door brought an envelope similar to the others. But this time, instead of money, Harutiun Khntirian found only a letter, signed, like the others, by the chairman of the Union of Armenians. However, the letter they found on the table when, confronted with the stubborn silence from within, they finally broke the door down, spoke not of the homeland and its illustrious consular representative but of a homeland impossible to represent since it had vanished from the map: "The Board of the Union of Armenians in Romania has decided as follows: the offices that the UAR has placed at the disposal of the consulate shall be closed, which decision is valid for the whole of Romania."

The suppositions were debated one by one, but none proved to be satisfactory. What all the theories had in common was that after receiving the letter, the Armenian consul, Harutiun Khntirian, had drawn the blinds and locked the doors. From the inside, insisted some. From the outside, insisted others. And they added: "How could he have locked them from the inside if there was a padlock on the outside?"

The door was broken down in the presence of a committee made up of His Holiness Archbishop Husig Zohrabian and Terenig Danelian, chairman of the Union of Armenians, accompanied by various gawpers gathered in the churchyard. They entered cautiously, prepared for anything, including the rigid corpse of Harutiun Khntirian. But they found no dead body. They did not have the patience to search for him in nooks and crannies or in the filing cabinets, where, among violet rubber stamps and orange seals embossed with the republic's coat of arms, Harutiun Khntirian might have hidden from this world, like a book mite. What they did find, written in ink so fresh that you might have sworn it had only just been committed to paper, was an Armenian translation of Mihai Eminescu's poem "Mortua est!"

But what does one padlock more or less matter? What is important is that nobody saw Harutiun Khntirian ever again. It was rumored that he committed suicide, seated at his desk, dipping his rubber stamp in the thin blood that trickled from his brow so that he would be ready to emboss it on the passports of the citizens of an imaginary republic. It was also rumored that he had wandered off into the wide world, heading eastward in the direction of the country that had abandoned him. Others told that Harutiun Khntirian had popped up again, his mind having gone somewhat astray; he was now a jocular, entertaining man who resembled not at all the conscientious functionary of the real and subsequently imaginary consulate. They said he was the author of satirical sketches and comedies and that he died, like any man with a sense of humor, at the age of almost one hundred. The only thing that can definitely be linked to the death of Harutiun Khntirian is the translation of Mihai Eminescu's poem "Mortua est!" It was published in the diaspora *Armenian Almanac* in 1941.

The time is now 1924, however. Feverishly reading reports on the Lausanne Treaty negotiations and vainly seeking some sign that the countries around the table might remember his own abandoned country, Harutiun Khntirian occasionally rubber-stamps a passport belonging to some Nansenian who has arrived in the second wave of refugees after the Greek-Turkish war of 1922. Since a stateless person applying for residence in Romania needed a certificate of ethnicity, issued by the Union of Armenians, and since the consulate was housed in the same building as the union, Khntirian was under the illusion that the applicant had not come to the wrong address, and he applied his increasingly pointless, increasingly worn, increasingly violet stamp to that person's documents.

As for Drastamat Kanayan, alias General Dro, he did not come to the wrong address; it was the consulate he was looking for. To Khntirian's disappointment, however, the only man who had come especially to see him did not require a rubber stamp. But to his delight, it turned out that he was not the only man in the world who stubbornly believed that the Armenian Republic continued to exist, despite the occupation, the shattered borders, the exiled governments, and the revolts that had been bloodily crushed.

And what was more, after Harutiun Khntirian disappeared without trace, slipping away between the pages of the files or dissolving among the dark crannies in the wall of his office, General Dro survived him in the conviction that the Armenian Republic had to exist somewhere and that it could be found if only you knew where to look. Whereas in his struggle for the lost Armenia Harutiun Khntirian wielded a rubber stamp, a flag pinned to a wall, and files trussed with ribbons, assisted only by his secretary Aram, General Dro wielded real arms, and consequently he founded the Armenian Legion. He unpinned the captive flag from the consulate wall, letting it flutter in the breeze, at the head of his new army.

Between two journeys the length and breadth of Europe, General Dro returned to Ploieşti to keep his army command in fighting shape. After he regaled them with accounts of his Armenian Legion as a new army of salvation, the general organized expeditions to the Strejnicu Forest. The expeditions were undoubtedly an occasion to have fun, with picnic baskets and bottles of plum brandy and wine. But they were also warlike expeditions, during which General Dro, on horseback and waving his flintlock, commanded an assault on the woods. The members of his group, ranging from avengers Misak Torlakian, Yervant Fundukian, and Simon Pilibbosian (the comrade in arms of Kevork Chavush) to Atam Altokayan of Ploieşti, obeyed his orders, roaring at an unseen enemy and shooting at the trees, producing cascades of falling leaves. After such victorious sallies against every possible enemy, from the Ottomans to the Bolsheviks, and without taking prisoners, the expeditionary force returned to the picnic baskets and bottles of *raki*, which Nshan Maganian had fiercely guarded in the meantime. Nshan Maganian, a teacher at the Armenian school, did not wield a weapon, but he participated with all his heart, thinking of the rebels of Zeitun from the time of his childhood.

The fact that those men, who had braved death on the battlefield or in guerrilla warfare, expended as much ferocity on shooting at trees and fighting phantoms hiding behind the trunks by no means diminished the joy of victory in Strejnicu Forest, which today is remembered as the place where Nicolae Iorga was assassinated by the Iron Guard in 1940, rather than as the site of an uninterrupted string of victories on the part of the Ploieşti Armenian Legion. After the war and the denouement brought by the Red Army, the group dissolved. General Dro and his closest comrades left Romania in the spring of 1944. Even the young lads, Anoush and Agop Kirmizian, who acted as shield bearers to the doughty wielders of flintlocks, were whisked away, first to Constantinople, in a Turkey still friendly with Germany, from whence they departed into the wide world, embarking on a ship to Marseille. Nshan Maganian, the Sunday school teacher, died in reclusion, too discreet to attract the attention of the new authorities but consoling himself with the fact that he had christened his only son among four daughters with the name Setin, after his native town of Zeitun. Those who paid with their lives included Atam Altokayan, in a way that proves yet again that history grins at us from ear to ear. Atam Altokayan made it to the front, but it would seem that the training he received in Strejnicu Forest had not been thorough enough since he fell prisoner to the Russians. In the prisoner-of-war camp he was recruited by the Red Army's Tudor Vladimirescu Division, and after August 23, 1944, he returned to fight the Germans on the Russian side. But after a while, even history stopped grinning and said enough was enough, putting a stop to Atam Altokayan's martial peregrinations the length and breadth of Eastern Europe, now against the Bolsheviks on the German side, now against the Germans on the Bolshevik side. Unfortunately for him, in a war that kept being turned back to front, Atam Altokayan could only be stopped by a bullet in the forehead, in the trenches around Bucharest.

His name is commemorated by our priests on Vartanak, the day of the martyrs, along with those members of the Armenian community who fell for Romanian independence in the two world wars. All the other advisers and companions of General Dro who were still in Romania were bundled off to Siberia en masse. Those who did not leave their bones there, since they were too young to have the wisdom to die, returned enfeebled, with soft, toothless gums, half-blind.

Grandfather Garabet, the fierce preserver of the secret of General Dro's arms, was not among the heroes of these stories. He also managed to convince others not to be swayed to leave. It was not easy, especially when it came to his brother-in-law Sahag Sheitanian, who was brought up in Constantinople by a grandmother who by night smuggled arms under her skirt in preparation for the Dashnak assault on the Imperial Ottoman Bank Headquarters. Grandfather carefully hid the Armenian newspapers that published appeals to enroll in the Legion. "Too much blood," he would say, probably remembering the obsessions of his mother, my great-grandmother Mariam, who, the more the cataracts occluded her vision, the more she saw blood, which had remained imprinted on her retinas from the massacres of her youth, throughout Anatolia, from Trebizond to Adana. Having become shaky in her old age, she cut her hand and did not know which was the blood in her veins and which was the blood of her visions. They found her glassy-eyed, curled up, drained of blood but with a peaceful expression on her face. She had been submerged in her own phantasms, as if under water. "Too much blood," said Grandfather. It was the summer of 1941, and he could not know how right he was to prove.

One day Mgrditch Musayan turned up in our town out of the blue, arriving from Constanța. The parochial council was convened. Full of enthusiasm, Mgrditch brought the message of General Dro. Grandfather was reserved and managed to persuade the others to control themselves. Musayan did not add anything to what he had said; he even seemed to sympathize with them. They accompanied him to the train station, walking with him along the straight road from the church, which was flanked by chestnut trees and the large houses of Armenian and Jewish merchant families, now requisitioned by German officers. They bid him farewell and thought that that would be the end of it. But the next Sunday, the Feast of St. Mary no less, when a large number of people gathered at the church to pray, and also to partake in the repast of beef and rice afterward, a military truck entered the churchyard, from which alighted eight soldiers in German uniform. They went inside the church, and the officer planted himself in front of them, close to the altar. The frightened congregation shrank back, and Father Dajad Aslanian faltered in his sermon. Then the soldiers took off their caps, and the officer fell in line with the others. Thinking the soldiers would not understand a word he said, Father Dajad continued his sermon, not from where he had left off, but urging the congregants, in Armenian of course, to stay calm and to place their trust in the Good Lord. Not knowing what else to say and reciting the Lord's Prayer, he looked at the soldiers more closely. On their chests they wore the German eagle with outspread wings, but on their arms they wore banderoles in the colors of the Armenian flag. The man in the officer's uniform was none other than Tatevos Bedrosian, the history teacher and head of the Armenian school in Constanța. He now went up to the priest, who stood stock still before the altar, and kissed his hand. Tatevos Bedrosian then turned to the congregation, finished reciting the prayer from the point where it had remained frozen on the priest's lips, and spoke to them about the homeland, about the lands occupied by the Bolsheviks, about the sacred duty to liberate those lands, urging the men to follow the example of the *fedayi* in the Caucasus Mountains and to enlist as volunteers in the Armenian Legion. He gave as an example the other seven men, all of them Armenians, former prisoners of war, but now soldiers of that strange army with its mixed insignia. The congregation gazed in astonishment, now at the German speaking Armenian, now at the German eagle on his chest, now at the banderole with the Armenian tricolor. They were uncomprehending and therefore fearful. At last, Tatevos Bedrosian turned to Father Dajad, from whom the only movement was the smoke rising from his censer. He put his cap back on his head; he gave a military salute, albeit avoiding the Nazi salute; and, followed by his men, he stiffly walked out of the church, but not before promising to return. The paupers gathered in the old graveyard were able to rejoice since after that nobody else had any appetite for the repast that was laid out.

Tatevos Bedrosian, the teacher who was now a German officer, did not return to Focșani since the Armenian Legion had been mustered in Holland, where it was quartered. Tatevos returned to Constanța, where in those days around ten thousand Armenians lived and where the chances of recruiting volunteers were therefore greater. He continued to hold meetings, and at one of them General Dro himself was in attendance. There is a record of one such meeting, giving the names of those who took part: Tatevos Bedrosian, head of the Armenian School in Constanța, history teacher; Garo Zartarian, industrialist, politician influential among the Armenian community; Mgrditch Musayan, vegetable grower, close associate of Dro; Hapet Kasparian and Vazken Kasparian, father and son, coffee traders; Khosrov Bedrosian, cereal farmer; Aram Sarkisian, retailer; Hovhannes Sahagian, teacher at the Armenian school. Those who, unlike Tatevos Bedrosian, did not manage to flee before the Russians arrived, were arrested one by one, and if they were not summarily executed, as happened in

Rostov and Kharkov, they were sentenced to long years of hard labor and deported to Siberia.

Nothing more was heard about Tatevos Bedrosian's soldiers; they probably died in the siege of Stalingrad. It was rumored that Tatevos managed to escape and went to Germany, a rumor corroborated by the fact that his wife and two daughters, Emma and Seta, also finally went there. Mgrditch Musayan was arrested and sent to Siberia. He was a religious man. His body died in the icy wastes of eastern Siberia. But he himself had the strength to survive, a tatter of soul clinging to withered limbs, until he received his last communion from Father Hamazasp Bedikian in Constanța. When commemorating the names of those who died in the war and in Siberia, instead of saying "died an untimely death, unshriven," Father Hamazasp was able to conflate the two deaths of Mgrditch Musayan and say, "died an untimely death, shriven."

Arakel, his son, later tried to find out what had happened to his father, that he might understand his suffering, his silence, and, after his return, his haste to die. Since none of the other men from Constanța returned from Siberia to tell the tale, Arakel Musayan ventured to write to the authorities once the times changed and once he had exhausted every other avenue of discovering his father's fate in the decade after the war. The reply from the post-Communist Romanian Intelligence Service concludes our story of the Armenian Legion in a way that allows no glimmer of light to slip through the chinks in the door:

> Romania—Romanian Intelligence Service, Public Relations Bureau, no. 70865, September 16, 2005. To Mr. Musayan Arakel, Constanța, no. 93, Boulevard Ferdinand, Constanța County. Re. your request, addressed to the RIS, Constanța County Section, registered as no. 3546158 on August 31, 2005. We inform you that, subsequent to checks carried out on archive materials surrendered by the former organs of the secret police, the following information was obtained: Musayan, Mgrditch, son of Mesrop and Chiuvage, born on January 25, 1891, in Turkey, was stopped and arrested by a Soviet officer and two Soviet civilians on June 6, 1945, being suspected of Armenian nationalist activity as part of the Dashnak organization. After his arrest, he was deported to the USSR and sentenced to 5 (five) years imprisonment and 5 (five) years compulsory residence in Siberia. On May 15, 1956, he was repatriated, moving into his former domicile in Constanța. The documents that we hold do not provide the number of the sentence or the court that handed down the conviction.

The signature at the bottom of the letter is an illegible wavy line, which suggests a wish on the part of the signee to remain as anonymous as the officer and civilians who instigated Mgrditch Musayan's arrest and the court that convicted him.

The Legion set out at the end of 1941. The names of the recruiters are not known for sure. The figures for the number of soldiers vary from eight thousand to twenty thousand. The difference in fact resides in our knowing how many dead we should add to those fallen in the war, who, unlike the usual dead, were unfortunate enough to be buried twice and are therefore all the more restless: once in the earth and once in statistics. In his passionate hatred of the Bolsheviks, General Dro overlooked three things. First, that the Germans would not agree to arm an entire division without gaining some advantage for themselves and that they were as little interested in the fate of the Armenians and Armenia, wherever it might lie, as the Allied powers had been after the First World War. The Armenian officers recruited from among Soviet prisoners lost their rank, and the officers of the Armenian Legion were recruited from the Wehrmacht. Second, if Hitler had no mind to let any other patch of Europe remain free, he can hardly have had the slightest intention of allowing an independent Armenia. The German Army had no more intention of liberating Armenia using the Armenian Legion than the Red Army had of liberating Romania a few years later, when, with the help of the Tudor Vladimirescu Division, made up of former Romanian prisoners of war, it instead became an army of occupation. Third, Dro ignored the fact that whether he liked it or not, the road to Armenia led through Stalingrad and the Don Bend, and he had no way of knowing what that would mean for the German Army.

When they were not machine-gunned in midair as they tried to parachute behind Soviet lines; when they were not hunted down one by one in the forests; when they were not starving and freezing to death on the snowy steppes or in the siege of Stalingrad, the soldiers of the Armenian Legion were summarily shot by the Russians. The repression traced back the whole of the route by which the soldiers of the Legion had come; those suspected of sheltering, feeding, or even cheering them were executed without trial. The Russians were unable to find General Drastamat Kanayan, even though they scoured Bucharest and Ploieşti in their zealous search. They suspected that he was hiding out in the mountains until the general himself, to spare them the effort, sent them a message from Beirut, where he had arrived safe and sound and as irrepressible as ever. From Beirut he traveled to the United States, where he died in 1956 and from whence, as I said, he returned to Armenia, after more than four decades, to be buried in a ceremony attended by tens of thousands on the field at Bash-Abaran.

Nobody said another word about the Armenian Legion, about General Dro's command center in Ploiești, or about the expeditions to Strejnicu Forest. Now, as I write *The Book of Whispers* and ask various people about what happened back then, their answer is that they do not know because their grandparents and parents never talked to them about it. In Strejnicu Forest, the grass has grown over the hoof prints of the general's horses, and wild honeycombs have filled in the bullet holes in the trunks of the trees. As for the arms of General Dro, if they ever existed and if they were ever buried, they at least proved to be of use when it came to fostering the illusions of those for whom no other hope existed. And in times like those, that was no small achievement.

5.

This story, which we call *The Book of Whispers*, is not my story. It began long before my childhood, in the days when they spoke in a whisper. It began even long before it became a book. And it did not begin in the Focșani of my childhood but in Sivas, in Diarbekir, in Biltlis, in Adana and the Cilicia region, in Van, in Trebizond, in all the *vilayets* of eastern Anatolia, where the Armenians of my childhood were born who are among the protagonists of this book. It began even long before that, with the legends the old folk of my childhood listened to and the fears they felt in their childhoods. In a time when there were as yet only two crumpled pages, bloodied more than read, the book continued to grow with the massacres of 1894–95 and the fierce resistance put up by the mountain folk of Sasun and the inhabitants of Zeitun, led by the Hunchakian Party and the *fedayi* of Van. It continued with the occupation of the Imperial Ottoman Bank headquarters by a band of twenty-five armed Armenians, led by Armen Garo, who took a hundred and forty bank staff hostage, threatening to blow up the imperial treasury unless the foreign powers intervened to stop the killing of Armenians, an act that the enemies of the Armenians have described as the first terrorist attack in history but which those who committed it described as an act of justice, aimed at drawing the attention of the whole world to a tragedy that, unfortunately, was only just beginning.

Or perhaps in its deepest part, *The Book of Whispers* begins with another book — the same as people are born of people, books are born of books and then grow up by themselves — a book written a thousand years before: *The Book of Lamentation* by Gregory of Narek. That a book was a guide to worship and that weeping was regarded as a salve against the times, often the only one, is also proven by the fact that this book of lamentation was used against illness; when every other cure failed, it was placed at the patient's bedside. The fact that it was called *The Book of Lamentation* and that this book is called *The Book of Whispers* does not mean that the journey from weeping to whispers has been one of cures. It means that in those days the people had not yet lost the freedom to weep and, as in Gregory of Narek's hymn to the divinity, that God was still close at hand. Between that weeping and these whispers, it does not mean that one suffering takes the place of another. Rather, it is merely the difference between weeping and stifled weeping. In the century of my birth, the amount of blood shed for just one teardrop was the same as the amount shed in a whole century of war back in those days.

But our story begins in the time when the chronologies become clear, when people begin to have names and faces, when we can find the houses where they lived and the streets where they walked, when we can leaf through the books they read, seeking to understand their thoughts from the corners of the pages they folded and the notes they wrote in the margins. The year is 1890, the year when Misak Torlakian was born in Gyushana, a little village of no more than two hundred souls, in the *vilayet* of Trebizond. Three years later, in Afion Karahisar, my father's father, Grandfather Garabet Vosganian, was born. The two could not have met in their childhood since Misak Torlakian's village was in the north, a few miles from the sea, while Afion Karahisar was in the center of Anatolia, and in those days the Armenians did not travel far. Children traveled even more seldom, only to the nearest town, as was the case with my maternal grandfather Setrak Melikian and his grandmother when they traveled to Erzerum and were saved. Nonetheless, young people traveled farther afield, to Europe, where they learned trades and foreign languages to broaden their minds and bring home money to a world still poor and biblical, where the folk came down from the mountain to barter with the inhabitants of the plain, exchanging wool and sheep's and goat's cheese for flour, fruit, and vegetables. And so it was that the Melikians, Grandfather Setrak's older cousins, arrived in Craiova. Not having anywhere to return to after their village was torched and put to the sword, they remained in Craiova. As I have already recounted, they discovered Grandfather Setrak working as an apprentice barber in Odessa, after which they found his sister Satenig in an orphanage in Aleppo. Grandfather Setrak opened a colonial goods store whose olive, cacao, and coffee crates, left over after the Communists confiscated it, I saw crammed in the larder, and that fostered the illusion that one day he might revive the business. Grandfather Setrak met my grandmother Sofia, whom he married when she was just sixteen. My aunt Maro was born, named after my grandfather's elder sister, who committed suicide by casting herself into the waters of the Euphrates, and later my mother, Elisabeta, was born, who gave birth first to my brother Melik (named after the family's legendary ancestor, a prince of Urmia) and then to me, Varujan, which in old Armenian is the name of a bird, not any particular bird but one that, like flight itself, is contained in every bird. I have a daughter named Armine, which means "little Armenian girl," and she will add to my ancestors, just as my grandmother Arshaluis, the wife of my other grandfather, Garabet, added to the inside cover of the Bible a record of the most important things that happened to her:

the burning of the houses in Pera; the escape by ship across the Bosphorus; the death of her father, Baghdasar Terzian, on the deck; her marriage, brokered by Father Ignadios; and the birth of my father, Berj. After which she wrote nothing more, reckoning that she would not live long enough to forget all the things that had already happened to her. It is sufficient to evoke two things about Grandmother Arshaluis: the gentleness with which she laid bread and *vospabour*, lentil broth, on the table, and the light and tranquility that suffused the air around her when she combed her hair.

In the photographs, my great-grandfather Kevork Vosganian seems a stern man with thick, twirling moustaches and round, black-framed spectacles. He was a functionary; he had beautiful handwriting; and, to judge by his appearance and the watch chain that hangs from his pocket, he led an orderly life. Sometimes he wore a fez, the same as I, his great-grandson, wear a hat in Europe. I never saw my grandfather Garabet wearing a fez, not even in photographs. In his youth he wore a hat, rather a modern one for the 1920s, and a long raincoat with a turned-up collar. It is funny to think of your grandparents when they were young: Grandmother, plump and mignon, with luminous green eyes and long, wavy hair tumbling delicately down her back, with chubby hands that formed dimples at the base of the fingers when she arched them upward to display her rings; and Grandfather, half serious, half romantic, a young man in his prime, with whom Grandmother was hopelessly in love for all the forty-five years they lived together. Grandfather went to Father Ignadios in Galați, who took out the list that he updated at the beginning of every year, striking a thick line through the names that had already been dealt with, adding new names, not to the end of the list but at various points and according to criteria known only to him. It so happened that Grandmother was at the top of the list of marriageable girls drawn up by Father Ignadios. Like any man in his prime, Grandfather believed he deserved the best, which is to say, the top of the list. So he took his older brother David as a chaperone, and they both went to the house of Heghine Terzian, who had two daughters. Both were beautiful, but only one, Grandmother Arshaluis, was of marriageable age. Grandfather brought with him a box of bonbons, tied with a bow, and a large bouquet of flowers, which the elder brother, David, was carrying when they arrived. Looking out of the window and believing that the suitor was David rather than Garabet, whom she found more attractive, Arshaluis hid in the larder and came out only after they implored her, reassuring her that the suitor was in fact Garabet. Garabet liked Arshaluis too, so everything seemed to be going according to Father Ignadios's plan. But shortly after that, my grandfather disappeared. Rumor had it that he had crossed the Danube to Silistra, where he had a lover. This proved to be true.

Arshaluis, as unmarried as she was inconsolable, fell ill, and neither smelling salts nor eau de cologne rubbed on her temples could revive her. But the fact of the matter was that Grandfather, quickly crossing the frozen Danube, had gone to Silistra not only to see his Bulgarian lover, but also to bid her a permanent farewell. When he returned, my grandmother, her nostrils inflamed from the smelling salts and emanating a strong whiff of eau de cologne, promptly recovered, arranged her hair as she ran down the stairs, and leapt into the arms of her fiancé. Father Ignadios, officiating at the wedding, took out his list and, after studying her carefully, silently and with great satisfaction added Aunt Armenuhi, my grandmother's sister, to his list.

When I look back now, at the same age my grandmother was when I was born, the memory of my grandparents in their old age has begun to blur. This is because Grandfather Garabet was highly skilled at preserving memories of himself. An artist by nature, he understood that the story of every man's life is only partly made up of what he experiences in real time while the rest is made up, in equal parts, of the things you remember, the things you hope, and the things you fear. Grandfather created a parallel life for himself, composed of photographs, numerous from his youth, fewer from middle age, and almost none from old age. Do not be deceived by the fact that *The Book of Whispers* speaks of the old folk of my childhood. Garabet Vosganian, one of the protagonists of this book, is not an old man, despite his age. As I grew up, my grandparents grew younger. Now, Grandmother is a beautiful young woman, her fingers sticky with grape juice, gazing at the sunset from the Asian shore of the Bosphorus, and Grandfather is a young man crossing the frozen Danube on horseback, returning from Silistra to ask for Grandmother's hand in marriage, as she sits with her mother Heghine and sister Armenuhi, who has not yet been included on Father Ignadios's list; they sit in their cramped little house in Galați, which, aside from the lack of grapes and toasted peanuts from back home, also differs in that the sun does not sink there but rather rises above the water, which is a river rather than a sea.

And a few lines farther down, my grandfather Garabet will have become a mere child. As the pages of the book write themselves, as they turn one by one, as I advance in age, my grandparents grow younger, and I will be an old man; I will rock them in their cradles, and we will die together.

Misak Torlakian, on the other hand, was never concerned about his own life; he even despised it. He was more faithful to his dreams than his periods of lucidity. He lacked charm; he was short and burly, with dark eyes and dark hair, which was also curly, doing his swarthy, hook-nosed face no favor. He was awkward, and this was why, even in his most passionate moments, he kept his silence. A companion more different from and more suitable for General Dro you could not hope to find. It is obvious why he could not have been more different. The reason why he could not have been more suitable is that Misak Torlakian, who led a harsh life and never backed down, was prepared to fight to the bitter end for the sake of Drastamat Kanayan's phantasms. Clumsy and exalted in his taciturnity, Misak Torlakian nonetheless had the tenacity and relentlessness of an avenger or, as his biographers were to say, for reasons we shall discover, an Armenian Nemesis.

Misak Torlakian was five years old when, during the reign of Abdul Hamid, the Ottoman Empire unleashed the first of the massacres. Starting in Trebizond, they spread to the other *vilayets* inhabited by the Armenians, reaching their climax in the south, near Adana. At the time Trebizond was a city of tens of thousands of people from various ethnic groups: Turks, Circassians, Kurds, Azeris, Greeks, Georgians, and Armenians. The city pulsated around its port, whence radiated straight streets and white, flat-roofed houses without courtyards all the way to the outlying districts. News traveled quickly and more often than not had to do with the life of the port and those who came and went by sea. This is what happened when Bahri Pasha, the governor of Van, stopped off in Trebizond on his way to Constantinople, having been recalled from his post at the insistence of the foreign powers, which had complained on numerous occasions about atrocities against the Armenians. The number killed at his orders is reckoned to be around one thousand, while more than five thousand fled in fear of further reprisals, leaving behind their houses and possessions. Famed for his brutality against the Armenians, the governor was greeted in the port of Trebizond as a hero by the Muslim population; he was cheered all the way to the center of town. Perhaps little Misak, holding the hand of his uncle Manuk Aslanian, was in the street at the time, mingling with the silent crowd of Armenians, who watched in alarm as Bahri Pasha made his triumphal procession.

Among themselves, the old folk of my childhood told the story of those events. The meetings, at which the women and children were not present, took place in the afternoons, over coffee. They must have been the same everywhere: in Bucharest, Constanța, Pitești, and Craiova; in the courtyard of Nshan Hazarian, the merchant from Buzău; and on the verandas of Moldavian houses. These were subdued conversations, like the ones at which I was present in my childhood in the yard of our house in Focșani, at no. 9, March 6, 1945, Street, with its wooden benches and pillowed armchairs arranged in a circle beneath the shade of the apricot tree. When the guest was from another town, the meeting would take place in the yard of the Armenian church. This is why the Armenian churches everywhere had large yards, and since the sites were at least two or three centuries old, the trees were mature enough to provide plentiful shade. Each told his own story or others' stories, taking responsibility for those no longer alive.

The story of Misak Torlakian began on October 2, 1895, at around five in the afternoon, when Bahri Pasha, accompanied by Hamdi Pasha, the military commander of Trebizond, arrived in the center of the city via the promenade. The sound of the shot could not be heard amid the din of the cheering and would have passed completely unobserved if Hamdi Pasha had not noticed that Bahri Pasha's arm was bleeding. It was stupid, Misak Torlakian was later to recount, but not with the fear of the child dragged away by the hand lest he be crushed by a crowd now yelling and running in every direction, while Bahri Pasha, surrounded by soldiers, was ushered to the shelter of a nearby coffeehouse. Rather, he recounted it with the coldness and wisdom of the *fedayi:* it was stupid to believe that you could kill a man with a revolver from that distance. You might hit him, but then you did more harm than good, which is what happened in that case. Uncle Manuk had no idea who could have done such a thing, nor did any of his *fedayi,* who, if they had got it into their heads to kill Bahri Pasha, would have taken aim at him with a carbine from one of the surrounding buildings. But whoever did it, deliberately or at random, the Armenians were held to blame, and Governor Kadri Bey of Trebizond *vilayet* demanded that they surrender the assailant. Even if they had known who it was, how could the Armenians have done such a thing? In any event, the assailant was never found, although the authorities subsequently boasted that they had caught and punished him.

The aftermath is not part of the story of Misak Torlakian. The events have been described in books and official documents, and the only thing that Misak might have added was the image of his village, burned to the ground by those for whom the massacres and looting in Trebizond had not been enough.

Trebizond was a lively port, from whence goods from the Orient were transshipped to Europe. This is why all the world's major powers had opened consulates in buildings whitened by the sea breeze. It must have come as a surprise to Kadri Bey, the governor of Trebizond, when, on the morning of October 5, 1895, a delegation arrived at his office. It was a delegation unique in its way, representing so large a number of nations that its like was not to be seen again until the signing of the Treaty of Versailles. But at the time, war did not yet stalk Europe, setting the continental powers at odds, so the diplomatic representatives of Britain, Austro-Hungary, Belgium, Spain, France, Greece, Italy, Persia, and Russia were unanimous in demanding that the governor of Trebizond take steps to protect the Armenian population. All that the governor could promise was that, by virtue of his official obligations, he would protect the diplomatic corps, which was another way of saying that the consuls should mind their own business. Having incited the city's poor, the authorities handed out arms, and, under the protection of soldiers and the police, the massacres began, according to eyewitness accounts, at eleven o'clock on October 8, to the sound of trumpets. The same unusual detail can be found in all the accounts of the massacres of 1895, which took place the length and breadth of Anatolia, from Trebizond to Adana: a blare of trumpets heralded the assault on the Armenian districts.

According to the official dispatch sent to the government in Constantinople, 182 Armenians were killed that day and 11 Turks. The estimates of the European consulates range from 600 to 800 Armenians slain, but otherwise they are in agreement on one matter: not one Turk was killed. Both the Orthodox and the Catholic Armenian bishops kept exact records, with lists of the victims' names. They counted 591 Armenian dead, along with 81 victims from the surrounding villages. Accustomed to precise record keeping, the bishops also drew up a list of the material damage: 135 shops looted; 1,167 houses destroyed; and losses of 134,608 Turkish lira. At this point in the story, Misak Torlakian, or whoever else might tell it, will shrug. As if it was of any importance how many cursed Turkish lira the Armenians' damages amounted to! Compared with the more than two hundred thousand who were to die by the end of 1895.

At the age when other children sit bent over their schoolbooks, Misak Torlakian witnessed the first executions decided upon by the court of the Armenian revolutionaries. Shortly afterward, he was given his first pistol, with which he wounded himself when he cleaned it for the first time. It did not frighten him particularly. Accustomed to blood, he did not make any distinction between his own blood and that of others, and unlike Grandfather Setrak, who held blood in affectionate worship, Misak Torlakian held blood, even his own, in contempt. His own blood warmed and soothed Grandfather Setrak, who, like Misak Torlakian, had seen so much bloodshed on the other coast of Anatolia. His own blood burdened Misak Torlakian. He would prick his legs, ropy with varicose veins, the consequence of long days lying in ambush in the mountains, and then he would watch, rocking back and forth, holding his forehead in his palms, as the blood trickled down to his ankles and shod the soles of his feet, like black socks. "There, you see," he would say. "It's too thick and too heavy. I have to strain for it to come out." This is why General Dro had such power over him because, unlike the others, who at such times moved away, believing him to be insane, the general, who was otherwise restless, would sit down and watch him in silence, overwhelmed by the same fascination with blood. When the blood, reaching the gaps between his toes, dried and blackened, General Dro would say, "Enough, Misak." Torlakian would give a start, look around him in bewilderment, as if awakening from sleep; and coming to his senses, with a certain amount of sadness he would take the strips of lint the general handed him and bind them tightly below his knees. He would then rise to his feet with a fresh and inexplicable liveliness; he would stamp his blood-caked feet on the floor, the way one might stamp off snow on entering a house.

Not inexplicably, his contempt for blood was accompanied by an attraction to all the things that brought death. As I said, at the age of twelve, Misak received his first pistol, from his uncle Manuk Aslanian. It was the only weapon he ever received as a gift; the others he acquired for himself, offering in return his own life and, with indifference, reckoning that the price he paid was lower than the value of what he received. In exchange for a carbine and bandolier of bullets to replace his pistol, at the age of fifteen he became a courier for the partisans in the mountains. Misak acted as a guide for the cargos of arms bought in Tiflis and Baku and smuggled over the mountainous borders.

Misak then fulfilled another dream, for which he once again offered his life in exchange, impassively placing it in mortal danger. He learned to fire a cannon, and, what is more, he was given command of his own cannon. But on the mountain paths, too narrow for a man to walk alongside a mule, the *fedayi* did not possess such a weapon. He obtained false papers, under a Turkish name, and at the age of nineteen joined the Ottoman artillery. His commanders marveled at his skill in handling weapons but without wondering where such a young man could have acquired such knowledge. And so it was that Misak Torlakian, a kind of Gavroche of the anti-Ottoman guerrilla fighters, rose to the rank of sergeant in the Ottoman Army, commanding a garrison of twenty artillerymen in the western fort of the city of Erzerum.

Once war broke out, Misak Torlakian's game of serving in the army came to an end. The tragic situation tore the masks from people's faces, and by the autumn of 1914, Misak Torlakian could no longer pretend. The Armenians conscripted into the Ottoman Army were stripped of their arms and sent to do hard labor on the railway lines. Many of them were killed before they reached the places to which they had been assigned. The others were worked to death. Misak filled a knapsack with as many bullets as he could carry, and slinging a rifle over his shoulder, he abandoned the fort in Erzerum under cover of darkness, returning to his native places by paths known to him alone. "Desertion" is probably not the most appropriate word for what he did since Misak did not run away—he never did that, not even in extreme situations; he merely reverted to being himself, tearing off his military stripes and donning the sheepskin jacket of the mountain partisans.

The time is January 1915. Misak Torlakian, raised in the midst of the avengers, decides to become an avenger himself. He builds a den in a cave up in the mountains, and beneath the snowy peaks he waits for the Turkish armies to withdraw after their defeat at the hands of the Russians. He then makes a decision so bold and so reckless that only solitude and youth could have inspired it: he decides to kill Enver Pasha, the commander of the defeated Ottoman Army and minister of defense in the government of the Young Turks. Calculating that Enver Pasha will cross the passes near his village in order to reach Trebizond and thence Constantinople by sea, Misak Torlakian lies in ambush, scanning the horizon. The stubbornness of his mind outstripped the powers of his body since his legs, as I said, were to be left permanently infirm from his lying frozen and motionless, and not even the torture of slicing and bleeding them would ever cure them.

We cannot know how the history of the twentieth century might have changed if Enver Pasha had ordered his weary and demoralized army to take the road through the pass to Trebizond and had come within range of Misak Torlakian's rifle at least for a second. But Enver Pasha—the diminutive commander who dreamed of being a Napoleon or Frederick the Great but who, after the defeat at Sarıkamış, where more than four-fifths of his one hundred thousand soldiers had perished from typhus and the freezing cold, like the army of his imperial idol a hundred years previously, was no longer so proud and reckless— sniffing the snowy peaks, probably sensed the danger. So he decided to abandon the road to the sea. He went via Sivas to central Anatolia and kept to the paved roads, although they were more inconvenient for his exhausted army and for his own high-heeled, feminine boots, but which at least had the advantage of open and therefore safer plateaus all around. Having returned to the capital, embarrassed by his own weakness and, like the other members of the triumvirate, Talaat and Djemal, seething with a thirst for revenge, Enver Pasha gave his first order: complete the process of disarming all the Armenian soldiers in the imperial army and transfer them to labor brigades.

Misak Torlakian remained in his mountain hideaway until the coming of spring. He finally realized that his wait was pointless and descended to the plain. It was there that he learned of the order to deport and execute the Armenian men in the labor brigades. He crossed the mountains once again, descended to the port of Trebizond, and found work as a sailor on a ship taking cereals across the Black Sea to Batumi. Thence Misak Torlakian traveled to Tiflis, where he met up with the political groups of the Armenian Revolutionary Federation, who pointed him to Yerevan and suggested he gather volunteers to join the tsar's army and assist in the liberation of the Armenians of the Ottoman Empire. He should do so as quickly as possible, before the Young Turks could put into practice their plan to deport and exterminate the Armenians of the eastern *vilayets*. Misak Torlakian was in a state of overexcitement, compared with which madness seemed like tranquility. He was forever to feel it thereafter, the same as General Dro did, especially when he had to persuade others to join him unto death. He recruited some fifty volunteers, cobbled together a platoon, and placed himself in the vanguard of the Russian troops. At the beginning of December 1915, leading the armies and casting himself madly into battle, Misak was the first to enter Trebizond after its abandonment by the Ottoman Army, which was incapable of withstanding the Russian juggernaut. He went to the Armenian quarter; he entered the coffeehouses; he searched the churches. Everywhere was deserted; the houses had been ransacked, the shop counters thrown to the floor, the doors of the churches ripped off their hinges, and the altars burned. But not because of the war since the rest of Trebizond's ten thousand houses were intact. From two or three stray people in rags, who crept mad-eyed past the blackened, bloodied walls of the Armenian quarter, Misak learned that the twelve hundred Armenian families of Trebizond had been driven out of the city. At the crossroads, criers with big drums had announced, shouting for all to hear, that by order of the Sublime Porte all of the Armenians were to take provisions for the journey and as many belongings as they could carry, and then they were to assemble at the southern edge of the city, where they would be mustered into convoys. Whoever disobeyed the order and was found in his house after sunset or anywhere other than the place from which the convoys were to set out would be shot or hanged in a public square to serve as an example to others. Those who wished to leave their children with Turkish families could do so, but the children would first be given over to the army, which would then allocate the children for adoption, making sure that the new families would not be known to the natural parents.

The convoys set out at the end of June 1915. So that the regular troops of the Turkish Army would not waste their time marshaling and escorting the convoys, they were accompanied by special troops. The idea of creating a force of irregular troops came from Dr. Nazim, one of the leaders of the İttihad, or Committee of Union and Progress, and, by an irony of fate, the minister of education. The special forces were to wreak havoc on the helpless deportees. The irregular troops—or rather the hordes intent on pillage, rape, and murder—were recruited from among prisoners who were released from jail if they enlisted. The prisoners readily accepted, and, as the bloody waters of the Euphrates and the carnage by the roadsides and the mass graves of Deir-ez-Zor were to prove, they diligently performed the task assigned to them. And when even they wearied of so much killing and raping, when there was nothing left for them to pillage, they simply abandoned the convoys, leaving them prey to the bands of Kurds who followed silently and patiently at a distance, waiting for the moment when they could fall upon the helpless masses. These were the same bands who, alongside the inhabitants of the slums, looted the abandoned Armenian houses and profaned the churches, ripping the gold frames from the icons and stealing the silver candlesticks. Finally, without even knowing why, or probably without any reason at all, they burned the churches to the ground.

Misak Torlakian was to discover all these things from the testimonies brought before the imperial court martial that was to rule on the Trebizond massacres in 1919. He learned that after they left the city, the men were separated from the women and children, and the women were then robbed and raped. He learned that some of the women were loaded onto barges, strangled, and thrown into the sea. He learned that before reaching Erzincan, most of those in the convoys died of hunger and exhaustion. The verdict passed by the court martial on May 22, 1919, was unanimous: the ringleaders of the massacres were sentenced to death. But this sentence, like many others passed by the court martial after the war, was never put into effect. Those convicted were helped to leave the empire by sea, in vessels placed at their disposal by none other than the ambassadors of European countries. Nevertheless, the sentence was to be executed in a manner that history was to judge in various ways but which those around Misak Torlakian and those who listened to the stories of the Trebizond massacres could categorize only as an act of justice.

In the vanguard of Russian troops, Misak Torlakian had arrived first but still too late. In Trebizond there was nothing he could do except weep or wreak blind vengeance on anybody who crossed his path. Since he chose to do neither of these, all that remained was to seek out survivors in the surrounding countryside. The convoys had left on June 25, so he could no longer catch up with them. When he was confronted with those silent streets, the smashed windows, the reek of burning that not even the wind could dispel, the overturned carts, and the stench of corpses, the first thing that came to his mind was to look for his family. We follow Misak Torlakian as he rides to his village, some six miles to the south, near the foot of the mountains. All their lives, the old folk of my childhood were haunted by searching, the same as they were haunted by the sound of the trumpets that they, in their childhoods, had heard in various places but that were always heralding the same danger. They were haunted not by the search for good fortune or the search to save their own lives but the search for others. Since the destruction and dispersal of 1895 and above all since 1915, a century has passed, but there are still grandchildren and great-grandchildren who are searching for each other. Fathers and brothers searched for daughters and sisters in the harems. Parents sought their children in the orphanages. Husbands searched for wives in the weaving factories of Aleppo and Damascus, where hundreds of women worked as slaves. Letters crisscrossed the globe. Questions were murmured in fear-stifled voices on the decks of ships and in the camps of the survivors. Desperate or resigned announcements were published in the pages of the Armenian newspapers on every continent. In my family, many sought one another; sometimes they found each other, even thousands of miles away, but most of the time they did not. Hundreds of thousands of families sought their members; a people searching for each other, after so many tragedies, for that reason seldom had the repose to find each other.

The image of a man who comes to a stop at the edge of a destroyed village is common to many of the stories told over coffee by the old folk of my childhood who fled to the mountains and returned to their native places in the second half of 1915. Apart from a few details, the stories resemble each other so closely that as we recount Misak Torlakian's return, it is as if we tell all the stories simultaneously. As I said, the only difference is in the detail. However, Misak Torlakian's story has something extra, something that most of the stories do not have, or that, if they do have it, is not so intense: hatred. The story of Misak Torlakian is not the story of a life but the story of a feeling. The thirst for revenge. The disregard of every precaution. The reckless act. For example, there is what he did on the afternoon of December 14, 1915. Misak walked reeling along the village lanes. He wanted to stop at the doors and shout, but he felt that it was futile. Their house had been ransacked, the doors had been wrenched from their hinges, the pillows slashed open, the floorboards ripped up, the pottery smashed. Those who had done the ransacking had had plenty of time; they had nothing to fear since the owners could not possibly return. Probably the moment when the hatred burst its dam was when he entered the room of his younger brother and sister and saw the splintered beds, the jumbled sheets, the broken toys. Misak leapt on his horse and galloped for two days and two nights without stopping until he caught up with the retreating Turkish Army at the pass. These were places he knew well. He followed the troops at a crawling pace. Under cover of darkness, when the time was ripe, Misak leapt from his hiding place onto the back of the endmost horseman, bashed him over the head, and dragged him back to his den in the same cave where he had waited in vain for Enver Pasha. Nobody turned back to look for that Turk, who, given his rank, turned out to be nobody of importance. But history has recorded his name: Ismail Bey. From him Misak discovered that the man responsible for the massacres in Trebizond was the governor, Djemal Azmi. It was also then that Misak heard for the first time the name of Behbud Khan Javanshir, an Azeri. Then, for weeks on end, driving Ismail from behind and tying him up at night so that he could not escape, Misak searched the mountains for his partisans.

Soon, Misak Torlakian's group came to number hundreds of partisans. They joined sides with the Russian Army in a deluded attempt to liberate the lands inhabited by the Armenians. Weakened by turmoil within the empire, by lack of food and munitions, and also by the soldiers' increasingly revolutionary mood, the tsar's army had ceased to be a trustworthy ally, and after Kerensky's provisional government took power, a retreat on all fronts began. Misak and his men followed the retreating army from the port of Trebizond, which the Turks quickly reoccupied. He crossed the sea to Batumi and thence took the road to Tiflis, which he had traveled once before. There he mustered a division of around a thousand soldiers, which in Yerevan joined the army of the fledgling republic. He fought against the Ottoman Army once again, this time under the command of General Dro, at Kars, at Alexandropol, at Etchmiadzin. He fell into an ambush with seven of his soldiers and, having been wounded, he held out until the general's troops regained their positions.

Dro asked him to remain in the ranks of the Armenian Army. But the First World War was over, and Misak Torlakian believed that what Armenia needed was administrators and skilled diplomats more than warriors. That the fledgling Armenia had a lack of administrators is proven by the manner in which the country was organized. As for diplomacy, in order to understand why the republic enjoyed so little support on the part of the Allied chancelleries, it is enough to cite that the Armenians turned up to the peace talks in two rival factions, not to mention their demand to rebuild a Greater Armenia as large as the kingdom of the Bagratids a thousand years previously. The Armenian warriors had done enough to ensure their fame, but they proved too few to stop the Russian and Ottoman Empires, now reinvigorated by socialist and republican movements, which, as they whirled in their waltz around each other, ground away the frail body of Armenia.

In the devastated yard of his house, Misak Torlakian had sworn an oath of vengeance. Among his own people, the oath could never be fulfilled. And so, barely having recovered from the wounds he had suffered in the battles of spring 1918, he set off for Constantinople. He sojourned for a few months in the ports of the Crimea, where he did everything he could to earn some money, from trading in tobacco to trafficking in foreign currency.

In the meantime, the war had ended. Foreign soldiers patrolled the streets of Constantinople. In 1919, under pressure from the Allies, the new Turkish authorities tried those responsible for the massacre of the Armenians before a court martial but not before spiriting the accused out of the country shortly beforehand. On the night of November 1, 1918, on board the *Lorelei*, a vessel under a German flag, the İttihad leaders departed for Malta and thence to various cities of Europe, mainly in Germany, Austria, and Italy.

On July 5, 1919, the five judges of the court martial unanimously found the leaders of the İttihad guilty of the mass murder of the Armenians. Sentenced to death were Talaat Pasha, the former grand vizier; Enver Pasha, the former minister of war; Djemal Pasha, the former minister of the navy; and Dr. Nazim, the former minister of education and creator of the special forces. At two separate trials, dealing with the massacres in the *vilayets* of Trebizond and Kharput, the governor of Trebizond, Djemal Azmi, and Behaeddin Shakir were found guilty and sentenced to death. After Kemal Pasha Atatürk unleashed his revolution and rekindled Turkish nationalism, sorely hit by defeat in the war, the zeal of the court martial judges waned. On February 9, 1920, the court martial in Constantinople handed a five-year sentence to Oğuz Bey, who on April 24, 1915, had headed the operation to kidnap a large number of Armenian intellectuals from the imperial capital, later killing many of them, including Daniel Varujan, the Armenians' greatest poet, aged just thirty-one. After that, the trials ended once and for all. Against the backdrop of the Treaty of Sèvres, which demanded the annexation of the eastern provinces of the Ottoman Empire to the new Armenian Republic, anti-Armenian feelings among Turkish political leaders and the heads of the army were rekindled.

The new authorities carried out none of the death sentences handed down to the leaders of the İttihad. The Turkish government never demanded their extradition from the countries to which they had fled, nor did the authorities of the countries in question, particularly Turkey's former allies, take it upon themselves to send them back to face their punishment.

When I first leafed through my grandfather's notes, which he and his brother-in-law, my godfather Sahag Sheitanian, used to study late at night, I did not understand much. They were a few yellowing pages sewn into a cardboard folder. It was clear that the pages had been bound in the folder with the object of preserving them for a long time. The notes were written entirely in Armenian script, apart from the years, which were in Arabic numerals. On the cover of the folder, written in block letters using a broad-nibbed pen, was a single word: Nemesis. I did not know anybody by that name or anything the word might refer to. And because I leafed through the folder hurriedly, during a short moment when Grandfather forgot to lock his bedside cupboard, I was afraid to ask. Perhaps it was a name after all, although it did not sound Armenian. I found the answer in the *Larousse* that Uncle Kevork sent all the way from Los Angeles: "Nemesis: ancient Greek goddess of revenge . . ."

The folder contained a number of pages written with a nib pen: lists of names, in two columns, and between them, joining the pairs of names, were recorded years. The names meant nothing to me. The ones in the first column sounded strange; all of them ended with "pasha." These names were followed by arrows, each with a year inscribed above it, and then other names, in the right-hand column, this time Armenian:

March 15, 1921, Berlin
Talaat Pasha → Soghomon Tehlirian

December 6, 1921, Rome
Said Halim Pasha → Arshavir Shiragian

June 25, 1922, Tbilisi
Djemal Pasha → Stepan Dzaghigian

April 17, 1922, Berlin
Behaeddin Shakir → Aram Yerganian, Arshavir Shiragian

April 17, 1922, Berlin
Djemal Azmi → Aram Yerganian, Arshavir Shiragian

June 19, 1920, Tbilisi
Fath Ali Khan Khoiski → Aram Yerganian

July 18, 1921, Constantinople
Behbud Khan Javanshir → Misak Torlakian

Many decades passed before I was able to understand the connection among those names. In a way, the cardboard folder was one of the protagonists of my childhood. Grandfather took it out of the cupboard only at night, when I ought to have been fast asleep. Adults often forget children's fears and curiosity. They forget that children rummage through every drawer, among papers; that they understand to the best of their intelligence, not daring to ask; and above all that they eavesdrop. This was what I did, pressing my eye to the crack in the door, fascinated by the whispers of my grandfather and his brother-in-law Sahag Sheitanian, as they bent over the folder with the yellowing pages, adding a newspaper clipping or a letter sent from far away.

There were no signs next to the foreign names. Later I understood that there was no need for any signs since all of them were dead. To the right of many of the Armenian names were inscribed signs that looked like crosses. But a few still had no sign next to their names. Among them was the name of Misak Torlakian, which I encountered there for the first time, during my childhood, via those yellowing pages. I only ever heard his name spoken once, in circumstances I shall later describe. But I never saw him. He came into *The Book of Whispers* with the strange circumstance of dying rather than living. And in fact he is far more present than might be believed since none of us knew how closely my grand-father's life was connected to that of Misak Torlakian.

The time is 1965, and the place is Focşani, a small town in southern Mol-davia, with thirty-nine thousand inhabitants and a food and a textile industry. The child I was then leafs through the pages of the cardboard folder, puzzled by the names, the dates, the various cities. The time is also 1895 and the place Trebizond, the city whitened by the salt sea breezes, where the trumpets blare, like they did before the walls of Jericho came tumbling down. The trumpets herald the massacres against the Armenians, massacres that will end three long months later, to the sound of the same apocalyptic trumpet blasts, in Adana, on the southern Mediterranean coast of Anatolia. More than two thousand vil-lages will be wiped from the map, and as if coursing along a trough between the two seas, the blood of more than two hundred thousand people will flow. The time is also 1915 and the place Gyushana, at the foot of the mountains; a village has been destroyed, reeking of death and charred wood, the same as all over eastern Anatolia and along the sandy desert roads leading down to Deir-ez-Zor. The time is also 1920, and Armen Garo, the leader of the men who attacked the Imperial Ottoman Bank headquarters two and a half decades before, now orga-nizes, assisted by Shahan Natali, the first Special Mission (Hadug Kordz), for which a special corps (Hadug Marmin) has been created. The fact that we are simultaneously in four different times—listening to the trumpets of Trebizond, the drums of the heralds that announced the order for the Armenian popula-tion to assemble at dawn twenty years later, with bundles for the journey, and the speeches at the Dashnak congress of the 1920s, which declared the need to exact a "toll of blood"—and the fact that all these have as their backdrop the whispers of my childhood should not surprise us. Time is a wild beast that runs with an arched back and whose paws leave a trail of prints, one after the other. But still, time runs on all four paws at once. How ridiculous, awkward, and un-true it would be to picture time only as the instant you are now experiencing. Obviously, I am simplifying things by comparing time with a four-legged crea-ture; time is something completely out of the ordinary, a millipede with a lion's head and a bird's beak but with a disdainful human smile, sprinkling the blood with healing powder or else raking it up so that it will not dry.

In its relentlessness and scale, Armen Garo's operation of 1920 can be com-pared with the operation Simon Wiesenthal was to carry out decades later, whose aim was not to leave unpunished any of the crimes committed against the Jewish people during the Second World War. But whereas Simon Wiesen-thal acted in the broad light of day, operation Nemesis remained completely un-known for another half a century, which is to say, until after the death of Misak Torlakian and my grandfather Garabet Vosganian.

If Simon Wiesenthal, a former prisoner at Mauthausen, thereby possessed all the more legitimacy to create a network dedicated to hunting down Nazi war criminals, then Armen Garo was certainly the man best suited to run the Special Mission. Karekin Pastermadjian by his real name, with a degree in agronomy from the University of Nancy, Armen Garo was just twenty-three when, on August 26, 1896, at the head of a commando of twenty-five men, he occupied the Imperial Ottoman Bank headquarters and demanded an end to the massacres of the Armenians. In his proclamation to the embassies of Constantinople, Armen Garo was to utter the historic words that marked not only the end of the nineteenth century, but also the century to come: "We are not criminals. But mankind's criminal indifference has pushed us to this act." Fearful that the whole treasury would be blown to smithereens and under pressure from the foreign powers, which had deposits of their own in the safes of the Ottoman Bank, Abdul Hamid, the bloody sultan, agreed to put a stop to anti-Armenian atrocities and allowed the commandos to be evacuated to Marseille on the personal yacht of the bank's director, Sir Edgar Vincent, but only after the surviving seventeen, having entrusted their three dead and six wounded to the Armenian community and keeping their revolvers, left on the shore their forty-five bombs and eleven kilos of dynamite, more than enough to reduce the treasury of the Sublime Porte to rubble.

Armen Garo drew up a preliminary list of more than six hundred names, men he regarded as guilty for the massacres and deportations. Since the number of the guilty far exceeded their resources to do justice, Armen Garo and Shahan Natali reduced the list to forty-one names. They then reduced the list again to the seven principal criminals, who had in any event been sentenced to death by the court martial. He obtained photographs of them and their families, which he gave to the group entrusted with carrying out the sentence.

The group took the name Nemesis: the goddess of revenge.

Over the course of the next two years, six of the seven criminals on Armen Garo's list were executed, shot by members of the Nemesis special corps. The exception was Enver Pasha, the minister of war, who, having once escaped Misak Torlakian's rifle, did not escape a second time; it was an Armenian who pulled the trigger but not a member of the Nemesis group, rather a soldier in the Bolshevik army.

The man who headed every list, regardless of how long it might be, was Talaat Pasha, minister of the interior. He was the one who had drawn up and sent by his own hand—a habit since his days as a humble post office telegraph operator—the telegram to the *vilayets* inhabited by Armenians, the telegram that unleashed the deportations. The man chosen to punish him was Soghomon

Tehlirian, a student who had served valiantly with the partisans. Above all, he had begun the series of revenge executions on his own initiative, in 1919, killing Talaat's agent Harutiun Mgrditchian with a bullet to the heart. It was Harutiun Mgrditchian who drew up the first list of three hundred Armenian intellectuals to be arrested on April 24, 1915, most of whom were subsequently murdered. April 24 was thus the day when the eventual killing of the Armenians' greatest poet, Daniel Varujan, was set in motion. And the Day of the Poet's Death became the day when Armenians all over the world commemorated the 1915 Genocide, which began in 1895 and continued in various forms until 1922.

Tehlirian completed his mission after a search that lasted almost six months. In Berlin, close to his home on Uhlanstraße, Talaat was shot with one bullet to the back of the neck. Soghomon Tehlirian first walked past him to make sure he had identified him correctly. He then spun around and pointed his pistol. It is said that first he called out to Talaat so that he would turn around, look in his eyes, and know exactly what was happening. But that is just a story; Tehlirian was interested in only one thing: not to miss. So preoccupied was he with not missing that he botched his escape. He was immediately grabbed by passersby who had rushed to the fallen man. Tehlirian put up no resistance but merely whispered, over and over again, "I'm Armenian. He's a Turk. Leave me alone; it's nothing to do with you . . ."

In Berlin Soghomon Tehlirian's trial began, and Armenians from all over the world came to the German capital, asking to testify or at least to attend the proceedings. Meanwhile, Armen Garo was training the other members of the group. Although he asked to be assigned to punish Djemal Azmi, the man chiefly responsible for the Trebizond massacres, Misak Torlakian was tasked with killing Behbud Khan Javanshir, who, as Azerbaijani minister of the interior, had been responsible for the Baku massacres of September 1918, which claimed the lives of more than twenty thousand Armenians.

Misak Torlakian, following the example of Armen Garo, put together his own team, which, in order not to draw attention, had to be no larger than two or three men. He chose Harutiun Harutiunian, a comrade in arms alongside whom he had fought under the command of General Dro and who had been in the same hospital ward as he after they were wounded in the battle at the foot of Mount Ararat. He then chose Yervant Fundukian, who, like Misak, was originally from around Trebizond and had also fought in Dro's army. The three conducted an intensive three-month search for Behbud Khan. But when they found him, it was by a fluke: a Dashnak militant recognized him on a street in Constantinople. It turned out that Behbud Khan was there in the capacity of trade representative of the Bolshevik government.

They drew straws: Harutiun Harutiunian and Yervant Fundukian were to shadow him and find the most suitable place, and Misak Torlakian was to carry out the sentence. A week later, the members of the commando group decided that the best place to shoot Behbud Khan would be in front of the Pera Palace Hotel, where he was staying. As two limousines waited for him at the entrance to the hotel at all times and as he never arrived or left at fixed times, the three members of the group decided to sit in the café opposite, playing endless games of backgammon or *gyulbahar*.

MISAK'S DREAM. On the evening of June 18, 1921, the two limousines pulled up at the entrance of the Pera Palace Hotel as usual. Behbud Khan got out, accompanied by five men wearing Bolshevik caps. But instead of entering the hotel, they decided to take a walk in the nearby public park, on the banks of the Bosphorus, where they sat down at a table by a refreshment kiosk. The three Armenians left the café, mingling with the crowd, breathlessly stalking Behbud for hours and hours. It was not until nightfall that the six men stood up from the table and headed back to the hotel. Running slantwise across the street, between the motorcars, Misak Torlakian caught up with them on the broad sidewalk in front of the hotel.

Behbud Khan turned and looked at him. This sequence is common to all the stories of the members of Nemesis: the moment in which the two, the man about to kill and the man about to be killed, look at each other. There is nothing more enlightening or more murderous than the two men looking at each other. The man about to die senses the danger, and his eyes fasten on the other man. And the man with the gun, despite his determination and tireless months of stalking, has a moment's hesitation.

The story of men is a story of deeds, of memorable words, but above all it is a story of looks, hard to describe, hard to decipher, but no less intense, no less real for all that. As for the looks of my old folks I know only what the photographs have recorded, looks deep and seldom smiling. As to the looks of my dead, insofar as a record has come down to us, I know only that they outlived the body; many of them died with their eyes wide open. And the photographs of the withered dead, with their gaping eyes, are all the more disturbing since, shrunken with hunger, exhaustion, and disease, their eyes remained whole, appearing huge and greedy in the diminished faces.

When Soghomon Tehlirian and Arshavir Shiragian and Aram Yerganian and Stepan Dzaghigian approached with their whitened knuckles gripping their Mauser pistols, the look in their eyes must have been insane because without fail they drew the attention of the men they pursued. It must have been the same with Misak Torlakian, too, as he approached and pointed his pistol at Behbud Khan before firing two bullets into his chest.

On the broad sidewalk in front of the Pera Palace Hotel, there were many passersby, enticed there by the breeze off the Bosphorus. On hearing the shots, they did whatever they could to save their lives: some dived onto the ground and lay flat; others hid behind trees or parked cars. Taking advantage of the panic, Misak Torlakian made a run for it, darting around the corner of the building and losing himself in the web of lanes behind the hotel.

We are the only ones who follow him. The others, probably ashamed of the fear that overcame them, are picking themselves up off the ground, coming out from behind trees and cars. They approach the man who has been shot, not knowing whether he is dead or just wounded. Misak Torlakian runs, still gripping his pistol, until he thinks himself secure in the darkness of the back streets. He stops to catch his breath, pressing himself up against a wall and closing his eyes. It is now that he remembers the dream. He was running barefoot over a plain, the plain at the foot of the mountains. His village was smoking, but to get there, Misak Torlakian would have to have changed direction since the village was always on the other side, although it was hard to say where because he could see it smoking whether he turned left or whether he turned right. But he could not turn aside to reach his village and help his parents and brothers and sisters because he could hear the rumble of hooves approaching. It was the white stallion of Behbud Khan Javanshir, becoming larger and larger, looming threateningly. He came at a gallop, but it was as if he did not wish to reach him; he merely harried him ceaselessly. The Azeri was wounded, his clothes were soaked in blood, but instead of weakening him, it only made him all the more ferocious. Misak was holding his pistol, and as he ran, he turned around to shoot. But his pistol turned into a whip, and he could not fire any bullet from it. He stumbled and fell; he got up and continued to run; his heart thudded to the rhythm of the galloping white stallion, which was smeared with the blood of Behbud Khan.

In the moment when Misak opens his eyes, he understands the full horror of the dream. "I didn't kill him!" something within him cries. He sees the revolver in his hand, and the fact that he did not throw it away as he fled is for him a second sign. Still half-submerged within the dream, still shaken by the revelation, he decided then and there that the only way to release himself from the dream would be to return to the esplanade of the Pera Palace Hotel in search of Behbud Khan Javanshir. Probably he then submerged himself in the dream once more since his recklessness showed not one flicker of lucidity. Misak Torlakian ran back the way he had come. The crowd thought he was somebody who had come running to see what had happened. But then he started to shove aside the people standing around the man on the ground. First, Misak Torlakian fired a shot in the air, and the shocked, frightened people drew back. Misak remained face to face with the fallen man. He fired another shot. This time, the barrel of his revolver did not turn into a whip; the shot rang out in his dream and in reality simultaneously; and the galloping of the stallion, which he had heard behind him and which thudded in his heart and eardrums, ceased. Returning to reality, Misak Torlakian fired another shot in the air to stop the stupefied bystanders rushing at him. Now lucid and as a result intent on saving his own skin, he fled among the cars, stepping on the people who had thrown themselves on the ground. One of the men wearing a Bolshevik cap tried to grab his leg; Misak Torlakian fired at him, wounding him. He took cover behind a car and kept his pistol at the ready until he saw that some French military policemen had appeared among the people who surrounded him. He placed his Mauser on the hood of the car and came out with his hands up. They handcuffed him. He was buffeted by the people who had been ashamed of their fear up until then and who were now punishing the man who had caused that fear. In the confusion, the French military policeman lost the keys to the handcuffs. The next morning, before Misak Torlakian could write out his statement, they had to remove his handcuffs using a saw.

6.

The Book of Whispers also had a silent part, which people hid not only from me or from those who preyed on them, but also from each other and even from themselves. The silent part of *The Book of Whispers*, which I could sense without being able to describe it, I discovered much later, when the people no longer seemed to be fearful. Not because the new times no longer had people who preyed on others, but because we had not yet become accustomed to them.

Aurel (or Aurică) Dimofte died on December 4, 1957, almost a year before I was born. His wife Anica used to bring us milk and cheese once a week, on Wednesdays, from Vadu Roșca. One day, she brought us a plate of *kollyva*, sprinkled with walnuts and cinnamon. I had not eaten boiled wheat prepared that way before. The Armenians are not great ones for *kollyva*. When the dead are commemorated, the women make a kind of halva from semolina fried in a pan, into which they mix walnuts roasted on the stove and raisins. Something similar to *kollyva* is made only at Christmas and Easter. It is called *anush-abur*. Like *kollyva* it is made from hulled wheat, but it is juicier and contains dried fruit. It is a sign of birth and resurrection rather than death, although all these things are connected, of course. The *anush-abur* was boiled in large cauldrons, spread on trays to cool, and then served in bowls, like a dessert. Probably because they had so many hundreds of thousands of dead to commemorate at the same time, the old folk of my childhood were forced to reduce their debts to the dead.

I ate *kollyva* for the soul of Aurel Dimofte. It was sweet and good. Grandmother asked Mrs. Anica whether many people had come to the memorial service. Anica burst into tears and told us that there had been no memorial service. They had placed the *kollyva* on the table, they had laid a place for Our Lord Jesus Christ, they had recited the Lord's Prayer, and they had sung "Eternal Remembrance," lifting their plates and rocking them in their joined hands. It was because Aurel Dimofte did not have a grave with a cross, and the priest was afraid to recite his name at the altar, in front of everybody. After Mrs. Anica left, her shoulder yokes swaying, Grandfather said to Grandmother in a whisper, "Don't ask her about her husband again. He was one of the ones in the uprising . . . Who knows where his bones are rotting now."

Without understanding them very well, I had heard Grandfather utter the same words before. They had been sitting under the apricot tree in the courtyard, drinking coffee and talking, looking through old photographs, reading the newspapers. They had uttered a name and then fell silent. And like the priest saying amen after the choir had sung, Grandfather had said, with a sigh, "Who knows where his bones are rotting now." I pictured bleached bones, crumbling at the side of the road, but I gradually came to know that, the same as water that overflows its banks finally drains into the earth, so too the dead still have enough life in them to scrabble at the soil and to seep down through its cracks, like a sleeping man reaching out his hand for the blanket to cover himself. The earth does not resist; it is good, it is healing, and it covers all.

To clarify this snatch of childhood memory, in which the only thing clear was the sweet taste of *kollyva*, I set out in search of Aurel Dimofte.

The time is 1949. The time is also November 1957, and the icy north wind has already begun to blow across the Siret floodplains, bringing an early winter. The time is also 1964, and with the other characters of *The Book of Whispers* I am eating the sticky *kollyva* with my fingers. And the time is November 2005; the times seem to have changed, except that the burden of being repressed and of speaking in a whisper has turned into the burden of being free and of not knowing what to say because you do not know what to say first.

In 1949, the characters are not those of *The Book of Whispers*; they dwell outside it. What is more, some of them are among those who decry books and goad the masses to toss them into the flames. In *The Book of Whispers* you will find the story of the day when they burned the books. But just as on the day of the Massacre of the Innocents they were unable to kill all the innocents, on the day of the burning of the books they were unable to destroy all the books. In the war between the authorities and books, although only the books perished, the authorities never won. It was because people wrote more than they had the strength to forget.

On seeing how arduous was their war against books, the new authorities discovered a new means for victory, one they had not previously employed: to set books against each other. Just as birds, when they fly across the seas, need a scrap of land on which to alight, so too books, in order to survive, in order to breathe, need people to read them, to open their covers, to turn their pages. Otherwise, just as happened to the new, raucous books written in the times when the people spoke in a whisper, they die of exhaustion, suffocated. But in those days the smoke of the pyres had not yet dispersed, the new books had only just begun to be written, and the Communist authorities were tugging at the end of eternity like a bell rope, flushed and bursting with pride at the deafening clangs. And as if that were not enough, they swelled the din with untiring staccato clapping and applause.

This must have been what it was like at the Plenary of the Central Committee of the Romanian Workers Party on March 3–5, when they decided to collec-
tivize agriculture. The wealthier peasantry had been worn down by the system
of compulsory quotas. The refusal to meet quotas was treated as sabotage and
machination against the state, punishable by confiscation of property and imprisonment. The same peasantry now had to be persuaded to relinquish their
land and a part of their agricultural annexes to the collective farms. The peasantry was divided into three categories: poor, middling, and wealthy, or kulaks.
The poor peasants were easily dealt with, but savage persecution began against
the middling peasants and kulaks. The Constanța region was the first to report
that collectivization was complete, followed by Bărăgan and Siret. All kinds of
rumors circulated about what had become of those who opposed, rumors that
were not groundless and that were spread deliberately in order to instill fear.

In the Galați region, Suraia and Vadu Roșca, the lands to the south of Focșani, were left till last. The locals were stubborn, there were few poor peasants,
and Suraia was one of the most populous settlements of Bărăgan.

There were two kinds of heralds of collectivization: the agitators and the advisers. A handful would be from the village, but most of them were outsiders.
Poor, landless peasants, accustomed to backbreaking toil and often relying on
alms; Gypsies who lived in shacks; and day laborers were given new clothes and
caps, and they were armed with cudgels cut from the trunks of old osiers. When
the first trucks arrived in Suraia, bringing food and drink—round loaves of black
bread; thick, salty sausages; barrels of wine to be doled out in tin cups—some
rejoiced, pushing and shoving to eat and drink right there by the truck. But
others felt only gloom. Nothing is for free, they thought, and indeed, those who
thought that way, even if they had not crowded around the truck to eat bread
and sausage, were to pay a heavy price for what they had not eaten.

We talk. The time is still November, but the year is 2005. Vasile Niculiță,
Gheorghe Porumboiu, Damian Pătrașcu, Sterian (or Sterică) Răducanu,
Gheorghe Mocanu. The host, Damian Pătrașcu's daughter, has brought cups of
wine and thick slices of *cozonac*. They make the sign of the cross and moisten
their lips with the wine, but after that they neither drink nor eat. They gaze with
mistrust, but also with curiosity, at the grown man, hardly able to believe that
somebody has come all the way from Bucharest to listen to their story. Except
that I am not a grown man, although I am six feet tall and have white, thinning
hair; nor am I from Bucharest but from seven miles north of there, from Focșani; and I am the child eating *kollyva* in remembrance of Aurel Dimofte.

All of a sudden Vasile Niculiță turns to the man on his right, Gheorghe Mocanu, and says, "Get out of here, you!" And then he says to me, "I'm not saying

anything till you get him out of here." Gheorghe Mocanu sits in embarrassment, prepared for anything, to remain or to be shoved outside. I was unable
to tell them apart, so old and withered were they, and I did not know why some
of the survivors of those times should stay but not others. But they knew. "Because he was one of the advisers," explained Porumboiu. "That means he was
one of the ones who went into people's yards and threatened them with jail and
crushed their fingers in the door if they didn't sign up for the collective."

A large number of agitators and advisers arrived, they recount, each talking
over the top of the other. It started in front of Culae Focşa's house, in Suraia.
There were about eight hundred agitators and advisers, says Sterian Răducanu.
No there weren't, says Ghiţă Porumboiu; there were about two hundred. Anyway, there were a lot of them, they finally agree. After they finished doling out
the food and drink and inflaming people's minds, they began entering the yards.
Those who didn't want to sign they bundled onto the trucks and drove down the
lane to the edge of the village, to make them afraid.

Vasile Niculiţă planted himself in front of Culae Focşa's house, barring
schoolteacher Gheorghe Mocanu's way. "Him who you see here, not some bas-
tard brought in from elsewhere, he was one of our own, Suraia born and bred,
and he led them from house to house, saying, 'He's all right, treat him nice;
he's stubborn, a few of you should go in at the same time, frighten his mis-
sus and kids, but guard yourselves.' That's what he said. What did he mean by
that 'Guard yourselves'? When you enter my yard, why should you guard yourself if your intention is good? Go on, tell me!" Gheorghe Mocanu, as old and
shrunken as the rest of them, says nothing, and as they wave their arms, he sits
with his shoulders hunched and his hands folded in his lap. "That's what I asked
him, I did. 'What are you doing bursting into folks' houses?' And he says, 'So
that you can sign the form to join the collective.' Back then," explained Vasile
Niculiţă, "he didn't play dumb like he does now; he had a voice because there
were a dozen of them backing him up, armed with clubs. So I say, 'Give me the
form to read!' 'Let's go inside your house,' says Mocanu, 'so you can read it in
detail.' I wasn't daft. I knew if I went inside, I wouldn't be able to get away. 'No,
give it to me here, in the lane. There's no reason that the woman and kids should
know.' And he gave me it. And he says, 'Sign here, at the bottom.' But I say, 'Let
me read it first! What's this "I hereby voluntarily join the collective farm"?' And
this Mocanu here he nods his head, as if to say it's obvious. But I say, 'If it's vol-
untary, why are you forcing us?' I didn't expect him to say anything to that; I
clouted him in the head and ran off into the thickets by the Siret floodplain.
And from there I went to my relatives' in Galaţi."

Vasile Niculiţă seemed to cool down after he remembered how he had clouted Gheorghe Mocanu over the head; he stopped asking for him to be thrown outside and even forgot about him. But Mocanu had not forgotten. He had not forgotten that he had had to pick himself up off the ground, his head ringing, in front of the Gypsies that made up his team of agitators. The next day, the advisers and agitators started going around in larger gangs. And when they came face to face with villagers armed with clubs, axes, and shovels, the outsiders retreated. Not having land, hearth, wife, and children to protect, they weren't as grimly determined as the locals. The villagers didn't chase them but merely watched in silence as they fled over the bridge.

But their joy was short-lived. On the evening of November 27, the ZIL jeeps of the militia arrived and drove through the village, while Dumitru Arbănaș, the mayor the Communists had appointed from among the village's more feckless, indigent inhabitants, pointed out the houses where the ringleaders of the rebellion lived. The peasants who hadn't had the good sense to flee were arrested at gunpoint—those who had been in the war recognized the machine guns and knew how unforgiving they were; they were tied up and thrown into trucks, like sheep, one on top of the other. The ones who fled were caught in the thickets, in the undergrowth, at their kinfolks'; or else they appeared later, brought out of hiding by hunger, cold, and fear or by the fear of their kinfolks, who had heard that they would suffer the same fate as the fugitives, or worse, if they hid them in their barns or cellars.

"Whenever I came home from Galați," says Sterian Răducanu, "I'd stop off at Piscu's; he was my godfather. The lamp would be lit, and he'd give me bread and bacon and a cup of wine. But this time, when I came back, there was no lamp lit, and the gate was padlocked. I pressed myself up against the fence because there was a truck with a tarpaulin at the end of the lane, a ZIL truck, and in each truck there were twenty or thirty men. Folk were peering from behind their fences, afraid. Nobody was brave enough to open his gate. I barely got away before somebody in one of the trucks saw me. But back at Vadu Roșca the sky was red, like it was ablaze. The village is burning, I said to myself; they've set fire to the village."

The advisers had learned their lesson and now stuck together. They went around in gangs, by the dozen. Two or three days after what happened in Suraia, leaving time for the rumors to spread fear among the people, they arrived in Vadu Roșca. They came in two trucks and went to the schoolhouse to spend the night there. But they had made something of an error: the people of Vadu Roșca were not frightened but enraged. The news had traveled quickly, and the peasants gathered with axes and torches, forcing them to take shelter in the school. That was what saved them because the peasants were loath to throw rocks at the school windows, let alone stuff burning straw in the keyholes to suffocate them inside or burn them out like rats, which is what the agitators themselves would have done. If it had been the mayor's office, they wouldn't have had any qualms; it would have been all the same to them; but because it was the school, or if it had been the church, they held back; they surrounded the building, holding their torches. If you hadn't known what was happening, you would have thought it was the Feast of St. Ignatius, the longest night of the year, when fires are lit so that the light might vanquish the darkness.

If it was a religious feast, torches and all, then it turned bad. The peasants overturned the vehicles in which the outsiders had arrived; they rolled them into the Siret River. The fires drove people to reckless deeds. Iosandru Areaua slashed the tarpaulin with his knife, as if he were stabbing the outsiders themselves; he raised the blade in the firelight, as if expecting thick blood to stream from it.

"It was wonderful," recounts Damian Pătrașcu; "Lord, how wonderful it was! I hadn't seen so many torches since I was little, on Easter night, just after the war. It was during the famine, but folk still found enough flour to make flat cakes, to plant lighted candles in them, and to send them floating down the Siret. And each recited the names of his dead, and the people all wept together; some wept in grief for the departed, some wept for joy that others were still here, but I wept for them all because I was still a young lad and I couldn't really tell the dead from the living. I like to look at people's faces in the firelight. They're nicer than in the sunlight, more alive. That's what I remember best about that night: the people's faces, lit up sharply, like they were carved from wood. But nicest of all was Dana, Radu's daughter, with her headscarf pushed back onto her shoulders and her hair falling loose; how beautiful she was! And she was laughing with her head thrown back. Who knows what those bastards in the schoolhouse must have thought, peeping out of the windows in fright? Especially when they heard the violin and the big drum, like on New Year's Eve. Aurel Dimofte was the first to throw his cap on the ground and shout, 'Let's dance, brothers!' And he stamped on the icy lane with his boot, and Ionuț Cristea joined in with him. 'You're right!' said Dumitru Stan. The fire had robbed us of our wits; we'd been carried away by the fear. And then all the others joined in: Ion Areaua; Crăciun's sons, Dumitru and Toader; Stroie; Marinică Mihai. It was their dance with death; they didn't know it at the time, but maybe they sensed it. We joined together in a circle dance, like on a holiday. We were dancing and whooping; we were inflamed. The next day, half of us were crawling on the ground, covered in blood, deafened by the rat-tat-tat of the machine guns, those of us that death hadn't already taken."

The circle dance broke up after midnight and the people went to their houses, washing their hands of the agitators in the belief that they had given them enough of a fright. When they saw the circle dance break up and the fires go out, when they heard the big drum move off into the distance, the outsiders poured out of the schoolhouse, thanking their gods that the tires on one of their trucks were still intact. They all piled into the truck, leaving behind their cudgels in their haste, but not forgetting that they had been in fear of being burned alive and not forgetting to wreak a terrible vengeance later.

Dumitru (Niţu) Stan had been at Stalingrad. He sensed that the calm the next morning boded ill. What was more, Sterică Răducanu had come to him before daybreak with the following news: "There's some cars with officers in Suraia. They're lying in wait. And when I came back from Piscu to tell our folk still in the village that they were going to come down on us again, a wee civilian in a navy blue overcoat pops out of the darkness, at the edge of the village, and he says, 'Where did you come from?' 'From Vadu Roşca.' He had a loud voice, but he couldn't say his words properly." He was to recognize that voice again later, more readily than the face, which he had not seen very well in the darkness. He was to hear it over and over again, until it became an obsession, making him relive that night and its terrors thousands of times, terrors associated with the lisping voice of Nicolae Ceauşescu, sent from Bucharest to quell once and for all the peasant rebellions in the Siret floodplain. "What you doing here at this hour?" "I've come to fetch my wife!" He said it without knowing whether the other man would believe it or not. But little did Nicolae Ceauşescu care about that. "What's going on in Vadu Roşca? Are there people with pitchforks and axes?" Sterică Răducanu turned aside a little to see whether the red glow of the torches from the circle dance was visible against the sky. But the sky was like a motionless, pitch-black bell. So he turned back and said, "Haven't seen any." "You smoke?" "I smoke." Ceauşescu gave him a cigarette and held out a lighted match. He held the flame of the match next to his face for a long moment. "He was getting a good look at you so that he'd remember your face," says Damian Pătraşcu. "That's what I thought too. He wanted a good look, but not only that. My legs had gone limp; I could barely stand up. 'Can I go now?' I said. 'Yes.' I left, tottering. He was watching me from behind, and that's why I didn't break into a run until I was a fair distance away. He didn't believe me. He knew I'd lied to him. When he looked at me holding the lighted match by my eyes, he wasn't looking me straight in the eye; he was looking to see whether my hand was trembling as I held the cigarette to my mouth. In other words, I was afraid because I was lying. He knew I'd lied to him." "Then why didn't he arrest you right there?" "Why would he waste time with me? He knew they'd arrest me the next day or the next week and that I didn't have anywhere to run. None of us had anywhere to run; they caught us and arrested us all, and a good few more besides."

Niṭu Stan listened to what Sterică Răducanu said and knew they were going to come; he knew there would be no way back. He went to fetch the others. In the lane, his son, who could not have been more than six years old, caught up with him and gave him the big knife for slaughtering pigs: "Dad, take the knife; don't let them kill you . . ." They gathered at the edge of the village, on the side where the road led to Focșani. Each had brought something: old carts, thick planks, boulders, unvarnished oak tables, stumps. "Climb up the bell tower," Niṭu Stan told Ionuṭ Cristea. "If you see them coming, ring the bell." "I told him. Better I hadn't; it breaks my heart even now because I sent him to his death. And he took Vasile Haralambie with him, a young lad not even twelve years old. Poor lad. When they found him at the bottom of the ladder, in the bell tower, they beat him black and blue. He trembled in a fever until Epiphany." It was silent, so there was still time. They positioned themselves by the truck the agitators had left there the night before. Next to it they piled up everything they could lay their hands on: carts, stones, cauldrons, tree stumps; they leaned planks against the barricade and plugged the gaps with wads of oakum to make it hold. Radu's daughter Dana climbed up onto the hood of the truck and crazily waved her headscarf like a flag. Niṭu Stan still had his old rifle, from the war, but it didn't have any bullets, so he shook it like a club. The others had brought whatever they had been able to lay their hands on around their yards: axes, pitchforks, shovels, cudgels for chasing off wolves, hedging bills for cutting withes. The old folks were standing in the church porch, praying; the women were whimpering behind the fences; and every able-bodied man in the village was at the barricade, scanning the horizon with narrowed eyes.

The wind had died down; not a dog was barking; not a bird's wing was flapping; not a crow was croaking. None spoke. Suddenly, the ground began to rumble. They felt it through the soles of their feet before they heard it with their ears. The branches of the trees began to tremble, although the wind had not stirred. "The tanks are coming," Niṭu Stan said to himself. He thought he had said it out loud, but looking around him, he saw the others were puzzled; they couldn't understand it, and all of a sudden he felt sorry for them and wanted to shout for them to run away—their barricade of planks and oakum was useless before tank tracks; they couldn't hide behind it from shells and machine guns— but before his voice could make itself heard, the large bell began to toll. The men looked at the bell tower in terror. The women's sobs caught in their throats. Dimofte's wife, who was large with child, covered her mouth with her hand. The old folks made the sign of the cross over and over again. The trembling of the air from the tolling bell combined with the trembling of the earth, and the people no longer knew which tremor was cursed and which was blessed.

Radu's daughter Dana was the first to see them. They were like a green streak across the horizon, looming larger and larger. With a single glance Nițu Stan knew that the stock of his rifle and the men's axes and tools, good for turning the earth and clearing the forest, would be completely useless against the two tanks that were nearing the bridge, surrounded by trucks of the kind that, as far as he could remember, were used for carrying heavy machine guns.

The tanks came to a stop and with them the trucks, after turning around so that their rear ends faced the barricade. The tarpaulins of the trucks were lifted to reveal the long perforated barrels of machine guns. From the trucks alighted a number of men in Securitate uniforms, led by the short man in the navy blue overcoat, wearing a military cap. They went to stand next to the tanks. The short man raised his hand, and the villagers thought he wished to address them. The bells stopped ringing.

The villagers took a step back. Next to Nițu Stan, Costică Arbănaș fell to his knees and bared his breast, tearing open his shirt. Next to him were Aurică Dimofte, Stroie Crăciun, and, gripping an axe, Ion Areaua. Then the others came, one by one. Perched on the cab of the overturned truck, Radu's daughter Dana stood stock still, clasping her headscarf to her chest.

Then everything happened at once. With a jerk, Ceaușescu lowered his arm. The bell started ringing once more, drowning out the whistling of the bullets, though flame and lead from the muzzles of the guns filled the air. The first to fall was Aurel Dimofte, first to his knees, looking in bewilderment at the blood gushing from beneath his palms, which were pressed to his chest, and then he collapsed onto his back, with his knees still bent, thrown backward by the bullets still cramming his body. Radu's daughter Dana was flung into the air like a rag doll. The force of the bullets left her hanging in midair for an instant, and then she crashed down onto the hood of the truck, her arms spread wide. As if by a miracle, the bullets missed the kneeling Costică Arbănaș, and he remained there motionless, empty-eyed, not even aware of his own sobs. Nițu Stan threw himself to the ground and rolled to the edge of the road, but then he went back to drag Stroie Crăciun after him, who kept moaning, "Stan, don't leave me . . ." until the blood gushed from his mouth, suffocating him. The bell continued to toll, and it was as if its chimes flowed over the whole church, turning its walls into resounding brass. The tolling bell became so deafening that the church rose into the air, its foundations floated on the horizon, and the sky itself became a brass dome, with a huge clapper striking the walls of the heavens. The machine guns strafed the belfry, but the bell continued to toll. The tanks slowly moved forward and then squashed the barricade like a molehill; planks and dead bodies clattered over the armor. The wounded dragged themselves out of the path of the tanks before they could be crushed under the tracks. All the machine guns were now firing at the belfry. A gigantic battle was being waged between the tolling bell and the whizzing bullets. Even if by now the belfry had been reduced to a tatter, its plaster pocked by the bullets, shredded, stifled in the powdery smoke of the whitewash, the bell rang on victorious until the cannon of one of the tanks slowly rose and released a shell aimed at its very heart. Ionuț Cristea had certainly been killed long before, and the bell had gone on swinging, battling alone. The tank finally killed the bell too.

After the bell fell silent, the bullets fell silent too. "It went on and on," they remember. "We thought they were going to kill us all." "It lasted just ten minutes," say others. "It was like hail, like a summer storm."

When everything else had fallen silent, the moans of the wounded could be heard. Up until then they had been moving targets, disjointed wads of cloth writhing with arms outstretched, kneeling, pressed up against each other (depending on which the bullets had hit), crawling, scrabbling with their fingernails, seeking a foothold on the icy ground, as if climbing a ladder; the weaker sought shelter in the arms of the stronger, the bloodied in other bloodied arms; the blood had begun to mingle so that you no longer knew which wound belonged to whom.

"We were huddling under the stairs of the belfry," recalls Vasile Haralambie. "By then the bell was tolling on its own, as if it were alive. Ionuț was dead, his hands still gripping the rope, his face and clothes covered in blood and plaster. With his white face, he was like one of the saints painted on the walls inside the church. Then there was a loud noise and a flash like a lightning bolt. The bell fell silent. The soldiers came. One of them took out his bayonet and unclasped Ionuț's fingers with the blade, to stop the rope from swinging."

"Then, like in a dream, I heard the bell tolling," remembers Ioniță Haralambie. "I thought I was dead and that I had arrived in heaven, but when I opened my eyes, I saw them climbing out of the trucks and coming toward us, the wounded, with their guns pointing at our foreheads."

"They poked the barrels of their guns in our necks, those of us who were still alive, to frighten us to death, like it hadn't been enough already," remembers Marin Crăciun. "With their rifles or with their boots they rolled over the ones who were dead so they were facing upward. But they didn't bother to close their eyes. Death had come so suddenly that they'd died with their eyes open."

"I was kneeling there, and I couldn't stop crying," remembers Costică Arbănaș. "Some people wet their pants in fear; I wet my face. I was sobbing, choking on my tears. They were scalding, gushing like blood. Two of them came up to me, and one poked his gun in my forehead, but the other one said, 'Leave him, can't you see he's lost his mind?' And I stayed like that until the afternoon; I can't remember anything else except that I toppled like a log in the lane and couldn't stop crying. When I came around, it was evening and it was deserted; there was nothing but a sickly smell of sticky blood. There was a light in the schoolhouse. I went over and looked through the window. They were beating people. The dead were in another room, piled on top of each other in a heap. It was only then, from the horror of it, that I stopped crying . . ."

"They dragged Cristea out of the belfry," remembers Lazăr Sandu, "and they threw him down from the roof. He fell with a thud, like a dead bird. Then they took his arms and dragged him into the middle of the lane. The place where he fell was like a red mushroom, and then there was a red trail, broken in the places where his head had jolted over some stones, like they were using him to mark out a boundary."

"Marinică Mihai died huddled up," remembers Ioniță Haralambie. "You'd have thought he was a sleeping baby if there hadn't been a puddle of blood under him. His dog came up to him and licked his cheek but felt he was cold and still. Then the dog sniffed the blood and started to lap it up. The poor dog wasn't to blame; the blood was still warm, and the dog—who knows? The dog sensed the blood was alive, and he recognized it. It lapped the blood for a long time; nobody chased it away . . ."

"My mother was holding her belly," says Ionică Dimofte, "so that she wouldn't miscarry me. I know all these things only from what I've heard in snatches because nobody wanted to tell the whole story from beginning to end. They'd say a few words, and then they'd freeze, as if it were happening all over again. They didn't want to remember, and that's why I began to remember it for them, when I was still in my mother's womb. My father, Aurică Dimofte, was one of the first to die. They took them, and they threw them on top of each other, like sacks from the mill. They heaped them in a classroom and left them there till nightfall. They loaded them on a truck after that, and nobody knows where they took them. It was so that people wouldn't be able to mourn them openly. They buried them elsewhere, at the edge of a graveyard, without crosses, without a priest, without candles. Later, some God-fearing people planted some makeshift wooden crosses there for them. It wasn't until after the revolution, thirty-five years later, that I found my father's grave, in Florești. I spoke to the old gravediggers. I recognized him by his clothes. He had a broad leather girdle in which he kept the deeds to his land. They buried him deeds and all. When I got the land back, I had to go to court with witnesses because the deeds had rotted. And I also recognized him by the bullet hole in his forehead."

"They thought I was dead," remembers Marin Crăciun. "They went to pick me up, and I moved. Then the wee man in the blue overcoat kicked me in the belly and swore at me. But I didn't say anything. I just groaned and cursed him in my mind. I cursed him really bad, him and his whole family. I cursed him for all our dead. And that's what happened in the end. Some say that it was because of the revolution, that Iliescu had to shoot him so that he wouldn't talk, but it's not true. It was because of that winter and our curse, the curse of the people of Vadu Roşca. Here's the proof: he died the same way he killed Dimofte's son Aurel, with the Securitate battalion from Tecuci. He fell to his knees exactly the same way, and they shot him so many times that he fell backward. He died on his knees like Aurică Dimofte. Except that Ceauşescu died a cursed death, with his hands tied behind his back. He couldn't even hold his hands to his chest, like Aurică had when he tried to push the gushing blood back inside. Don't ask me anything else because I can't hear; they beat me over the head so much that all I can hear is a buzzing to this day. The last thing I can remember hearing on this earth is Ceauşescu's swear word."

"They interrogated us for two days. They'd ask us a question, and then they'd beat us," remembers Damian Pătraşcu. "After they beat one unconscious, they'd grab another. Who started the rebellion? Had anybody come from anywhere else? Did we know anything about the groups in the mountains? Who were the leaders? Who thought of the barricade? And then they'd start all over again. After that they took us to Galaţi. They kept kicking me in the mouth until they broke all my teeth. In the middle of January the trial began at the Constanţa Military Tribunal. Then they took us to Gherla Jail. All of us from the ages of fifteen to twenty-five they locked up for the crime of terrorism against the state, Article 199 of the Penal Code. For two years we didn't have the right to receive food parcels or letters. Our kin mourned us as if we were dead. And if we weren't dead, then what were we?"

"They let us out in the autumn of 1964," remembers Gheorghe Porumboiu. "When we arrived in the village, nobody came out to greet us. People looked at us over their fences. Only the dogs came up to us and licked our legs. We were trembling with cold and hunger and from all the beatings. But the dogs recognized us; they didn't bark at us. In the end, the people got used to us. But we didn't tell any stories, and nobody asked us. This is the first time."

"When the floods came this summer," remembers Marin Crăciun, "folk said the Good Lord wanted to wash away the dried blood that was left in the cracks between the stones from fifty years ago. It's been fifty years. But that wasn't it because blood has to be softened with blood before you can wash it away. That's why the floodwaters took Marin Dobre, Ionel Crăciun, Neculai Dimofte, and a few others who were on the barricade and who survived back then, in '57. They escaped the bullets, but they didn't escape the onrush of the water because they were old and couldn't cling on to anything. But I say that God couldn't do a thing like that. He knows that the blood is in our minds first of all. Maybe the wound will heal when He takes all of us, one by one, but maybe not even then . . ."

In Vadu Roşca eighteen were convicted; in Suraia, fifteen; in Răstoaca, forty; and in Cudalbi, fifty. They were young; they did not die in prison. But nor can the life they lived after that be called life. On the morning of December 4, 1957, there were forty-eight wounded in Vadu Roşca. There were ten dead: eight men; a woman, Radu's daughter Dana; and a bell.

All were buried in unmarked graves, the same as the other dead, our dead, whom we commemorate on April 24, the day of the massacres. But they were also uncommemorated and therefore even more alone. I was a child. Their graves were scattered, and nobody knew where to shed a tear for them. The others were still in prison, in Gherla and Aiud. Dimofte's wife Anica and the other widows had to do backbreaking work to bring up their orphaned children, who for a long time afterward were treated as the offspring of bandits. But what mattered to me at the time, in the shade of the walnut tree at the back of the house, was the *kollyva*, which was so good and so sweet, all the sweeter since the dead remained uncommemorated and therefore pined for this world.

" If there are dead who are uncommemorated," said Grandfather Garabet, "and if their graves are unknown and have no cross to mark them, then we shall commemorate them along with our dead who have no cross." And because Dimofte's wife Anica knew figures better than letters, thanks to her trade in cheese, she recited their names for Grandfather, who wrote them down on a scrap of paper: Dana Radu, Aurel Dimofte, Ionuţ Cristea, Dumitru Marin, Ion Arcan, Dumitru Crăciun, Toader Crăciun, Stroie Crăciun, Marin Mihai.

Afterward Grandfather squeezed those names among the names of our dead written on the sheets of paper, although there was room for them since the diminished bodies of the dead, especially those without a cross and without commemoration, occupy less room in this world than the bodies of the living.

When I talked about the mages of my birth, I committed an injustice in naming only Angheluţă, whose fingers, dusted with white icing sugar, shone like candles; Bobîrcă, enveloped in shadows that rustled like the glossy black olives he endlessly poured from one sack into another; Mercan, the merchant who dealt in air; and the halva vendor, who receded into the distance as he came nearer and who cut slices as even as time.

The gifts of the mages also included the salted, toasted walnuts of Harutiun

Frenkian. Of all of them, he was the one who kept the secret of the mages most closely. All I can remember about him are his gifts.

In *The Book of Whispers* I have kept for myself the place usually reserved for the storyteller, who is a chance presence only. I am not a character in *The Book of Whispers*, and in my absence things would have turned out exactly the same. The only difference between myself and the others who read this book is that I am its first reader, a condition that, as I said, is merely one of chance.

Or perhaps the destiny of being the storyteller—which is to say, the first reader—was bestowed on me by the Four Mages—of Light, of Shadow, of Air, and of Time—as well as by the fifth mage, about whom we shall now learn: Harutiun Frenkian, the mage of fruit.

These are the fruits of our customs, Grandfather Garabet would say. First of all, the apricot. Apricot orchards have always blossomed on the plains below Mount Ararat, and it was not until the early Middle Ages that the first travelers took apricot stones and branches to the rest of Europe. When every living creature was given its name in unchanging Latin, the apricot received the name *Prunus armeniaca*. Its color is part of the Armenian flag, a background against which the other national symbols stand out in relief. Naturally, that is not why an old apricot tree stood in the middle of our yard in Focşani, but that must be why we loved it more than any other fruit tree and why the soft couches on which we chatted and drank coffee were placed beneath its round canopy. Grandfather used to say the orange of the apricot is the color that can be seen from the farthest distance and that such a choice proved wise for a scattered people like ours.

The second fruit is the pomegranate. The fruit of fruits. As round as an apple, as large as a quince, as tart as the fruits of Jerusalem, with a skin as thick as a tropical fruit's and seeds clustered like grapes, which, when crushed in the fist, release a juice the color of blood. Through our blood we are kin to the pomegranate. The apricot is the fruit of those who stay together. But the pomegranate is the fruit of solitude and exodus. Since it has blood like a human, the pomegranate can also have feelings. The pomegranate can suffer from yearning. It can abide untouched for long periods. Of all the fruits, and given its blood, it is the one most suggestive of sacrifice. And of all the fruits of the earth, it was the pomegranate that chose to accompany my old folks' old folks on the roads of death, down to Deir-ez-Zor in the deserts of Mesopotamia. Sahag Sheitanian, the husband of my grandmother's sister, my godfather, told the story of the pomegranates that the fleshless ghosts of the convoys passed from hand to hand, each taking one seed and keeping it on his tongue, enigmatically cool in the scorching heat of the sands. It is because it served as nourishment for the convoys in the desert that the pomegranate has precisely three hundred and sixty-five seeds, one for each day of the year. Had God not chosen the lamb among all other living creatures as the symbol of sacrifice, He would certainly have chosen the pomegranate. You cannot bite into the pomegranate as you might an apple; you cannot pluck its berries as you might a bunch of grapes; you cannot eat it all at once as you might a strawberry; but you can drink its blood, as the Tuareg still drink the blood of lambs in the desert to survive. The pomegranate: the silent lamb of the Lord.

And then there are the fruits that are houses: the walnut, the hazelnut, the almond, the pistachio. The walnut was my first teacher. I clambered among its thick branches, and we read together. I turned the pages for both of us, and that is why the iodine stained my fingers with its yellowish-green, stickily darkening blood. I wanted to be a walnut tree when I grew up; I did not think that growing up could mean anything other than being a walnut tree. It was not true, as I later learned. The tree that was born in the same moment as I was in fact a birch.

The mages were not the discoverers of amber, myrrh, gold, or cakes of salt. Nor was Harutiun Frenkian, the mage of fruits, the discover of fruit houses, of concealed fruits. They arrived with my old folk and with the oriental scents that wafted around them, seeping through the cracks in the door. In the native places, everything—pilaf, *imam bayildi* with minced meat between roast eggplants, *sarayli*, sweets, halva, baklava—had the taste of toasted hazelnuts or walnuts, around which swirled the aroma of ground coffee boiled over a low flame in a narrow-necked copper pot. On the convoys' journey to Deir-ez-Zor, the sand crunched between the teeth like ground, roasted hazelnuts, remembered Sahag Sheitanian. "When we were dizzy with hunger," he said, "we thought the sand dunes were mounds of ground walnuts or hazelnuts or that they were semolina halva, in which bronze-colored chips of toasted hazelnuts glinted. The mirage was of no use to us. It didn't allay our hunger. It just made us all the thirstier." We have a photograph of Grandfather Garabet and Uncle Sahag, with Grandmother Arshaluis and her sister Armenuhi, the two of them plump in their bathing suits, with trunks that covered their thighs but tops that left their chubby shoulders bare. On the back it says, "Us at Carmen Sylva, 1932." "We had a hard time convincing you, Sahag," laughed Grandfather, "to tread on the sand. You walked on tiptoes, like you were treading on hot coals." "It was like semolina halva," repeated Sahag. "There were many of us, and in that place we needed a lot of halva for our requiems. Even the scorching heat smelled of toasted walnuts."

And so it was that the aroma of toasted walnuts everywhere followed the sweat, the blood, the sticky palms, the fevered brows. Death, when it came, smelled of toasted walnuts, and when we commemorate our dead, their memory also smells of toasted walnuts, ground and mixed into semolina halva.

From the bowl of walnuts that was my birth gift, every May, the widow of Father Dajad Aslanian took a few walnuts for the requiem halva. Up until 1968, the year when Grandfather died, if we also count the funeral and the forty-day memorial service, the walnuts were added to the commemorative halva ten times. Grandfather thought it was appropriate that Father Dajad's widow should make the halva since she was the last to be included in the will of old man Harutiun, or Hartin, as his name was written in Romanian documents to make it easier to pronounce.

THE STORY OF HARTIN FRENKIAN'S WILL. Usually the story of a will begins after the death of the person who writes it; as a joke the bequeather hides the will from his legatees or couches it in cryptic language, to reward the cleverest and most persevering of them, and not to mention disputes over wills. None of these were the case with old man Hartin's will. For more than two decades, Hartin Frenkian and his will lived intertwined lives. When he wrote it in August 1938, Hartin Frenkian had no way of knowing his will, the most generous ever conceived in twentieth-century Romania, would die with him. Alongside the arms of General Dro, Mantu's tuba, Misak Torlakian's Mauser, and the bell of Vadu Roşca church, old man Hartin's will is one of the protagonists of *The Book of Whispers*.

Like many of the characters in this book, Harutiun Frenkian was born in Anatolia, in the year 1873 and in the town of Erzerum to be precise. The year of his birth has no other purpose here than to help us calculate that when he appeared at my birth, *daidai* Hartin, the mage of fruit, was already eighty-five. He was therefore not only the most generous, but also the oldest of the mages.

In the autumn of 1914, the Ottoman Army began conscripting men in preparation for the war. If we follow Hartin Frenkian from the crossroad where he decided to take the seemingly reckless course of going overseas under an assumed Greek name rather than to be enlisted along with the other Armenian men, then we will easily see he made the right choice. If we follow the other men from Erzerum, who did not come to the same crossroad, then this is what we will find: since the Turks were allies of the Central Powers, the men enlisted in Erzerum were sent to the Caucasian front to fight the Russians. In December 1914, the Armenian soldiers were withdrawn from the front, under suspicion of being in league with the Russians; by then, Armenian partisans were already fighting against the Turkish Army. The Armenian soldiers in the Turkish Army were disarmed in January 1915 and sent to labor camps. By the beginning of February, there was not one Armenian soldier in the Ottoman forces on the

Caucasian front. Disarmed, wearing tattered uniforms with the epaulettes torn off, guarded by Turkish soldiers, the men returned to Erzerum. The foreign travelers and diplomats in the city gave accounts of the fate that befell many of them: eighty to a hundred men were taken from the camp, surrounded by Turkish soldiers and officers, and were shot and bayoneted to death. The remaining men were taken to Sebastia, along with another two thousand from other labor camps. Shackled together, they were sent over the mountains to the railways of the Bozanti region. In the mountains, with barely imaginable savagery, they were killed and hurled down precipices. Among the Armenians there are no survivors' accounts since there were no survivors. All we have is the manuscript written by Father Knel Kalemkelian, the bishop of Sebastia. Of the men enlisted in Erzerum in September 1914, not one escaped with his life. There are no indications of suicide attempts, and for this reason we may conclude that all were murdered. Death was everywhere. Suicide would have been a pointless gesture.

An Armenian first and an Armenian of Erzerum second, Hartin Frenkian had no intention of risking his life for the empire. He packed his bag one night in September 1914, boarded the train to Constantinople, and there he took work on a merchant vessel bound for Constanța. Since it is the only business you can start with little money and from which you can make fast earnings, especially when you have come from foreign parts and have the advantage of knowing the price differences among various goods and are gifted with a persuasive tongue, Hartin Frenkian cobbled together a shop for himself in Constanța, selling coffee, spices, and sweetmeats. He knew nothing about his family back home. In my childhood, I never heard him talk about the people back home. In my collection of stamps, steamed off envelopes, which stood in for a family album, I did not have any stamps from Turkey. We had nobody to write to in that country since there was nobody who could have answered. When he entered the city at the head of a Russian army in the winter of 1915, Misak Torlakian found only two families still alive, out of the fourteen thousand Armenian inhabitants of Trebizond, sitting dazed in the ruins of their houses. Of the forty thousand inhabitants of the Armenian villages around Trebizond, only a thousand still lived, hiding in the forests. At dusk, they came out to scavenge for food in the devastated villages, daring to show themselves only a few months later, when they saw the vanguard of the Russian troops. Erzerum was the *vilayet* of my grandfather Setrak Melikian and Hartin Frenkian; of the more than two hundred thousand Armenian inhabitants of the three cities of Erzerum, Erzinga, and Bayburt and the Armenian surrounding areas, including Zakar, the village of my mother's family, the vanguard led by Misak Torlakian found only twenty-two Armenian survivors, hiding in a church and praying to God that they be spared the fate of those in Urfa, where the Armenians were locked inside the church and burned alive. Dressed in rags, weak with hunger, and almost blind from the darkness of the crypts, the twenty-two Armenians were taken over the border to Yerevan by Misak's volunteers.

In the spring of 1916 Hartin Frenkian would not have found any living relative, neighbor, or acquaintance to write to among the more than two hundred thousand Armenian inhabitants of his native *vilayet*. The Ottoman authorities had foreseen such a situation as early as the beginning of 1915, just a few months after Frenkian had fled in fear of enlistment. It was called the plan to liquidate the Armenians and was conceived by Talaat, Behaeddin, and Nazim: "Families whose members manage to flee will be suppressed; measures will be taken to prevent any relations with our country." Almost a century later, we are able to testify that in this respect the governor of Erzerum staunchly did his duty.

Cut off from the world in which he had grown up, Hartin Frenkian toiled in the middle of the world that had received him, becoming a leading merchant in Constanţa after the First World War; he was even elected vice president of the city's Chamber of Commerce and Industry. He expanded his colonial goods store. He then founded a chain of stores and opened his own wholesale warehouses near the port. With the Great Depression looming, Hartin Frenkian made the business coup of his life: from America he imported unrefined sugar, which he decided to process himself. One after the other, he bought sugar factories at knockdown prices. The first was in Chitila, at the edge of Bucharest, which he chose because it was the same age as he, having been founded by Nicolae Bibescu in 1873. Then he bought factories in Timişoara and Arad. Not having a family of his own, his life was his ledgers, with their pages divided down the middle by a vertical line, with incomes in blue ink on the left and expenses in red ink on the right, and with the total at the bottom, in blue or red ink, depending on his luck. He was a good boss. He built houses for his workers; he helped them by paying wages in advance and giving them loans, particularly if they had children; he worked shoulder to shoulder with them. Behind the factory in Chitila he planted orchards of walnut and apple trees, among which he strolled with pleasure, picking and eating the fruit right there under the trees, with the same pleasure as when he was a child.

He became very rich. A part of his wealth remained in his sugar factories, in his beet fields, in his unrefined sugar warehouses, in the molasses trade he did with the distilleries and animal farms, and in his colonial goods stores in Bucharest and Constanţa. Apart from that, Hartin Frenkian remained faithful to his Anatolian upbringing, which held that the only genuine wealth is counted in gold and jewels, as these alone remain untarnished by time. That was what most of the Armenians from those impoverished lands did. In those lands, what little money they had was the more precious for being counted in gold pieces. And they were not wrong. When they saw the Red Army coming, it was not at all hard for them to stuff their jewels in a bag and set off for Constanța in the middle of the night, where they stowed them in the dark belly of Onik Tokatlian's vessel the *Transylvania*. Lying hidden all through the journey among the sacks of goods, which hid their glitter, the jewels alighted in Marseille, whence they traveled to North and South America. But the new times struck down the oldest Armenian families without mercy; their ancestors had arrived in the time of Alexander the Good and Stephen the Great or even earlier, before any *voivode* arrived in Moldavia to demand they seek their permission to trade, and all their money was tied up in manor houses and estates.

Hartin Frenkian's jewels were well guarded in safe number 78 of the Romanian Commercial Bank. In 1945, Onik Tokatlian urged Hartin Frenkian to leave Romania. Onik Tokatlian had the advantage over Hartin Frenkian, having seen during the war the effects of communism on its home ground in Odessa, Sevastapol, and Poti. But Hartin Frenkian refused. He thought himself too old to start life all over again. "And in the end," he told Onik Tokatlian, "it's too much to flee twice in one lifetime." And so Hartin Frenkian chose to remain faithful to his will.

He had indited it with nibbed pen in the summer of 1938, using lined paper so that the round, awkward letters of a man still not accustomed to the Latin alphabet after so many years would remain straight. Sometimes he forgot to indent the paragraphs or start sentences with a capital letter, but he did not make any spelling mistakes in Romanian and also displayed a mastery of the grammatical rules.

In his will, Hartin Frenkian requested that his goods be administered by a foundation to be named for him. But since Armenians are long-lived and death was tardy in arriving, he set up the foundation himself in 1943, endowing it with everything needful.

Hartin Frenkian's will had two provisos for its execution: the first was that he be dead, and the second was that the laws in effect when he made his fortune be unchanged. Unfortunately, neither of these conditions was met when the time came.

It was in 1948 that Hartin Frenkian realized for the first time that a tardy death could be as bad as an untimely death, like the one that had befallen his family in Erzerum. On June 11, 1948, the Nationalization Law was passed, giving the state title to Frenkian's factories. It was something new to him. He had put on his smoking jacket and gone to the Bourse, hoping to find out what was going on. But the authorities had surrounded the Bourse. The brokers had rushed outside, throwing away the money in their pockets in fear lest they be searched. On the sidewalk of Strada Doamnei there was a gleaming carpet of gold coins, guarded by soldiers, while the passersby gazed in astonishment. Troubled, Hartin Frenkian went back to Victory Avenue, to his three-story house at no. 72, in front of the Royal Palace. (Today, the spot where the house once stood is an open space populated by various statues.) The passersby looked in puzzlement at that tall man, who held his back straight despite his age and who was wearing a smoking jacket. He was a man in stark contrast to the drab gray clothes, the military tunics without epaulettes, the slouching walks, and the scuffed shoes that could now be seen on Victory Avenue, a street where fewer and fewer motorcars and carriages now passed and the people were more hurried and suspicious than before. In that moment, Hartin Frenkian began to live the life of his last will and testament. A young man stopped him, waving his arms in front of him and probably bringing him back to reality for the last time. "Why aren't you at the factory?" asked Frenkian, as if that still had any importance to him. "I've just come from the factory," the man said, as if trying to excuse himself. "They sent me to tell you not to go there any more. They're coming to arrest you. They're waiting for you at your house . . . They're look-ing for you everywhere." "And what is your name?" asked the old man calmly. "I'm Ştefan Niculescu, Mr. Frenkian. The stoker . . ." Hartin Frenkian nodded. "I know you. You're a hard-working lad. I've put you down for a tidy sum in my will. Use it wisely; open a workshop for yourself . . ."

The young man took him by the arm and diverted him away from his house. He took off his overalls and helped Hartin Frenkian to pull them on over his ele-gant jacket with the silk collar. After taking him past the Matache Market and then to the hotels by the Northern Station, the young man begged him once again to disappear and never come back. Hartin Frenkian was left sitting on a bench in the park opposite the portico of the Northern Station. He kept looking at the oily blue sleeves of the overalls he was now wearing. He was clutching to his chest the briefcase in which he kept his will, which contained a neat list of the numbers of the safe deposit boxes containing his jewels, share certificates, and treasury bonds.

Despite his being a man of seventy-five, or perhaps precisely because of that, his desire to live proved stronger than his bewilderment. Carefully looking around him, straightening the overalls that concealed his smoking jacket, Hartin Frenkian went into the station and bought a ticket to Focşani. He huddled on the wooden bench in the corner of a third-class compartment, giving a start whenever the door opened and every time the train stopped in a station, looking fearfully along the platform at the military patrols and breathing a sigh of relief when the train set in motion again. Frenkian did not know that he had nothing to fear, not because the rumor they were coming to arrest him was untrue but because the secret police had such a long list of people to arrest that they would hardly bother to search vile-smelling train carriages for him. His first impulse had been to give himself up and to explain, showing them his will, that he was not one of the exploiters since he had decided, in clause ten of the said will, to sell his factories and to share the money among his employees, each according to his wages and the number of years he had worked. But since they wanted to arrest him for what he had done during his lifetime rather than what he was to do after his death and since the will also included all his safe deposit box numbers and the names of the banks where they were held, Hartin Frenkian decided to abandon the plan. And a good job too: his will was worthless as long as he was alive, and the state had confiscated all his factories anyway; his generosity in sharing them with his workers would therefore have been treated as an attempt to loot state property.

After a train journey of more than five hours, among a swarming, raucous crowd, something thitherto unfamiliar to him, Harutiun Frenkian arrived in Focșani, got off the train on the side opposite to the station entrance, and walked to the Armenian cemetery, where he sat down on a bench beneath the chestnut trees in front of the chapel. As he waited for darkness to fall, he must have espied the Seferian vault, and he must have thought that had he followed Tokatlian's advice and left in 1945, he would now have been with Seferian in Buenos Aires, and the sale of his jewels would have provided him with a comfortable old age or—why not?—he could even have started a new business because nowhere in this world is there such abundance as to leave no room for spices from the Orient. We would be mistaken if we thought that he had any regrets. In the souls of my old folk I have sensed pain, melancholy, and lives not lived to the full, but I have never heard them voice any regret. They accepted life as it was, they did what they thought had to be done, and that was that. Aged seventy-five, Hartin Frenkian, rather than meditating on how and when death would arrive, must have been thinking about how he could fill the void of a death late in coming. He perhaps thought of old man Seferian, without envying the fact that his body was alive and walking around on the other side of the world while his tomb lay vacant on this side, and certainly without knowing that a portrait of Onik Tokatlian in dress uniform could be found within, lit by a votive lamp. After darkness fell, Hartin Frenkian walked down Cîmpineanu Street. He crossed the railway tracks and carried on down Tanners Street. He walked past a church, turned down Snowdrops Street, and then into a little street that bore a new name, significant to our story: "March 6, 1945, Street, the date when the first democratic government was established."

"What's with you, *baron* Harutiun?" Grandfather must have asked, in his surprise at seeing him. And Frenkian's answer must have compounded that surprise: "I'm here to rewrite my will . . ." As Frenkian was twenty years older than he, Grandfather might, for good reason, have believed that the old man had lost his mind. "You've come a hundred and twenty miles to rewrite your will . . ." Despite the unusual situation, Frenkian seemed very calm. "I have pen and ink, but I need a table at which to write . . . and a chair on which to sit . . ." "Couldn't you find a table and chair in Bucharest?" "Obviously not . . ."

Grandfather Garabet was about to ask him another question, but the old man held up his hand to stop him, sat down, took the will out of his briefcase, unscrewed the cap of his pot of ink, and asked to be left alone. There was no difficulty in that since everybody in the house was asleep at that hour. He then laid a few sheets of lined white paper on the table, dipped his pen into the inkpot, and wrote: "Codicil." For a time he gazed vacantly, in the light of the gas lamp, before lowering his eyes to his will, rereading it in full and without haste. Finally, he took up his pen and wrote: "I who am the undersigned Hartin B. Frenkian fully maintain the previous will and testament that I filed at the notary office of Ilfov Tribunal, registering petition no. 75075 on August 31, 1938, but with the following modifications and additions." He turned to Clause 10 of his will and read aloud: "As sole owner of all the shares in my companies, I enjoin that after the end of my life the universal legatee shall convene a general meeting to decide upon the liquidation of the companies. The sum resulting from the liquidation of the companies shall be divided among all the clerks in my employ at the time of my death, proportionally to the gross monthly wages of each." He then wrote in the codicil: "The stipulations laid out under Clause 10 of my will regarding my companies, my sugar factories in Chitila, Timișoara, and Arad, are hereby revoked." Then he went and knocked on a door: "Get up," he told my grandfather Garabet. "I need a witness." "Shall I call Sahag too?" asked Grandfather so that there would at least be someone else with whom he could make head and tail of it all later. "No. Sahag has a big mouth. So. Look here: written and signed by me this day of July 31, 1948, in Bucharest." Grandfather did not object to the time or the place, both of which were wrong, but that night, nothing else seemed to fit either. "It's to confuse them," explained Hartin Frenkian. "Let them believe I'll be in Bucharest on that date." "All right," agreed Grandfather. "But where will you be?" "In the mountains, up beyond Vidra. At Niculae Filimon's sheepfold. I'm going to become a shepherd. I'm positive they'll never think of looking for me up there." He carefully laid the sheets of paper one on top of the other inside his briefcase. Grandfather fetched himself a chair and sat down in front of him. "Who are 'they,' Uncle Hartin?" Frenkian leaned toward him across the table, and whereas he had been speaking in a whisper up to then, now he spoke almost silently: "The secret police . . . The truth is that they want to lay hands on me, to arrest me . . . It isn't enough that they've stolen my factories . . ." "A shepherd, you?" Hartin Frenkian shrugged. "In the end, what else are we, Garbis? What were my grandfather and your grandfather and your grandfather's grandfather if not a nation of shepherds? Maybe it would have been better if we had stayed up there in the mountains; we should never have come down to the plain, to the cities. Look how we ended up . . . What with one thing and another, I'm going to stay up there, above Vidra, until my affairs arrange themselves. How long can this madness possibly last? The Americans will come, and they'll chase away the Russians and all their Communists." "I should have fetched Sahag," said Grandfather. "He'd have liked that bit about the Americans." "I'll be off now," continued Hartin Frenkian. "Before people are out and about. Otherwise you'll find the secret police knocking on your door tomorrow. Have you got any gold?" "Where would I get gold?" shrugged Grandfather. "I paid all my gold to buy the land for this house, and the rest I spent on food. Sahag paid two gold Napoleons in Craiova for a sack of wheat . . ." On the threshold, Hartin, half a head taller (though Grandfather himself was six feet tall), straight-backed, white-haired, and with bushy eyebrows, laughed and patted him on the shoulder. "Garbis, my lad, I've got mounds of gold pieces and jewels; you could stick your arms in them as far as the shoulder. It's all written down here." He patted his briefcase. "That's why they're looking for me. And that's why they're not going to find me." He left before the break of day, with Grandfather following behind him. They took the first train to Odobeşti and then the narrow-gauge steam train that carried woodcutters up to Panciu, on the way to Vidra. "You go back home now. I'll manage. And in any event, it's better you don't know if anybody asks you. Filimon knows me. I sold him molasses for his animals. He won't trust you." Grandfather watched him walk into the distance, looking completely out of place in that rustic setting in his smoking jacket, now starting to look shabby, and his muddy gaiters, clutching his briefcase to his chest, like a schoolteacher.

The storyteller is now in some difficulty. He cannot follow Hartin Frenkian along the mountain paths from Vidra to Tulnici and then to the Putna Cataract by way of Lepşa. The paths are narrow, difficult to follow if you do not know them. The people in those parts are solitary and mistrustful. The summers are short and shady, the winters long and icy. The only thing we know about Niculae

Filimon's sheepfold is that his shepherds took their sheep from the hills up into the mountains, occasionally to Țifești, occasionally to Strãoane or Fitionești, occasionally to Crucea de Sus, climbing as far as Mount Nereju and sojourning under Moșinoaia Monastery. Hartin Frenkian finally found Niculae Filimon, or rather the sheep breeder found him, after learning that an old man wearing strange clothes had been asking about the sheepfold, knocking on people's doors and asking for a bed for the night, but preferring to sleep outside on the porch than to share a room inside with other people. He learned that the old man had a briefcase tied to his wrist with a thick piece of string but that it did not seem to have any money in it. The man seemed to be mad. But if he was mad, then he was not the only one; on seeing the madman in one-eyed Anghel's tavern, Filimon embraced him with the greatest respect. The other customers saw that Filimon showed equal respect in not sitting down until the old man had taken a seat, and when he left, he opened the door for him and went out behind him. With steep mountain trails in his Armenian blood, Hartin Frenkian climbed to the sheepfold and then followed the flock through the mountains and over the hills of the Carpathian bend. He wore a sheepskin coat over his smoking jacket, which he stubbornly refused to part with. He tucked his trousers into his leggings. When his patent leather shoes wore out, he swapped them for army boots with corrugated soles. Under his voluminous sheepskin coat there was room for his smoking jacket, whose silk collar was fraying and whose elbows were wearing thin. He wore a broad leather girdle, beneath which his will, pressed against his skin, was better protected than ever, although it had started to yellow at the edges as it absorbed the ever more depleted sweat of his aged body. When one evening the Paraginã brothers and Vasile Sava came to fetch food for their men, Niculae Filimon was not embarrassed to have Hartin Frenkian by his side. Ion Paraginã circled them, took out his pistol, and pointed it at the old man. "Who's that?" The shepherd, who was the same height as the old man, went up to Paraginã and with one finger pushed the barrel of the pistol aside. "Put it away, Ion. The old man's one of our own. He's hiding from the secret police." Ion Paraginã turned to his brother Cristea, pointing at the clothes visible beneath Hartin's unfastened sheepskin coat. "I wouldn't wonder if he used to be a minister." "He's more than that," said Niculae Filimon. "He's a kind of king. He's the king of Romanian sugar." The brothers took their sheep bladders, filled with cheese, and their wooden tubs of butter and vanished, but not before sending Vasile Sava to scout the surrounding area. The next time, Cristea Paraginã came alone. "It's all right, sir," he told Hartin Frenkian. "I asked Timaru, and he told me he'd heard of you. And he told me to tell you to stay up here longer because the secret police are arresting folk like you in droves." Then, because night had fallen and they had lit the fire, and because Hartin had finished doing the sums in Niculae Filimon's ledger, and above all because he had heard the other man call him "sir," which was something unusual in that world of goat herders and shepherds, he ventured to ask, "But what about you—who are you?"

Paradoxically, in the middle of the winter frosts, sleeping on plank beds among rugged strangers, learning a new occupation, and accustoming himself to life above the tree line, Hartin Frenkian spent one of the most tranquil periods of his life in the winter of 1948–49. He received no news from the outside world, but via a family in Vidra, where my grandparents had stayed for a time during the war, he sent a scrap of paper to my grandfather. On it he wrote only the initials of his name in Armenian script so that Grandfather would know he was alive.

They sat around the fire, sometimes without talking, sometimes telling stories or making plans for a future that only there, among the snows, closer to the sky, seemed possible. They sat with the Paragină brothers, Vasile Sava, Captain Mihai Timaru, Gheorghiță Barbu, and sometimes Brother Filimon Tudose from the Moșinoaia Monastery, but most often with Cristea Paragină, who came for food and brought Amăriuței, a lad from Crucea de Sus, to keep watch next to the packs by the side of the road in case anybody came up the valley. Cristea Paragină had taken a liking to the old man. Hartin Frenkian told him about the places he had been, about the mountains and plateaus of Anatolia, about the swarming city of Constantinople, and about the ports of the Mediterranean, while Cristea listened in enchantment, scratching with his bayonet in the frozen earth. He told him about the salons of Bucharest, about the Oriental Ball at the Military Club, about the royal family when they arrived to open the ball, about what the ministers wore, about the stock exchange and the major industrialists of the Chamber of Commerce. Cristea told Hartin Frenkian about their hidden dens, the oldsters' den and the young 'uns' den; about how they had amassed weapons for the uprising; about the other bands of partisans in the mountains of Rodna, Făgăraș, Vîlcea, and the Banat, who were waiting for the signal to descend to the plain together once the Americans came. Truman had won the election, Cristea informed him one November evening, bringing the news. "He's against the Russians . . ." "Churchill is really against the Communists," said Frenkian. "It won't be possible without Churchill." Around the fire, in the forests above Vidra, Hartin Frenkian and Cristea Paragină discussed world politics. They drew maps on the ground, Cristea with his bayonet, the old man with the tip of his shepherd's crook, maps in which the Russians and the Red Army withdrew to the steppes and the Allies occupied Eastern Europe and the Balkans.

Most of all, Hartin Frenkian liked the stories about the golden bull of Stephen the Great. "These lands belong to us, the descendants of Vrâncioaia," said Cristea Paragină, and the others, whoever might be with him at the time, would voice their agreement. "All the forests as far as the mountaintop, beyond Soveja, at Lăcăuți, have been ours for five hundred years. The men of Vrancea shouldn't let themselves be cowed into joining the collective. All this land is theirs, and it oughtn't fall into the hands of the outsiders." Once, when both brothers came, accompanied by Timaru, they showed the old man the golden bull; Frenkian gazed at it in enchantment. He could feel his will, his own golden bull, burning against his skin, and he was about to show it to them, but he stopped himself, rejoicing in his own mind that he had met such men, who had such reverence for heirs and legacies.

But the joy of evenings around the fire and stories about faraway worlds came to a sudden end. Almost a year had passed. One evening in mid-October, Cristea Paragină arrived alone, tottering, and collapsed by the fire. They had been betrayed by infiltrators. Securitate troops had surrounded them. They knew about their dens and their secret entrances and exits; they knew everything. Ion Paragină had been wounded and arrested, Vasile Sava too. They had shackled Timaru hand and foot. There were two trucks. Cristea and Gheorghiță Barbu had escaped, pressing themselves to the roof in the darkness. They had descended by a shortcut and waited for the trucks, but they had been afraid to open fire, lest they kill their own men. Cristea Paragină lay for two days, with Filimon and Hartin Frenkian tending his wounds as best they could, after which he vanished. Reprisals had begun in Vrancea. Fifty men were arrested and taken to Galați in chains. They shot Amăriuței and tied his body to the rear bumper of the truck, dragging him through the village. By the time they got to the other end of the village, the body was nothing but a ragged hunk of flesh, but at least they had the decency to toss it in a ditch and cover it with soil so that the dogs would not devour it.

One evening, almost a year later, Cristea Paragină returned to the sheepfold, as if resurrected from the dead. His eyes were sunken in their sockets, his cheeks stubbly, his voice cracked. It was then that Hartin Frenkian, after letting him eat his fill, decided finally to show him his will.

The uprising had been crushed. Securitate trucks patrolled the village lanes, headlights blazing. They stopped anybody they caught outside after dark. If they found anybody carrying more food than he and his family could eat in a day, they interrogated him. Whoever had weapons of any kind at home, a rifle or a bayonet, had to turn them over; otherwise he would be shot. And they were not joking; they shot a number of men. "But they didn't find the golden bulls," said Cristea Paragină. "Nor will they ever find them . . . That much at least." All he knew of his brother and Mihai Timaru was that they were alive and had been sentenced to life imprisonment. "They hated them too much to kill them and send them to heaven," he said bitterly. He was hiding out with a friend, Gheorghe (or Gheorghiță) Bălan, in an abandoned mill in Gura Lepșei, above the Putna Cataract. The two men looked at each other, one with a white beard and the appearance of a biblical patriarch, the other with the downy cheeks of a young lad. It was then that Hartin Frenkian opened his sheepskin coat and the smoking jacket that had once been black and glossy. He lifted his flax undershirt and showed him the girdle. "I'm putting you in my will," he said. "You're a good lad. I'm giving you a million lei, not today's lei, which aren't worth two bits, but real, prewar lei . . . A million lei in banknotes, treasury bonds, shares, whichever you prefer . . ." "What would I do with all that money, sir?" said Cristea Paragină, blinking. "Can't you see how we live up here? And who would accept prewar money?" Hartin Frenkian thought for a few moments. "Here's what we'll do. I won't leave you bonds, although their time will come again—you'll see. I'll give you gold. And jewels." "I think we've all completely lost our minds, sir," sighed Cristea Paragină, although he liked the old man; he even loved him, mad as he was; he loved him more than before. In the end, the times were insane too, and the wind whistled through the trees, foretokening snow. "Come back tomorrow, at dusk," said Frenkian. "In the meantime, I'll ask somebody to bring me pen and ink from the valley. On a piece of paper I'll write the numbers of the safes at the National Bank. When you hear I've died, go and take the gold. Gold is valuable at any time. You can exchange it for guns and wait until the Americans come. You're a good lad; you have time." And before the younger Paragină vanished into the forest, he said, with a sigh of relief, "Tomorrow evening. Don't forget . . ."

It was one of the things that Cristea Paragină never forgot because he did not have time to forget it. At dawn, soldiers surrounded the abandoned mill. Cristea tried to escape, running out the back, where there was a barbed wire fence. He did not manage to scale it. Riddled with bullets, he was left hanging from the fence, his hands impaled on the metal thorns. Gheorghe Bălan was taken to Galați in chains and savagely tortured so that he would reveal where the golden bulls were hidden. To lose your temper is only human, and confronted with Gheorghiță Bălan's obstinate silence, even one of the brutes torturing him lost his temper, drew his revolver, and blew his brains out. They say his name was Varlaam, but that may or may not be true. There was no investigation, so nobody bothered to find out. Anyway, all the torturers were much alike.

Hartin Frenkian prepared his pen and inkpot; from his leather girdle he took a sheet of lined paper, and on it he wrote: "Codicil. I who am the undersigned Hartin B. Frenkian fully maintain the previous will and testament that I filed at the notary office of Ilfov Tribunal, registering petition no. 75075 on August 31, 1938, but with the following modifications and additions." He then laid the pen aside, screwed the cap back on the inkpot, and waited. Meanwhile, the wind had started to blow. The mountain cocks took shelter inside holes in the tree bark. The snows came. The ice glinted glassily and then softened. The icicles snapped. The snows dissolved and flowed down the mountain. When spring came and the stags descended to the river, mingling with the sheep, Hartin Frenkian knew that he had been waiting in vain. He stuffed the pages back inside his girdle and put the inkpot in his pocket. He continued to count the seasons, the sheep, and the skins of cheese taken to market in Focșani. Sometimes he would find pages from the newspapers, wrapped around smoked sausages or crumpled up to provide padding for bottles packed in boxes, or blown on the wind. He would smooth them out and read them at length, trying to picture the reality behind them. The news arrived with a delay, but one item arrived on time, two springs later—namely, the news of Stalin's death. That spring Hartin Frenkian would reach the age of eighty. "It is time," he decided. With a cutthroat razor, he shaved off his beard, peering into a shard of mirror. He discarded his sheepskin coat, and, as best he could, he brushed his smoking jacket, which had turned white with wear and which was baggy at the elbows, stiff with sweat under the arms. He bid farewell to shepherd Niculae Filimon and made his way back to Focșani by way of Vidra, Panciu, and Odobești.

"As you can see, Garbis, I'm still alive," he said, entering the yard of our house in Focșani and thereby preempting any other question. He still tried to hold his back straight, but he had aged. The steep mountain paths force you to walk with a stoop, and it is hard to straighten your back at that age, especially if you have to keep a lookout at all times. His face was furrowed, roughened by the cold, and his left hand had a slight but uncontrollable tremor, although he kept his hands clasped together to stop it from showing. "I need a room," he said. "In the buildings in the churchyard," suggested Grandfather. "There's a room in the old schoolhouse, next to Minas the blind man's. If it doesn't bother you . . ." It did not bother Hartin Frenkian. He asked only that the door could be securely locked at night and that the room have a table and a chair. "Yes, it will," said Grandfather. He wanted to ask him whether he needed the table that he might write his will, but he thought better of it. He had anyway noticed that the old man kept his hands clasped over his girdle, and he understood why. "How do you make your living, *baron* Hartin?" "How do you make yours, Garabet?" "I'm retired. I draw a pension from the state . . . It's not a lot . . . To tell the truth, given how much they took from you, the state ought to give you something back." "The state . . . that's no good," said Hartin Frenkian with a shake of his head. Otherwise, he seldom shook his head; most often he nodded, not at what other people said but at his own thoughts. "What can you expect from the state? I think I'll go into trade again." "Trade?" said Grandfather in amazement. "What world are you living in, *baron* Hartin? The shops from the old days have closed; it's not the trade you once knew; nowadays it's all state trade." Hartin Frenkian leaned forward slightly, and, in a voice low enough to enter the pages of *The Book of Whispers*, he said, "Are you dead, Garabet? You're not dead. Am I dead? I'm not dead, thank God. Then trade is not yet dead either. And customers can always be found."

Sometime after that, when my grandfather went to keep him company first thing in the morning, he found him reinvigorated, rubbing the shoulders of his smoking jacket with a wetted brush. "I'm off to Bucharest to fetch some goods," said old man Hartin, but Grandfather Garabet refrained from asking what new madness this might be. "All I want is for you to give me the money for a third-class train ticket. I'll return the money to you in a month." As Grandfather made no immediate response, Hartin, after the harsh life he had led in the last few years, imagined that his hesitation was a refusal. He took Grandfather by the collar—only now did he feel how badly the old man's hand trembled—and said, "Sit down. If you don't believe I'll be able to give you the money back, here's what we'll do. You'll give me the ten lei now, and I'll put you down in my will for a million of those good prewar lei. We'll write out the codicil right now. Ten lei, Garbis; think about it; after I die, you'll be a rich man!" "I didn't say I wasn't going to give you the money," replied Grandfather Garabet. "And don't talk about death any more. We'll live and we'll see."

They lived and they saw. Hartin Frenkian took the train. This time it was less crowded because this time there were no demobilized soldiers, no war invalids reduced to begging, no Moldavians with rolled-up sacks on their way to buy grain in Oltenia, no refugees of every variety. Traveling calmly this time, Hartin arrived in the Northern Station. He went to the Bassarab Station, and from there, paying with the last of his small change, he took the train to Chitila. Night had fallen. Hartin Frenkian went to the sugar factory. He did not dare approach. He gazed at it from a distance, filling his nostrils with the smell of burned beets and molasses. Then he went around the back, where, untended but still bounteous, the walnut and apple orchard had borne fruit. He placed his cloth sacks under his head for a pillow and slept until dawn. When he woke up, numb with the chill of night, he shook out the sacks and started to gather the fallen walnuts, selecting the choicest specimens.

The tranquil splendor of a neglected but still fruitful orchard is, like all splendor, only apparent. The guard who kept watch to make sure that the workers did not pilfer sugar, smuggling it out of the factory by tossing it over the fence at the back, also cast a glance at the orchard from time to time, if only for the sake of a change; instead of greening copper pipes and gray roofs, he could gaze on the large, round canopies of the walnut trees and the sloping foliage of the apple trees. This time, however, he spotted Hartin Frenkian, which was not hard, since the old man did not bother to conceal himself as he searched among the grass, and even from a distance his black clothes made him stand out. "Hey," shouted the watchman, who, like anybody who has grown old in his job, sought to obtain the maximum effect for the minimum effort. "Get out of there!" But being elderly, he was unable to shout loud enough, and the other elderly man's ears were not sharp enough to allow him to hear. The watchman cupped his hands to his mouth and shouted again, while Frenkian calmly continued to search for walnuts in the grass. To spare himself further effort, the watchman picked a piece of wood up off the ground and threw it in the direction in which he had been shouting, this time with greater success since the walnut picker paused and looked around him, searching for the source of the noise and straightening his back in order to do so. On seeing the outline of that man arching his shoulders in a way so familiar to the workers at the sugar factory, the watchman froze, still holding the next bit of wood he had been about to throw. What happened next would have been incomprehensible to any onlooker. It was not the thief caught in the act who ran away, but rather the watchman. As he turned tail, he even forgot to drop his bit of wood. As may be suspected, he did not run toward the walnut thief but to the management building. Frenkian watched him as he ran, and when he reckoned he was far enough away, he shook the mouth of his sack to make the opening larger and absorbed himself in his search among the weeds once more. This was why he failed to notice when, a few minutes later, a group of men approached. Marching at their head was the man who seemed to be in charge, wearing a navy blue suit and a cap. He was the director, as they would have called him in those days. They came to a stop a few paces away and gazed at the old man in silence. Reaching for a walnut, Harutiun Frenkian saw them. He gave a start and straightened his back, although not sufficiently to allow him to stand completely erect. Rather, he stood in a slanting posture, ready to make a getaway. They looked at each other, recognizing each other, but embarrassed to address each other. The man with the look of a director about him bent down and picked something up from the grass. To Hartin Frenkian, after that long embarrassed silence, the sudden gesture seemed threatening—they were about to throw stones at him; they did not even want to dirty their hands with him; he had seen the like in childhood, when they had thrown stones, almost killing people, and now they were going to drive him away in a similar, shameful fashion. He wanted to run, taking his sack with him. However, the other man did not raise his arm behind his shoulder ready to throw but stretched out his hand. In his open palm lay not stones, as the old man had feared, but walnuts. Faced with this unexpected gesture, the old man looked all around him, and then he looked at the walnuts in bewilderment. The man in the cap took two steps forward, holding out his open palm. Frenkian straightened his back, becoming the tallest among them once more. He quickly took the walnuts from the man's hand, fearful lest he change his mind. "I know you," he said. "You are Ștefan Niculescu. The stoker, a good worker . . . I put you down in my will, even then . . ." He looked around him. "All of you . . . If I die, the factory is yours. But you have to be bold enough to ask for it. And if you like, you can sell it after that; I wrote in my will how you should divide it up . . . But it would be a shame; it's a good factory; you just need to take care of it . . ." The man with the cap made a sign to the others, who, following his example, bent down and began to gather walnuts. The taller men shook the trees to make things go more quickly. The sacks soon filled. Niculescu, the stoker or director or both the one and the other, brushed his palms, took off his cap, and essayed a kind of smile. Then he told the watchman to carry the sacks of walnuts to the station for the old man. He did not try to shake his hand since in any event he was clutching his cap, but by way of farewell or apology, he said, "Come again . . . sir . . ."

Frenkian did not come again. But he made an arrangement for the factory watchman and workers to fill his sacks and bring them to the station for him. Hartin Frenkian asked them all their names, made a codicil, and put them down in his will. The workers were delighted with all that money on paper and thanked him kindly, but they would not have been satisfied if the old man, instead of giving them tens of thousands of lei in his will, had given them each two or three lei to buy themselves a tot of schnapps at the station buffet. But Hartin Frenkian was as generous with his money after death as he was thrifty with it during his life.

In particular, he was thrifty because his business was barely getting under way. For a few days he shut himself up in his little room in the yard of the St. Mary Armenian Church in Focșani, munching stale bread dipped in linden tea, and then he walked the streets taking short steps, looking in the shop windows; he roamed the grocery stores and taverns; he entered and asked the vendors one thing and another; he conferred with Sahag Sheitanian and others who still kept shops in those times adverse to trade or who had once been shopkeepers and, even though they had lost their premises and counters, still knew a thing or two about trading.

"It's time I went into a new line of business," he decided. "It's not the best time for candies. In troubled times like these, people prefer to drink away their sorrows than to suck lollipops in the holidays. They'd rather buy salty snacks, which give you a thirst, than sweetmeats, which do the opposite."

And so it was that Hartin Frenkian, once the king of sugar, now became a trader in salty snacks. From Mercan, the mage of air, he picked out a few large jars with chipped rims, which meant he could take them for free. In them he tossed a handful of coarse salt and poured boiling water and in them he left the walnuts to float for two days. After he removed the walnuts from the salt water, he toasted them on a hob and set off to do the rounds of the taverns, selling toasted salty walnuts, which were just the thing to go with a mug of beer or a tot of something stronger. Since the shops selling colonial goods had disappeared, and with them peanuts in their shells or roasted with salt, Turkish hazelnuts, pistachios, and almonds, Hartin Frenkian did not have any competition. The tavern keepers looked askance at the vendors of pumpkin and sunflower seeds and at the customers who munched them, spitting the husks on the floor, so Hartin Frenkian's trade in salted walnuts did quite well. In the morning, when the taverns were closed and the tavern keepers were polishing their counters, wiping down the sticky tables; when the drunkards were sleeping it off, clarifying their blood, Hartin Frenkian would stand on the pavement in front of the Armenian church and sell his walnuts by the mug. On holidays, he would go to the Armenians' houses and sell them by the teacup rather than the mug so that the price would not seem too high—ground walnuts for *sarayli*, baklava, and *anush-abur*. Since the initial investment was negligible, the trade in walnuts did quite well, so well, in fact, that by the time winter came, Hartin Frenkian was able to afford a shabby overcoat from Weissmann's second-hand shop by the meat market, an overcoat whose stitching was fraying but that was warm. Now snugly wrapped up, Hartin Frenkian ventured to extend the scope of his trade. Before the major feast days, he huddled up in the night train to Bucharest, bartering a handful of walnuts for a seat in the chilly third-class carriage. He went straight to the Armenian cathedral on King Carol I Boulevard, which was now called Republic Boulevard, where he sold his walnuts. "It's more of an obligation," as he explained to those who could not quite understand the point of his journeys. For the more exacting Armenians of Bucharest he selected the choicest goods and presented them in a more enticing way. He carefully cracked the walnut shells with a small cobbler's hammer, borrowed from Anton Merzian, and removed the two hemispheres of the kernel intact and still adjoined to each other. Now, as I write *The Book of Whispers*, half a century after those Armenian holidays and the long chats the Armenians used to have in the churchyard after the service, there are still plenty of people from Bucharest who remember how Hartin Frenkian would enter the church and from his overcoat pocket would take a few candle stumps (which he had probably borrowed from Arshag the bell ringer in Focşani), how he would light them and stand just inside the entrance to the church, since the police would have moved him on if he had stood outside. There, inside the entrance, he sold his extraordinary walnuts, which were as round as pigeon's eggs. The men who now, as we read *The Book of Whispers*, are embarking on old age but who were small boys at the time, know that their parents barely said a word to old man Hartin Frenkian in his shabby overcoat with his bag of walnuts. They were embarrassed to hand over a few coins for a cup of walnuts to the man they had known so well in the days when his tattered smoking jacket shone as new. Since they were embarrassed, they sent their children to buy the walnuts for them. In that way Hartin Frenkian came to know all the children by their first names; he would give them an extra walnut to munch on their way home. Afterward, he returned to the train station, avoiding the center of the city, lest he meet somebody, other than the Armenians, who might recognize him. He took the night train back, and if he had time beforehand, he would pop into a few taverns next to the station. But he walked with shorter and shorter steps, leaning against walls to catch his breath, putting on his overcoat earlier and earlier in the autumn and shedding it later and later in the spring. Wherever he could, he sat down; he was growing harder and harder of hearing, and he learned to tell coins apart by touch because his vision had dimmed. From time to time, he would ask the names of his more generous customers; the names of the friendlier tavern keepers, who used to give him a bowl of hot soup and bread; the names of people he sensed were more woebegone than he; and in the evening, with his nose pressed to the paper and his pen dipped in ink diluted with water, he would add a codicil, including them in his will. The only thing that had remained genuinely alive was his will. The final change dates from 1958, when he added generous customers and Armenian paupers, the final name being Mariam Aslanian, the widow of Father Dajad, whom he granted forty thousand lei at the 1938 value, which would have been worth more than the whole of her pension to her dying day. One evening, in February 1959, Hartin Frenkian entered our yard; he probably saw me and talked to me in his bouldery Erzerum Armenian; perhaps he gave me a walnut; I don't know. Of all the mages, as I said, he was the only one I remember only through his gifts.

The same as in all the fundamental moments of their lives, when the Armenians of my childhood felt the need to endure, to preserve, or to explain, Hartin Frenkian turned to photography. Like all Armenians who, on the eve of separations, battles, massacres, departures in the convoys, and therefore on the eve of their meeting with death, felt the need to put themselves in a safe place, had photographs of the living part of them made, Hartin Frenkian asked Grandfather to take his photograph. But since the living part of his body was his will, he asked him to make a photographic copy of it. That night, in the winter of 1959, Grandfather photographed Hartin Frenkian's will page by page; he photographed the codicils, the notices in the *Official Gazette*, everything. After Grandfather carefully developed them, they gathered together the photographs, still moist and sticky, and placed them in another folder, which the old man entrusted to him for safekeeping, and Grandfather promised he would do everything exactly as he had asked.

It was a hard winter, particularly after Epiphany. It was not as snowy as the winter of 1954, when they threw the loaves onto people's roofs directly from the bread truck on the street. The people then climbed up into the attic and opened the skylight to retrieve the bread because the wall of snow outside their houses reached up to the eaves. But trade is trade, and even if the train station customers wanted mulled wine and boiled plum brandy more than beer and spritzers, Hartin Frenkian continued to do the rounds of the taverns, and during the day he watched the steam puffing from the engines; he dozed more than he traded. In the evening, wetting his ink pencil on his tongue, he totted up his incomes and expenses in the pages of the ledger, comparing the totals with the coins knotted inside his handkerchiefs, like little sacks of gold pieces. If we take into account that the old man always wore the same clothes, ate sparingly, heated his stove with twigs gathered from the graveyard; if we consider that his expenses were very low, then the king of sugar's commerce with walnuts was profitable. But even so, when they finally decided to break the door down and found him glassy-eyed, curled up like a frozen bird, it proved not to have been profitable enough since the coins knotted in handkerchiefs were not sufficient for a coffin and a cross for his grave. Since Anton Merzian and Krikor Minasian had been at loggerheads ever since they opened workshops next door to each other on Main Street, in order for them not to find a fresh bone of contention there in the room where Hartin Frenkian had died, the first thing they did, even before they closed the dead man's eyes—"Let him see us count it," said Agop Aslanian the parish accountant, "to show we don't steal from the dead"—was to unknot the handkerchiefs, count the coins, and check the amount against the total in the ledger. "Everything is in order, Hartin," said Father Varjabedian; "may God illumine your soul." At the end of that flawless accounting, which concluded Hartin Frenkian's transactions with the world, the priest closed the dead man's eyes. Mariam Aslanian, the widow of the previous priest, offered to look for some other, more decent clothes for him in her husband's wardrobe.

but Grandfather stopped her. In accordance with his own wish, Hartin Frenkian was buried in the black suit that had once been a smoking jacket but that from such long wear now crumbled between the fingers like old paper. Since they could not patch it, they found a white sheet, a kind of shroud, which they pulled up to beneath his chin, over the black suit and his hands, which lay folded on top of his will.

At the dead man's side, Grandfather unfolded the bundle of papers and in a slow voice intoned all the parts that Hartin Frenkian had underlined, wishing them to be read out after his death. "I who am the undersigned Hartin B. Frenkian, not having ascendants or descendants, entail that on my death my estate should be dealt with as follows: I establish the Hartin Frenkian Foundation, bequeathing to it full title to my property in Bucharest, no. 72, Victory Avenue; the jewels in safe no. 78 at the Romanian Commercial Bank; 178,000 shares in the Arad-Chitila Company; 72,000 shares in the Banat Company, deposited in safes 1392, 1398, and 1400 at the Romanian Commercial Bank and in safes 2231 and 2361 at the National Bank of Romania, and all the shares in Romcolind; ten million lei in land bonds kept in my strongbox; and any other personal property, real estate, receivables, or shares, wherever they might be, in this country or abroad, that I now possess or will possess at my death. The purpose of the foundation is as follows: to build and run a hospital in Bucharest with a minimum of eighty beds, endowing it with modern furniture, equipment, apparatus, and instruments; to build and run in Bucharest a home for poor Romanian Orthodox schoolchildren from the countryside. I bequeath to the Romanian Academy the sum of 15 million lei with which to invest in real estate. From the income thus earned the academy shall provide scholarships for poor and meritorious Christian Orthodox Romanian pupils. I bequeath to the Ministry of Education funds with which annually to build a primary school with all the necessary furniture in villages in the countryside. I bequeath to the Armenian General Benevolent Union in Paris fifty thousand lei . . ." Grandfather read on for another quarter of an hour, the whole list of buildings, land, and money left to churches, universities, various public institutions, and employees; the long list of beneficiaries, old partners, bishops, notaries, and administrators; as well as the newer legatees—the tavern keepers, customers, paupers, and good Samaritans. Then he folded up the will and made the broad, sweeping sign of the cross performed by a man who has kept his promise. It was only natural that Anton Merzian, the man who spoke only in questions, should ask one now: "About how much money would that be in total?" Grandfather shook his head and weighed the pages in his hand, as if he could gauge the size of the sum that way. "I reckon about a billion lei . . ." "A billion, you say?" said Merzian, to whom it seemed unimaginable. "That's a thousand million," explained Agop Aslanian, the accountant, the son of the priest's widow Mariam. "A million, you say?" asked the cobbler, still puzzled. "In other words, a million times a thousand." "Aha, a thousand, right?" asked Anton Merzian. "A billion," repeated Krikor Minasian, unable to understand it since it was not a word he had ever uttered, and he looked in amazement at the peaceful face of the old man, stretched out in a coffin so narrow that it sooner resembled one of Mercan the empty bottle dealer's packing crates.

Having hastily been washed, and for that reason still showing ink pencil stains on his fingers and at the corners of his lips; dressed in his worn, crumbling, parchment-like suit; placed in a coffin made from thin, rough, unvarnished planks, Hartin Frenkian was buried in the spring of 1959. Father Varjabedian nasally muttered the hymn of remembrance *I veri Jerusalem*. The few people assembled around the coffin bore themselves as if it were a business to be got over with; none sighed or shed a tear. Only Mariam, the priest's widow, wept, not for the old man or the legacy she would never come into but because she had done so at every funeral since her husband's death.

7.

"Do not harm their women," said Armen Garo. "Nor the children."

One by one, all the members of the Special Mission gathered at the offices of the *Djagadamard* newspaper in Constantinople. They had been selected with care. The group had been whittled down to those who had taken part in such operations before, working either alone or in ambush parties. "I trust only a man who has killed before," Armen Garo had declared. They were given photographs of those they were to seek out, wherever they were hiding. Their hiding places might be anywhere, from Berlin or Rome to the steppes of Central Asia. Broad-shouldered, bull-necked Talaat Pasha, the minister of the interior, was a brawny man whose head, with its square chin and jaws that could rip asunder, was more like an extension of his barrel chest. In the lower part of the photograph, his fists, twice the size of a normal man's, betokened pugnacity. Beside him, fragile, her features delicate, his wife wore a white dress and a lace cap in the European style, so very different from the pasha's fez. Then there was Enver, a short man made taller by his boot heels. He had haughty eyes, and his slender fingers preened the points of his moustache. He was proud of his army commander's braids, which, cascading luxuriantly from his shoulders and covering his narrow chest, were meant to disguise the humble beginnings of a son whose mother, in order to raise him, had plied one of the most despised trades in all the empire: she had washed the bodies of the dead. In one of the photographs, his thin, possessive, but nonetheless timid arm encircles the delicate waist of his wife, Nadjeh, a princess of the imperial harem and therefore a daughter of the sultan. And in another photograph, Enver, the son of the woman who washed the dead, the son-in-law of the sultan, strains to look haughty; his face set rigid, he stands between portraits of his idols, Napoleon and Frederick the Great. Then there was Djemal Pasha, the Lepidus of that martial triumvirate. Ordinary in appearance, if he had not worn the epaulettes of a naval minister, he would have gone completely unnoticed, although he made painful efforts to match the brutality of Talaat and the haughtiness of Enver. Then there were Dr. Nazim and Behaeddin Shakir, the ideologues of the Union and Progress Party who had come up with the idea of releasing criminals from the prisons. Enrolled in armed units, the criminals were to guard the convoys of Armenians and slaughter them at the crossroads. We do not know how beautiful their wives were; they were plump and had black hair, but their features are hard to make out since the only photographs we have of them are from their youth and show them with veiled faces, weeping by the coffins of their husbands after the avengers had completed their mission. And the others, Djemal Azmi, prefect of Trebizond, Behbud Khan Javanshir . . . Armen Garo picked up the photographs of Talaat and Enver, pictured with their wives. He looked at each of his men in turn: Soghomon Tehlirian, Aram Yerganian, Arshavir Shiragian, Hratch Papazian, Misak Torlakian.

"Do not kill the women," he repeated. "Nor their children."

The date when that meeting took place is of no importance to us. *The Book of Whispers* is not a history book but one of states of conscience. This is why it tends toward translucency and its pages are pellucid. It is true that in *The Book of Whispers* there are many precise dates, which specify the very day, hour, and place. The pen moves swiftly, but sometimes it decides to linger, waiting for the reader and me to catch up, and then perhaps it goes into greater detail than necessary. Each additional word illumines, but precisely for that reason it diminishes.

And so even if we were to strike from it each list of years and each tally of days, *The Book of Whispers* would still preserve all its meanings. Such things have always happened to people everywhere. In fact, at its core *The Book of Whispers* remains the same for all time, like a chorale by Johann Sebastian Bach, like a narrow gate through which people pass, stooping or huddling close to each other.

"Above all else, they killed our poet," said Shavarsh Misakian.

The newspaper offices had escaped the disaster as if by miracle. In any event, after the slaughter that began on April 24, 1915, when hundreds of intellectuals were arrested and the greater part of them slain, all the capital's Armenians had taken it to be a miracle when the deportation order was rescinded. They had been about to share the fate of the other Armenian communities, driven from their homes and plundered of everything they owned, although their fate would have been even harsher, for unlike the Armenians of Van, Sivas, and Adana, their convoys would have had to traverse the whole of the Anatolian plateau on their way down to the deserts of Syria, where, unless they were first massacred by the gangs of armed criminals or the bands of nomads, they would have died of hunger and cold amid the expanses of makeshift tents, in the desert where the scorching heat of the days and the freezing cold of the nights claimed their equal share of victims.

Outlawed in 1915, the central press organ of the Armenian Revolutionary

Federation, called *Azadamard* at the time, reappeared in 1918 under a new name, albeit one that evoked the first: *Djagadamard*. Shavarsh Misakian was the editor-in-chief; he had returned to take up his old job. He sat in a corner. He was not a member of the Special Mission, but he possessed the authority that Armen Garo and Shahan Natali needed, an authority lent not by his stature but rather, given his drooping left shoulder and crooked head, precisely by his lack of grandeur. It was his infirmity that made him imposing because it reminded others of the stubbornness with which he had endured torture in the military prison where he was taken in March 1916 and where, a few months later, he tore himself from the hands of his tormenters and hurled himself from the third floor into the courtyard below. He had survived his serious injuries and was released on November 27, 1918, when the capital was occupied by troops. But his broken body had taken upon itself the crookedness of the world, a reminder to all that he had been delivered from the fear of death.

Their enemies knew that in order to annihilate them as a people, they would, without fail, have to kill their poet. To an oppressed and threatened people, the Poet becomes the leader. Daniel Varujan had been arrested along with the other intellectuals on April 24, 1915. He was tied to a tree and stoned to death, then abandoned to the scavenging animals and the phantoms of the night. Legends tell that he is alive still. During the burning of Smyrna some told that for an instant they had glimpsed his face in the blazing mirrors. The only thing that we can deduce from these legends of the resurrection of Daniel Varujan is that although we know the site of his passion, bound to the trunk of a tree, to a living cross, we do not know in what place his grave might lie. As we have proof of his death and even know the name of his executioner—Oğuz Bey, the captain from Çankırı—but have no knowledge of his grave, we may be tempted by the thought of his resurrection.

Others of those arrested on April 24—for example, two members of parliament, Krikor Zohrab, the member for Constantinople, and Vartkes Seringulian, the member for Erzerum—ended up in the deserts of Syria, in Urfa and then Aleppo. Roessler, the German consul in Aleppo, tells us of them in a letter to Wangenheim, the German ambassador: "Zohrab and Vartkes effendi are in Aleppo and are part of a convoy headed for Diarbekir. It spells their certain death: Zohrab has a heart condition, and Vartkes's wife has just given birth." About the crimes that took place when my grandparents were children I have learned many things, not so much from the accounts of the survivors as from the boasts of the killers. How great the difference between the timidity of those who are slain and the arrogance of those who slay . . . For example, we learn that they were stabbed with bayonets. Vartkes had his brains blown out. Zohrab had his head smashed in by rocks. Their bodies were then cut to pieces and abandoned. Had anyone bothered to bury the countless dead of those days, he would not have been able to recognize them from the mangled remnants of their bodies.

But life goes on. The name of the place where Daniel Varujan was killed is Tuna. Before being led away, the poet told the others, "Take care of my newly born son. Let him be baptized Varujan."

"We will avenge them, both him and the others," said Armen Garo, looking fixedly at Shavarsh Misakian. "This is why you shall not harm their women or their children. We are not robbers of the dead or killers of women."

They were in the first circle.

"Armen is right," said Shavarsh Misakian. "Follow the example of General Dro."

At the time, Dro had not yet become a general. He was aged just twenty-one in February 1905, when the three-day massacre began in Baku. The Tartar bands killed thousands of Armenians. And Prince Nakashidze, the tsar's governor, despite the warnings and then despite the Armenians' cries of desperation, not only did nothing to protect them, but even supplied the attackers with weapons. The Central Committee of the Armenian Revolutionary Federation sent word to governor Nakashidze that the party had sentenced him to death. The young Drastamat Kanayan, whom, under the name General Dro, we met earlier, was given the task of executing the sentence.

On the appointed day, Dro waited for the governor's procession on a narrow street where the Cossack outriders would be unable to flank the prince's carriage. He had the bomb inside a bag, hidden beneath bunches of grapes. But when he saw that the prince was accompanied by his wife, Dro hesitated and finally abandoned the plan, merely watching them as they passed. He waited until nightfall. In the returning carriage the prince sat alone. When the cavalcade reached a spot opposite where he was standing, Dro hurled the bag into the carriage and then ran as fast as he could. The explosion was terrible. Together with Nakashidze, a number of mounted guards in the governor's retinue were blown to pieces. Taking advantage of the panic, Dro managed to vanish. That night, his comrades smuggled him across the border into Turkey, and there he remained for nine years, until the beginning of the war.

"But at the time, Dro could not imagine what was going to happen," said Arshavir Shiragian.

Nobody could have imagined. The Armenians' leaders had helped the Young Turks seize power, believing they would put a stop to the bloody atrocities of Sultan Abdul Hamid. Vartkes effendi, who went on to become the member of parliament for Erzerum, had sheltered Halil Bey in his home during the counterrevolution. The same Halil Bey would later order him killed. And as a bitter irony of fate, whereas Dro had believed that a woman should not pay for the sins of her husband, thirty years later, in Omsk, Stalin ordered that Dro's wife, along with one of their sons, be killed in payment for her husband's deeds.

"In Trebizond," said Misak Torlakian, "hundreds of women, along with their children and their old folk who were unable to walk, were embarked on rafts and taken out to sea. The women rejoiced, in the midst of that tragedy, when they were told that they would travel part of the way by sea, as it would spare them further exhaustion. But the next day, the rafts returned to the shore empty. The women had been drowned in the sea. The same thing happened at Unieh, at Ordu, at Tripoli, at Kerasonda, and at Rize. From Gyushana, my village, not one woman reached Meskene, Rakka, Ras-ul-Ain, or Deir-ez-Zor in the convoys, which means they all died on the way, of hunger, or by a bullet, or by the knife."

"In Kharput *vilayet*," said Soghomon Tehlirian, "in June, the notables were killed, and then the men were taken from the towns and the villages. The death marches were made up of women, old folk, and children only. At Arabkir, the women were embarked on boats and then drowned. The Armenian children from the German orphanage were drowned in the nearby lake. The women from Meskene were killed on their way to Urfa, and their bodies were thrown in the river. On the road between Sivas and Kharput, the mutilated bodies of the women massacred on the eastern bank of the Euphrates lay by the side of the road and in gullies for months on end. There were too many of them to bury. Their skeletons could still be seen in the middle of 1916. Of the almost two hundred thousand souls in the convoys, only a tenth reached Ras-ul-Ain and Deir-ez-Zor."

"The first women to reach Meskene, Rakka, and Deir-ez-Zor," said Aram Yerganian, "were the bodies that floated down the Euphrates. Throughout July of 1915, the surface of the Euphrates was strewn with water-bloated bodies, with heads, arms, and legs pell-mell. The waters of the river were reddish, a sight such as if it were then that death itself was born."

The circle of those who bore witness grew wider.

"Corpses are constantly to be found on the Euphrates," said Roessler, the German consul in Aleppo. "The corpses are all tied together in the same way, two by two and back to back. This proves that it is not a matter of random killings but a general plan of extermination hatched by the authorities. The corpses float downstream in increasing numbers. Mainly women and children."

"More than six hundred Armenians," said Holstein, the German consul in Mosul, "mainly women and children, driven out of Diarbekir, were killed while being transported down the River Tigris. The rafts arrived empty in Mosul yesterday. For a number of days corpses and human limbs have been floating down the river. Other convoys are on their way, and probably the same fate awaits them."

"Through Aleppo," said Guys, the former French consul, "since May, convoys of thousands of people have been passing. After a stay of two or three days in the places specifically set aside for them, these unfortunates, for the most part women and children, receive the order to head to Idlib, Mina, Rakka, Deir-ez-Zor, or Ras-ul-Ain, to the deserts of Mesopotamia, places destined, as all believe, to be their graves."

"Thousands of widows, Armenian women from the Van *vilayet*," said Jackson, the American consul in Aleppo, "accompanied by not a single adult man, are approaching Aleppo in a deplorable state and half naked. Like the other ten to twenty groups that have passed, these are convoys made up of from five hundred to three thousand people, leading behind them children in an indescribable state of wretchedness."

Roessler once again: "In connection with the Armenians of Kharput, it has been reported to me that in a village south of the town the men were separated from the women. The men were slaughtered and abandoned like that on each side of the road, along which the women were forced to pass."

"It may be believed," said Aram Andonian, the man who collected the accounts of the survivors, "that the hundreds of children in the Deir-ez-Zor orphanage may as well never have existed."

It was not until near the end, at the furthermost point of the road, that the authorities believed they had found the solution to a problem that had thitherto seemed insurmountable: how to kill without leaving behind the bodies of the dead. Not because it made them feel guilty in any way but because the hundreds of thousands of mangled bodies with blackened skin on their bones, floating down rivers or lying at the bottom of gullies, although they filled the convoys coming up behind with despair and readied them for death, nonetheless interfered with the circulation of road and rail traffic and thickened the air with the miasmas of death; they prompted protests from the Arabs, who were no longer able to use the rivers for drinking water, and they brought pestilence. To avoid such drawbacks, the killing of the children in Deir-ez-Zor would have to be the perfect crime.

The orphans, brought from Meskene and the other places where refugee camps had been pitched, were driven through the desert to Deir-ez-Zor. Imagine a convoy of hundreds of disfigured children, wearing nothing but rags and staggering barefoot through both the searing heat and the chill of the desert, their shoulders covered in bleeding, maggot-infested wounds, driven onward by horsemen lashing them with whips and rods. The dead and those in their death throes were tossed into the carts that accompanied the convoy. The place they finally reached is called Abuhahar. By then only three hundred children were able to keep their legs under them; the rest, the majority, were transported in the carts. In the foothills of the mountains at the edge of the desert, the soldiers brought the convoy to a halt, and the carts were unloaded on the plain. The soldiers surrounded the area, waiting until nightfall. At dusk the birds of the desert arrived. Drawn by the scent of blood, then by the wheeling of the other birds, and then by the croaking din and the snap of flesh ripped from the bone, the vultures and ravens of the desert swooped on bodies that, even if still alive, no longer had the strength to fend them off. Above all else the birds went for the eyes, the cheeks, and the lips, which were all the more enticing given that the flesh on the bodies had grown so lean. For two days flock after flock of birds settled on that haggard plain at the foot of the mountains, and the children were left prey to the beaks and the black, steely talons. It was the horrified Arab nomads who told the tale. And the man who commanded the soldiers, Corporal Rahmeddin, was promoted with unusual swiftness to the rank of commandant of the Rakka gendarmes.

The other children, who lay sick and hungry in the Deir-ez-Zor orphanage, were loaded into carts one freezing December day. The moribund were thrown into the Euphrates; the river, swollen as it was at that time of year, quickly swallowed the emaciated bodies. After a journey of twelve hours through the desert without food or water, the convoy's commandant, who we know was called Abdullah but who liked to be called Abdullah Pasha, found three different means of exterminating the children. But because he sensed hesitation in the eyes of the soldiers, he first grabbed a two-year-old boy and showed him to his men. "Even this little boy," he said, "has to be killed, the same as all the others his age. Otherwise one day he will grow up and seek out those who killed his parents, and he will take his revenge. This is the son of a dog who one day will come to find us and kill us!" And whirling him around in the air he then furiously smashed him against the rocks, crushing him before he had time even to groan.

Some of the carts they lined up one next to the other, cramming into them as many children as they could. In the middle they placed a cart full of explosives, which, once detonated, turned the children into ash. Those no longer able to walk they laid out on the plain. They scattered petrol-soaked hay on top of them and set it alight. And the others, for whom there was no room in the carts, they pushed inside caves. They stopped the mouths of the caves with brushwood and dry grass, which they torched, suffocating the children. They left the charred bodies at the bottom of the caves.

But not even the perfect crime can be wholly perfect. A little girl by the name of Ana took shelter in a nook in one of the caves, where, thanks to a crack running through the mountain, she found a streak of air. So she survived, and when the fires had gone out, a day and a night later, she went outside. For weeks she wandered, as far as Urfa, where she was taken in by some Armenian refugees, and she told them the story of the slaughter of the innocents.

From the third circle comes the voice of Djemal Pasha, minister of the navy, alarmed at the large numbers of corpses floating down the Euphrates. And then he is indignant at the fact that the routes of the death marches might interfere with the running of the railways. It was then that the Turkish authorities understood that no matter how perfectly the system for exterminating the Armenians might have been designed, it nonetheless had a defect: it left behind the bodies of the slain. Reshid Pasha, the prefect of Diarbekir, strove with all his might to rectify this flaw: "The Euphrates has little to do with our *vilayet*. The corpses floating down the river probably come from the *vilayets* of Erzerum and Kharput. Those who die here are thrown into the bottom of caves or, as is more often the case, they are sprinkled with petrol and burned. Rarely can sufficient space be found to bury them."

Let us return to the first circle.

"You did not see the places where the convoys met," said Hratch Papazian, "or to be more precise, what was left of them. At Deir-ez-Zor. Thousands of tents made of rags. Women and naked children, so weak with hunger that their stomachs could no longer hold down food. The gravediggers tossed them into carts pell-mell, the dead and the dying together, so as not to waste time. At night, the living blanketed themselves with the dead to keep warm. For a mother, the best thing that could happen was for a Bedouin to come and take her child so that it might escape the mass grave. Dysentery made the air unbreathable. With their muzzles, the dogs rummaged in the burst bellies of the dead. In October 1915 alone, more than forty thousand women passed through Ras-ul-Ain, guarded by soldiers. There was not one man among them. A crusade of martyred women. All along the railway line were scattered the mangled bodies of women who had been raped."

"Of the 1,850,000 Armenians who lived in the Ottoman Empire," said pastor Johannes Lepsius, "around 1,400,000 were deported. Of the other 450,000, around 200,000 were spared deportation, in particular the populaces of Constantinople, Smyrna, and Aleppo. The advance of Russian troops saved the lives of the other 250,000, who took refuge in Russian Armenia, a part of whom died there of typhus or hunger. The others kept their lives, but they were banished from their native places forever. Of the 1,400,000 Armenians deported, only

10 percent reached Deir-ez-Zor, the final destination of the convoys. In August 1916, they were sent on to Mosul, but they were to die in the desert, swallowed up by the sands or crammed into caves, in which the dead and the dying alike were set on fire."

They fell silent. The circles had closed around Armen Garo. He looked at Shahan Natali, at Shavarsh Misakian, and then at all the others. He took the photographs and handed them to the men who sat in the first circle, to each according to his mission.

"But even so," he repeated wearily, "do not kill the women and the children."

To the old Armenians of my childhood the place where they lived seemed accidental. To some of them even the time in which they lived seemed accidental, except that time was harder to deceive. And for that reason, time, peeking out from the pages of the photograph albums, from old clothes, or from over their shoulders, ended up transforming them one by one into an event.

As place was therefore nothing but a convention that you could ignore when the circumstances were not particularly threatening, my old folks were fascinated with wide-open spaces. They used to talk as if they could be in different places at once. This probably helped them to survive when it seemed the hardest thing possible, but it also helped them to die when there was not much else to do.

In this respect, my grandparents had different attitudes, however. Grandfather Setrak, my mother's father, seemed never to be bored. His elder brother, Harutiun, had been put to the sword in front of him, and that had given him the chance to flee, to escape with his life. But because somebody else had died in his place, he reckoned that in some way the life he lived was not his own or that it was only half his own, a kind of borrowed life. Because another had died that he might live, he repaid that debt by living for others. He lived for his daughters, Elisabeta, my mother, and Maro, whom he named after his sister, buried in the soilless grave of the River Euphrates. He lived that he might give gifts to the poor children, to provide money for the weddings of the lads from his shop, to clothe the naked and feed the hungry. He gave food to the Soviet Armenian prisoners of war, who were made to do hard labor under the Antonescu regime. Under the Iron Guard regime he was slapped around, accused of being a Jew, and only the crucifix he wore at his throat saved him from much worse. He was slapped around after the Communists came to power, accused of being a member of the Iron Guard, but this time the crucifix he wore at his chest was of no use to him; quite the contrary. But as Ecclesiastes says, the bread cast on the waters returned after many days, and one of the Armenian prisoners on whom he had taken pity now returned, this time as an officer in the Red Army, so the stinging of his slapped cheeks and the confiscation of his shops were the only bad things to befall him. The Communists let him keep one of his houses and were indulgent enough not to send him to prison for being the bourgeois exploiter he was. That it was not possible to prove whom he had exploited was another matter entirely, but the Communists did not let such niceties get in their way. To them, it was enough that my grandmother had a fur coat, that they had a piano at home, that they went to the spa at Olănești in the summer, and—to make matters worse— that Grandfather used to organize get-togethers serenaded by folk musicians at the Chez Pasha restaurant on Sundays. Having become a night watchman at the Brothers Buzești Lycée in Craiova, my grandfather Setrak had plenty of time to ponder all these things during his sleepless nights. Things that also included the notification he received in 1942, to the effect that on the orders of the marshal he and his entire family were to be interned at the prison camp in Tîrgu Jiu, along with other stateless Nansenians. The order was revoked, and Grandmother unpacked the thick coats and woolen stockings, hers and the two girls,' but she left Grandfather Setrak's inside a wooden suitcase. Having almost ended up in a prison camp, now he was to be conscripted. He bid his family farewell and went to Bucharest in the spring of 1944, where his career as a soldier in the Romanian Army, like that of the other recruits in the Nansenian company, lasted precisely three days. History does not record how shopkeeper manners adapted to army boots and tight-buttoned collars. The company did two days of training, and on the third day, they saw real-life action, when the railway station opposite their barracks was bombed. With the barracks thrown into chaos and the recruits milling around in confusion—recruits more apt to do a trade in military equipment than use it in combat—the Romanian company made up of stateless Armenians evaporated. Seeing that nobody gave them the order to fall in line, the Armenians scattered.

So Grandfather Setrak, who in the space of just a few years had experienced so many different states—having got rich and been reduced to penury; having been slapped around, called a Jew, interned in a prison camp, conscripted, and demobilized; having been slapped around again, called a bourgeois, and demoted from the bourgeoisie—had every right to believe the world made no sense. According to my grandfather, whoever believed the world was other than senseless did not understand anything. To demonstrate how absurd the world was, his clinching argument was the proof most readily available—namely, the example of his own death. First, he let himself be hit by a motorcar in front of Purcicarul Fountain while he was returning from the Old Market. Then he fell on his head from the roof of his house on no. 4, Strada Barați while he was trying to repair the eaves. He succeeded the third time, when he died of cold in the winter of 1985, because the Communists were economizing on gas; to make the best possible savings, they would cut the supplies for days on end, just when the frost was at its bitterest.

To a man who had cheated death by a hair's breadth so many times, nothing could seem more absurd than dying because the Communist state was economizing on gas, and therefore Grandfather Setrak died with tranquility stamped on his features. He was buried in Craiova's Catholic cemetery, not because he was a Catholic but just so things would continue to be senseless.

By contrast, Grandfather Garabet believed that all the things in the world had a meaning. Unlike Grandfather Setrak, who had spent his childhood in an orphanage and working as an apprentice during what ought to have been his school years, Grandfather Garabet had attended the agricultural lycée in Constantinople, which at the beginning of that century was no small achievement. He knew a lot of things. He was inventive and studious. To the exasperation of Grandmother Arshaluis, not for anything in the world would he have exchanged knowledge for shopkeeping aptitude. As a result, whereas Grandfather Setrak raked in money from coffee, olives, cacao, and raisins, as a shopkeeper Grandfather Garabet was always bankrupt. At least he would have been if his brother-in-law Sahag Sheitanian had left him to his own devices. But being bankrupt all the time was not his only trade. Grandfather Garabet was also a church cantor, a violinist, a motorcyclist, a calligrapher, a photographer, a painter, a teacher of music and Armenian, a portraitist, an embroiderer, and an impromptu musician. In other words, he plied all the trades that do not make you much money. All in all, when they made their reckoning with the world, my family came out even: Grandfather Setrak prospered, Grandfather Garabet squandered. Communism leveled all that: Grandfather Setrak was no longer able to prosper, and Grandfather Garabet was no longer able to squander.

But since for Grandfather Garabet the worldly side of things, the side that could be measured in coin, was unimportant, his life did not change very much with the arrival of the Communists. In fact, when it came to what they had done previously, the lives of the Armenians of Focșani did not change very much. He who was a watchmaker remained a watchmaker. He who was a cobbler remained a cobbler. He who was a grocer continued to sell groceries. The bell ringer remained a bell ringer, the doctor a doctor. And the priest did not discard his cassock, of course. But whereas the trades remained the same, the tradesmen suffered. For the mechanisms the watchmakers repaired were no longer Swiss but Russian. Patent-leather gentlemen's footwear and ladies' high-heeled shoes gave way to clunking boots that were cobbled again and again until the soles ended up thicker than the uppers. There were still sweetshops, but from the shelves the delicacies now vanished: Turkish delight, halva made from *tahin, leblebi*, tins of Van Houten cacao, sacks of coffee, candied tropical fruits, and chocolate-coated almonds. In their stead appeared dough coated in fat, cardboard-like wafers, and very dry biscuits whose crumbly cream filling used to flake off. Only the sugar candies, when they caught the light, preserved a tiny, stubborn gleam of their former glory. Assisted by Arshag the bell ringer, Father Dajad Aslanian, rolling up the sleeves of his cassock, hid the church books and treasures in the old crypts. It was not until a number of years later that he cautiously took them out, one by one, and finally he retrieved the most precious treasure of all: the silver bird whose beak sprinkled chrism on the holy water at Epiphany. The chrism was that sanctified by St. Gregory the Enlightener himself in the year 301, it having been topped up every seven years ever since. The church bell was now silent and pensive. Arshag would ascend to the belfry, not so much to pull the rope as to talk to the bell, which answered him in silences of varying profundity, like an organ from whose pipes you inhale rather than blow air. He also ascended to gaze through the south-facing window, which was narrow enough to use as a gun slit but tall enough to allow you to see as far as the edge of town and whether the Americans were coming. Through that south-facing window he espied no Americans, but through the north-facing window he did espy the Russians coming down the road from Tecuci. And more than ten years thereafter, during which time the south-facing window kept its silence, it was also through the north-facing window that Arshag watched the Russians depart, heading down the same road to Tecuci. This time, the other members of the parish council were there with him, and he let each look out of the window in turn. But by then it was too late; the red flags had put down roots, and the hammers and sickles had become part of the plasterwork so that to remove them from the frontons you would have had to rip away the wall. Lingering longer than the others, his face pressed against the small windowpane, Sahag Sheitanian put it well when he said, "If we are to be free, then rather than their leaving and our remaining, we should leave and they should remain." It was a misty morning following upon a rainy night. The Russian soldiers soon vanished. The earth caked their boots in mud, so they left no dust in the air behind them.

And the doctors were still doctors, but the same as in any other war, having promiscuously buried the starving, those with bleeding wounds, those shivering with typhus, and those that wept for all the rest, now they were inundated with births, children who, in that topsy-turvy world where the sun set in the east, were born already old.

So my grandfather Garabet Vosganian situated himself at an equal distance from all the different things that were happening. He wanted to understand the world, so he looked on it as repeatable, and he let his models live in his stead. His model of suffering was Komitas the monk, whom he began to resemble as he grew older; he ended up resembling him so well that when I first saw the death mask of Komitas, which is preserved by the Mekhitarist monks on the Venetian island of San Lazzaro, I was shocked by the uncanny likeness. For my grandfather, Father Komitas was perhaps not only a model of suffering, but also a model of madness.

He would often sit motionless, murmuring to himself. We did not know what he said; Grandfather did not let us come near. Those pages remain blank in *The Book of Whispers*. Sometimes he would lock himself away in his room and sing. He had a baritone voice that nimbly rose to a high tenor, exactly like the voice of Komitas, which astounded Vincent d'Indy, Camille Saint-Saëns, and Claude Debussy. He would sing, accompanying himself on the violin, straining the bow against all the strings at once so that it sounded like a quartet.

Komitas was arrested on April 24, 1915, the same day as his friends, the poets Daniel Varujan, Rupen Sevag, and Siamanto. He was wearing his archimandrite's robes but without the hood, whose pointed tip symbolizes Mount Ararat and which is worn by every representative of the Armenian Church, from monk to Catholicos. His hood and his cape he gave to some needy members of the convoy. Vehicles took them almost as far as Çankırı. Komitas mingled with the crowd, trying to soothe their suffering as best he could and urging them to keep faith in God. At night, he kept apart and began to murmur. At first, his fellow travelers thought he was praying. However, he was not praying but talking to somebody, and if God was that somebody, then the words, unwonted for a monk, were reproachful, like an inverted psalm. One day, he saw a woman about to give birth, but before he could reach her, a soldier ripped open her distended, throbbing belly with his bayonet. From that moment hence, Komitas fell silent, like Andrey Rublyov faced with the cruelties of the Tartars five centuries before. He spoke but once after that. At first the others thought he was joking, but then they realized that the reins of Father Komitas's mind had slackened. He stopped in the road and told the others in the convoy, "Do not hurry! Let the soldiers overtake us . . ." Then, as Daniel Varujan was being led away to his death, Komitas gave voice for the last time, not talking but singing. First he sang the psalm "Lord, forgive me!" but in a harsh voice, as if expecting God to beg forgiveness of us, and then he sang "Krrunk" (The crane). And when he finished, he burst into laughter. His peals of laughter were heard the whole night through, rasping and angry, like a rotten scrap of cloth that you keep tearing into shreds, folding it and tearing it anew. Many of them, including Daniel Varujan and Siamanto, were killed then. Not knowing what to do with him, Oğuz Bey sent Archimandrite Komitas to Constantinople in the end. He knew how to kill people who fell to the ground or who tried to flee; he killed people who prayed, who begged for mercy, who wept or cursed, but he did not know how to kill a man who laughed.

And Komitas laughed continuously. It was a laugh the likes of which had never been known before, that took upon itself the tears of the suffering but defied the killers; that laughter showed that there was nothing left of Komitas to kill.

He never recovered. His friends sent him to a sanatorium in Paris. He died twenty years later, and his laughter and his tears were reconciled on his death mask. His face is tranquil, the same as my grandfather's was, as if death were just a way station, as if you were leaning against the rim of a cool well and gazing within.

Grandfather Garabet would sing "The Crane," a song that told of the native lands, after which he did not burst into laughter but fell silent. He knew what he was doing since the traces were left on the canvas. My grandfather's laughter was made of pigments. He would brush the pigments onto the canvas—at random, as I used to think—or else he would dab them with his finger straight from the palette. And when the roars of laughter were irrepressible, he would squeeze them onto the canvas straight from the tube. Black and orange were the dominant colors. Grandfather would study them carefully. It was his way of understanding himself. In his effort to understand, Grandfather had his own methodological standards for each separate thing. He decoded himself through colors, for example. Above all else, energy means light. Light is a combination of colors, and by the spectrum you can understand what distance it has traveled, what body emanates it, what time of day it is. It is the same when it comes to a man: you place a prism of glass in front of him, you look at him, and there is your spectrum. "Here I am," Grandfather would say, looking up close at the jagged furrows of pigment, even touching them, so as to see not only the colors and the flow of the lines, but also the smoothness or roughness of the paint.

They were among his few moments of participation. Other than that, he would look at things patiently, painstakingly. Even when he was eating, so that he might understand the nature of the food, he used to chew each morsel up to thirty-three times. He said that that was the required number of chews if you were to make anything of the taste and meaning of each foodstuff, on the one hand, and if you were to break down the food sufficiently to protect your stomach, on the other. To tell the truth, that point at which he made himself equally distant from all things was also equally distant from himself. It is a different kind of madness to view yourself with the same curiosity and detachment as you might examine the trees in the garden or the chronology of a war, from the vantage point from which all things can be viewed from outside themselves. As is plain to see, Grandfather took Father Komitas as his model of suffering not to imitate him but to mirror him. Whereas the madness of Father Komitas was internal, the madness of Grandfather Garabet was external to things.

For that reason, my grandfather, who believed the world existed only so that it might be understood, used to say that once you learned yourself by rote, once you became so predictable that you could recite yourself by heart, like a poem, with a beginning and an end, with even a rhyme scheme, then the time had come for you to die.

If during their passage through this world Grandfather Garabet Vosganian understood and Grandfather Setrak Melikian failed to understand, then my godfather Sahag Sheitanian suffered. And if for Grandfather Garabet the foremost understanding—which is to say, self-understanding—came from his encounter with combined pigments and for Grandfather Setrak non-self-understanding came from his encounter with the slaps he was dealt with a vengeance, for Sahag Sheitanian self-suffering came from his encounter with Yusuf.

8.

THE STORY OF YUSUF. In *The Book of Whispers* there are no imaginary characters since all of them have existed in this world in their own place and time and under their own name. There is one character alone who might seem imaginary, given that his existence gradually transforms *The Book of Whispers* into a self-replicating reality, like two parallel mirrors. I often write about the storyteller of *The Book of Whispers*. In my tale, the storyteller tells of *The Book of Whispers*. And in the telling of this new book, there appears once more the storyteller who tells the tale. He tells of the storyteller and his story. If the order were reversed and we came to the final storyteller, the one who does not have the defect of describing himself, and if we were to move away from him and toward me, then we would have the dream, then the dream within the dream, and so on. But in this way, writing about the one who writes, while he in turn writes, stooped over the manuscript in which there is also a character named the author, it is as if we were gradually going deeper, like those toys made of hollowed wood, the *matryoshka* dolls that Old Man Musayan brought back from Siberia, losing count of the years and forgetting that in the meantime his son, Arakel, was already old enough to be drafted into the army.

Of all these real-life characters, some of their names you will find in the history books; others you will find only in *The Book of Whispers*. Although more often than not it tells of the past, it is not a history book, for the history books tell of the victors. Rather, it is a collection of psalms; it tells of the vanquished. And among the characters of the book there is also one who did not exist, but in spite of this fact or precisely because of it, he too bears a name: his name is Yusuf. This Yusuf was nothing more than a borrowed name, and he exists in *The Book of Whispers* only because of the fact that, despite not being part of the book's fabric, he is nonetheless the key that opens the door to the room of the most grievous chamber of the liminal era, a chamber with bare walls gouged by fingernails, with buckling floorboards and earth heaped haphazardly in mounds, like the earth of graves dug in haste. And the graves dug with the greatest haste are mass graves.

The living and the dead belong to the heavens and the earth. Only the dying belong wholly to death. Death walks among them; it is tender and takes care not to snap off the state of dying too soon. They are its fresh shoots of rice. The state of dying is an initiation into death. From Mamura to Deir-ez-Zor, for a distance of more than 180 miles, an entire nation traversed the seven circles, which is to say, the road of initiation into death. And it was at the end of this road that Sahag Sheitanian met Yusuf.

MAMURA. THE FIRST CIRCLE. The road runs straight for the length of the railway line. The entry into the first circle was made on foot, the circle of the death marches that gathered the Armenians from the most various of places, from European Anatolia, Smyrna, Izmid, and Adrianopolis or from the *vilayets* of eastern Anatolia, from Trebizond, Erzerum, or Kharput. Seen from afar, as they walked huddled together, their heads bowed, they looked like pilgrims. Except that pilgrims are driven by their faith, not by soldiers thrusting them from behind, butting them with their horses' muzzles, herding the stragglers back into line with blows of the whip. Sahag Sheitanian's family had five members: his grandmother, his parents, himself, and his younger sister. The two older children, Simon and Hayguhi, had been smuggled to Constantinople. His mother, Hermine, was a fiery woman. She was still steady on her feet. She held her arms around the children and walked in a straight line, keeping to the middle of the column to shield them from the horses' hooves but also to shield them from the sight of the crows pecking the corpses by the side of the road. They had some money. Rupen, the father, kept it hidden under his shirt. With a part of the money, they had been able to pay for a kind of ticket, or rather they had bought the goodwill of the stationmaster in Izmid, and they had boarded the train that traveled the Eshkisher-Konya-Bizanti-Adana route. Halfway to Mamura, the army halted the train, having placed a barrier across the railway track. But even if the journey on foot, across rocky wastes and a scorching plain, was to be exhausting, their lives were saved when the train stopped, as there was no room in the cattle trucks in which they had been crammed, their food had run out, and no one had given them water. The dead still remaining in the cattle trucks were those who had only just breathed their last since all those who had died on the way had been pushed out of the moving train onto the embankments.

Thus they were fortunate twice over: first, because they had not had to travel for hundreds of miles on foot, and second, because they had been released from the cattle trucks when they were all on the verge of death by suffocation. But most of the convoys, particularly those from the eastern *vilayets*, did not have any such luck. Those people made the whole journey on foot. Some of them, the wealthier folk, managed to get hold of carts and mules. Because of the exhaustion, the cold, the hunger, the raiding parties, and the massacres, of the almost one and a half million people deported, half a million died before they even reached the edge of the first circle. And then we may add those who did arrive, not on their own legs but borne on the waters of the Tigris and the Euphrates.

In September, the nights begin to grow cold, but the fierce heat of the day is unrelenting. They herded them onto open ground by the railway station in Mamura. As far as the eyes could see, folk erected makeshift tents from whatever they could: blankets, clothes, sheets. Most of the tents hung from just four sticks and spread over an area of about ten square feet. The faded tent fabric was proof against the sun and the rain but useless against the cold. Sahag counted with his eyes the ramshackle tents; there were so many that their farthermost limit could not be glimpsed. They were pitched at the edge of the town, on the other side of the railway track. There was a reason for this: it was easier to guard the railway track, and it meant that none would dare to go into the town for bread. They still had meager provisions. They ate in haste, watchful, in the shadow of their tents, so as not to be seen by the others.

Now and then, scattered groups tried to approach the railway station but were driven back into the camp. But in the end, the soldiers stopped threatening them and allowed them to go about their business. Some went from tent to tent, helping those within to carry away their dead. And so that the dead would not be left all alone, they laid them one next to the other. Later, when the dead had multiplied beyond measure, they laid them one on top of another. And so it was that death built mounds that surrounded the camp like watchtowers. The animals snorted from hunger and at the smell of death. They were mainly mules, tethered to carts or carrying bundles on their packsaddles. The mules proved to be the most resilient. The horses had died either of thirst or having broken their legs on the mountain paths. The dogs kept apart. They sensed in the eyes of the people the same hunger, the same state of being harried. Together with the flocks of crows, the dogs waited patiently for evening to fall.

The family slept huddled together to keep warm. In the daytime, they undressed and hung out their knotted clothes overhead. They had agreed to share their cart with a betrothed couple from Konya, and the men took turns pushing it from behind to help the mule. The woman offered to darn their sheets, strengthening them against the gusts of wind. She was traveling with her fiancé. They were to have wed, but the wedding guests had died on the road behind.

Sahag's mother had two pots in which she collected rainwater. When the water had almost run out, they wiped their lips with the rags they hung out at night so that the hoarfrost might moisten them.

When the host of tents extended too far, threatening to spill over the railway track, and when the number of corpses was so great that the air was thick with the stench of death, the soldiers descended on horseback among the tents and forced a few thousand folk to take to the road once more. The tents caved in under the horses' hooves; the people were herded to the edge of the field with blows of the whips. When they did not manage to cram their things into their bundles or to fold up their tents, the horsemen made haste to set light to the roofs of dry fabric.

Their turn came at the end of October. For a hale man it would have been a five-hour walk to the next stopping place, but it took them almost five days.

ISLAHIYE. THE SECOND CIRCLE. The road led through the Amanus Mountains, over the crests, then down into Islahiye, on the banks of a river. When they reached the second circle, the first snows began to fall. Many were clothed in thin rags, and they had only the sweat-soaked dust that thickened their clothes to keep them warm. They threw the blanket over the mule, and for the whole way they wrapped themselves in the sheets. They abandoned the cart, which no longer had room to move along the narrow paths, and the men carried on their backs as many of the chattels as they could. When it grew a little warmer, they tore a sheet into strips and tied it to one another so that they would not lose their footing and slip among the steep precipices. The mountain path was clean, and clean it remained even after the convoy had passed, for those who fell, having reached the end of their strength, were thrust with prods of the walking stick into the ravines. The old woman rode on the mule, which helped her to survive the journey, unlike many others, who died of exhaustion or collapsed dying and tumbled down the rocks. When they came down into the plain, the convoy was met by a band of a few dozen armed Kurds. At a signal, the soldiers guarding them blocked the way ahead, leaving the convoy powerless to advance. The folk came to a stop, gazing in fear as the horsemen fell upon them, brandishing their muskets and sabers. The plateau was narrow, with mountains behind, precipices to each side, and the horsemen before them. It is a scene we know from hundreds of accounts. Convoys of mostly women and children, abandoned defenseless, scattering over the plain, each person seeking to escape, not knowing that when you break away from the throng, you become the easiest prey of all for horsemen bent on plunder and slaughter, be they the murderers the Turks had armed and released from prison for that very purpose, be they the Kurds, Chechens, or Bedouins. Rarely did they attack at random. More often than not, they were informed of the convoy's time and route, and the soldiers had orders to move aside, leaving the horsemen to do their work. Sometimes they merely plundered and seized the young women, but more often than not, they slaughtered them to the last man. There was no general rule. They might kill you for your money or jewels or else because you had nothing to give them. The best thing to do was to curl up into a ball or lie down and pretend to be dead. If you were lucky enough not to be trampled under the horses' hooves, you might survive until the horsemen tired of chasing moving targets, until night fell and they went away, whooping and grasping the struggling women slung over their saddles. Behind them they left a plain dotted with corpses, from which those still alive would slowly be climbing to their feet in a daze.

The fiancé of the woman they had befriended was also killed. Around his neck he wore a worthless but shiny necklace, which a horseman coveted and did not take the trouble to steal from him other than by chopping off his head. They were forced to leave him there, prey to the wild animals.

Dragging the wounded behind them, it was not until daylight that they reached the plain at Islahiye. On either side of the entrance to the camp there were two mounds of corpses, mainly children. They unpacked their tents. The food was almost gone. In the morning, mounted soldiers streaked across the plain, tossing loaves of bread at random over the tents. The people swarmed, grabbing at pieces of bread, fighting for their share. Toward noon, the camp grew quiet. The people crawled inside the tents, keeping watch over those whose death was near.

The soldiers kept their distance, for the oppressive smells of death were no longer sweet but sharp, presaging the spread of dysentery. The commandant of the camp summoned the men that still had strength and ordered them to collect the dead. In those autumn months, at the Islahiye camp starvation and dysentery caused more than sixty thousand deaths. The commandant ordered the corpses to be left at the edge of the camp for two or three days before burial. Exposed to the wind, the dead dried up and shriveled, taking up less space, and in this way there was more room in the mass graves.

Then, they moved their tents closer together so that the raiders, especially the Bedouins from the surrounding villages, would not have room to move between them. They did not fear one another, for none of the deportees stole money or gold, not having any use for them. The things they might have coveted—flour, sugar, or cured meat—had long since run out. At the foot of the walls or along the embankments, their animals searched for tufts of grass. Those wracked within by dysentery lay curled up, awaiting death. The others chewed long on the pieces of crumbly bread tossed from the galloping horses.

A miraculous and at the same time terrible thing happened: the snow came. They rushed outside the tents with outstretched palms. They still had enough life in them for the snowflakes to melt in their cupped palms so that they could lick the drops from between their fingers. Then, when they saw that the snowfall was thickening, they waited for it to settle and licked it from the ground, together with the dogs and mules. More than the others, Sahag drank his fill, for he had noticed that the snow thickened the most and lasted the longest on the brows of the dead, which were colder even than the ground.

But with the snow came a bitter frost that froze the earth, turning to jagged folds the sheets from which the tents were patched together. It cleansed the air. The putrefaction of sundry creatures abated, and the miasmas settled on the ground as hoarfrost. The people huddled together, gathering inside the most capacious of the many tents. And there they managed to scrape together a fire from a few chips of frozen wood. They crowded together, even if they managed only to see the feeble flame from afar.

Those at the point of death were so emaciated from hunger and scorched by the cold that when they dragged them between the tents by the arms or legs, their ankle and wrist bones broke, snapping like dry twigs.

When the snows melted, the convoys began to form once more. The heavens grew damp, and the rain began to fall. The roads were mired in mud. They tied strips of sheets around their feet; otherwise their bare soles would have stuck in the ground, and the people no longer had the strength to tear them from the mud. Beneath the drizzle that blurred every outline, the new journey lasted almost a week. They were unable to count the dead, for on this misty road no one could see anything but the bluish mist of his own breath. The flesh of those who fell, soaked by the rain, was as soft and sticky as clay. They were trodden underfoot by those that came behind. Their flesh was churned into black dough and swallowed by the mud of the road. Nor did the rain cease when they arrived.

BAB. THE THIRD CIRCLE. The plain of black tents stretched along a strip of land a few miles from the town. This was deliberate, as it prevented the deportees from going into the town. Because of the clayey soil, pools of slushy water had begun to form, and all was transformed into mire.

They did not manage to make a tally of the dead left behind on the road because they were overwhelmed with those that were now dying within the deportee camp. The men, as many as remained, organized themselves into two groups. Some of them handled the lugging of the dead bodies outside the camp and the digging of the mass graves. The dead were harder to lug in the third circle; because they were as dry as the crumbly soil and the cold had sapped their bones, they absorbed water and bloated. The veins of the waterlogged corpses burst, causing them to turn red like raw meat. Swollen and unwieldy, they took up much space, so besides the fact that the earth was sticky, the graves also had to be made larger.

The second group of men roamed the plains, approaching the town only as far as the rubbish pits and the edge of the paupers' quarters, searching for food, which more often than not consisted of carrion flesh. Some, those still nimble, threw rocks at the crows or hunted the dogs that hung around the camp and that after nightfall scrabbled at the hastily covered graves in search of flesh that had not yet rotted.

Thus the epidemic of typhus broke out. It struck the children first. It covered their cheeks in red blotches, which, because of the squalor, swiftly turned into open wounds welling with blood and the sweat of fever. Then it passed to their mothers, who were unable to refrain from clasping their feverishly shivering babies in their arms. Only the winter frost prevented the plague from spreading to all. But the cold also meant that there was no hope for those that fell ill. From fear of the sickness, the soldiers kept their distance, and only rarely did they venture among the tents through the sleet to toss them a loaf of bread without dismounting. They no longer thought of wiping the mud off the loaf. The lucky ones who got a piece of bread ran to share it with the people in their tent, or else they crouched with their heads hanging low, grasping their crust and gobbling it without chewing, lest another rush at them and wrest it away from them.

From time to time, the women in particular, who would lose their minds out of pity for the dying children, would venture to the edge of the settlement to beg for food or to seek a safer shelter and clean bedding. When they were not shot at, they were driven away with rocks and clubs.

The woman with whom they had set out on the journey fell ill. She lay huddled, and they could do nothing for her but heap on her shoulders all the bedding they had. One day, the man of the Sheitanian family came back with a dead crow, which he had hunted as the bird lurked with its flock by the mass graves. The man had a wild glint in his eyes; his hollow cheeks were covered with tufts of crinkled hair; his clothes were nothing but tatters, and to stop them fluttering in the wind he had tied them with a piece of string, wrapped round and round his body from his chest to his waist. In place of boots he wore two strips of knotted rag, with two pieces of wood for soles. This caused him to walk disjointedly, shuffling, now and again lifting his soles to step over a ridge. In order to hunt, he did not need to run, nor would he have had the strength to do so. The dead things needed only to be carried away. It was enough to cast a rock at the dogs and crows; they were cumbersome, as the camp had stuffed them with food aplenty. And then he had but to crush the head with the same rock or swiftly to wring the neck. Which is what Rupen Sheitanian had done; the bird's neck was unnaturally crooked. On seeing him like that, Hermine clasped her children to her breast, and, harrowed, she whispered, "Ur es, Asdvadz? (Where art Thou, Lord)?" "God is dying, woman," said the man. "Look; even His angels have died." And he tossed the black bird into the middle of the tent.

Using damp twigs, they struggled to kindle a smoky fire and then singed the flesh of the plucked bird. But it did not help the sick woman, whose shrunken stomach could no longer hold down the food. She vomited the only morsel she managed to swallow, and unable to quell her spasms, she died shortly thereafter, having suffocated. "It is the sign of the black angel," murmured Hermine. "It is a different and more cursed sign," said Rupen, "if God kills even the black angels." And he looked up at the gray sky, he looked down at the miry earth, and he looked at the drizzle and the mist of the camp that blurred sky and earth together in one greedy, murderous haze. They slung the woman over the mule so that she dangled on either side like a pair of saddlebags, and Rupen took her to the edge, where the bodies swelled and distended gelatinously. But first he unclothed her and shared her garments with Sahag's younger sister, to protect her from the cold, and with the young woman from Konya, lest the Bedouins lust after her if they saw her naked.

No matter how hard the local people tried to avoid the deportees, driving them away like dogs with whatever they could lay their hands on, shouting "Ermeni! Ermeni!" so that others would come out and throw rocks at the creatures that hesitantly approached, their arms outstretched, no matter how hard they tried to avoid them, the typhus still spread through the town. Then the Arabs mustered their warriors and fell on the camp, furrowing it with their horses' hooves, slaying the people with sword or bullet, driving them away with the flat of their swords or with blows of their cudgels, setting fire to their tents. The same as always, the soldiers looked on, impassive, willingly accepting the assistance that the bands of warriors lent famine, dysentery, and typhus. The slaughter lasted the whole day, and the warriors swore to return if the next day the deportees did not move on their way, no matter where, as long as it was far away from the houses of the town.

Although the instructions said that the camp at Bab had to be kept in isolation until the coming of spring, because of the local discontent, the convoys once more set under way. It was January 5, although this was not known for a fact; nobody had kept a tally of the days, and because no day could be distinguished from the next by any sign—such as Sunday mass, for example—they perceived only the passing of the seasons and even then only with approximation. The only precise tally to be kept was that of the dead. The Turkish soldiers cut notches with their bayonets in the pole nearest to each place where the corpses were dumped. But even this tally ceased to be kept when the typhus raged and the dead began to be brought by the cartload and emptied straight into the mass graves.

They tried to reckon the arrival of Christmas by the length of the nights, but because the sky was always gray and overcast, the nights seemed longer than they really were. And the dead multiplied because it was in the night that the dying mainly gave up the ghost. But because the next day the first convoys set off and they were unable to know how many would reach the journey's end, the few priests among them, who could be told apart from the others only by their longer beards, decided that that night would be Christmas Eve.

Those who still had candle stumps lit them. Hermine said, "Let the light be visible." They burned the whole candle, scraping up the warm wax with their fingers and smearing it on their palms. They would also have to preserve a taper for the night of the Resurrection. "By then," said Rupen, swaddling the soles of his feet, "we will all be dead."

MESKENE. THE FOURTH CIRCLE. So that it would not stray near Aleppo, where there was once more a risk of contamination, faced with the growing hostility of the local populace and at the express order of Djemal Pasha that the deportees should be kept far away from the railway, the convoy avoided the most accessible road, via Aleppo and Sebil, and cut across tracts of wilderness, via Tefridje and Lale. A man in good health might have made the journey from Bab to Meskene in two days if we take into account that he would have been able to enjoy a restful night in the caravanserais of Lale, that he would have been able to eat his fill, and that he would have had mules to carry his water skins. It took the death marches that departed from Bab more than ten days to make the same journey; sometimes it took more than two weeks.

After they left Bab it began to snow again. As they did not keep to the main road that led to Aleppo and as snow covered the whole expanse, the convoys often lost their way. The soldiers would take a bearing and then turn them back in the right direction, pushing them forward with their horses' muzzles. Nor was it hard for them to lose their way because those that made up the convoys—even the hardiest, those that walked at the front, breasting the wind—went with their eyes downcast, looking up only seldom, not at the road, which they reckoned endless, but at the sky, to seek some glimmer of light, a sign that the snow would stop or merely a sign, any sign. They wrapped themselves in all the fabrics and bedding they still had, tying them around their bodies with string to keep the wind out. The thickest blankets they reserved for their feet, fashioning booties for themselves that they soaked in cooking oil, if they still had any, or in puddles of petroleum, the better to keep the snow out. The convoy had set out in a compact huddle, but now, as it began to tire, it straggled for almost half a mile. The soldiers were content merely to shove them, no longer attempting to hurry them; those that were beaten with whips or canes fell to their knees rather than quickening their steps. When they fell, it was taken as a sign of rebellion. These the soldiers killed with blows of the cane to the back of the neck, thereby saving bullets. They would fall senseless in the snow, a fall that was the same thing as death. Then the soldiers gave up, letting them advance according to their strength. The exhausted ones moved more and more slowly, falling to the back of the convoy. It was harder and harder for them to lift their feet out of the snow. Finally they would remain motionless, planted in the snow, their legs too frozen to allow their knees to bend. They died standing up, their arms akimbo, having been blown into that position by the wind; they died like black, withered trees. The governor of Aleppo, alarmed at the large number of bodies that, if left by the roadside, would have brought the plague to the city, sent carts after them. Sometimes, the carts would find them a few days later, still standing, their frozen arms creaking in the wind. At first, the gravediggers took fright. But later they quite simply plucked them from the snow, like trunks whose roots had withered away, and they said to each other that the earth must be glutted with the dead if it had left these people to die standing up.

They slept in abandoned caravanserais, sometimes remaining there for two days at a time so that they might gather a little strength. With the carts for the dead sent from Aleppo there also came a few sacks of *bulghur*, a kind of husked wheat, which was shared out among them, each receiving enough to fill his two cupped hands. At Tefridje and then at Lale they saw from afar a host of large shelters, with sheet-metal roofs resting on poles, some of them even having brick walls, and they rejoiced that they would be able to find protection from the cold. But they were not allowed to go within a few dozen yards of the shelters. Lest the road to Meskene remain strewn with the dead, the authorities had decided to set up such shelters in the Aleppo *vilayet* and amass the dying therein. They did not receive any care but were laid on the ground to die, fifteen to twenty in each shelter. The state in which they arrived was so pitiful that they were too feeble even to turn over on one side or the other or to brush the swarms of bugs from their faces. They died in the same posture in which they were laid, often with their eyes open since their eyelids were too shrunken and withered to cover the whites of their eyes. For this reason, the camps had only a few guards, without pistols but armed with clubs and rocks to keep away the dogs, the hyenas, and the crows, although they displayed little alacrity in the performance of this duty.

The joy of approaching such places, which they thought had been prepared for them against the onslaught of wind, rain, and snow, turned to bewilderment and then horror when the convoy was brought to a halt on the outskirts of the shelters without being allowed to proceed any farther. At each of those way stations, the convoy was met by a band of soldiers, headed by a petty official and a man dressed in black, whom the others addressed as *doktor effendi*. He made all the people in the convoy stand in a row, at a distance of one pace from each other, so that they could not prop each other up. Some collapsed straightaway, making the task of the *doktor effendi* the easier. For he had come to tend not to the living but to the dead. To eliminate the risk of so many corpses strewn along the road, especially given that Aleppo was full of foreign consulates ready to send dispatches to the imperial courts of Europe, the *doktor effendi* indicated the moribund who were there and then bundled away to the shelters and beaten if the life in them put up any resistance. The *doktor effendi* gauged each of them, pointing his finger at those that showed the rash of a fever, those that were already shivering from every limb, those whose cheeks were deathly pale and whose eyes were sunken in their sockets or whose mouths were flecked with greenish-red froth from their perforated, wheezing lungs. At each of the two camps for the dying the convoy thinned by around a tenth. Of those that had set out from Bab, around a third did not make it to Meskene. Many gave up the ghost at the two way stations for the moribund, while the bodies of others lay scattered along the roads, their flesh melting with the snow and seeping into the streams, their bones crumbling to gravel.

In Meskene, at the boundary of the fourth circle, the convoys once more met the Euphrates, which was a flowing tomb for thousands of deportees. At the bend in the river, beyond Meskene, the corpses from the north accumulated, those that the waters had not dragged down or that the fish had not yet torn to shreds. The bodies were hauled to the bank with boat hooks. Because the earth was frozen and the corpses were too many to bury, they were sprinkled with petrol and set alight. The black smoke was visible from the camp at Meskene. Although the deportees knew why the smoke was so thick, knew why the pyre was so wet that it could only smolder, knew what floated down the river, still they went to the riverbank, knelt down, and greedily drank water that tasted like lye.

Some pitched their tents yet again; others took shelter in abandoned tents. The same as always after the appearance of a new convoy, the number of dead swelled before receding to the usual figure of five or six hundred a day. The cold had softened somewhat, particularly in the daytime, but the nights were just as bitter. The rains and the snows had abated and were to become ever more infrequent the nearer the convoys came to the desert. The air too became drier, making the breath of the dying rasp the more noisily.

The camp was harshly guarded. The few that managed to elude the guards were captured on the plain by the town, and then they were dunked up to their necks in the cold river and left on the bank in the wind. If they survived, they were sent back to the tents, where, shivering and delirious, they perished soon thereafter.

All of a sudden, the mule knelt down and refused to drink. It had been a good animal. Rupen stroked its forehead tenderly for a long time, and then with a rock he struck it repeatedly in the same place. The children wept, but they wiped away their tears when they tasted the sweetness of the meat, which was not stringy, like that of the crows, or bitter, like that of the carrion. It lasted them a few days and lent them strength. They also received a fistful of *bulghur*. When they raised their eyes wondering at that gesture of kindness, they learned the reason from Kior Hussein, the same man who punished those that tried to escape by plunging them into the icy water: "I don't want you to die here. We have problems enough as it is. The earth is sticky, hard to dig. You will die anyway. But leave this place on your own legs and go into the desert. There, nobody will have to tire himself out because of you. The wind and the sands will bury you."

Then they understood that those who received a portion of grain in their cupped palms were to continue their journey. They let them go down to the river and drink the brackish water, which, like the Jordan, was to acquire the taste of human flesh. The *bulghur* was a fleeting remedy for innards parched by dysentery. And in their bellies the water swelled the grains that had been swallowed unchewed, making them feel achingly ravenous but sated at the same time. For the body craved strength, but shrunken by starvation, the stomach swelled, ready to burst walls thinned by so much grinding away at nothing.

Sahag had grown thin. His ankles were only a little thicker than his wrists. His mother meted out what was left of the sacks of flour and sugar bought in the station at Konya from traders who, knowing where they were going and adding their desperation to the price, had asked three times what they were worth.

They ate in the evening so that they could sleep since Hermine had observed that hunger is harder to endure in the night, when the body is more focused on itself. At first she gave an equal portion to all and then more to the children and less to the adults. And at Meskene, she gave nothing to the old woman, who, one evening, made a sweeping sign of the cross, turned her face to the wall, and died huddled. The next morning they loaded her on the cart for the dead and rolled her into the mass grave. As there was nobody to wash the dead, to watch over them and fold their arms across their chests, there was no reason for them to press rags soaked in hot water on their joints in order to straighten their bent legs and arms. And even if they had bothered to soften the shrunken, frozen gristle of the joints, it would have been in vain since the bodies were not laid neatly in the mass graves side by side but tumbled on top of one another pell-mell. "We should have kept her until the afternoon," said Hermine. "By then the graves would have filled up and they would have laid her on top . . ." Rupen made no answer but merely shrugged. He no longer spoke; he would lift his shoulders, and the women did not know whether that was now his manner of speech or whether he was stretching his increasingly stooped back.

The old woman had chosen the right moment to die. The next day, soldiers surrounded their corner of the camp and drove them on their way once more. With the mule dead, the old woman would in any case not have been able to travel and would have been dragged to the carts transporting the dying back toward Lale. There, the only things that were plentiful were the swarms of gnats and the patience with which the dying were laid in a row and left to die.

DIPSI. THE FIFTH CIRCLE. Ordinarily, it was a good five hours' walk from Meskene to Dipsi. But it took the convoys more than two days. For the first time their footsteps met the sandy lands that betokened the closeness of the desert.

The carts that collected the dead and dying no longer accompanied them. From time to time, the gravediggers that collected the dead would wait for the winds to whip up the sands and cover the mounds of naked, blackened bodies. But the two days the journey lasted were calm. The sky had cleared, and the winds had died. The corpses lay at the edge of the road, a large part of them lacerated by animals. Among the dead bodies were the dying—women and men exhausted by the journey, by hunger and thirst, children who could not understand what was happening to them—and they waited to die, leaning against rocks or withered trees. This effort to remain seated was their final effort in the fight against death because otherwise, if they lay at the edge of the road, the sand would have covered them, smothering them.

The camp, made up of thousands of tents, was situated in a valley on the right bank of the Euphrates. Those who chose that place, surrounded by hills, had calculated that the relentless stench of death and the sharp reek of dysentery and typhus would have less chance of spreading. The distance between Meskene and Dipsi was shorter than between Bab and Meskene, and for that reason, the governor of Aleppo had not set up the midway shelters for the dying that he euphemistically named *hastane*, which is to say, hospitals. But given the exhaustion of those in the convoys, arriving after a two-day journey of sand and then mountain passes, the whole camp at Dipsi was called a *hastane*. And it deserved its name since in the few months in which it served as a concentration camp, more than thirty thousand people died there.

The so-called hospital was completely lacking in medicine, and the only staff were the Armenian doctors among the surviving deportees, who were helpless to do anything except put a name to an illness, when it was not otherwise obvious, and estimate the number of days until death. The concentration camp at Dipsi was one of the deepest levels of the initiation into death, not so much because of the large numbers who gave up the ghost there as much as the even larger number of those who, having been infected there, were to give up the ghost farther along the road to Deir-ez-Zor, the place where the seventh veil of death fell away.

It was now March. The rains had ceased. From time to time, at evening or dawn, a blanket of cloud would gather. Spring will have arrived unnoticed for the deportees, who looked around them more and more seldom and even then with fear, alerted by the clatter of horses' hooves or the whoops and the muskets of the Bedouins. This was why they looked mainly at the ground. And that was how they discovered it was spring. Near Abuhahar, Hamam, Sebka, and Deir-ez-Zor, where the trees became more and more sparse, spring arrived unawares, when the tufts of grass began to sprout. At first, they did not know how to eat them; the sharp edges of the long fine blades made their gums bleed, and they choked on the stringy strands. Then, the wisest and most patient among them showed the others the art of eating grass. You had to crumple the strands into a ball in your palm, on which you then sprinkled a little salt to moisten the clump of grass. You did not chew it all at once but let it soften in as much saliva as you could gather in your dry mouth. You kept it like that in your ravenous mouth for a few minutes, until it turned into a kind of paste, like pottage. When there was no more grass to be found, Rupen ripped up the roots and washed them in the waters of the Euphrates. He cut them into little pieces, and once they had been soaked in water for a few hours, they could be eaten.

It did not rain, but the sky was not serene. The nearness of the desert lifted a kind of haze, which the dust stirred up by the wind held in suspension. The dogs and the wolves had dwindled, and in their place appeared hyenas. They were harder to catch, swifter and more accustomed to the dryness of the desert. And their corpses could never be found, for when a hyena felt its end was nigh, it vanished into the desert whence it had come. The crows remained. They were hard to hit, for in the nacreous haze they could not be told apart from thin air, in which white angels could not be told apart from black.

Since the grass dwindled because of the miasmas, as well as the Turkish soldiers' horses, which grazed at the edges of the camp, Hermine and Rupen, after agonized thought, decided to send Sahag to act as one of the couriers.

My grandfathers, Garabet Vosganian and Setrak Melikian, did not sing songs of the deportation in their moments of solitude. Nor did the other old Armenians of my childhood. The poems we read as children, the songs we heard, told mainly of the *fedayi* who had fought in the mountains, not of the massacres and the deportations. In silence did the convoys descend each level of the initiation into death. Perhaps it was because the inner suffering was too strong to allow anything to pierce through to the outside. Perhaps it was because they did not believe that anything would come afterward.

But since nothing pierced through to the outside, the deportees wrote for themselves. The manuscripts that have remained from the seven circles of death were written during the journeys of deportation wherever a piece of wood was to be found, a milestone, a tree trunk with yielding bark, a wall. For a long time, until the rains washed them away and the winds erased them, the Armenian letters and words written or carved on wood and stone remained. Those who went before left tidings for those that came behind. And if there was room, those that came behind left their own words. In the camps pieces of paper circulated from hand to hand. They were not signed, from fear of reprisals, nor were they dated. There was no need. The reality, with the exception of the snow that turned to mire and the mud that turned to swirling dust, was unchanging.

The tidings described the realities of each circle of death. Those who bore these tidings were the couriers. They were picked from among the young boys, who were more agile and could creep unseen. And to give them the strength to make their journeys quickly, they were given provisions. Some never returned; either they were incorporated into the advance convoys, which meant the distance until their death was shortened, or else they were killed on the way. For this reason, the couriers were always volunteers and chosen from among the orphans, because few parents chose to part with their children that way. The man who decided at that end of the death marches was named Krikor Ankut. The man at the other end, at Deir-ez-Zor, was Levon Shashian, a responsibility he held until he was killed after enduring unimaginable torture.

Krikor Ankut measured up the young boy, with the flat of his hand shoving his chest, but Sahag found the strength to keep his balance, not to fall. The man therefore decided the lad was suitable. The journey to Deir-ez-Zor would have taken around six days on foot, but as the couriers traveled mainly by night, taking shelter in hollows in the riverbank by day, the round trip lasted more than two weeks. Sahag learned the name of the man at the camp in Rakka who was to provide him with further provisions to reach Deir-ez-Zor. Rupen and Hermine stood to one side and watched, not knowing whether what they had decided would be to their son's advantage or whether it would spell his death. Somebody stood guard outside the tent; another had brought a jug of water. Hermine carefully washed Sahag's back, and then the boy lay face down with his arms spread. Krikor Ankut dipped his quill in the inkwell and slowly wrote on the boy's skin, filling his back down to his rump with large letters that were as plain as possible, both to make the task quicker and to spare the boy, who bore the scratches of the quill without flinching. The fact that his skin was stretched tautly over his bones made the task easier. For a short while, the boy lay motionless to allow the ink to dry. Then, they mixed earth in the basin of water and made a thin mud, with which they smeared his back. Anointed with mud, he was only a little dirtier than he had been before. They asked him whether he knew how to swim. The boy answered that he had grown up on the bank of the Bosphorus. Then Krikor traced the road to Deir-ez-Zor for him in the earth. "Travel by night. Keep to the bank of the Euphrates, and do not stray from it. If you have no other escape, throw yourself into the water and endure as long as you can, until the water dissolves the ink and washes it away. They must not see what is written there. Likewise when you return. Above all when you return."

On behalf of the boy, Hermine received the provisions for the journey. She set aside a handful of grain and rice for his younger sister, and then she embraced him, and he vanished into the night. They did not bid each other farewell. Having seen so much death around them and accepting it as an unavoidable reality, they had long since bidden each other farewell.

Sahag did exactly as he had been asked. He meted out his meager food, he endured three days, but he did not stop at Rakka, fearful he might never be able to leave. When he arrived at Deir-ez-Zor, he sought out Levon Shashian, who wiped away the mud and read Krikor Ankut's message. He cleaned the boy, inscribed fresh letters, and then smeared his back with a layer of mud mingled with ash. On his return, Krikor Ankut first gave him a cup of water and a fistful of *bulghur*. He told the women to wash him, and after he had read, he asked to be left alone. With his own hand he wiped away the text on the boy's back, embraced him, and said, "Do not tell anybody what you saw at Deir-ez-Zor. Most will not believe you, and then it will do you no good. Go back to your parents." When they saw him, Hermine took him in her arms and wept, not so much in joy at having him back as in pity.

In mid-April, the camp at Dipsi was broken up, and the final convoys set out along the course of the Euphrates. Mounted soldiers and gendarmes surrounded the camp, rushing between the tents, striking with canes and whips, driving the people from the shelters toward the edges, where the convoys were forming. When all those still able to stand had run from the tents, driven before the horses, leaving the dying behind them, the signal to depart was given. They had been walking for almost an hour toward the hills, turning their heads back toward the hospital camp at Dipsi, when they saw thick smoke rising. The shelters had been sprinkled with petrol and set alight. From the color and shape of the billowing smoke, they realized that along with the tent fabric there also burned human bodies, withered or yet moist, moribund, pell-mell.

RAKKA. THE SIXTH CIRCLE. The harsh journey lasted more than a week. By day the heat was scorching, but the nights were exceptionally cold. They walked ever more slowly, tottering. For those dazed files of people, impassive to the shouts and the lashes of the guards, at least there was no longer any danger of their being attacked by armed bands, for they no longer had anything to pillage. But at the way stations, the Arabs would approach, buying girls with little bags of grain. The convoy kept to the right bank of the river and finally reached Sebka, the camp on the bank opposite Rakka, from where the town was visible like a miraculous and forbidden realm. The waters of the Euphrates slaked the thirst of the deportees, but there were fewer and fewer chances of their finding anything to eat. From time to time, the gendarmes would gallop past and toss them bags of food sent by the foreign consulates or Christian charities. Tossed at random, most of the food was wasted. The people tugged at the bags of flour and sugar, and the powder sifted away between their fingers. Other food aid, such as chickpeas and rice, was inedible because the people no longer had teeth. They swallowed them without chewing, but their stomachs did not have time to digest them, either because of long disuse or because of dysentery. Rupen no longer went hunting; dogs were scarce, and the wolves went in packs. On no few occasions the packs attacked people as they scavenged in the rubbish, devouring them. Rupen went with the others to collect the dead bodies. He helped to dig the mass graves, a task made easier now that the earth was neither hard nor sticky. It was enough to move the sand aside with your spade. But the task was harder given that the graves had to be much deeper. Otherwise, the wind would have winnowed away the tops of the graves, lifting them like lids and exposing the dead.

There was nobody to pray by the mass graves. All the methods used to kill the Armenians, on the roads of Anatolia, from Constantinople to Deir-ez-Zor and Mosul, were later used by the Nazis against the Jews, methods that ranged from convoys taken to isolated and easily encircled places to be slaughtered to the concentration camps where the dying were shot, starved, plunged in icy water, or burned alive. The only difference was that in the Nazi camps the prisoners wore numbers, and that macabre numbering augmented the horror of the crimes against the Jewish people. The dead resulting from the endeavor to annihilate the Armenian people were not as numerous, if comparisons can be made between crimes on such a scale, but they were numberless. The names we know are mainly those of the murderers—the governors, the camp commandants, the pashas, those with the ranks of *bey, ağa, çavuş*. The victims rarely have names. Shedding its vestments circle after circle, never was death closer to its naked core; never was death so nameless.

Traditions have yet to be invented when it comes to the digging of mass graves: how they should be dug; how the dead should be laid therein; whether the men should rest at the bottom, the women in the middle, and the children above; how they should be washed; how they should be clothed; what kind of prayers the priest should say and of what eternal rest he should speak; what kind of cross should be planted; how many arms that cross should have and what should be inscribed thereon. There is no tradition as to all these things. Each mass grave has its own laws, and the only thing that makes them alike is the haste with which they are dug. And this precludes the idea of lasting customs since where there is haste, there can be no tradition.

Graves are given names and they are adorned in order that the buried should not be wholly forgotten. The mass graves were made so that the dead tossed into them would be forgotten as quickly as possible. Mass graves are history's guiltiest part.

Around this nameless core of death I have traced seven circles; its epicenter is Deir-ez-Zor. Within their area, whose outer circumference passes through Mamura, Diarbekir, and Mosul, more than a million people died, around two-thirds of all those who died in the Armenian Genocide. We know that they were there and that of those who entered the circles of death, of those who were not forcibly converted to Islam, sold as slaves, or taken for the harems, almost none escaped. Anybody could die anywhere. There is not one family of Armenians in this world that does not have a member who vanished in the circles of death, as if dragged down into a whirlpool. Therefore, you can pray at the edge of every mass grave in the sure knowledge that somebody who belonged to your family is laid there.

Rupen knew how to do a thing well. Death was a refuge for the humiliating plight of the living, and the mass graves were a refuge for the embarrassing situation of the dead. But there was also another reason why Krikor Ankut, along with the other leading men, decided to hasten the removal of the dead from the tents and the digging of the mass graves. A few days earlier, they had removed a faceless corpse from inside a tent in which lived a large family. They gazed for a long time at that corpse, whose face looked as if it had been eaten away by rats. But in the camp there were no rat holes, and therefore there were no rats. They all understood, but they said not a word. They did not need to swear an oath of silence, sensing that nobody would be able to speak of something so gruesome. When similar cases began to abound, the men decided to make an inspection every morning and evening so that no corpse would remain inside the tents for long.

New garrisons were sent to Rakka and Sebka from Aleppo. The soldiers and gendarmes kept their distance from the camp. The camp was not hard to guard. At its northern edge was the riverbank, and the Euphrates was hard to cross even for a man in good health. To the left and the right stretched the plains, on whose open expanse there was no place to hide, and to the south was the desert. And indeed, with the exception of the boy couriers, few managed to flee, losing themselves among the motley crowds of the markets in Rakka and thence traveling in a direction opposite to that of the convoys, to Bab and Mamura or north to Urfa.

But the soldiers were not only guarding the people. They also guarded the wild animals and even the birds. The inhabitants of Rakka and the tribes of Bedouins were fearful of the plagues that stalked the convoys of deportees. For this reason, the governor of Aleppo had forbidden gravediggers from outside the convoys to approach, and the carts that were sent to the camp were abandoned to the deportees. And finally, when the deportees themselves did not kill them for food, the horses were shot to prevent them from bringing back any of the diseases that, having raged unopposed, had now become incurable.

As they stood and gazed toward the tents, polishing their boots, currying their horses, cleaning their guns, the soldiers, in their fresh uniforms, looked ready for the parade ground. Their faces were invisible to the deportees because they were too far away, and when they did come closer, to toss them aid, they did so galloping past on their horses. Anyway, their faces were of no importance.

The feeling was mutual. To the deportees, the soldiers had one and the same face, and to the soldiers, the deportees were devoid of any face and even any human quality, given that they had been given the order to shoot, without mercy, any man, bird, or beast that tried to leave the sixth circle.

The deportees were more and more exhausted after months of hunger and ordeal. The soldiers, on the other hand, were more and more rested since the deportees were easier and easier to guard and the way stations were more and more frequent. And what made the incongruity even starker was the fact that as the deportees became more and more ragged, the soldiers' uniforms became fresher and fresher, shinier and shinier, and their horses more and more bedizened.

The men had managed to organize themselves in such a way that they were able to collect the dead as quickly as possible. The arrival of new convoys from Abuhahar and Hamam was immediately followed by the extension of the network to collect the dead. They had begun to work at the same pace as death. But this was ill omened since death, finding itself trumped, quickened its own pace. And then it gave the soldiers to think. They realized that in the camp at Sebka the people had begun to obey a rule other than death's, and the man who was courageous enough to defy death might defy anybody in the world. So they hastened the departure of the convoys to Deir-ez-Zor in order to throw them into disarray. But the corpse collectors from the camp at Sebka reassembled their teams; they reorganized themselves, most of all from fear, not the fear of death but fear of themselves.

This ability to organize, so unwonted for a camp of ragged, almost moribund people, could be tolerated at Sebka, where there were thousands of tents, but it would have become dangerous at Deir-ez-Zor, at the center of the seventh circle, where the deportees were in the tens of thousands.

This is why one morning the commandant sent word that all the men between the ages of fifteen and sixty were to assemble at the edge of the camp. They were to be sent to dig earthworks. And of course, they would be given food and drinking water. They emerged from their tents, and some believed that since they were going to be sent to work, it meant they were needed and that consequently they would be spared. Others were hesitant, and they went only after the soldiers threatened to come for them on horseback. Others still, such as Rupen, went impassively. Ever since he had become a hunter of angels, without caring overly much about whether they were black or white but only about the stringy flesh beneath their feathers, Rupen had become empty inside; he lived only to protect his children. And this is why, when Sahag came after him, thinking that boys of fourteen might be accepted into the ranks of the men, Rupen stopped him and slapped him twice, which bewildered the boy but was sufficient to quell his impulse.

But still others stubbornly tried to hide, such as the husband of the woman in the adjacent tent, whom they had befriended. Together the couple formed a single whole, which is why each of them, man and woman, could pass for the other. Tall, with narrow hips and small breasts, dressed in man's clothes, she did not attract the soldiers' attention when the convoys formed, and she managed to conceal herself from those who seized the women. And the man, who was thin and whose cheeks were without down, whose hair had grown long and wild, dressed himself as a woman, waiting anxiously lest they searched the tents. But that did not happen. When the men were lined up and counted, it was decided that five hundred was a satisfactory figure, so the order was given for them to set off.

In any event, the proportion of men in the convoys had dwindled. During the march to Deir-ez-Zor, the men were the main targets of attacks by war parties. In some places, so that no mistakes would be made, the death marches were segregated from the outset, with the men being slain during the journey in ambushes by bands of warriors or even by the soldiers meant to guard them. So the greater part of the convoys was made up of women, children, and old folk. Almost all the old folk perished, unable to keep up with the others on the way to Sebka. Some of the convoys, above all those that came from the west, had traveled almost six hundred miles to that place.

The two slaps, dealt not in anger but in desperation, were Sahag's last memory of his father, Rupen Sheitanian. The men were taken south into the Syrian desert and shot. After that death returned triumphant, spreading like a puddle of green silk above the camp.

It was late spring when the convoy set out again, taking Hermine and her two children and the two lovers with it. The waters of the Euphrates had subsided and grown clearer. As the *vilayets* along the two tributaries of the Euphrates had by then been emptied of Armenians, the bodies floating down the river had also dwindled, and no fresh corpses took the place of those devoured by the fish or swallowed by whirlpools or snagged on the banks. Like any other grave, the Euphrates had closed and once more made room for life.

If the journey from Meskene to Deir-ez-Zor had taken a different route, then the deportees would probably have long since died of thirst, especially now that the torrid heat had arrived. But the river that had for so long mingled the water of life with the water of death now provided limpid water. And so it remained all the way to Deir-ez-Zor, where the Euphrates abandoned the convoys to their fate, descending to meet the Tigris.

DEIR-EZ-ZOR. THE FINAL CIRCLE. The convoy was made up of indistinct little shapes. In the wind, they seemed flimsy, a flock of fluttering birds rather than a column of people. The photographs taken by the foreign travelers who managed to get near the convoys or who came across those left behind to await their death, helpless at the side of the road, show mainly children on the way to Deir-ez-Zor. The death march to the seventh circle was a kind of children's crusade. They shared the same fate as every other unarmed crusader. The children in those photographs are skeletal, their torsos withered, their bellies hollowed, their bones jerking like steel springs above their concave abdomens, their arms and legs having tapered to the thickness of twigs, their heads disproportionately large, like the sockets of their eyes, in which the eyeballs bulge from their orbits or sink into the back of the skull. The children gaze without any expression on their faces other than vacancy; they gaze as if from another world; they do not stretch out their hands; they do not ask for anything. In their eyes there is no hatred; they have lived too little to understand or to condemn. There is no imploring because they have forgotten what hunger is; there is no sadness because they have forgotten the joys of childhood; there is no oblivion because they have no memories. In their eyes there is nothing. Nothingness: a small, half-open window to the other world.

When a woman collapsed, it was also a death sentence for her child. More often than not, the child would cling to its mother, and they awaited death together. With horror, Hermine noticed the rash of typhus on her little girl's cheeks. In a short while, because of the scorching heat, the red blotches would spread. Hermine walked onward, clasping her little girl by the shoulders and weeping. Sahag wanted to help her, but his mother would not let him come near, to protect him from the disease. She did not even touch him but would examine him with her eyes as he slept, seeking signs of the illness, her heart in her throat. In terror, she thought to discover the signs. But then she breathed easy; they had been merely blotches left by the dust, which, soaked in sweat, had taken on the color of dried blood. She refrained from embracing him in his sleep. She caressed only the little girl, without caring whether she too would fall sick, quite the contrary: the thought of allowing her to go to the other world unaccompanied terrified Hermine, who, not knowing how she might cure her daughter, prayed that they would die together.

The journey from Sebka to Deir-ez-Zor was the longest and most frightening of all, a march of almost sixty miles. Since the desert heat had begun to bother the mounted soldiers, who dozed in their saddles next to the convoys, which dragged their feet across the scorching sands, they decided to travel by night, and in the daytime they waited by the riverbank, where there was still an occasional cool breeze. The few men remaining pitched makeshift tents to fend off the murderous heat. Some would be gripped by madness as they slept; they trembled and writhed, and the others would hit them to waken them, preventing them from suffocating in their sleep. Others lost their minds while awake and wandered off, but they did not get far since having lost the reflex of self-preservation, they were felled by bullets.

The convoys had no shadow. By day, lying on the ground, they left no shadow, or else where they found a patch of shade, they would wrap themselves in it like a blanket. By night, as they groped their way, stumbling over rocks or falling into sinkholes, they became their own shadows. The convoys were so weak that they no longer had the strength to leave a shadow, to pull their shadows behind them like a fisherman's net. It took the shadowless convoys almost two weeks to travel from Sebka to Deir-ez-Zor.

The camp was on the right bank of the Euphrates. Here, the tents were in the tens of thousands. Deir-ez-Zor was the ultimate center where such a camp was established. From Deir-ez-Zor there was no transit to any place in this world.

For this reason, the deportees were given nothing to eat. As vegetation was sparse and the men who might have killed animals of the desert lured by the corpses had also dwindled, the hunger became unbearable. Their bodies were so weak that even the diseases spread with the greatest slowness; the organism did not have enough vigor even to nurture a disease. Those sick with typhus no longer ran a fever because they had stopped producing antibodies. The other diseases retreated, leaving starvation to gnaw away at their bellies, to stretch their skin over their bones and dry out their innards.

Incidents were fewer and fewer. The camp commandant had discovered Levon Shashian's group, which had organized not only the living messages that the orphans carried on their skin from one camp to another, but also a system for supplying food and medicine, as much as they could come by, and the same system as in the camp at Sebka, whereby teams of men managed to bury the corpses, keeping pace with death. Levon Shashian had been taken from the camp and murdered with bestial cruelty by none other than the commandant himself, Zeki Pasha. Any organization on the part of the deportees within the camp was suppressed, and in this way, in the opinion of the soldiers, any danger of revolt vanished. The camp succumbed to lethargy. The army's fear of revolt perhaps seemed unjustified since the soldiers were well equipped, rested to the point of boredom, and armed to the teeth, while the deportees were more and more skeletal, ragged, and irresolute, drunk with death. But the soldiers were genuinely afraid, and the authorities in Aleppo and Deir-ez-Zor were too. The soldiers had learned to fight other soldiers, and their weapons were designed to dispatch enemies afraid of death. Weapons had yet to be invented that could strike fear in those who were no longer afraid of anything. Exhausted, eaten away by hunger, the deportees were unaware that their reconciliation with the thought of death constituted their formidable strength. Although this power of fearlessness in the face of death increased with every new circle, the journey through the seven circles of death was not one of revolt. The journey of the convoys was sooner one in expectation of death. Death, wandering through the camp, had become one of them; death itself was one of the victims of the circles of Deir-ez-Zor.

Only a muted murmur seeped to the outside. A German traveler who managed to see the deportees at Deir-ez-Zor from close by was left deeply troubled not so much by the obvious things, which the photographs reveal in all their horror, as by a single detail: in that dreadful place he did not see any people weeping. Or rather, he did not see what we normally understand by a person weeping—that is, he saw no tears.

But it is not true that the people did not weep. Rather, they wept differently. Those who still had the strength to sit upright rocked back and forth; the others wept with their wide-open eyes staring up into the sky. But the weeping was a kind of uninterrupted groan, in a low voice, which, repeated by thousands of chests, made a droning sound. The weeping was not the streak of tears running down the cheeks but a sound. That drone, flowing endlessly and tuning itself to the surroundings, came to sound like the hum of the wind among the dunes or the swirl of the waters of the Euphrates. The weeping did not ebb for an instant, until the convoys were taken from Deir-ez-Zor to the plateaus where the last deportees were killed. That dry weeping took the place of prayers, and of curses, and of silence, and of confession, and for some it even took the place of sleep. Many fell asleep weeping in that way. Others died weeping, with their weeping still thrumming in their stilled chests, like a note in an organ pipe. I heard that weeping when Grandfather Setrak used to rock back and forth on the chaise longue in the garden or when Grandfather Garabet used to lock himself up in his room and his violin fell silent.

At first, the weeping groan irritated the soldiers, especially given that combined with the waters and the wind, it seemed to come from everywhere at once. But then they got used to it. The drone proved more reliable than any sentinel; as long as it flowed evenly, it meant that nothing untoward was happening. It would have stopped if the people had found some other occupation than dying or lamenting their dead. It would stop, said the soldiers, if the deportees revolted or if they all died. But apart from the cases of madness, which most often ended with a bullet to the chest in the expanses around the camp, they did not revolt. When it came to dying, however, they did not die as quickly as before. It seemed that death itself, having lived among the deportees for so long, had come to love them. Although the camps were dismantled a few months later and the deportees were mostly killed in the meantime, the drone did not cease at Deir-ez-Zor.

But by then, their ears alert to that noise that carved a riverbed for itself wider than the Euphrates, the Turkish soldiers were not very worried when it came to guarding the camp at Deir-ez-Zor. To the south and east there was no need for guards since there was only desert. Anyone who tried to flee in that direction would have no chance of survival. Nor was there any hope of escaping over the Euphrates, which bordered the camp.

For a time, Deir-ez-Zor was the destination of all the convoys, without the authorities having made any decision as to what was to be done next. Probably they expected that the convoys would gradually disappear on the way so that Deir-ez-Zor would be just a kind of lazaretto where those who did manage to arrive would quickly give up the ghost, a kind of *hastane*, like at Tefridje and Lale. Despite the plentiful opportunities to die, a few hundred thousand deportees stubbornly clung to life. Or rather, they had quite simply forgotten to die. The camp became increasingly crowded and hard to control, not because of the people but because of what rained down on them and what they stirred up—namely, diseases and miasmas. As the authorities in the imperial capital wanted a hasty and definitive solution to the Armenian question, Deir-ez-Zor became a transit point rather than a destination. However, the transit was not between two camps but between this world and the next.

Of all the manifold forms of suffering, hunger proved stronger than disease or pain. Lacking any source of food; providing only chance sustenance, such as grass, berries that set the teeth on edge, wild honey, and the carrion of wild animals, the camp at Deir-ez-Zor succumbed to a state of hallucination. The skeletal bodies went down to the Euphrates to drink water, walking unsteadily, and then they sat back down in the scorching heat, rocking back and forth, groaning, as if feeding on the light, like plants. Some, losing all discernment and all sense of anything but hunger, put in their mouths whatever came to hand: the bark of trees; rags saturated with the salty taste of sweat or feces; feces that, because of starvation, were hard, sparse pellets, like a goat's. After the killing of Levon Shashian and those who labored at the mass graves trying to provide shelter for the dead, the corpses once more began to linger inside the tents. Once more, faceless corpses began to appear, bodies without arms or legs. Those who did the rounds of the tents every few days to remove the mutilated or decomposing bodies were no longer shocked. Some even did so with an ulterior motive; having been hunters of crows and hyenas, they were now hunters of the dead. This is why those inside the tents eyed them carefully and did not entrust their dead to just anybody.

Even so, the task did not prove easy. It was increasingly difficult to distinguish the dead from the living. The living lay motionless for hours at a time, and often they fell asleep with their eyes open, going blind in the blazing sunlight that burned away their eyeballs. And the dead would sometimes give a start because of the large differences in temperature between night and day; their limbs would soften in the sunlight and then contract in the frost at night. So they began to collect the dead at random, and some would return from the edge of the mass grave, awoken by the jolt of having been thrown on top of the others.

When the signal was given, the convoys began to form once more. Some were driven east, toward Marat and Suvar. Others marched west, in the direction of Damascus. But whichever the direction, the outcome was the same. Once they arrived on a plateau that the advance guard reckoned suitable, the soldiers moved away, encircled the convoy, and fired their muskets from every side. When none were left standing, they inserted their bayonets into the muzzles of their guns, drew their sabers, and did butchery, making sure that the blade finished off what the bullet had missed.

Hermine was waiting for death, holding her daughter in her arms. The little girl was increasingly convulsed by chills; at night Hermine covered her with her body, trying to warm her. Sahag managed to obtain a handful of green dates and even a pomegranate that had fallen from a soldier's saddle. They ate the sour-sweet seeds of the pomegranate one by one, holding each under their tongues for a long moment. In the other tent, the two lovers were suffering from starvation without being able to search for food since the woman refused to let her man go outside lest the soldiers see him and kill him. They seemed to feed on each other, and clinging together they endured until one evening, when they released each other from their embrace and stood up. They took off their clothes, and the woman handed them to Hermine. "Clothe the child with them," she said. "She is trembling with cold." They were completely naked. Hermine gazed at them in wonder, not because of their nakedness, which, like anything else that might happen to the body, was nothing unusual in the camp, but because they were ineffably beautiful. They had a strange light in their eyes, their hair lay smooth around their foreheads and shone, their flesh was of a ravishing whiteness, her thighs and chest had ripened and become rounded, and his muscles had knitted together and tautened around his bones. The light was beaded on their shoulders, and they cast no shadow around them. "We have come to say farewell," he said, but it was as if his lips did not move. Then he took his woman by the hand, and they moved into the distance. For a long time, they were able to see their receding outlines, perhaps also because of the luminous contours their bodies had acquired. They were so radiant and so impassive as they seemingly floated over the sands. Hermine and Sahag waited, straining their ears for the noise of the shots. But nothing happened, not even after darkness fell, enveloping the clay and the wax of their bodies. All that remained was an indistinct scent, like the smoke of smoldering myrrh or amber. "They have escaped," whispered Hermine. "I will go to call them back," said Sahag. "They will die in the desert out there. Nobody has returned alive from the sands." Hermine made a sign for him to sit and she went over to him. "Leave them . . . They are beautiful and without sin. I keep thinking that Rupen is right." She spoke of her husband in the present tense, as if he had gone far away but would return, although by then Rupen had been killed along with the convoy of men from Sebka. "Rupen is right. God is dead. Let them go on their way. Here, where you saw them for the last time, at the edge of the Deir-ez-Zor camp, is the boundary of the Garden of Eden. The gateway to paradise is but two paces away. We have returned to whence we set out at the beginning of the beginning. But in the meantime the world has turned bad. Perhaps they will start the world over again and they will create a different God."

Sahag peered into the darkness, where the conjoined bodies of the man and the woman flickered one last time and were extinguished. And all of a sudden a breath of wind bathed the boy's brow, fresh and rustling. It was as if the sands had parted before the two and from the earth fruit trees pleasing to the eye had sprung up. The two arms of a far greater river joined before them: the Tigris and the Euphrates. And the man, walking in the garden watered by those rivers, left behind him his kin, his father and his mother, and he clove to his woman, and they were made one flesh.

But here, among people, as the convoys of hundreds of people were led to the execution sites on the plateaus, on the way to Suvar or Damascus, new convoys arrived from the west, descending to the last circle of death. In that July of the year 1916, throng separated from throng, throng joined throng, and despite the continual coming and going, the size of the camp at Deir-ez-Zor remained the same, as if it were motionless. The surrounding lands had filled with bones. The final frontier had been crossed. The living served the dead, whose burial was their only remaining occupation. The dead served the living, keeping them warm, like garments, in the frosty nights and providing communion bread to those who had gone out of their minds with hunger.

With wild eyes, Hermine gazed at her daughter. The blazing heat of summer began to kill people, drying them up, sweating away their bodies' salts. The living and the dead, who were alike in their motionlessness and in the spasms that convulsed them from time to time, now also began to resemble each other in the dark, dry color of their faces.

Given the pace at which the executions followed upon one another, the concentration camp would be cleared by the autumn of that year. Even without the executions, nobody would have survived until winter given the conditions at Deir-ez-Zor. That summer, it was the children who died above all. Many remained unburied among the tents, huddled, blackened, naked carcasses. Hermine impatiently waited to be included in one of the death marches; she did not hope for anything, but she longed with all her soul to leave that place. Her open eyes motionless, the child would whisper from time to time, "I'm hungry!" When the child's groaning became continuous, mournful when she exhaled, rasping when she drew air into her chest, Hermine set out among the tents. An hour later she came back empty-handed. "They didn't give you anything, did they?" the little girl asked in a dull voice. She shook her head, her eyes vacant. "Afterward, don't give them anything of me," the child went on, smiling sadly. Hermine lifted her hand to her mouth, so harrowed that she forgot to drive away the boy when he approached his sister to caress her. She looked at him in a manner wholly unaccustomed and then grasped him by the wrist. "Come!" she said in a new voice. She dragged him outside the tent toward the edge of the camp, upstream, where the Arabs brought their animals to drink. On the riverbank, she stood with her son, praying that it happen as quickly as possible.

The Arab that approached looked at them without kindness. But at the boy he looked with curiosity. As Hermine and the boy spoke Turkish, they could have made themselves understood in those words common to all the expanses of the Mohammedan faith. But there was no need. It was well understood what was afoot. The circumstance had been repeated thousands of times during the death marches and at the edge of the camps. And to make things clear, Hermine let go of Sahag's hand and pushed him one step forward, keeping her hand on his shoulder, lest the boy bolt back the way he had come. Despite his weakness, Sahag did not seem to be afflicted by any disease, and the Arab, by way of agreement, took out a little pouch of flour and handed it to the woman. She received it, cupping it in both hands. Then, feeling himself released from her grip, Sahag tried to flee. But the Arab caught him by his waist and his neck and threw him over his horse like a pair of saddlebags. He leapt up behind him, and giving a whoop, he galloped away. Hermine stood rooted to the spot for a long time. She thrust her hand in the pouch and stuffed a fistful of flour in her mouth to stifle her scream.

For a time, the boy languished inside a different kind of tent, one much larger, furnished with carpets and unintelligible inscriptions on the walls, in which lived people who spoke a hoarse, guttural language, who looked on him with indifference but brought him food, wiped the sweat from his brow, and changed his sheets. When he became strong enough to travel, they lifted him onto a horse, and then they made their way deep into the parched lands where their only occupation, when they were not pillaging convoys, was tending the fires in which the camel fat sizzled by night and searching for water by day. Sahag's only clear memory of those days was of the men's doleful prayers and the white garment he received, a garment streaked with blood from the painful mutilation of his member, although he failed to understand why this new pain provoked smiles and satisfaction on the faces of the others. With his white, bloodstained garment he also received a new name: Yusuf. (Nobody asked what his old name had been.) But that was to his advantage later, when they sought him, traveling as far as Urfa and Diarbekir. Not knowing whom to ask after, they did not find him.

Yusuf became a capable young man. He learned to lead the camels to water, holding their bridles. He learned to ride; he became inured to dry victuals, and faced with the sandy expanses, he learned patience. He received man's clothes; he had his own horse, the only creature to which he could speak Armenian; and he knelt with the others, at sunrise and sunset, at midday, as they murmured words that sounded like a prayer. He might have remained a skillful horseman of the deserts, with his body already steeled by the circles of death; with his long eyelashes that protected his eyes from the sands; with his swarthy face, honed against the harsh wind; and with his black, curly hair, a good shield against the scorching sun. The fact that he did not speak Arabic was to his advantage. Nobody pestered him with questions, and he did not have to tell the story of his life. He did not have to pray to a prophet who had revealed himself to him by bloodying him and thus could preserve for himself the other who had revealed Himself having been bloodied.

He could have been a good horseman of those expanses, and one day he might have become the chief of his own tribe. In winter he would have gone down to the shores of the Red Sea, almost as far as Medina, and, at least once in his life, as far as Mecca, and then, via Jerusalem and Damascus, he would have gone back up to the places he knew so well and farther still, to the mountains, to Ras-ul-Ain and Mosul. But Yusuf remained aloof, and the others, content that he was capable, left him in peace and did not interrupt the unintelligible conversations he held with his horse.

Yusuf lived that life in bewilderment. But enlightenment came to him all of a sudden, as happens when the questions are not precise. They had reached Mosul. It had been a good day. They had sold goat's cheese and camel hide. In the tent it was warm and peaceful, and there was a scent of toasted meat, but before sitting on the pillows around the fire, they counted the gold pieces they kept in purses with drawstrings. Then the women admired their gifts: amber, fabrics, and jewels. The master of the tent grasped the most beautiful of the jewels in his fist and then, opening his fingers like a magician, gave it to the youngest of his women. She tied it around her throat, and twisting this way and that, she joyously danced around the fire to the sharp sound of the pipes and the rhythm of the tambourines. The droplets of fat made the fire spark and sizzle; faces shone and lengthened in the light of the flames; the rhythm of the tambourines joined with the handclaps; and the woman danced in a circle, carried away by her youth and the joy of her jewel. The boy saw her when she drew level with him, swaying her hips and shaking her breasts from the base of her shoulders. The talisman on its gold chain, worn in full view and proudly, was his mother's, and the boy remembered the modest gesture with which she used to conceal it under her clothes. Nobody noticed when he slipped outside the tent. His mind whirling, the only thing he could do was run wildly. Not even he knew what he was running from. He ran until he was out of breath and fell to his knees. And feeling the need to be released from his body, he began to scream.

He sat on the sand, and rocking back and forth, he screamed at the top of his lungs. By the time the scream faded, giving way to the Deir-ez-Zor moan, to dry tears, Yusuf had died. He had been an unhappy, alien, silent creature wandering in places unknown to him and among gods in which he did not believe. Yusuf had been born from blood and was slain by a scream. But he was not slain as happens when a body kills another body, piercing it from the outside inward. Rather, Yusuf had died pierced from the inside outward, by the very body to which he had been added, like a white, bloodied garment.

Stripped of the new garment, with Yusuf lying at his feet like a cast-off rag, Sahag returned to the tents. But this time, no longer a son of the tribe, he came surreptitiously, hiding in the deep shadows, avoiding the fires and the tent openings. He went to the animal pen and slowly untethered his horse. They trod silently over the sand. The horse followed him without sensing any change, obeying him, sniffing him, since Yusuf had never existed for the horse. Later, galloping hooves could be heard, but by then horse and rider were far away.

He headed west, in the opposite direction to the death marches, but alas, the return journey, back through the circles of death, from death to the resurrection, was not a journey back in time. On the contrary; climbing the levels one by one, from the depths into which he had fallen, as if down a well, he found only the traces of the convoys, survivors begging at the side of the road, new and terrifying names given to the ravines whose scree consumed the bones, children of his nation wearing *shalwars* and with Yusufs growing within them, as if in nests. Many times he wanted to go back to the tent, to kill the Arab, beneath the eyes of his women and children, and to take back his mother's talisman. Then he told himself that the Arab bore no guilt. The man who had ripped the pendant from his mother's throat was elsewhere, and he would have to wage too great a war to find and kill all those like him if he were to be certain that his mother's killer had been punished. The Arab had ultimately proven to be his benefactor, and it was not his fault that the times had cheapened human life so much that the Bedouin had set the boy's life at a pouch of flour.

At Ras-ul-Ain, Sahag reintersected with the railway line that he had left two years before, on the way to Mamura, climbing out of a cattle truck, his face swollen and scarlet from the lack of air. He sold his horse and traveled for a day and a night, huddled in the corner of a carriage, as far as Izmid. On the way back he found no pointer to show him the way. For a time, his journey was by train and by boat, which took him west to Bazargic and then to Silistra.

As long as he was fleeing, the memories left him in peace. When he finally settled, in Silistra, he became a grocer's apprentice, and later he opened his own shop. Later still, he began to look for a wife, but until he found her, he tarried with the girls that waited for the sailors in the port. The Bedouin robe he had once cast to his feet came to life, hissed like a snake, and set out on Sahag's trail. And so it was that one evening he saw the face of Yusuf looking back at him in the gaslight, mirrored in the window. Sahag gazed in horror as Yusuf danced to the sound of drums and flutes, as his white desert dweller's garment swished; as he held his member in his hands and rubbed it, cavorting savage-eyed; as he ejaculated not seed but blood. Sahag could find no other way to dispel the apparition than by grabbing a tool and striking the window. But Yusuf only chortled. His face shattered; it multiplied in a thousand other faces and seeped into the room. When Sahag came to his senses, he took a good look at himself; at his savagely distorted face; at his clothes in disarray; at the not yet flaccid, still mutilated member in his hand. He understood that Yusuf had entered him and that not by breaking windows and covering the mirrors could he fight against that transparent face.

Sahag and Yusuf hated each other, but they knew that they were forced to live together. Yusuf suffered tenfold the torments to which Sahag had been subjected, as he had to endure the worship of an alien savior and the gentle commandments of that savior's faith. But he avenged himself on that foreign tribe in the only way he could, which is to say, through the member that bore his birthmark, poisoning its seed. Bound to that seed, forever to remain barren and dwindling with the passing of the years, Yusuf also dwindled. In my childhood, Sahag Sheitanian was an old man. That is why I never knew Yusuf.

Each of his halves was accustomed to waylaying and hating the other. Each waited for the other to fall asleep before it struck. But as fate would have it, they always fell asleep together, and only in dreams did they truly become separate, for the two halves were unable to dream at the same time. The more his other half dwindled, the greater became the resignation of Sahag and his wife, Armenuhi, at not being able to have children. Split in two, inured to hating and unable to store away his hate in the nooks and crannies of his soul, Sahag began to hate others. First of all he hated those like Yusuf. But as very few around him were like Yusuf and as his unconsummated hate gnashed like the fangs of wild beasts (which have to rend; otherwise they grow until they end up piercing their own skulls), Sahag poured out his hate on the Bolsheviks. The unhoped-for opportunity arose after the war. Previously, the only Communist in Focşani had been a bibulous greengrocer whose sole political activity was to hurl raucous, slurred curses at the king and his dynasty on May 10, until the authorities became wise to it and arrested him at the crack of dawn, before he could awake from the previous night's drinking bout. But after the war, the town filled with Communists. Sahag used to call them Communist highwaymen. The Communists repaid his affection with their usual generosity, which is to say, they looted his shop and then, when there was nothing left to loot, they confiscated the entire premises. Sahag only rejoiced. "Take it all!" he shouted, waving his arms and jumping up and down on one foot. "Loot these!" he cried, throwing tins of Van Houten cacao at them. "You forgot to take these!" he yelled, tossing bags of coffee beans, which scurried over the pavement like cockroaches.

He came up with the idea of putting the Telefunken radio in the Seferian crypt, and in the night he used to go there by himself to listen to Radio Free Europe in the cemetery. In the summer of 1958 he watched avidly as the departing Red Army battalions vanished down the highway to Tecuci. He sat unbudging for hours in front of the saucer-sized screen of Mrs. Maria's television set, over the road from our house, watching the live broadcast of Gheorghe Gheorghiu-Dej's funeral, hanging on every detail, cracking sunflower seeds, drinking beer, cheering as at a soccer match. "The Russians poisoned him with radiation," he said, albeit this time without any hint of reproach for the Russians. "They did his gallbladder in!"

And it was also Sahag Sheitanian who was the first to succumb to the fascination of maps. Uprooted from the places of their childhood, the old Armenians fled; they emigrated; they crossed deserts, continents, seas, and oceans; but they never really traveled. Journeying through the world was for them a part of sadness, not curiosity or joy. That is why they preferred to travel over the expanses of maps, like book mites.

The cartographic plates were like a fissure in the real world; they opened into a different dimension. On those maps, the wars always had a different ending than in reality, the *fedayi* came down from the mountains and crushed the armies, the prisoners managed to escape from the concentration camps, and the warriors broke out of the encirclements. The Americans landed in the Balkans, English paratroopers dotted the skies, and the Russians retreated into the depths of Siberia. And of course, Armenia stretched from the Caucasus to Tyre and Sidon, from Anatolia to Lake Urmia, as in the time of Tigran the Great, in the last century before Christ. The world was made of interlayered maps, studded with arrows indicating troop landings, liberations, routs, retrocessions, glory, and triumph. Of all those maps, to them the least remarkable and therefore the least noticed was the one laid directly over the grass—in other words, reality itself.

For that reason, on his maps different treaties held sway, and the wars had different outcomes. The Treaty of Sèvres held. The Yalta summit never took place, and Stalin's carefully sharpened pencil did not carve up Europe. Sahag Sheitanian and the other Armenians of my childhood were men of maps rather than men of this world. Sometimes they were so impassive, their eyes gazed so far away, that it was as if they had been rolled up like maps and vanished from the earthly plane.

In the *Book of Whispers* every aroma, every color, every flicker of madness has its own magic. The guide to the various realms, the magician of the maps, was Mikael Noradungian. The others would stand around him, watching wide-eyed as he smoothed the continents beneath his palms. Wise and silent, my grandfather would sit there too. Like nothing else, the maps proved that there was in fact a meaning behind the chaos of the times. Anton Merzian would forget to ask questions, and in front of the maps, where there was room for all, he would no longer argue with Krikor Minasian. Ştefănucă Ibrăileanu, Mgrditch Tcheslov, Agop Aslanian, Vrej Papazian, Ohannes Krikorian, and all the others would piously approach, allowing themselves to be guided to that new Bethlehem, where salvation took the form of a map. Sahag Sheitanian would gaze, overwhelmed by the wonder of it. These were the only moments when his twisted innards unclenched and he was reconciled with Yusuf.

9.

THE STORY OF MIKAEL NORADUNGIAN, THE MAGE OF MAPS. Noradun-
gian was a kind of mage of perpendicular worlds. His life was made up of frag-
ments rather than lived as a continuum; it was more like the line of life on a
wrinkled palm. That is why nobody remembered him the way you usually remember people, which is to say, where they were born, what they did in life,
whom they were friends with, whom they were enemies with, or how they
died, the last of these being a way of understanding what the others leave unex-
plained. The greater part of his life unfolded among these stories. Noradungian
was always situated outside his own life, and we can sense his presence by entering the rooms he has just left.

Mikael Noradungian was born in 1873, the same year as another character
in our stories, Hartin Frenkian. And as we shall see, their lives, resembling each
other only in places, were to have the same turning point seventy-five years later,
in 1948.

Noradungian came from an Armenian family whose surname was rare. In
The Book of Whispers we have not come across any other characters with the
same surname apart from that family from Agn. And it was no ordinary family.
At the beginning of the twentieth century, although Armenians, they occupied
some of the highest positions in the Ottoman Empire. Under the tutelage of
his two uncles, Gabriel and Asadur, Mikael Noradungian had gone to Constantinople, where he had founded a successful business. And since many of
his customers were Armenians from the eastern *vilayets*, he also opened an inn
in Constantinople's Galata quarter, which caused a veritable buzz, the same as
the inn opened by another Armenian, Manuk Bey Mirzayan, had in Bucharest
a century earlier. My great-great-grandfather Khachadur Melikian used to stay
at that inn in Galata when he was visiting the shores of the Bosphorus and rode
through the streets thronged with folk from every conceivable part. When, on
the eve of the Balkan Wars, Gabriel Noradungian, a teacher at Constantinople's
law school and close associate of the Young Turks in the Revolution of 1908,
was appointed foreign minister by the Sublime Porte, his nephew Mikael became an undersecretary of state in the Ministry of Communications, at a time
when "communications" meant the post office and telegraph. In that position

252

he must have worked with Talaat Pasha, the erstwhile telegraph operator who was obsessed with planting telegraph poles throughout the empire, the same Talaat who, rising to become a central figure in the administration, ordered that all Armenian high dignitaries be dismissed in 1914 and then, a year later, that they be deported, along with the entire Armenian population.

But since Mikael Noradungian did not tell any stories about himself, we know nothing about any connection with Talaat Pasha; we merely suspect it. However, the connection does seem to have been real since otherwise Mikael Noradungian would not have been one of the first to sense what was afoot and would not have put himself out of harm's way. Gabriel Noradungian resigned his post at the Foreign Ministry in 1913, and his nephew Mikael, in the Department of Post and Telegraph Offices, did likewise. At the beginning of 1915, they went to Paris, where they looked after Armenian émigrés, and the old minister began to write his memoirs. His nephew Mikael, having been initiated by his other uncle, Asadur, climbed the rungs of Freemasonry one by one, reaching grade thirty-three by 1909. He was a founding member of the Supreme Council of Turkey, even hosting the Founding Convent of the Grand Lodge of Turkey at his inn in Galata.

Mikael Noradungian came to Romania in the autumn of 1920. The meeting took place in the house of Armenag Manisalian. They also invited Harutiun Khntirian, the consul of the Armenian Republic; Krikor Zambakchian; and Grigore Trancu-Iaşi. Grandfather expressed reserve. He did not believe in secret societies. He believed in meanings, not secrets. When people do not understand but are embarrassed to admit it, they invent secrets. "What would have become of Christianity if it had remained a secret?" asked Grandfather. But Sahag Sheitanian, prompted by the pain in his guts, urged him to go: "Anything that doesn't take account of borders is good for us," he said, "until the Greater Armenia is rebuilt. Look at how Bolshevism and Pan-Turkishness are expanding, how they fight against borders." But that was to happen much later, when, old and resigned, at a crossroads in life, Mikael Noradungian, who had remained within the narrow, tenebrous circle of Freemasonry all his life, was forced to emerge into the light. But in the autumn of 1920 Mikael Noradungian did not reveal to the others that he had a special mission to fulfill in Romania, which was why he needed to have an audience with King Ferdinand.

During that time, Noradungian did not sit around idly. Back in those days, people did not set much store by learning a trade from books. They served an apprenticeship in the trade allotted to them. If the trade was more complex, they became journeymen and then replaced the master, carrying on the business. When their abilities were innate and obvious, they went into business for themselves from the outset, crafting or trading without a workbench or counter at first, lugging their tools or goods from door to door. A trade was not something chosen willy-nilly; there had to be a place for it on the part of both craftsmen and customers. This meant that a place had to be found, in the same way that the diviners searched for a spot to dig a well using a hazelnut switch. In this respect, the Armenians were a nation of hazelnut switches. A history of the ways in which the Armenians who arrived in Romania after 1915 dedicated themselves to trade and the crafts, of the ways in which they found nooks for themselves in a world unfamiliar to them, might substitute for the business textbooks of today and suit every possible reader. And the way in which Mikael Noradungian developed his businesses would form a central chapter in such a history. He did not start from scratch but rather put his previous businesses back together again, unencumbered by the political implications, which in any event he held in contempt. After selling arms to Tsarist Russia during the war and then to the Whites during the Civil War, he sold arms to the Bolsheviks after the Whites were defeated. In Romania he represented the Levant Company and was a seasoned hand in that world of bribes and venality, winning major orders for the army and railways. He continued to trade, opening a company office on Victory Avenue in Bucharest, just a stone's throw from Hartin Frenkian's building on Palace Square. And, of course, he continued to do what he had learned in the empire: he ran postal and telegraph services, holding a managerial post at Bucharest's telephone company.

In addition to these activities, which demonstrated that he was a major businessman and, according to the certificates issued by the Ministry of the Interior granting him Romanian citizenship, a man who had "done significant services for Romania," Noradungian also fulfilled the mission for which he had come to Romania on behalf of the Supreme Masonic Council of France. By the end of December 1922, Mikael Noradungian had reinitiated the thirteen members of Romania's Supreme Council of the Ancient and Accepted Scottish Rite, and with the blessing of King Ferdinand he brought about a revival of the Romanian Masonic Order. In March 1923, Noradungian signed the high decree for the publication of the statutes, constitution, and general regulations of Romania's Ancient and Accepted Scottish Rite. He then accepted the highest degree in Romanian Freemasonry: grand sovereign commander of the Supreme Council, thirty-third degree. Given that Romanian Freemasonry allowed only ethnic Romanian leaders, the title was honorary, however.

There is always something that eludes any biography, all the more so if that biography is mysterious, like the one we here recount. That something is the passion shared by men as different as Grand Sovereign Commander Mikael

Noradungian, General Drastamat Kanayan, dealer in colonial wares Sahag Sheitanian of Focșani, and so many others mentioned or merely hinted at in *The Book of Whispers*. There is the story of Yusuf. There are also other stories that gave rise to strange creatures that dwelled in the souls of the old Armenians and that took advantage of every opportunity—a window, a mirror, an aroma, a name, a photograph—to reveal themselves. But of all of them the story of Yusuf is the farthest reaching in its scope. Each man had his own means of replicating himself as a kind of Yusuf since each of them had survived. Each therefore bore the guilt of not having died together with the others. Through the guilt of having survived, each carried in himself what he strove with all his might to keep closed, like a door, but which, no matter how hard he braced his shoulder against it, sometimes burst open. As can be seen, through that half-open door gusted the breeze of madness. The same as in the case of Sahag Sheitanian, in the case of Mikael Noradungian that draft of air was part of a brightly colored world: the world of maps, floating and swooping through the sky like kites.

Noradungian was a member of the artist rather than the warrior caste. Unlike General Dro, he did not believe that Armenia should be liberated come what may; rather he nurtured the conviction that the country could only be free in a free world. Noradungian did not believe it was an appropriate solution to set one enemy against another in the hope of ridding yourself of at least one of them. And this is why he did not agree with the general's plan to found an Armenian legion. What is more, he did not hide his hostile feelings toward Nazi Germany. That is how he ended up at the top of the list of those to be deported to the Tîrgu Jiu labor camp, a list that also included my grandfather Setrak Melikian, whose wooden suitcase stuffed with scarfs, undershirts, and woolen socks Grandmother Sofia had already packed.

Noradungian and General Dro agreed on the same solution only after the disaster at Stalingrad, when the Armenian Legion was annihilated and the Russians, with a terrible thirst for vengeance, were scouring the Crimea for the survivors. Their solution was as simple as it was illusory, as we shall see: the Americans. But Noradungian had a plan completely different from the usual vision of American salvation; unlike all the others, who tirelessly read the newspapers, sat with their ears pressed to the radio, or greedily swallowed all kinds of rumors or, like Arshag, sat motionless gazing through belfry windows as they waited for the Americans to come, Mikael Noradungian hatched a different plan: instead of the Americans coming to us, we would go to the Americans. He had conceived it before the war, on the eve of Carol II's royal dictatorship, when Freemasonry was forced to lie dormant. In short, Romania was to declare itself the forty-ninth member of the United States of America. This idea, which turned the Monroe

Doctrine on its head, was to be applied in the simplest possible way: Romania would adopt the U. S. Constitution, the best of all possible constitutions since it was Masonic in origin, and the country would accept the dollar as its national currency, which was strong not only thanks to its purchasing power, but also thanks to the Masonic symbols on its promissory notes. The advantages were numerous: as part of a republic, Romania would be able to get rid of Carol II and to avoid looming dangers such as Germany, on the one hand, and the Soviet Union, on the other. But since Romania was not a bale of hay that you could lug on your back from the north of the Balkans over the Atlantic and since the idea was eccentric to say the least—if not downright insane in Francophone Romania, which had its own heroes and which in its entire history had only ever encountered America in the movies—Mikael Noradungian decided that his plan was unachievable precisely because it was too simple and therefore not grandiose enough. After the fall of Stalingrad, both Mikael Noradungian and General Dro, the one joyfully, the other bitterly, realized that of the two enemies warring between themselves only one now remained, the more dangerous of the two—namely, the Soviet Union—and they agreed that the American solution was the only one possible. Each wished to solve the problem in his own way. General Dro vanished in the spring of 1944. In his house with the Armenian insignia on Strada Popa Soare in Bucharest he left behind Partogh, the bell ringer of the Armenian cathedral, a man whose nose had been squashed by a soccer ball at the beginning of the century, when he was the goalkeeper for Fenerbahce. Partogh was to water the flowers, air the house, open the street-facing windows, and turn the lights on at night so that nobody would know that General Dro had boarded a ship to Beirut and from there embarked on the long voyage to New York and then Boston. So convincingly did the bell ringer embalm the dead house that when the Russians reached Bucharest at the end of August that year, they spent almost a month searching hundreds of houses, imprisoning, torturing, deporting, or shooting whoever crossed their path before they finally accepted that Drastamat Kanayan, general of the armies of sacrifice, had slipped through their fingers.

On the other hand, Mikael Noradungian had a mission to fulfill in Romania that had been entrusted to him a quarter of a century earlier and that nobody had rescinded: to keep the flame of the Romanian Masonic Order burning. Since the mission could be fulfilled only if he stayed in the country, Noradungian continued to come up with all kinds of solutions for bringing the Americans. After the plan to integrate Romania with the United States and hoist the American flag above the seat of government on Metropolia Hill came to naught, Noradungian concluded that its failure was due not to the fact that it was insane but, on the contrary, that it was not insane enough. For this reason, after the defeat at Stalingrad and the German retreat, Noradungian conceived a truly spectacular plan to counter the Bolshevik peril. When he saw that Romania could not be unified with the United States, Noradungian, together with Constantin Bellu, the treasurer of the Romanian Grand Lodge, reworked the plan, this time trying to unify Europe, or as much of the continent as was possible, with a view to subsequently joining it to the United States of America. Through this project Noradungian remained loyal to his two commitments — namely, Freemasonry and Romania; he imagined a European Masonic Union that would then be transformed into a United States of Europe and, for greater security against the Russians, incorporated into the United States of America.

We can imagine how Sahag Sheitanian must have felt when he entered the room of maps on his every visit to Bucharest. These were the only times when Sahag and Yusuf stood next to each other, without enmity, without hate, and this the only place, in front of the vast expanses they had crossed together and that in the world of the maps could be encompassed with a single sweep of the arm. In the beginning, the countries were colored differently on the map. But as the unionist project took on life, one color filled increasingly wider expanses; it flowed along the Mediterranean, bringing salvation as far as the Bosphorus, and from there it continued in the footsteps of the ancient Greeks, over the ruins of Troy, Ephesus, and Miletus and farther still, beyond the seven circles of death, down to Deir-ez-Zor, the western edge of the Garden of Eden, now a churning desert waste that ground bones to sand. Sahag lingered for hour after hour in that room, gazing at the maps with the fascination of a despairing man for whom they spelled salvation in the absence of any escape.

In one respect, however, the incorrigible dreamers Mikael Noradungian and General Dro were mistaken: they believed that it was enough to have convictions in order to succeed in the end. General Dro seemed convinced that he could liberate Armenia from Bolshevism with just one legion made up of a few thousand men, half of whom were untrained, the other half prisoners motivated only by the desire for release. By virtue of the same crusade against Bolshevism, Noradungian firmly believed that the unification of all the nations of the Mediterranean and Balkans could be achieved by extending the jurisdiction of the Romanian Supreme Council to the other countries, with the Grand Mediterranean Lodge going on to transform the Masonic union into a European and then a trans-Atlantic union.

Whereas General Dro's ragtag Armenian Legion was massacred in the Crimea, Mikael Noradungian's Masonic union was to prove somewhat more fortunate; it was never put into effect. This does not mean that the maps did not

continue to display their colored expanses or that Noradungian did not continue, stubbornly and alone, to advocate his plan, even after the Russians arrived, bringing communism with them. While the people around him were
seeking safety, fleeing the country, Noradungian was knocking on the doors of
foreign military missions and legations, promising Masonic support for a new
Allied war against Bolshevism.

Then two things happened that relegated Noradungian's project to the world
of maps once and for all. First came the reply of the American legation: "For the
time being, nothing can be done, inasmuch as the understanding among the
major powers places Romania within the Soviet sphere of influence." This reply,
from those who ought to have been the plan's chief supporters, dazed Noradungian. He refrained from relaying it to the people who came to see his maps. He
did not realize that the Americans' reply was moot since it mattered increasingly
little to them whether the union would ever be achieved. What mattered to
them was the illusion more than the reality; the maps mattered more than the
world and its treaties, its fronts. And if the world had come to resemble those
maps, then they would probably have dreamed up different maps.

Fortunately for him, Mikael Noradungian did not have much time to brood
on his own suffering since the second disaster arrived hard on the heels of the
first, albeit couched in carefully crafted words, as if on the part of somebody
who wished to help. There was no impediment to the continued existence of the
Masonic lodges, Ana Pauker told him, inviting him to the Ministry of Foreign
Affairs. What was more, as proof of the high esteem in which the lodges were
held, Noradungian received a list of front-ranking members of the Communist
Party who were to be inducted into the order. Even if the discussion was ami-
able, conducted in the awkward, stilted Romanian spoken by Ana Pauker and
Mikael Noradungian, each according to the habits and accents of the native
lands and the foreign parts in which they had resided, Noradungian understood
that the Communist Party wished to place a noose around Masonry's neck and
employ it to its own ends, particularly in foreign affairs. With Armenian caution
and the wisdom of his seventy-five years, Mikael Noradungian feigned great
satisfaction with this proposal; he did not fawn, but he was sufficiently convincing for them to allow him to leave without clapping him in handcuffs. He even
agreed to found a Masonic lodge especially for the Romanian working class.
The joy he confessed to Ana Pauker was so sincere that as soon as he got back
home, he summoned all the thirty-third degree brothers and decided to put
Romanian Freemasonry into hibernation.

As the secret police began to search the archives and prepared to arrest all
the authors of that utopian plan for a United States of America and Europe,

258

Noradungian chose the course most conveniently to hand for a man of his venerable age. He took to his bed, and all those who visited him in those years, to pump him for information about the archives, agreed that the old man could not have long to live.

Among all the people who came to his bedside, one alone had been called there by Noradungian himself. That man was Levon Zohrab. It was to him that Noradungian gave the maps, carefully wrapped in cloth. As a result of a circumstance that *The Book of Whispers* shall describe to us, Levon Zohrab decided to pass the maps on to Sahag Sheitanian, the brother-in-law of my paternal grandfather, Garabet Vosganian.

A STORY WITHIN A STORY. LEVON ZOHRAB, THE CONCEALER OF THE MAPS. Of all the protagonists of *The Book of Whispers*, Levon Zohrab perhaps felt the greatest guilt at having survived. Unlike Misak Torlakian and others who, on returning home, found nothing but the stench of charred timbers and ownerless chattels jumbled among chunks of plaster hacked out by axes, Levon Zohrab was an actual witness to events. His father, Krikor Zohrab, a member of parliament for Constantinople, made him swear he would do exactly what he asked of him, and then, before opening the door to the Ottoman police, he made him hide behind the drapes, ordering him not to come out until it was over. Levon heard how they burst in and, after Harutiun Mgrditchian, who had come with them, confirmed that Krikor was the Armenian deputy, they arrested him. It was the morning of April 24, 1915. That same day they arrested Daniel Varujan, Siamanto Vartkes, Father Komitas, and the other Armenian leaders. A few years later, it was Levon Zohrab's testimony that convinced Soghomon Tehlirian to kill Mgrditchian in a manner regarded as the most appropriate possible: by shooting him in the heart before the eyes of his family. At the time, however, Levon Zohrab did not think of revenge but only of the shame he had endured hiding behind the drapes, a helpless witness to his father's arrest.

Levon Zohrab is not only the protagonist of this story within a story, but also one of the protagonists of the convoys that followed the convoys. He set out on his father's trail, scouring the route taken by the convoys. He lay in wait for the files of deportees; he mingled with them when they were not so closely guarded, trying to find those arrested on April 24. He stayed at inns, talking to the captains of the gendarmes. But because he moved on foot, while Krikor Zohrab and Vartkes effendi, the two Armenian deputies, were taken by train and then car to Aleppo, he always arrived too late. In front of him, no matter how quickly he walked, there was always another convoy, as if they were strung out on a rope, with one pulling the next behind it. In Aleppo he learned of his father's death.

An officer recounted to him the stories of a comrade who boasted of having killed Zohrab and Vartkes effendi with his own hand, and he described in detail the dreadful torture to which the two had been subjected. Levon Zohrab tried to identify the place; the thought that his father's bones lay strewn gave him no rest. He reconstructed what he could from the officer's drunken tales and finally found some places that fit the description. He hired two locals with a cart and the necessary tools and set off in search of his father's remains. But in those expanses you stumbled on bones at every step. And because of the large differences between daytime and nighttime temperatures, because of the winds and the scorching midday heat, the corpses had blackened; the skin had fallen from the bones, making it impossible for him to identify any body as resembling his father. So he began to bury all the bodies he found, in the hope that one of them might be his father. He did this for a number of weeks, until the locals refused to go with him any more no matter how much he paid them, since they feared his glassy eyes and the zeal with which he examined the decomposing bodies, seeking marks of violent death to match those he knew from the story of his father's murder. Levon Zohrab continued on his own for a while, but finally he stopped, exhausted and disturbed by the eyes that watched him, by the quiet or angry rumors and whispers that wove themselves around him, which held that he was a madman or even a robber of corpses.

Like the other tens of thousands of refugees who chose Romania for their destination, Levon Zohrab arrived in the port of Constanța, a motley, lively place where goods from all four corners of the globe intersected; where money went round and round like in a whirlpool; and where, if you wished to flee, you could hide yourself better than anywhere else.

But Zohrab managed to flee from everything but his own restless wandering. He chose a life of toil and poverty in the midst of the dock porters, who were simple, brutal folk. He then worked on the railways and in construction, reckoning that the penitence of endlessly digging and filling in holes was the most suited to the burden of having remained alive while his father's body remained unburied. The biggest torture, however, was not the penitence itself but the inability to complete it. Since the construction work required all kinds of materials, from gravel to bricks, and those materials did not always arrive on time, Levon Zohrab, a man accustomed to having things go smoothly, contacted a number of Armenian traders from Constanța and set up a building materials warehouse. In a short time, he laid down his spade and took up trade. Not without disquiet, Levon Zohrab observed that in place of the penance he had taken upon himself, he was starting to grow rich. But the hardest to bear was the fact that he could not stop. The money brought him no comfort. On the contrary, the money grew and grew with unstoppable ease, augmenting his guilt at remaining alive. The Armenian survivors distanced themselves more and more from the suffering that might have healed them, growing steadily rich. Such was also the case with Armenag Manisalian, the Israelians, the Seferians, Avedis Varteresian, Terenig Danelian, Krikor Zambakchian, Hartin Frenkian, Hovsep Dudian, Mikael Noradungian, and many others. And so it was with Levon Zohrab. The force that drove him to get rich, to come up with the means of increasing the difference between purchase and sale price, was far more powerful than the desire to remain humble and poor and thereby to redeem the sin of having survived. The more the unhealed wounds within him bled, aggravated by the serrated edges of the silver coins, the more the money piled up, and, converted into gold and jewels, the more heavily it weighed on him. Helpless to oppose the urge that flowed through his veins, he expanded his business and moved to Bucharest, where he met Mikael Noradungian. Noradungian explained to him in detail that the best means of enriching yourself in Romania was to do business with the authorities, and if you wanted to save time and bribe money, the thing to do was to become a member of the government yourself. And so it was that Levon Zohrab came to run the state tobacco monopoly and a string of tobacco factories.

We do not know how much wealth Levon Zohrab amassed. Perhaps he himself did not know, as he was not much concerned with counting money, or perhaps he was terrified by the power it brought with it. Nor is it possible to count how much he had by the end since, unlike Hartin Frenkian, he made no will. For reasons that are obvious, when they confiscated everything from him in 1948 and sacked him from the tobacco monopoly, they did not bother to make an inventory of his accounts, his bonds, his petty cash. An old man driven out of his houses, his automobiles, and his director's chair, taking shelter in the servants' mansard of his residence on Boulevard Dacia, Levon Zohrab once more had time to meet his father. But now, either because his aging soul was less prepared to cope with penance or because he was older than his father had been when he died, his pain was all the more atrocious since now he looked on his father with the tenderness he would feel for a younger brother whom he was all the more indebted to protect.

After he became his father's elder brother, Levon Zohrab's conversations with himself were interrupted twice. And the third time, ready to die, he interrupted them himself.

The first interruption was Mikael Noradungian, who gave him the maps. "It's over," he told him in the elegant Armenian he had learned in Constantinople at the Robert College. He told him he had put Freemasonry into hibernation.

and had begun to seek safe places for its most valuable insignia. The most precious of all these, for Mikael Noradungian, proved to be the maps; the secret police had to be prevented from finding them, whatever the cost. "Why me?" asked Levon Zohrab. "Because you understand. The maps will be safe with you. The secret police don't have any business with you; they have taken everything away from you already." They had taken everything apart from his phantasms, in other words. But like Noradungian, Levon Zohrab shared his phantasms with nobody else, so not even the secret police, with their brutal skill at searching things out, would have been able to find them and take them away from him. "But I'm almost as old as you," objected Levon Zohrab. "And as alone." "You will pass them on when the right time comes. At least your solitude won't raise any suspicions." It was the last time they saw each other. When the trial began and the interrogators asked about the maps, nobody knew where they might be since neither of the two men were alive, and the maps, although they still existed, were not to be found.

Mikael Noradungian was mistaken, however. The Communist regime did still have business with Levon Zohrab. That was because—and here Noradungian was again mistaken—they had not taken quite everything away from him; he still had his honor. Since the eyes of his father, as he had seen him from behind the curtain, had remained seared on his mind, they regarded him sternly and unblinkingly for the rest of Zohrab's life, preventing him from doing anything that would have besmirched the family name. And this is what the Communists demanded from him after a time: his word of honor. In the summer of 1948, four men in leather coats burst into Levon Zohrab's attic. They forced him to sit down at the table, pressing down on his shoulders. In fright, Zohrab thought it must be about the maps and chided himself for having answered the door. But the men were not looking for any maps. They were not looking for anything that could be hidden beforehand. They were looking for what could easily be found since it was there in full view: the telephone. They took it from the bedside table and placed it on the table in front of him. There were footsteps on the stairs, and then another man entered the room, wearing not a leather coat but a flimsy summer suit, which was also out of keeping with his burly body. He did not have the alarming facial expression of the others. On the contrary, he doffed his hat in front of the petrified old man, displaying a politeness that, although it could be regarded as over the top in the circumstances, did not seem at all forced. And unlike the others, the newcomer, placing his hat next to the telephone and remaining on his feet, perhaps out of respect, perhaps because he did not intend to stay long, smiled, saying, "I'm Chivu Stoica," as if that explained a number of things all at the same time. On hearing that name, Levon Zohrab was about to get up, but the other men's hands pressed down on his shoulders again, pinning him to the chair. Chivu Stoica cast them a reproachful glance and then turned to the old man: "There's no need to be afraid, Mr. Zohrab." He called him "mister" without a trace of irony, accepting the differences between the worlds to which each belonged, even if his world was the newer and was now master of the old. "We don't mean you any harm. We're not going to arrest you or take away any of your possessions. All we need is your word of honor."

Chivu Stoica took a piece of paper out of his pocket and smoothed it on the table in front of the old man. "Do you know what this is, Mr. Zohrab?" The old man put on his spectacles and read it. Then he handed the piece of paper back. "It's a telephone number in Turkey," he said. "You know this telephone number well, don't you, Mr. Zohrab?" smiled Chivu Stoica, although now less amiably. "Our men include former workers from your tobacco business, close associates even. They say you often called this number . . ." Zohrab looked at him; the other man's smile had faded from his face. "If I die," thought the old man, "the maps will be lost; I promised Mikael Noradungian to preserve them." Other than the maps and his father's piercing gaze, Levon Zohrab had nothing. With a sigh, he said, "It's the telephone number of the director of the Bank of Turkey . . ." The smile spread across Chivu Stoica's face once again. He lifted the receiver and handed it to him. "Call him . . ." "What could I say to him, especially under the present circumstances?" "We have many enemies, Mr. Zohrab . . . After nationalization, Romania's accounts at foreign banks were frozen. In the port of Constanța we have a number of Turkish ships waiting to unload ore. We can't pay them except in cash. The captains are threatening to raise anchor. And the country has great need of that ore . . ." "But what can I do?" "You can call the director of the Bank of Turkey . . . We need three days to get the money together. We'll also pay interest on it. Make him accept the delay . . ." "How much money is involved?" asked Zohrab. On the back of the scrap of paper with the telephone number, Chivu Stoica wrote a series of figures. The scrap was barely wide enough for so many digits. Zohrab read them, wide-eyed in amazement. "And how will you guarantee to pay this sum?" "With your word of honor, Mr. Zohrab." He picked up the receiver once more and added, "I warn you that one of these men was picked because he can speak Turkish." Chivu Stoica carefully dialed and brusquely demanded that the operator put him through to the number on the scrap of paper. Levon Zohrab then took the receiver and spoke. Stoica looked at his subordinate quizzically; the henchman confirmed that everything was in order. Zohrab spoke for a few minutes and then put down the receiver. "It's fine," he said. "The ships will wait . . ." He remained motionless while the man in the flimsy suit put on his hat, this time forgetting to bow, and then vanished through the door, with the others clomping down the stairs after him.

Zohrab turned the telephone toward him, lifted the receiver, and dialed a number, slowly, straining to remember it. He could not believe what he had done. On the other hand, his father, Krikor Zohrab, would have been proud of him, perhaps for the first time, even seeing him like that, in an attic with a shared bathroom down the hall, at the top of a narrow flight of stairs that remained his only channel of communication with the world and that, for some time, nobody had climbed except the postman to bring him his pension and the men we have just described. And perhaps precisely for that reason, his father would have been proud of the fact that merely his word of honor, given in the unsteady voice of a man surrounded by four secret policemen whose pistols could be guessed at from the bulges on their hips, had proven to be a guarantee stronger than any an entire state could provide.

Sahag Sheitanian arrived the very next day, early in the morning. He did exactly as Levon Zohrab had instructed him over the telephone: he walked past the house a few times, as far as Gemeni Square and back; he stopped a short distance away, in front of Ioanid Park, and examined the street-facing windows, waiting for a twitch of the curtain. Only then did he climb the stairs, trying not to make any sound. They sat down facing each other: Levon Zohrab and Sahag Sheitanian, bound together by the same memories of the circles of death. "It is the same as if you did bury him," said Sahag Sheitanian. "Who knows? You did everything you could." "I shouldn't have left him alone," whispered Levon Zohrab. "He was almost an old man. I should have gone with him." "They would have killed you as well." "In a way, they did." "Here's the thing, baron Zohrab," said my godfather, Sahag Sheitanian, leaning across the table. "The two of us carry the same suffering, you for your father, I for my mother. Here's what I think: it was the only thing we could do. And it was better for them too that way. If you really love your parents, you have to let them die before you."

But at least this time, the reason Levon Zohrab had asked him to come was different. He told him about Chivu Stoica's visit of the night before. Sahag Sheitanian stared wide-eyed: "The Bank of Turkey? You mean . . . the Ottoman Bank, baron Zohrab? The one Armen Garo wanted to blow up during the time of Sultan Abdul Hamid?" "I was at school with the director; we remained friends. They knew that." "Now that you've helped them, things will be better for you. They ought to be grateful to you." Levon Zohrab smiled sadly: "I have another three days to live, Sahag. Exactly as long as the respite they asked from the bank. The one who ought to be grateful to you becomes your worst enemy. Especially when it's not a man but a state, as in this case. Think about it: the

Communist regime, with its party, its secret police, its prisons, and the tens of thousands of people queuing up to become Communists, has shown itself to be weaker than the word of a single man and, what's more, a man who is a class enemy. I'm a burden to them. After the captain of the convoy receives the money and they unload the ore, they'll come for me, and probably they won't even bother to arrest me."

He stood up and went to the corner of the room, where he opened a door giving onto a kind of closet. "I made a promise that I have to keep," he said. "Lift those floorboards in the corner there. Carefully, so you won't damage what's underneath . . ." Sahag uncovered the hiding place, removed Noradungian's rolled maps like a baby from a font. He clutched them to his breast. "Take them," said Levon Zohrab. They're yours; you love them the best." He stopped Sahag in the doorway. "Do you really think it was a proof of love that I let my father die before me?" "No. It proves you love him because you didn't die at the same time as he, before his eyes. That's the rule of this world: we bury our parents, and our children bury us." "Which wasn't the case for the two of us," old man Zohrab smiled sadly. "Neither on the one side nor the other; am I not right, Sahag?" It was not Sahag who replied but Yusuf, with a grin glimmering in Sahag's guts, addressed to another Yusuf, who answered from the old man's gaunt chest, dancing wildly over the eastern expanses of the maps, among the unburied old folk and the unborn children.

As he had promised and now released from his oath, old man Zohrab was the first to die, without waiting for the murderous expression of the Communist regime's gratitude. Death had spared those people in their youth, even against their will. And because it had shunned them then and because, for that reason, they had been forced to relive others' deaths in their memories and nightmares, death decided that if it had been invited the first time but had not come, then the second time it would come only when invited, and promptly too. This is why death gave this gift to many of the Armenians of my childhood; it served them, in their old age, loyally, flickering in the votive lamp, wafting in the steam from the coffee, curling up inside the wrinkles of the sheets, trickling down the windowpanes, slipping through the cracks in the door, and when they invited it, it came; it lay down in their beds; it covered them with its shadow; and as they died, it lent them a peaceful face. Levon Zohrab died sitting at the table, with his head resting on his left hand and holding the telephone receiver in his other hand. In the end, that telephone had been the proof that he had led a worthy life. We do not know whom he wanted to call on the telephone or if anybody answered. There is no evidence that anybody else visited him, apart from death, of course, which remained by his side to the last, lowering him from the cross and mercifully embracing him.

The second to die was Mikael Noradungian. Death was hesitant around him. He lay bedridden for a long time, until death finally came to know him, after the mysterious life he had led. Death does not like strangers; only after listening to his whispers and mutters, observing his nightmares, rummaging through his papers, and reconstructing his memories from the wrinkles on the pillow did death become familiar with him; only then did it enter him and know him. He was buried on the last day of the winter of 1951, accompanied by only a few of the thirty-third degree members of the Supreme and Final Council, which he had revived almost three decades before. Bishop Vazken Baljian did not view their wish kindly. But he had to accept it, especially since it had the blessing of the authorities themselves, which, by indulging it, wished to avenge themselves on the dead Noradungian for the enmity the living Noradungian had borne them for the fact that he had put Masonry into hibernation just as the Communists were about to lay their hands on it. Noradungian had to be punished. How can you punish a dead man other than by throwing into doubt any positive memories of him? And how else could the Communist authorities avenge themselves on an enemy other than by displaying indulgence toward him and suggesting that what might have seemed opposition was in fact submission, with the Communist regime feigning sadness at having lost a friend? But the few people who knew that Noradungian had put Masonry into hibernation not in order to destroy it but to protect it from humiliation, hoping for better times, came to the funeral and honored him. And as I said, Bishop Vazken agreed to the Masonic symbols that were carved on his tombstone and the inscription beneath them: "All-Powerful Grand Sovereign Commander of the Supreme and Final Thirty-Third Degree Council of Romania"; and further: "Twenty-Seventh Descendant of the Pakraduni Dynasty," which meant that this Armenian from Agn, who became a merchant in Galata, then a minister in Constantinople, the gray eminence of Romanian Masonry, dealer in arms and illusions, was the last scion of the great Armenian kings of one of the minor and major Armenias that had been founded, flourished, and perished between the corner of the Mediterranean and the triangle between Lakes Van, Sevan, and Urmia.

In those days, Sahag Sheitanian was a man in his prime. On Grandfather Garabet's advice, he took the maps to the parish offices and put them where nobody would look for them but where anybody could find them: in the vestments trunk. While Arshag the bell ringer kept watch, carefully scanning the surrounding area, they would go there sometimes to ponder the maps, dreaming of revived frontiers. This is why Arshag never saw the maps. Rather, accustomed to watching the flight of the birds, he sought frontiers in the places where they are always shifting and therefore unmarked. Minas the blind man would run his fingers over the maps, sensing the frontiers with his fingertips. Then he would place his index finger on the eastern border, where the route of the convoys had come to an end. "Everywhere I see at least a glimmer of light," he said. "But here, in this place, there is darkness. Bring a lighted candle and place it here." Anton Merzian asked whether it wouldn't be better to take the maps to the Seferian vault, where they would not be in any danger. Krikor Minasian, who never missed an opportunity to laugh at the way Merzian said stupid things in that interrogative way of his, reckoned that if they were to go by the cowardly Anton Merzian, then they ought to bury the maps rather than hide them in a vault. The others had no opinion either way. The only thing they all agreed on was that the Americans, instead of wasting time in Korea, ought to head to the Balkans as quickly as they could, with MacArthur at their head. Sahag Sheitanian, who kept the keys to the parochial offices and who was therefore able to open the trunk and look at the maps from time to time, lit a candle on a saucer, placed upside down in the east corner of the room, even if that meant Minas the blind man would come; of all things, even the brightest, Minas was best able to distinguish candles. They both gazed with large, dark eyes since each saw in his own way, which neither could communicate to the other. "You can't look at maps in a vault," said my grandfather Garabet. "It's not big enough. When you spread out the maps, after they've spent all that time rolled up, they feel a need to breathe. And besides, you can't really look at a map if you stoop like a cripple and grope for it. You can look at it only if you're standing up straight. Hunching up isn't appropriate to the splendor of maps." So the maps remained in the vestry trunk, and from time to time, on the eve of the big feast days, the men came and looked at them. In time, the maps started to yellow at the corners. They came to smell of old vestments. The men would take out the maps as if they were a monstrance and would fall silent in their presence. The circle around the maps began to thin out, until the only old Armenian of my childhood who remained was Sahag Sheitanian, and next to him, rather than Minas the blind man, stood Yusuf, who had aged all too quickly, who was now withered, trembling from every joint, and just as blind as Minas. Having grown accustomed to him after all that time and feeling sorry for him, Sahag would guide Yusuf, showing him the way back to himself so that Yusuf could climb back inside his body and rest.

One night something extraordinary happened. Sahag Sheitanian dreamed of Yusuf. In the dream, Yusuf was asleep, lying on his mattress of dried, aromatic herbs in the white tent pitched in the desert. Twisting and turning in his sleep, Yusuf was dreaming of Sahag, who was also asleep in a tent, his tent of patched sheets in Deir-ez-Zor, but it was a bigger Sahag, wearing a white, bloodstained tunic. Sahag called out Yusuf's name in his sleep, he called his blood by its name, and he dreamed of Yusuf asleep. In that way, each sinking deeper into the other's sleep, Sahag and Yusuf met for the first time, in a dream. Only then did Sahag know that Yusuf, for the first time identical with him, was dead. It was a sign. He too died not long after that. Not many remained to go to the funeral, apart from us nephews. We did not find the maps in the trunk when we took the cassocks and vestments to Bucharest's Armenian Museum. They had existed for as long as they were different from this world. As the continents were divided up anew and regrouped, entire swaths of the maps began to turn white and then quite simply vanished. Europe began to unite, piece by piece, sheltering itself beneath a protective carapace. The Berlin Wall fell; Armenia was liberated, although of its three lakes it retained only Sevan and now stretched only as far as the plain below Ararat. Minas the blind man had died long ago, wrapped in the shroud of his vision of Kevork Chavush and mourned by his daughters Luisa and Armaveni. The maps began to acquire the same whiteness as Minas's eyes; as the world regained its health, the maps developed cataracts. Like other dreamers, Mikael Noradungian, Levon Zohrab, Sahag Sheitanian, and the others pictured the reality that precedes reality, and that merely made them feel all the more alone in this world.

I do not know what disease Sahag Sheitanian died of. Some say it was old age, but for the Armenians of my childhood, old age was not a disease. Death invited him into its arcade and let him choose from its shop windows the manner of his death and the moment when it would happen. He picked the precise moment when the maps turned completely white and when there was nothing left to tempt him. That was his revelation: the apocalypse of maps, the day when the maps descend to earth.

10.

Torn from the clutches of the angry mob, Misak Torlakian was covered in bruises, bleeding; his clothes were in shreds. He was taken to a dark cell and shoved inside. He huddled on the cold floor. He closed his eyes and lay motionless the whole night. The white stallion had returned, now peacefully grazing on the plain. It was saddled, but the rider was nowhere to be seen. Misak approached, and the horse sniffed him. It did not rear up on its hind legs but merely gave a short whinny and moved away.

In the morning he was handed over to some soldiers who took him to another prison, keeping him under close guard as they walked along the side streets. The new cell was no different from the one in which he had spent the night, but he shared it with other prisoners: a young Macedonian, an Arab arrested for murder, and a Russian Bolshevik arrested for spying. His cellmates took care of him, gave him water, and then laid him on the only mattress in the cell. Later, they were to testify on his behalf.

One of the jailers turned out to be an Armenian by the name of Parsegh. He gave him fresh clothes and sent word to Armenians abroad that Misak Torlakian was alive.

The news was made public a week later, when, following a series of summary interrogations and a confrontation between Misak Torlakian and the victim's brother, it was announced that the trial was about to begin and that he would need a lawyer. The Armenian community straightaway found Hmayag Khosrovian to represent him.

Contemporary accounts say that Misak Torlakian was apathetic during the trial. He sat motionless, seeming not to hear the witnesses and answering in monosyllables when he was asked questions. He did not even flinch when the witnesses for the defense described the circumstances of the Trebizond massacres of 1895 and 1915 or the Baku massacres instigated by Behbud Khan Javanshir.

His lawyer, Hmayag Khosrovian, had defended Soghomon Tehlirian in Berlin not long before. Calling a large number of witnesses from all four corners of the globe, whose testimonies made a strong impression on the court, the defense argued not for the innocence of the accused but for his acquittal on grounds of his mental state and lack of discernment at the time of the assassination. Soghomon Tehlirian had been proven to be epileptic, his mind having been affected by the traumas he had experienced during the deportations. Although his crime was obvious and Soghomon Tehlirian did not deny it, the court finally decided to acquit him.

Hmayag Khosrovian employed the same strategy during the Constantinople trial. Soghomon Tehlirian really was mentally infirm, although not so infirm as to be unaware of what he was doing since he was driven by the obsession of finding and killing Talaat Pasha. But it was harder to portray Misak Torlakian as an epileptic or schizophrenic; he was a country lad with a robust constitution, hardened to the harshest situations. Hmayag Khosrovian tried to coach Misak Torlakian, teaching him how to feign mental illness. But faced with his client's evident inability to feign anything, he concluded that a waking Misak Torlakian would never convince anybody he was not in his right mind. Khosrovian therefore decided that it was the sleeping rather than the waking Torlakian who was ill.

Even given the conditions for leniency created by harrowing testimonies of the deportations and massacres of the Armenians, as well as the fact that the court, from the guards all the way up to the judges, was made up of Englishmen, the lawyer knew that Misak Torlakian would have no chance of escaping a conviction for premeditated murder in the face of the irrefutable evidence that he had cold-bloodedly killed Behbud Khan Javanshir. And there was a single sentence for premeditated murder: death by hanging. It was clear that Khosrovian had to come up with something; otherwise, in the eyes of the foreign journalists there to report on the trial and in the eyes of the witnesses from all over the world, Misak Torlakian would be nothing but an avenger without a cause, a body jerking and then hanging from the noose, with a small fissure between his atlas and axis vertebrae. Of all the methods of execution, hanging is the least heroic.

Before doing battle with the prosecutors, Hmayag Khosrovian therefore decided to do battle with Misak Torlakian's silences. He had long interviews with the accused; he looked at him as he sat silently, staring vacantly, rubbing his wrists after the cuffs were removed. He let him pace up and down the room without interruption. First he told him about himself, about his murdered relatives, about Soghomon Tehlirian, about how Tehlirian had stalked Talaat Pasha. He refrained from telling him about Operation Nemesis, although he was one of the very few, outside Armen Garo's circle of volunteers, who knew about it. Those who knew strictly kept the secret. He sensed that if he hinted at things he seemed not to know about but ascribed to them their correct meaning, then he might win Misak Torlakian's trust. Gradually, Misak was drawn out of himself by the lawyer's stories. Starting from where his own memories overlapped with Hmayag's, he began to tell his own story: about Trebizond; about his fascination with weapons; about the first man he killed and then the others; about his lying in wait in the mountains in the hope that Enver Pasha's army would come through the pass; about the Armenian vanguard of the Russian armies and how they found the devastated Armenian quarter of Trebizond; about his village, Gyushana, and its burned houses; about his younger siblings' room, where the sheets lay crumpled under chunks of plaster and charred timbers. He told him about his dream of the bloodied white horse, which reared on two legs in front of him as he stood pressed up against the wall but which did not crush him under its hooves, which meant that Behbud Khan Javanshir was not the rider but rather the burden from which the white horse demanded Misak release it, and this was why it pursued him in his dreams.

He said these things in a low but passionate voice. And then Hmayag Khosrovian knew that at last he was on the right path. Operation Nemesis could not be invoked in court; it could not be revealed that the group's leader had entrusted Misak Torlakian with the mission of killing Behbud Khan. Rather it had to appear to have been his own personal decision; it had to have been pure chance that brought the stocky, curly-haired Armenian face to face with the huge Azeri. Leaving the rest unchanged, the lawyer decided to shift the story of the massacre of Misak's family from the outskirts of Trebizond to Baku, the capital of the ephemeral Trans-Caucasian Republic. It was not hard. Misak was very familiar with the Armenian villages around Baku.

Then there was the dream and the bloodied horse. Khosrovian did not ask Misak whence came his conviction that the horse belonged to the pursued rather than the pursuer. When Misak spoke of his nights, his eyes once again became crazed, and he seemed to wish to escape from the dream, even if escape meant a less than enticing reality. In short, Hmayag Khosrovian decided that Misak Torlakian was a lunatic. And his somnambulism would have to be meticulously constructed.

Before the confrontation with Major Charles Davis, the physician the judges had assigned to evaluate Misak Torlakian's mental state, Hmayag Khosrovian asked for the help of some Armenian physicians, to whom he explained in detail how his client's somnambulism not only manifested itself in nocturnal episodes, but also had potential effects during the daytime. As all Torlakian's close relatives had been killed during the deportation, it was impossible to demonstrate whether or not insanity ran in his family. His apathy during the daytime could be put down to headaches, a natural consequence of the stresses placed on his cortex, which was turned inside out like a glove during his sleep. It was harder to prove the nocturnal episodes, and since the court was in session only during the daytime, witnesses were required. The only possible witnesses were his cellmates. This is what saved Misak since if he had been alone in his cell, all his efforts at feigning madness would have been futile.

Torlakian asked for the help of his three fellow prisoners: the Arab, the young Macedonian, and the Russian Bolshevik. First of all they used their cups and fingernails to scrape the wall until they had collected a handful of powdery plaster. Since the external signs of the illness could not be faked, the Russian, adept in the art of torture, ripped his shirt into strips and tightly bound Misak's hands behind his back. The Macedonian held out the crumbs of plaster in his cupped palms, as if he were offering the Armenian water to drink. Then, while the Arab held Misak by the scruff of the neck so that he could not avert his face, the Macedonian scrubbed his cheeks with the granular plaster. Misak's cheeks whitened and swelled, bleeding as if having been shaved with a blunt razor. But that was not enough. He was groaning and trying to free his hands so he could press them against his lacerated cheeks, but they took him to the top of the steps leading to the cell door. His hands had to remain tightly bound. A sleepwalker does not use his hands to protect himself since he is oblivious to any danger. They pushed him from the top of the steps. He tumbled down the steps, again and again. And only when his shoulders blackened with bruises and his nose had been broken on the edge of the steps, since he was unable to protect himself as he fell, only then did his cellmates decide it was enough. They unbound him, but he lay motionless, groaning. The Macedonian ground the plaster finely, mixing in crumbs of moldy green bread. Adding water, he made a greenish froth that he spread over the lips of the wounded man, most thickly at the corners of his mouth, where it had to dry and leave a crust. It was in this state that the jailor found Misak in the morning, as the other three looked on indifferently. Called as witnesses for the defense, the cellmates told the same story of a lunatic who often walked and talked in his sleep, except that this time the nightmare had been worse than on other nights. Torlakian had walked into the walls, climbed the steps, slammed himself against the metal door, fallen time and time again. "Why didn't you wake him?" "We tried to other times, but no sooner had he fallen asleep than he would start all over again. He wakes up by himself but only after the nightmare comes to an end. But anyway," they added, "why should we care?"

How skilled was the mutilation of Torlakian and how convincing the portrayal of him as a lunatic can be divined from the deposition of Major Davis: "If we take into account that his father was insane and his grandmother was a sleepwalker and if we likewise take into account that he sees before his eyes the image of his murdered parents and loved ones, then this proves that he is not in his right mind. There are testimonies that he is a sleepwalker; I myself saw him with froth around his mouth, and it is well known that after a bout of sleepwalking this is one of the symptoms and likewise that such bouts are followed by a depression that exhorts him to murder, for which the patient is not responsible since he cannot understand the meaning of his actions."

The trial ended with this deposition. The sentence was pronounced two weeks later and was strikingly similar to that handed down a few months previously in Berlin at the trial of Soghomon Tehlirian, who had been accused of murdering Talaat Pasha: "The accused is guilty of murder, but the court finds he is not responsible since he was mentally disturbed in the moment when the crime was committed."

Torlakian was sent back to prison, but this time to a cell that he did not share with anybody else. He even had permission to exercise in the prison yard. One night around three weeks later he was brought to the office of the chief warden. Civilian clothes were waiting for him. The photograph shows he has lost weight; the clothes hang limply from his shoulders, and he holds his hands in front of him, still numb from the grip of the cuffs. He looks like a bank clerk. To add to the utter discrepancy, he has been given a European-style necktie, with a small knot, and they have even put a hat on his head, making him look like a kind of Charlot. The bank clerk guise would have been convincing if he had not been flanked by four guards, two Turks and two Englishmen, all four in military uniforms. The guards conducted him to the prison gate, where a military car was waiting for him, with its headlights unlit. Only the two English guards climbed inside with him. The car made its way to the port, sticking to side streets, and came to a stop at a distant quay where a Greek vessel was berthed. Misak Torlakian was locked inside a cabin. The English guards stood on the quay, pistols at the ready, until the ship gave the signal to cast off. When the ship was far enough away to prevent any attempt at his swimming back, no matter how reckless, the captain unlocked the cabin and informed Misak that they would be docking in the Piraeus, where he would be free to go anywhere he wished, apart from Turkey. He would be arrested if he ever set foot in Turkey. As fate would have it, Misak was to see the port of Trebizond again, once from out at sea and once from the plateaus of Mount Ararat, now on the other side of the border, but he never set foot on Turkish soil again.

Using the meager amount of money he had received, Misak Torlakian went from the Piraeus to Athens. Nobody was following him. For the first time in his life he did not have to be wary; for the first time, he did not have to stalk anybody else. He could do anything he liked now that he had nothing else to do.

At the age of thirty-three, Misak Torlakian found himself empty-handed, and he experienced his freedom as a burden. He went to the Armenian church, he mingled with the immigrants, but they now had other worries; they had to survive, which they managed to do by selling *pastirma* and *sujuk* on street corners. Life shoved them from behind, and they had no time to look back.

Awaking groggy from the tension of the last few years, Misak Torlakian found the world painfully indifferent. He went north, to Thessaloniki, where he hoped to meet some of his comrades. He met them; Armenians were everywhere in those days in the ports of the Black Sea and the Mediterranean, many of them only just having arrived with the latest waves of refugees following the war between the Turks and the Greeks. Misak Torlakian mingled with them; he sought the comrades in arms of General Andranik and General Dro, the members of the Dashnak Party. The same as in Athens, Misak Torlakian proved to be of no use to anybody. He was even an embarrassment, like any other hero who had not died early enough.

He sought work. He had run out of money. For the first time, hunger did not inflame his fierceness for the struggle. Rather, he experienced it as a human need, and for this reason he saw it as shameful. He had never worked in the ordinary sense. Ever since he was an adolescent, the tools of his trade had been weapons, the Mauser in particular. He had fought with those arms, but he had also cleaned them, repaired them, admired them, become accustomed to them; he had been not only a fighter, but also a workman with weapons.

In Europe the guns had fallen silent. Moreover, the continent was ashamed of how many arms it had. The governments were talking about a league of nations; the armies had been disarmed; the soldiers had been demobilized and laid down the weapons of war. It might have been the same for Misak Torlakian, but he had been a soldier in an army that had given birth to its own generals, an army that, with the exception of a short interlude in the spring of 1918, had not served any government, but rather a people, and whose forces were counted not in divisions but in scattered bands. He too was a kind of soldier; he might have been demobilized and sent home except that he had no home to go to.

As long as he traveled from one place to another, nobody asked him anything. But when he decided to rent a little room near the port, the place where he might find work from one day to the next, two soldiers knocked at his door. In the meantime, Greece and Turkey had made peace. Whoever had been expelled from Turkish soil was not welcome on Greek soil. Torlakian was put on a train and taken to the Yugoslav border under armed guard. In Belgrade he searched for Soghomon Tehlirian in vain. It was better that he did not find him since Tehlirian had ceased to be the fighter he knew from secret meetings at the *Djagadamard* newspaper office in Constantinople. As often happens, after tension beyond the limits of human endurance, Soghomon Tehlirian, not having had the inspiration to die, was left drained of strength for the rest of his life. As we shall see, this did not happen to Misak Torlakian. His first encounter with death had been when he was just a child, in the squares of Trebizond. Not only had he seen it dwelling in a cold, motionless body, as is usually the case. Not only had he seen the dead image of death. He had encountered the living death, which walks in people's midst, which runs with the crowd: death in its most brutal and unexpected form.

Finding no place for himself in a world that was growing peaceful, shoved back and forth by the authorities of different countries, lonely, driven by the same strange fascination for Romania that had affected so many others, Misak Torlakian traveled by train for one day and one night and arrived in Bucharest during a blizzard one morning in the month of February 1922. Asking passersby the way, on streets covered in snowdrifts through which the trams could not run, he first went to the Armenian church on King Carol I Boulevard, and from there he went to the Armenian Consulate, where Harutiun Khntirian embraced him. It was the first time anybody had embraced Misak Torlakian since he and his comrades from the Nemesis group had bid each other farewell in the summer garden in front of the Pera Palace Hotel, after which he had crossed the road to catch up with the huge Behbud Khan Javanshir. Khntirian's embrace was sincere. Now that the Bolsheviks had occupied Armenia, fewer and fewer people sought him out, so Harutiun Khntirian, a shopkeeper without customers, warmly welcomed everyone who crossed his threshold. His inkpads had dried out from disuse, and when Khntirian gave Misak Torlakian a sheaf of useless identity documents, he had to press his rubber stamp as hard as he could. From Armenag Manisalian, Torlakian also received a certificate of ethnicity. He had never imagined he would have to produce papers proving he was Armenian, but Manisalian reckoned that the documents he had received on his release from prison were perhaps not the most suitable to present to the Romanian authorities. Endowed with these new identity papers, some of which proved he belonged to a people without a country and others of which placed him under the protection of a state that no longer existed, Misak Torlakian remained in Romania for two decades.

Unlike other protagonists of *The Book of Whispers*, Misak Torlakian did not get rich. He did not even manage to put together the smallest business. Since so many others in his situation were drawn to the ports, where, between two blasts of a ship's whistle, life could start afresh at any time, Misak Torlakian went to Constanța. Levon Zohrab was there in the same period; probably their paths crossed on the docks, among the heaps of sacks and the piles of planks, but we have no information as to whether they met. And the proof that such a meeting did not take place resides in the two men's very different destinies: Levon Zohrab got rich, first trading in construction materials, then in colonial goods, whereas Misak Torlakian, so skilled at handling weapons, was completely unskilled at handling money. With a small sum sent by Armen Garo from Boston and in memory of his family's occupation in the village of Gyushana, south of Trebizond, Misak Torlakian bought six cows and set up a small farm for himself. He banded together with Aram Yerganian, the fiercest of the members of the Nemesis special operation. And so it was that in peacetime, when those who had wounded were seeking fresh opportunities to wound and those who had been wounded were seeking a respite for healing, the most obdurate of the avengers, who had roamed Europe from Rome and Berlin to the Caucasus on the trail of the murderers of the Armenian people and had executed the death sentences handed down by the court martial, dedicated themselves to raising cattle in a village named Topraisar, near Constanța. But after a few strenuous months of cow-milking, Torlakian and Yerganian threw up their hands in defeat. That surrender came as a relief to both the one man and the other. Sullen after being vanquished by the cows, Misak Torlakian decided to avenge himself on their kind, finding work in a tannery. But the cows, this time in the form of stinking hides that had to be flayed, tanned, boiled, smoothed, and trimmed, proved to be just as implacable, and Misak Torlakian continued to live a life of grinding poverty. In a colony that was paving its way to prosperity, the Nemesis avengers remained alone and impoverished. Deprived of the jingle of coins and the sweet languor that a comfortable trade would have brought, garbed in poverty and silence, Misak Torlakian preserved the freshness and restiveness of his hatred intact.

It was around this time that Misak Torlakian first met my grandfather, on April 23, 1923, to be precise. Misak, whom the Constanța bureau of the Armenian Revolutionary Federation had provided with a suit, had left his job a few days earlier in order to rid himself of the thick reek of tanned hides, and together with Tatevos Bedrosian, the director of the Armenian school—the same man who in the 1940s was to don a German uniform with an Armenian tricolor armband and do the rounds of the Armenian churches in search of volunteers for the Legion—he arrived as a delegate at the convention of foreign branches of the Dashnak Party. He had been feverishly looking forward to the convention, at which he hoped to put his life back on its usual track.

For a long time after that, Misak Torlakian strove to remember the faces of those people from all over the world. The men he remembered from the mountain paths; from the secret meetings of the Dashnak bureaus in Trebizond, Tiflis, and Baku; from the detachments of volunteers in the vanguard of the Russian Army or the flanks of the Armenian Army at Sardarabad; from the group named after the goddess of revenge, who now wore beards and tied back their shaggy hair with a ribbon; they spoke in short sentences; they shared the same fate, dead or alive, as if nailed to the same cross, one on top of the other. They recognized each other by the insane glint in their dark eyes, the dry, glittering eyes of men who are sleepless or who, when they do sleep, are still awake in their dreams. Now those men were unrecognizable to him. Nor did they seem to recognize him. They wore tight city clothes; they had freshly shaven cheeks and pomaded faces; they exuded the bittersweet, stinging reek of the druggist's shop; they wore their hair swept back and thick with brilliantine; they drawled when they spoke and rounded off words with the suffix "-*tiun*," abstract words that suggested they were apt sooner to debate than to make decisions, let alone take action. Misak Torlakian, ashamed of his clothes, of the eau de cologne he had rubbed on his cheeks and hands to disguise the stale stench of tannery fumes, of his worn old shoes, withdrew to the sidelines and sat listening in amazement. None of those present had sat with bated breath in the public gallery of the courtroom in Constantinople; otherwise they could have testified as to the equally stony appearance, ravaged mien, and absent gaze that Misak Torlakian had displayed during his trial. And when Hovhannes Katchaznouni, the head of the republic's first cabinet of ministers in 1918–19, began his speech, Torlakian sat hunched in his chair, like a black spider. He dug his fingernails into the arms of the chair and looked around him in despair. Once again he entered the parallel reality where he was followed by the whinnying white horse whose neck was caked with blood. In the parallel reality, the memory of people died later than the people themselves. So too people's voices. Katchaznouni spoke without stopping and looked around the room, as if wishing to unburden himself. Torlakian knew him from the time when, after the vote of the National Council in Tiflis, it was decided to withdraw Armenia from the Trans-Caucasian Republic. In the spring of 1918, he had come to Yerevan as prime minister of the new republic, which Misak had defended.

"There is nothing left for the Armenian Revolutionary Federation to do," said Katchaznouni. "The Dashnak Party has run its course. During the war, the bands of volunteers"—this word pained Misak most of all—"acted without the accord of the party, mainly because they could not be reined in except following organized action . . . We lost all sense of reality, and we allowed ourselves to be carried away by our dreams to the point of delusion . . . Our party wished to control everything, ending up a dictatorship, and the parliament was just a fiction. The republic ought to have sought a common language with the Turks.

Was the arrival of the Bolsheviks a calamity for our country? There was no other power to take its place. Had they been any longer in coming, then we ourselves would have asked them to come. The Bolsheviks are needed in Armenia . . ."

Misak Torlakian did not hang around for the debates; he did not even wait for the end of the speech; he slipped outside; he walked without knowing where he was going until he reached a deserted street corner, leaned his forehead against a wall, and wept. He did not feel alone but abandoned, even among his own. He now said what he would have liked to shout out loud in that room. But his choked, tearful, sobbing voice was angry rather than sorrowful. This is how my grandfather Garabet Vosganian found him. He was striking his forehead with his palm, like at the Wailing Wall. Grandfather placed his hand on his shoulder, a gentle gesture. Grandfather had never lashed out at anybody because the world had never caught him off guard. But Misak Torlakian turned to him, his face contorted with fury, tears glistening on his cheeks. Unlike Grandfather, he had never flinched from confronting the world; there was nothing more for him to think about; he knew enough to urge him to take vengeance. Shed blood does not dry; it remains as a border, and he was the border guard. On one side of the border were the victims; on the other, those who must be punished. Neither bank of the river should be higher than the other. God forbid the blood burst its banks. My grandfather smiled at him, and perhaps Misak, with his furious and at the same time tearful face, took that smile as a mockery. It is true that the old Armenians of my childhood did not smile very often. Many of the things they experienced were sad: the memories, the songs, the new dead, even the feast days.

Even though the things they recounted, sang, worshiped, shared, and partook of were sad, the old Armenians of my childhood were not sad. It is true that they did not smile very often, but nor did they weep. Smiles and tears come from puzzlement and disquiet, from a certain ambiguity. But the old Armenians had clear eyes; they were neither sad nor happy; they were calm. Their joys and sorrows were like bridges across moods more nebulous. Their joy was genuine precisely because their sorrow was genuine. I saw them laugh, but rarely did I see them smile. Grandfather, for whom living largely meant understanding, was also tempted by nebulous moods. He did not try to steer the world from evil to good but from unclear to clear. For him, the nebulous moods were an expression of freshness. This is why he smiled, and because he had the strength and the charm to smile, others regarded him as their leader.

But that was to happen in the Focșani of the 1960s and in fenced-off places, be it our tree-dotted garden, be it the cemetery, where stone crosses grew alongside the trees. But the time is now the spring of 1923, and the place is a side street in Bucharest. One of the men, Misak Torlakian, is standing with his head pressed against the wall, as if he were resting it on a pillow. Obviously, he is a lunatic, as lawyer Hmayag Khosrovian would have pointed out. In tears, Misak Torlakian felt like a man lost, and the other man, Garabet Vosganian, smiled. "I don't yet understand," he said to himself. "He's mocking me," said Misak Torlakian to himself, "or he feels sorry for me, or he's pretending to feel sorry." Any of these reasons were enough for him to attack my grandfather. Since Garabet Vosganian was taller by half a head and since he was deft at avoiding blows, Misak Torlakian was unable to land a punch. Later he said that he had not even been trying to, but Grandfather was not so sure. Misak grabbed him by the collar of his raincoat and pulled him toward him, hissing, "Don't tell anybody you saw me crying!" "Who would I tell?" asked Grandfather, still smiling, but now awkwardly. "I don't know. Don't tell anybody," Torlakian hissed, threateningly. "Men like me don't cry." "Who are the men like you?" Grandfather asked, although there was no need. "They're few, but they exist . . . We're the ones who don't forget. The others can cry all they like . . . Now swear you won't tell anybody!" Grandfather was no longer smiling. "I swear," he said.

Misak Torlakian slowly released him, smoothing the collar he had crumpled in his clenched fists. He held out his hand for him to shake. "I'm Misak Torlakian," he said, "from the village Gyushana, Trebizond *vilayet*." "I'm Garabet Vosganian, from Afion Karahisar." They shook hands. Using his sleeve, Misak Torlakian then wiped the tears from his cheeks, and he was healed. Through that oath, Garabet Vosganian became the keeper of Misak Torlakian's tears. And as *The Book of Whispers* will tell us, my grandfather kept his oath until his dying day.

For Misak Torlakian, the year 1923 was to be a year of tears. To make sure he would not forget it, destiny twice caused him to weep. But the second time, Misak Torlakian wept alone, kneeling in the sand, facing the sea.

THE STORY OF THE FINAL VISIT TO TREBIZOND, IN THE YEAR OF TEARS. Pick a day from your life and let that day be the one that explains, the day that best describes the meaning of your entire life. For Misak Torlakian that day was May 24, 1923. He was not carrying a weapon, and he was not driven by a desire to kill, which means that only what was written in the folder in my grandfather Garabet Vosganian's cupboard could explain Misak Torlakian's life. What was more, on that day, he was holding not the Mauser with which he had been inseparable since childhood but a child's toy, something that might puzzle the reader of *The Book of Whispers*. But it will be puzzling only if you do not read the story to the very last page.

Perhaps with a presentiment that that day would be the one that explained his life, Misak Torlakian lived it intensely from dawn to dusk. He slept fitfully, twisting and turning. He awoke shortly after midnight; he washed his face in the basin; he shaved in the light of the lamp, peering into a shard of mirror; and he smoothed his harsh locks, running wet fingers through his hair. He put on his best suit and brushed it; he polished the toes of his shoes to a shine, straightened the knot of his necktie, smoothed the collar of his coat, and put on his hat. In that shard of mirror, he saw his flashing eyes, and rather than being satisfied with himself, he was afraid. He went out of the house and took a deep breath of the salty-sweet air that pervaded the tanneries district. It was as if something was lacking. He buttoned his coat and then unbuttoned it again. He thrust his hands in his pockets. He grasped the narrow brim of his hat, not knowing what to do with it next. He suddenly understood that all that getting ready had been a way of making the time pass, a way of finding pointless occupations to put off his meeting with the seashore. He went back home, took off his new clothes, and strewed them all around, as if repudiating them. He put on a pair of canvas trousers and a colored shirt, rolling up the sleeves. Then Misak Torlakian set off down the long streets of Constanța, which run perpendicular to the sea.

He watched the distant gray blobs of the dockworkers tying ropes and moving back and forth on the quay. He listened to the burble of the water as the fishermen's broad-hulled boats set off to sea. He sat motionless with the sea breeze on his face, whose edge was then softened by the first rays of the sun.

Accustomed to lying motionlessly in wait since his days in the mountains, gazing at a point on the horizon, he did not sense the others until one of them said hello in Armenian. It was then that he saw that dozens of people had gathered around him and that their number was growing. They moved aside to allow the priests to come to the front. The women stood at the back, wringing their hands. Nobody spoke since all of them would have told of the same thing: the story of waiting, in which the only detail that differed was the name of the child being sought. The authorities had stretched out a thick rope to prevent the crowd from approaching the quay. Now that it was fully light and the mist had lifted off the sea, the ship could be seen on the horizon. Misak Torlakian gripped the rope until his knuckles turned white. Another two hours elapsed before the ship moored at the quay. A number of officers, whose uniforms Misak recognized as Turkish, disembarked and handed the port authorities the passenger lists. Two by two, holding hands, the passengers were counted and made to stand in rows of forty. There were four hundred in all. The disembarkation took more than an hour. The passengers were children. Seeing that strange shore and the motley crowd on the other side of the thick ropes, they were afraid and felt a natural impulse to huddle up against each other. This reaction seemed to pain those who had been waiting for them long hours. They stood in silence and watched. Sensing they were being watched, the children took a step back, closing ranks; the people watching, desperately seeking familiar features among the small, anxious faces, took a step forward, longing to embrace them.

The ropes tautened. The men there to keep order braced themselves against the people's chests. All it took was for the line to break in a single place; the people surged forward and ran toward the children.

To those children, people running toward them could only spell danger. They were accustomed not to expect anything good; they had been through experiences that they could not understand; they had been rounded up from the roadsides or taken from the covered wagons that carted the dead. Some had been taken from their dying mothers' breasts. Others' parents had entrusted them to the authorities or benevolent foundations to spare them the journey of death. They had lived in church orphanages, scattered from Adana to Beirut, or they had been used as labor in the weaving shops of Aleppo and Damascus. When they no longer remembered their own names, they were given borrowed names to go with their borrowed clothes; they were quiet and watchful, gazing with narrowed, suspicious eyes. They could not be adopted by Muslim families since they had already been registered as Armenians. It was peacetime, and the foreign diplomatic missions would have protested against such forced Islamization. Nor could they be left to their own devices because as they grew up, they might remember or even understand, and that would have been a threat to the authorities, which found no better solution than to get rid of them. Appeals were sent all over the world. The four hundred children who had survived the circles of death and were scattered throughout the orphanages were taken to Constantinople. The Armenian community in Romania, responding to the appeal through Armenag Manisalian, president of the Union of Armenians in Romania, asked to take them. The children did not know this, and that was why they were frightened at being taken across the sea from one shore to another.

Standing in front of the children who had disembarked from the ship was a man with white hair who held a little girl by the hand. He was Sarkis Srentz, who was to be the director of the orphanage at Strunga during its three-year existence. Next to him was a churchman. From his pointed hood and the large cross that hung over his chest, he seemed to be a high-ranking bishop. Only later, when Armenag Manisalian approached him and kissed his hand, did the people discover that he was one of the bishops who had remained in the midst of the Armenians who had survived the massacre in Constantinople as if by miracle. He was Bishop Knel Kalemkelian. He made no gesture to stop the surging crowd.

He merely raised his hand and made the sign of the cross, murmuring, "Der voghormea"—Lord have mercy. Nor did he have any reason to stop the crowd; the children had been brought there so that they might find either their own families or succor among other families. Hanging around each child's neck was a piece of cardboard with his or her name written in Armenian. Those whose families had sent them to safety during the convoys or who were old enough to know whom to mourn, knew their first names and surnames, which were written on their pieces of cardboard. Those who had been found next to their dying mothers or who had been dumped at the roadside, too little to know what was happening and escaping with their lives precisely for that reason, had only first names; these were borrowed names, or rather adjectives: Andranik for a little boy, Anush for a pretty girl, Lopig for one who was chubby.

On seeing the bishop and on nearing the first row of children with cardboard placards around their necks, the crowd hesitated. Looking at the children more closely—at their gray, impoverished, clumsily stitched clothes; at their over-large boots without laces; at their earthen faces scarred by pustules because of their poor diet; at their hands, which they kept joined together to hide their uncut fingernails—the women covered their mouths with their hands, and the men, awkward in such situations, stood to their rear. It was the women who had the courage to approach. Each had come looking for somebody; each had a child who had been lost during the deportations, her own or a relative's; and each hoped to find that child alive. But because some of them did not know how to read Armenian script; or because the letters were traced clumsily on the cardboard placards, probably by the older children; or because they had forgotten the children's features after so many years; or because their features had changed, the women approached and peered closely. Some of the mothers, who knew they would never find their children, began to sob; others, as they reached the final row, sighed, their hopes having been shattered. Some of the women had come simply because they felt it would be better for the children if they found someone there to meet them; they had prepared parcels of food and sweets, which they handed out to the children at random. Unaccustomed to such gestures, the children took the parcels only after insistent urging. As the sun climbed to its zenith, Sarkis Srentz was about to shout impatiently at the crowd to hurry up, but Bishop Knel stopped him. He had seen the convoys with his own eyes and was accustomed to their slowness. Armenag Manisalian was patient too, watching from the steps of his house on the seafront. He did not approach the bishop to thank him or receive the documents entrusting him with the fate of the four hundred orphans until after each of those who had waited for them had walked along the final row.

Misak Torlakian felt a lump in his throat when he saw the children disembark, two by two, holding each other's hands, and then line up quietly in ten rows of forty to be counted again and to allow those who had been waiting for them to study them closely. He wanted to run to them among the first people in the crowd, but he decided it was best to let the women go first, knowing that a mother's longing is strongest. He went up to Bishop Knel Kalemkelian, who stood erect, his face calm, watching as the file of mothers flowed along the motionless rows. Torlakian kneeled and kissed the bishop's hand. "Astvadz oknagan, srpazan," he said; God help us, holy father. And Knel placed his hand on top of his head, whispering, "Astvadz bahaban, dghas"; the Lord preserve you, my son. With that blessing, Misak Torlakian approached the first row. His younger brother would have been around twelve years old by then, but he did not know what a boy of twelve looked like; at that age, he had been a rifle carrier and guide for the *fedayi*; he had not lived among other children and did not know how to tell them apart by their age. He could think of his brother only as he looked the last time he embraced him, after his desertion from the fort at Erzerum, when he had quickly gone to his village, Gyushana, to bid his family farewell before crossing the frontier with Russia. At the time, in 1914, Kalust, which in Armenian means "the one to come," was three years old; he was a sleeping little boy, with curly hair tumbling over his face, smelling of milk and water from the well. He now had to look for a boy of twelve, and it disconcerted him. He moved along the rows slowly, carefully reading all the names, even if the children were girls or were too young to be his brother Kalust. He moved so slowly that the people behind pushed him or moved him aside, and the children, troubled by the man's sharp gaze, looked up at him in surprise before quickly lowering their eyes, as if wishing to hide. He moved slowly so that the rows would not peter out too quickly and so that the hope of his search would not come to an end. In a way, with their sad eyes, with their unnatural stillness, which was more like rejection than submission, the children all resembled one another. On the other hand, none of them seemed to be that little boy of the Torlakian line whom, had he known what was going to happen, Misak would have taken with him as his own son, by right of the twenty-year age difference between them. The nearer he came to the final child, the more slowly he moved, without looking over the children's heads, in order not to anticipate or shorten the wait. He stopped in front of a lad who might have been the same age as his brother, and his cardboard placard was inscribed "Kalust." Only a first name, without a surname. Which meant that he was one of the children who had been found. It was not his own name; perhaps he had been rebaptized Kalust in the makeshift orphanage chapel. He looked at him for a long moment. The lad looked aside, embarrassed or perhaps weary of all the people who had passed in front of him. He had been given an apple, which he had half eaten; he held the core in his hand and the juice trickled between his fingers. Misak Torlakian wanted to say something, but he did not know what: "Do you remember who your parents are? Where you are from? Do you remember me?" But not knowing which question to ask first, he took from his pocket the toy he had found in the ruined house and that the child could not possibly have remembered. He stooped toward him, holding the toy in the palm of his hand, and the lad turned to look at him. Biting his lip and holding back his tears, Misak Torlakian slowly withdrew his hand and clenched the toy in his fist. The lad looked at him with soft, friendly hazel eyes, but his brother Kalust had had large blue eyes, unnaturally blue for a family of swarthy Armenians from the mountains. In the end, not one child proved to have Kalust's eyes, too unnaturally blue to survive in circumstances such as those. Misak Torlakian moved away and went on looking to the end. When the two crowds separated, Armenag Manisalian went to the port and signed for the children. Bishop Knel blessed the children and the crowd once again and handed the captain the documents. Torlakian watched as the children were put on carts that slowly drove away. He watched as the silent crowd was left behind, with a few people waving, not at anybody in particular but at the vanishing faces. He watched as a man and his wife walked away from the crowd. In his arms the man held a little girl. He was Nshan Maganian. Hoping for a miracle, he had come to look for a daughter who was buried in the deserts of Mesopotamia. He lifted his wife, Azniv, onto one of the carts and then their little girl, Anahid, born in their country of adoption. He then paid his penance, walking behind the carts for two hundred and fifty miles, as far as Strunga, outside Jassy, where, in an abandoned manor house, Manisalian had fitted out an orphanage for the four hundred children. By the time Misak Torlakian decided to look for the lad named Kalust, it was too late. The orphanage stayed open for just three years. Lists with the names of the children were sent all over the world. Many found relatives, scattered all over the globe, and made the journey back to Constanța before crossing other seas to other shores. Others were adopted. Finally, teacher Nshan Maganian gathered together the orphanage archives and went to Ploiești.

Misak Torlakian was the last person left on the shore. The quays had emptied, the fishing boats had returned to harbor, the ships' gangplanks had been raised, and the lights had been turned out. He knelt down and wept, long and deep, a mixture of weeping and talking, like that of those who went down into the circles of death around Deir-ez-Zor, as my grandparents did. He talked as he wept, telling stories, uttering curses; it was a weeping that did not release him but clutched him to itself. He gazed out to sea, his hopes dashed, and for that reason his lips murmured words that were unclear. It was late at night when he set off to his impoverished room, accompanied only by the memory of his brother Kalust's blue eyes, the eyes of him to come, and by God's blessing, given by Bishop Knel, but which, unfortunately, lingered for only an instant on the crown of Misak Torlakian's head.

"For a while I believed that Hovhannes Katchaznouni said those words about the Bolsheviks to protect you from Stalin," Misak Torlakian told General Dro. "I thought he wanted to get in with the Bolsheviks so he could save you. As it was, he went to the Soviet Union, to the Bolsheviks, and you came back safe from there!"

Misak was among the first to find out, from Tatevos Bedrosian, that Dro had been released and had arrived in Romania. He believed it was the hand of God, and the horse of his dreams neighed and reared up on its hind legs. He rushed to Buzău, spending the night with merchant Hazarian, and early in the morning he climbed aboard the train from Jassy, feverishly searching for him in every compartment. Dro was wrapped up in a Russian sheepskin coat. Misak recognized him by his beard, which he held proudly, and by his fiery eyes. "Is it going to be like before, general?" he asked him feverishly. "Like in the good times . . ." "It's peacetime," said General Dro. "In times like this, it's hard for us to win back our borders in battle . . ." "But how much longer do we have to be patient?" asked Misak Torlakian, disconcerted. "Until the next war, Misak," said General Dro. "To anybody who has come from there, it's clear that Russia is too poor to last long in peacetime. There'll be war, Misak, and the next time we have to be on the winning side."

They arrived at the station in Bucharest. Misak guided him to the Armenian Consulate. Harutiun Khntirian welcomed them with full honors, which is to say, he unfurled the tricolor, hung up the portraits, lined up his rubber stamps, and moistened his inkpads, as befitted the true representative of the government of the Armenian Republic, and at the back of the drawer he hid the dispatches from abroad and the newspaper clippings of the various proclamations made by the various governments in exile. They all arrived: Siruni, Saruni, old man Harutiunian, the Hovnanian brothers. General Dro addressed them in his shrill but powerful voice: "You ask me whom we should fight first. I answer you without hesitation: the Bolsheviks. The Turks killed our bodies, but the Bolsheviks kill our souls. We have to save our souls because once our souls have been redeemed, we will be able to revive our mangled bodies!" These words caused Misak Torlakian to rejoice. But they also meant a death sentence for Dro's family, held hostage in Siberia by Stalin. Those who listened to him, if they did not die in the peace between the two wars or during the war, were all arrested by the Red Army too; they died in the vast expanses of Siberia, or they returned bent double, half-blind, inhaling the icy Siberian wind through their nostrils.

"Peace is for victors," said General Dro. "What use to us is peace? It is harder to live vanquished in peacetime than in wartime. At least war gives you another chance. Let us then count the peace as the prelude to another war. That way we will preserve our hope."

General Dro's words had a magnetism they found hard to resist, if any of them wanted to resist. Rather, they let themselves be carried away by the vibration of his words; they dreamed of a Greater Armenia that would unite, within a rhombus, the three lakes, the arc of the Cilician Mediterranean, and the kingdom of Tigran the Great, all the more so given that the speaker was the hero of Sardarabad. Then they returned to their businesses, to the desks of their banks, to the chambers of commerce, to the goods warehouses and grain silos. They followed the stock exchange index and compared the ratings for gems with the ratings for bonds and shares. Having cured themselves of the fear of war, they dispersed, to enjoy in secret the blessings of peace. And those who were not teachers at the Armenian school or custodians of the library continued to get rich, adding to the list of benefactors inscribed on the marble plaque of the Armenian cathedral, and when the plaque filled up, they built public fountains; they donated printing presses; they founded orphanages, houses for boarding pupils, and libraries. They dispersed, each following the direction of his new occupation. Misak Torlakian remained at Dro's side, clinging desperately to the general's words and dreams.

When Dro went into the oil industry, using money he had received from America and with the help of his former comrades in arms, Misak Torlakian became a kind of administrator. He did not swerve from the promises of his youth. He learned that in those times, there were more weapons than those that had barrels and triggers. He administered Dro's oil businesses with the same feverishness as when he had carried rifles for the *fedayi* in the mountains long before, with the same love as when he had looked after his first Mauser, and with the same excitement as when he had learned to fire a cannon in the fort at Erzerum.

He saw oil as a weapon and could sense it sloshing in the bowels of the earth when the derrick pumped it to the surface. He took the same pleasure in the viscous rustle of the petrol coursing along the pipelines as he had in the explosions on the battlefield. With the money he set aside, he bought rifles from Noradungian, who still had contacts in the arms trade. He lined them up on racks, taking them out when Dro organized martial expeditions to the forest at Strejnicu, where they rode against invisible enemies, spraying the branches of the trees with bullets, churning up the leaves, before coming to a halt, panting, rejoicing in their sweat, which, in the absence of blood, reminded them of the whirl of battle.

General Dro continued to give his bellicose speeches, and Misak Torlakian nestled in the illusions they created. He traced a circle around himself, within which the war continued, with all its excitement and danger. There were others on the continent who drew similar circles around themselves, within which they armed and kept fierce resolve. The pressure from inside those circles caused them to expand until their edges touched. And then Europe went to war again.

Misak Torlakian had fought in the First World War on the Russian side, against Turkey's ally, Germany. After the new Russian government pulled Russia out of the war and its army retreated from the territories it was occupying in Anatolia and the northern Caucasus, Misak enlisted in Armenia's new army and was wounded, as we know, in its early and only glorious battles. In the Second World War, things were exactly the opposite. Misak Torlakian fought on the German side against Russia. He did so with the same zeal, and he chose his allies and enemies according to the stance they took with regard to Armenian territories. Those who occupied those territories were enemies; those who wished to liberate them were allies. "But the Germans don't want to liberate them," Vartan Mestujan, director of the *Ararat* newspaper, repeatedly told him. "They don't want to liberate Armenia; they want to conquer it for themselves . . ." And disconcerted, Misak looked to General Dro as usual, seeking his help. The general, who had spoken so many times before to so many leaders of every rank and so many crowds, had an answer for everything, and above all he had the gift of persuasion. They would gather around him; the general would stand up, smooth his beard, teeter on tiptoes when pronouncing a stressed syllable (which he also pronounced a third higher), and stick his thumbs in the armholes of his waistcoat to make it look all the more theatrical when he turned to look at the listeners standing at the edge of the audience. "We know this, and we also know that Wangenheim was content merely to send dispatches to Berlin, while closing his eyes to all the atrocities of the Young Turks. But even if the Germans want to occupy Armenia, it will be hard for them because Armenia is far away. We need to fear our neighbors; they're the ones who have always been our misfortune. What harm did Alexander of Macedonia's Greeks or Marcus Antonius's Romans ever do us, apart from dragging off our kings into slavery and chopping their heads off? But compare them with the Assyrians and Babylonians, the Medes and the Persians, the Parthians and the Arabs and the Tartars and the Turks and the Russians."

As long as the German Army was farther away than the Bolsheviks, who lurked beyond the Dniester giving ultimatums, Dro's words found numerous supporters, and they joined his armed forays into the Strejnicu Forest with raucous enthusiasm. Even after the German Army entered the country, given that its soldiers were disciplined and its requisitions moderate—not to mention the fact that they even built roads and improved the communications network—the idea of supporting an Armenian Legion incorporated into the Wehrmacht found supporters and even fanatics, such as Tatevos Bedrosian, the director of Constanța's Armenian school, who was bold enough to display the Armenian tricolor on the uniform of an officer in the 812th Battalion of the Wehrmacht. When Marshal Antonescu threatened the Armenians with deportation because of their less than warlike attitude and when the German Army showed itself to be more than indulgent toward the perpetrators of the pogroms against the Jews, the Armenians of Romania continued to swoon over General Dro's patriotic speeches, and they continued to weep over the songs of exile, but they refused to enlist in the Legion. And even though the Legion had command centers in both Berlin and Ploiești, the Armenians of Romania now tempered their fervor when dreaming of Armenia.

As we have seen, Misak Torlakian did not possess what you might call an instinct for self-preservation, and you might even say he was completely reckless. But he did have an exceptional instinct for self-preservation when it came to his ideals. Often, this second, heightened instinct made him despise the first. Life, perhaps with the exception of the interval he spent in Romania, had placed him in permanent danger, but the greater the danger, the safer his dreams and enthusiasm. In 1941, Misak Torlakian decided to accompany General Dro to Germany. Since he was not a man of maps and strategies, he left it to the general to make arrangements with the Germans as to establishing the Legion, while he himself went from camp to camp, questioning the Soviet prisoners and drawing up lists of Armenians. After that it was up to the general to talk to the prisoners and fill them with enthusiasm. Misak wanted to enroll in the Legion and train its soldiers, but he was informed that at the age of fifty he was too old for that. The German Army was proud of its achievements. The time had not yet come for veterans of the First World War to be called to arms. Excluded yet again, Misak returned to Ploiești, changing train after train as he traveled across an occupied, convulsed Europe.

The situation back in Romania had changed. War had broken out with the Soviet Union, galvanizing General Dro and the founders of the Legion. Thenceforward the nights would be dark, for fear of Allied bombing raids. Food rationing was introduced, and queues appeared at the shops. Some, like Arshag Svagian, who had done a black market trade in jewels, now sold food and fuel under the counter. For a time, the nightly bombing raids did not hit Ploieşti or the oil refineries. The town and its industrial zone were plunged into pitch darkness. The Germans had built a cardboard replica of the town and its refineries, which were lit up at night and looked real from the air. The Allies zealously bombed the replicas, delighting in the clouds of dust that rose from the pulverized cardboard. So great was the pleasure they took in their unhindered bombing that they never even wondered how the buildings could be replaced overnight or why the inhabitants foolhardily kept their lights burning all night long, while the anti-aircraft batteries, German though they were, fired off one or two desultory rounds, as if deliberately trying to miss. That was until six airplanes got lost on the way back and in the morning found themselves flying over the real city. Before the anti-aircraft guns could shoot them all down, they managed to wreak havoc.

Misak Torlakian took it as a sign. He pricked the ropy veins around his ankles and unburdened himself of the thick black blood; he closed his ledgers, now useless because of the burning oil wells and the mangled pipes of the bombed-out refineries. He picked the best pistols from the rack and went to Berlin. Some say it was then that the arms were buried, but the men he left behind did not wonder about them, fearful lest they learn the answer. Misak Torlakian, General Dro, Tatevos Bedrosian, Simon Pilibbosian, and the others decided to march east with the Legion, each infected with the other's illness and some of them even dying the others' deaths. And the same as in any other situation where death makes an unexpected, random choice, their departure left behind legends. Even today, The Book of Whispers tells one of them: the legend of General Dro's arms. Never to be found and therefore numberless, those weapons armed many more in their inner foolhardiness and rebellion than they could ever have done if they had been unearthed.

Misak Torlakian lived in close proximity to death his whole life, and like every man who has lived on a frontier, he often unwittingly breached border restrictions. From heedlessness he would cross into the realm of death and return just as unawares. He would sense he had crossed the border by the sudden chill in his bones and the stiffness of his joints, by the cold sweat that beaded his brow, and by the blood that blackened the corner of his lips, but more often than not by a strange melancholy. A mood of melancholy had never left him since his adolescence, when he had killed his first man. It is hard to say what melancholies afflicted Misak Torlakian on his journeys of thousands and thousands of miles from Berlin to Warsaw, from Rostov on Don to Simferopol, from Stalingrad to Armavir. But his prevailing feeling was one of stubbornness: his own stubbornness and death's. Death never peeled itself away from him; it followed him closely; it perched on his shoulder, like a monkey, giving short squeaks, turning somersaults; it walked swaying behind him, with the snuffling sound of a sweating mare; it rubbed up against his legs with its russet, vulpine back; it swooped around him like a bird.

Confronted with the various guises of death, he was puzzled not so much by their cruelty as by their meaninglessness. Death ought to have been meaningless only to those who were inured to the thought of dying and who received death in their own beds. A reconciled death was therefore meaningless. For Misak, death, or at least the death that accompanied him, was always meaningful; it was always an explanation. Only death as sacrifice could redeem. Some sacrificed; others sacrificed themselves or were sacrificed. Sacrifice was the only way in which life could conquer death. A cause worthy of sacrifice: that was what had guided Misak Torlakian's life ever since he was a boy, from when he carried weapons up the mountain for the comrades of Njdeh and Kevork Chavush and until he agreed to join Operation Nemesis. Death could not be a reconciliation but an undertaking.

But what shocked Torlakian, during his journeys across the Russian steppes, when he fought against the depression provoked by the endless expanses; against the dust storms of the scorching summer, which stung the cheeks, choked engines, clogged the horses' nostrils, dried the saliva, and crunched between the teeth; against the mire, which bogged down cart wheels, and coiled its tentacles around the soldiers' ankles, dragging them down; against the autumn rains, which dissolved flesh from the bone and rotted bark from the trunk; against the frost, the snow, and the north wind, which froze everything and made even hallucinations gleam glassily; as he fought all these, what shocked Torlakian was the overwhelming meaninglessness of death.

He sensed it for the first time in Warsaw. His faith in the German ability to bring order was shaken when he saw the ghettoes of the Polish capital. He experienced intense puzzlement at the mass executions, whose purpose he could not fathom, since death, like life, has a right to uniqueness. The mass executions and the mass graves were to him a mockery of death; you could be at enmity with death, you could fear it, you could scorn it, but you were not allowed to mock it.

For a time, Misak Torlakian and the group with which he had set out from Berlin traveled for a long distance behind the front line, until the Armenian Legion reached the north Caucasus. Authorized by the papers he had been given in Berlin, Misak reviewed the convoys of prisoners, managing to liberate a few Armenian soldiers, who went off to swell the ranks of the Legion. He traveled down through Bessarabia into the Crimea, where, finding a few acquaintances from his time in Russia during the First World War, he opened a few local branches of the Dashnak Party, which had been banned by the Bolsheviks. He held out hope that the party branches would be able to provide protection to Armenians after the war and then help to liberate Armenia, this time from German occupation. As the German Army's advance became increasingly difficult, Misak moved closer and closer to the front. He reached it in the winter of 1942, when the German Army was encircled at the Don Bend. Torlakian's instinct helped him remain outside the trap, and while the two armies gathered for the battle of Stalingrad, like bees inside a hive, he took advantage of the opportunity to travel to Armenian territory. In that war, in which victory was becoming ever more illusory, Torlakian nonetheless won a personal victory. He went to Armavir, on the plain of Ararat, and one clear morning he was able to admire the two peaks of the mountain, Sis and Masis, in all their splendor: two crests garbed in snow, hanging from the sky, higher than the mists at the base of the mountain could rise. The peaks hung suspended, shining unreal, like two bodiless heads whose bodies lay on the other side of the frontier, on Turkish soil, while the mountain itself, depicted on so many Armenian battle flags, too tall to be haltered, rejected that humiliation of history.

In the meantime, the Armenian Legion entered the thick of military operations. After administering the occupied zones for a time, replacing German troops transferred to the siege of Stalingrad, General Dro decided that the Legion should fulfill its destiny to drive the Bolsheviks out of Armenia. As the front was advancing with great difficulty, the general saw fit to overtake it, and the only way to do so was to parachute behind enemy lines.

The idea, captivating in its recklessness, proved to be disastrous. At Simferopol, Misak Torlakian bade a sad and hopeful farewell to his friends, alongside whom he had fought in the mountains of Anatolia, on the battlefields of the First World War, and in the army of the Armenian Republic; with whom he had dreamed in Ploiești; and with whom, as in the case of Simon Pilibbosian, he had been in league under the protection and at the urging of the goddess Nemesis. They spent the whole night talking. Misak, who found it increasingly difficult to tolerate the ban on his fighting in the Legion because of his age, embraced Simon Pilibbosian and the others, and then he sat down by the radio to wait for news.

As I said, it was a disaster. With so many Soviet soldiers having become soldiers of the Wehrmacht only out of fear, it is possible that they were betrayed. Perhaps they did not choose the landing sites well enough, or perhaps the nights were not dark enough. Or perhaps destiny, bored with so many wartime rolls of the dice, decided to quash from the outset so hopeless an endeavor.

Very little has been said about the Armenian Legion. Those who have said anything at all have been mainly detractors who prefer to view it as the 812th Battalion of the Wehrmacht, with its center of command in Berlin rather than Ploiești. The fact that it was a legion of Armenian volunteers more than a division of the German Army is also proven by the manner in which it ceased to exist, through an act of collective suicide. There are animals—lemmings, for example—that commit suicide by throwing themselves into the sea when they multiply too greatly for the earth to support them. Such a law probably also applies to some nations whose aspirations are greater than the Earth allows and that collapse under the burden of their own dreams; this might explain, from beginning to end, the illusion nurtured by a group of Armenians from Ploiești and the tragic destiny of the Armenian Legion.

And so the soldiers of the Legion were parachuted behind Russian lines. Those who were not picked off one by one in midair, plummeting to the ground like dead birds, wrapped in their parachutes like shrouds, were machine-gunned when they landed or were captured later, wild-eyed and weak with hunger.

Simon Pilibbosian's group managed to reach the ground. The radio apparatus went on transmitting for a while but then fell silent. This is why we know what happened to Simon Pilibbosian. He broke his knee when he landed with his parachute. After giving the order for all those who had landed safely to spread out, Pilibbosian leaned against a tree, propped his rifle against the ground, and shot a bullet into his head. The others did not have his courage, and since there was no radio to broadcast what became of them, they did not enjoy posthumous glory. Of the soldiers of the Armenian Legion who parachuted behind the front line, there were no survivors. Those who were not killed by bullets were swallowed up by the endless expanses. And those who had not yet left or who did not manage to escape from the second encirclement, which was in the Crimea, were hunted down one by one, along with the hard core of the Dashnak Party. I referred to the second encirclement as being in the Crimea because in the first encirclement, at Stalingrad, the Armenian Legion did not fall; it could not be trapped between two fronts for the simple reason that it had leapfrogged over them. In the long and various lists of the victims of the Second World War, the Armenian Legion added to the ranks of neither the prisoners nor the wounded but swelled only the ranks of the dead.

As long as the Russian front was in retreat, it was easier for Misak Torlakian to cross the lines from one side to the other and even to make his pilgrimage to Mount Ararat. When the Germans surrendered at Stalingrad, the front moved back in the other direction, and the Russians began to advance. Fascinated by the boom of the guns and blindly driven by death, to which he was tethered, with one leading the other, Misak remained close enough to the firing line to be trapped in the encirclement of Odessa. It was there that he met Onik Tokatlian, the captain of the *Transylvania*, which ferried the encircled soldiers to safety. Tokatlian offered Misak a place on board, but Misak declined. "It would be too simple," death whispered to him, adding, "You can't take the place of a soldier. It would be like shooting him in the back."

Refusing to accept salvation by water, Misak Torlakian managed to escape by dry land. Since it kept so close to him, death guarded him against bullets. He was in the habit of talking to death; he gesticulated, murmured, and spoke to dead friends, and death answered him on their behalf. With great difficulty, he managed to board a truck that slipped through a breach in the encirclement. He then traveled through the Ukraine to Czernowitz among the carts carrying refugees, among the endless columns of soldiers and military vehicles, which occasionally stopped and fought a rearguard action, and amid the shelling of the convoys. He did not veer from the path of the front line for one moment, nor did he move faster than it did. It was as if he could not travel away from Mount Ararat unless shoved from behind, always waiting for the moment when things would turn back in the other direction so that he might place himself in the vanguard of the troops once more, as he had thirty years previously, at the siege of Trebizond. But things did not turn around, and the Russian offensive shattered every illusion. One unsettled evening in the spring of 1944, General Dro gave them the order to take the shortest road to Berlin, recommending that they think of nothing except saving their own skins.

Misak Torlakian returned by the same turbulent road, crowded with people, beneath a sky foreshortened by rain and thronged with shells, and he was overwhelmed by the meaninglessness of death once again. Meaning imposes limits. But since of all the things in this world, the other person becomes the most dispensable in wartime, people died innumerably. In its accounting with death, of all the centuries of the Christian era the twentieth thus proved to be the most wasteful.

Focşani train station was not on the shortest road to Berlin, and Misak Torlakian did not seem to have come there to carry out any order. He had come to say farewell. Accompanied by Grandfather Garabet, he walked down Station Road, where the chestnuts were not yet in leaf. They entered the yard of the Armenian church. "Stay," said Grandfather Garabet. "We'll find something at which you can make a living . . ." "There's no place here for me. Soon the Russians will be coming. And then, if they ask you, you'll have to say you know me. In Simferopol and Rostov on Don, they shot everybody they found in the houses where I'd stayed. In the end you don't have to find something for me to do; I know wha

I have to do. If I think about it, I've never known how to do anything else . . ." "You did what you had to do," said Grandfather Garabet. "There is a time for everything. They almost hanged you for it. You yourself said that different times are on the way. What with one thing and another, Misak, peace is going to re- turn." "Who decides on our behalf whether there'll be peace or war?" said Misak Torlakian gloomily. "Who asks us whether we want peace and under what con- ditions?" "The world wants peace," said Grandfather in the soft voice he used when delivering a verdict. "Sometimes people are in too much of a hurry, and that's how wars start. But also because they're in a hurry, people get tired and start to pant, and that's how peace returns." "War means panting; peace means panting. Where's the difference?" "In the rhythm, Misak. The difference is in the rhythm. You fought; you killed; you did your duty. It's time to take it easy." "That's not true," said Misak. "Don't go by Armen Garo, when he wept in front of us. He's grown old. And don't go by Hovhannes Katchaznouni either. He's grown old too. Simon Pilibbosian is dead, so he'll never grow old. He kept the whole list, from which Armen Garo and Shahan Natali chose just seven or eight names for Operation Nemesis. Simon gave me the list before he left on the mis- sion. He put a bullet in his head, and so he left me the list as his dying word. There are forty-one names on it. Understand? Seventeen of the men on the list have died of old age already; six died by a bullet or the noose, as they deserved. There are eighteen left. Who concludes the peace in this war of ours?" "He who forgives," said Grandfather Garabet. He rarely smoked, but he accepted the cigarette Misak Torlakian offered him. The moment had come, and they had found the only thing that they could share together. "There's something else we can share," said Misak Torlakian. "This story." He took from his pocket the wooden toy horse and rubbed it on the sleeve of his coat. But he was unable to polish the mane since the wood was old and the paint had chipped. "It's all I have left from Kalust, my younger brother. I found it in his room, among the rubble, when I returned to our village. I was the one who gave it to him. I carved it from walnut wood with my bayonet. I didn't know why I dreamed of Behbud Khan, pursuing me on a bloody horse, or why the horse didn't crush me under its hooves. At the time I thought it was because nobody dies in his own dream. I thought that if I killed the Azeri, the dream would vanish. But it didn't com- pletely vanish; the horse remained, and I still dream of it. In my nightmares, others ride it and torture it." "Everybody who escaped from there has his own nightmares," said Grandfather. "We will only be rid of them when we die, not by causing other people's deaths. I have a son, and that helps me. Maybe you ought to settle down and do the same." "I'm too old for that, Garbis. If I was too old to lie on the front, where the dead are the most handsome and youthful, then I'm too old to have children. We were persecuted for some unknown guilt. Who can say that the persecution won't stop at us, that it won't be passed down to our children? Think of our grandparents and parents. Maybe we have it in our blood. Maybe victimhood is passed down from father to son." "But Misak . . ." said Grandfather. Misak interrupted him with a wave of his hand. "Garbis, I didn't come here to seek your advice. I don't have any doubts, so I don't need any advice. And I don't feel lost, like I did twenty years ago, so I don't need comforting. I came only to say farewell, only to see you, that's all . . . I'll send news from time to time, by a method you'll understand . . . And now, let us part here, in front of the church, like two men. Parting at the train station is for lovebirds . . ." He paused by the church gate and looked back at Grandfather, who was sitting beneath the chestnut tree, on Minas the blind man's bench. "Tell the story to nobody except Sahag. The blood in everybody's veins looks the same, and if you let it flow unchecked, you won't be able to tell victim and murderer apart. I'm sure he'll understand."

"What is going to happen now?" asked Sahag Sheitanian. In the meantime, Misak Torlakian had vanished. His passing through Focşani had gone unnoticed, and nobody came to ask after him. In May General Dro vanished also, and then Tatevos Bedrosian, along with his entire family from Constanţa. The founders of the Armenian Legion had either died in Russia or fled to Germany; none remained in Romania. Once the hard core had vanished, the Red Army counter-espionage services enlarged the circle, and, particularly in Bucharest and Constanţa, they began to make arrests. My grandfather was almost arrested on Christmas Eve, when he was carrying the box of shoes collected in church, but either the truck was too full or the Russian soldiers were still groggy after a sleepless night swilling vodka. Pulled back by Sahag Sheitanian, Grandfather managed to run, with the soldiers shouting behind him in the distance. As for Misak Torlakian, if the Russians were still looking for him in Romania, it meant that they had not found him elsewhere, so he was free to expend his passion on Simon Pilibbosian's list, while the horse galloped through his dreams.

"What is going to happen now?" asked Sahag Sheitanian. "We reckon there will be peace," answered Grandfather Garabet, "because that's the way it ought to be. On the other hand, there have been so many wars, all mixed up together, that the peace treaties can't quell them any more. Since you can't summon all the people to negotiate peace treaties, it means that some of them will go on waging war." "What kind of peace would that be?" asked Sahag, sensing Yusuf rustling and swelling in his bowels, about to be born.

11.

"What is going to happen now?" asked Sahag Sheitanian, looking over the fence. After the king's appointment of Petru Groza as prime minister, our street had hurriedly changed its name from the rather uninteresting "Cupboards" to "March 6, 1945, Street, the date when the first democratic government was established." The street name was just the part with the date; the rest had been added for the benefit of the street's residents, who had no idea what was happening. "What is going to happen?" asked Sahag Sheitanian, peering down the road at the men in leather coats who had come to arrest his neighbor Carol Spiegel. On March 6, 1945, Street, that was the event with which the first democratic government made its debut.

"What is going to happen now?" Sahag Sheitanian's grandmother had asked fifty years previously, as she walked down the side streets of Constantinople, smuggling pistols under her voluminous skirts for Armen Garo's men on the day they occupied the Imperial Ottoman Bank headquarters. "What is going to happen?" asked the other parents of the old Armenians of my childhood, from Trebizond to Adana, all over the Anatolian peninsula, from the shore of one sea to the other, as they heard the trumpets at dawn, which the Turkish Army blew to summon the rabble of the cities before they devastated the Armenian quarters. And they were to ask the same thing twenty years later, when they heard the drums beating at the crossroads and the cries of the heralds, as drawn-out and strangulated as the muezzin's call to prayer from the minaret of the mosque, announcing that in three days all Armenian families were to leave their homes, taking with them only as much as they could carry by hand, and that they were to assemble in convoys at the eastern gate of the city. The question remained on their lips until the hardiest of them had descended through all the circles of death down to Deir-ez-Zor. "What is going to happen now?" the few survivors had asked, the inhabitants of the cities on the European coast of the Bosphorus, whom the smoke of the fires in Christian quarters from Smyrna to Constantinople had driven to the ports, to the crowded decks of the ships, and whose direction home was marked by the dead thrown overboard, wrapped in white cloth, boundary markers of a road on which there was no traveling back. "And now, what is going to happen?" they had asked, showing their stateless persons' passports to foreign officials, sleeping piled on top of each other in makeshift shelters, toiling in drudgery by day, peddling whatever they could, slowly building up small shops in which the waft of oriental spices replaced the stifling smoke of the fires. What was going to happen? When war caught up with them again, they watched as the Germans and their allies grew harsher; once the eastern front opened up, at night they covered their windows with black card, and they stuffed their suitcases full of warm clothing, waiting to be deported. When the front came back in the other direction, they hid behind their fences, peeping at a different victorious army, which stole people's pocket watches to hang around their necks like medals, raped girls in people's yards, and smashed the windows of the pharmacies in search of medicinal spirit, which slaked the thirst of soldiers parched by the screech of death and the wind off the steppe. "What is going to happen?" they asked when they had to hide their hard-earned gold in the chinks between the tiles of their stoves, under their floorboards, beneath their vegetable patches, or inside their dog kennels; when they began to conceal their bonds and shares in the woodpile; when they heard and saw the men in leather coats kicking doors down in the middle of the night, hauling away the people inside, who at that hour were in their pajamas and slippers, like my uncle Yervant Hovnanian was when they came for him. They lived asking themselves that question, and what they saw all around them—the convoys filling the mass graves or vanishing in the sands of Mesopotamia, the baying mobs, the convulsed lands, and the crashing skies—ought to have been sufficient answer for them. But the question was asked in fear, and even if it arises from old suffering, fear demands new answers since, inexplicably, every new fear is accompanied by a new hope.

Precisely because he knew this, Grandfather Garabet refrained from giving an answer and contented himself with a shrug. They did not even expect anything more; they would have been disappointed if Grandfather had answered their question. They asked each other only in order that they might feel less alone. And in any event, like those who came before them, they sensed that the answer was always elsewhere.

Nonetheless, an answer did come and from the man they least expected: old Anton Ferhat. They were sitting on the chairs in front of the chapel of the Armenian cemetery, on the other side of the railway tracks, and from colored plates they were eating *halva* made by the priest's wife from fried semolina mixed with toasted walnuts, raisins, and cinnamon. The Seferian family vault was a short distance away. It had not yet become the secret meeting place of the parochial committee. Next to them were two freshly dug graves and a single wooden cross, on which two names were written in yellow paint.

Old man Ferhat was renowned for his niggardliness. He was not the only one who was obsessively thrifty since most of the old Armenians of my childhood, sitting there holding their plates of fried halva, were careful with their money. But Anton Ferhat was no ordinary miser. His miserliness was uncommonly creative, which helped him not only to avoid outbursts of generosity, but also to come up with arguments to explain a world based on his principles as being the most open-handed of all possible worlds. In short, the deeper he sank into miserliness, the more tenderly was he touched by his own generosity. He kept strict accounts of all his goods, and he stubbornly resisted any diminution of his wealth, remaining obdurate in the face of any temptation to charity. But here was Anton Ferhat, making the charitable donation of his answer to the question. He did not break with his principles, however, since by way of an answer he gave the only thing that, although he possessed it, he had not recorded in his ledgers, the only thing that, once given, did not reduce his wealth. That thing was his life.

"What is going to happen now?" they asked, and the first to answer was old man Ferhat, not singly but together with his wife. Where once she had squeezed her broad hips into the armchair in front of the table laden with good things, now she squeezed into the grave alongside her husband's. If we were to be absolutely fair, it was Dikran Bedrosian who gave the first answer, long before people started asking questions about the coming times. However, the others believed that what had happened to Dik Bedrosian could not be taken as a potential answer to a permanent question but rather as a cruel lesson resulting from the stubbornness with which he had always sided with the Bolsheviks. That was why Dik Bedrosian had been left with the tic of rubbing the bare wrist of his left hand, as if he still could not believe what had happened to him, thus leaving it up to Anton Ferhat to give the first answer. Like Bedrosian, Ferhat was silent, but his silence was that of a dead man and therefore far more eloquent.

The old man's death came not so much from his creative miserliness as from the symbol of that creativity: the plum tree at the bottom of his yard. The Ferhat family used to organize copious lunches, mainly at the initiative of the respectable Mrs. Ferhat, who, as she tended to the pots bubbling on the stove, would heave a sigh from the bottom of her well-fleshed lungs and say, "It's bad to be hungry!" Evidently, the meal was for Mr. and Mrs. Ferhat only. Afterward, sitting with her enormous bottom clamped in the vise of the armchair, in front of a mound of empty plates that glistened with grease, Mrs. Ferhat would heave another sigh, concluding, "It's bad to be hungry, and it's bad to be full!" The guests would arrive only after the siesta, once the remains of the lunch had been cleared away. From August to October, the Ferhats treated their guests to a dish that was always the same but which nonetheless varied: a bowl of plums, greenish and the size of apricots at first but riper and riper as autumn wore on. The rest of the year, the same bowl would be filled with prunes, whose curative properties the Ferhats never tired of praising. Well, it was from the branches of that highly useful plum tree that old man Ferhat heard an alarming rustle one September evening. He took his gun, and with the desperate ardor of a man about to lose all he held dear, he tiptoed to the plum tree, inserted a cartridge, and pointing his shotgun at random, he threatened to shoot. This summons, more sudden than determined, affrighted the intruder. A young lad fell crashing out of the tree, amid falling leaves and plums, and pressed himself up against the trunk, trembling and holding his hands in the air. Now master of the situation and seething with indignation, Ferhat ordered the lad to strip naked, and making the direst threats should the situation ever repeat itself, he shoved him out into the street, poking him in the back with the barrel of the shotgun. After that event, the plum tree continued to produce fruit unhindered for many years, a decade at least. When the Russians came, they set about confiscating everybody's guns, and Mr. Ferhat, fearful like any miser of the harshness of the law, surrendered his shotgun, demanding in return a receipt with his name on it so that, at least in theory, he would be able to balance his books, his property rights would be respected, and the gun might be restored to him one fine day. And his expectations were rewarded, albeit not in the manner he might have wished. In the meantime, the young lad had become a grown man, and since thievery, the occupation to which he had dedicated himself from an early age, was one that reaped dividends in those murky times, he joined the new political police; he was given a leather coat, boots suitable for stamping up and down stairs and kicking doors and people's stomachs, and the right to look through all kinds of official documents, such as the register of confiscated weapons. Anton Ferhat's name was at the top of that register. We do not know the secret policeman's name because nobody has looked for it, but the readers of *The Book of Whispers* have identified him as being one and the same as the thieving young lad. Old man Ferhat's body was found stripped naked. His mouth was stuffed with prunes, whose healing properties had no effect since Anton Ferhat bled to death without anybody in the street hearing his moans. The man had knocked at the door, and Mrs. Ferhat had opened it. Asking who he was and what he wanted, by way of an answer she had received a bullet in the chest and another in the forehead. Troubled not by the shots, which were common enough in those days, or by the noise of the fall, muffled by Mrs. Ferhat's softness, but by the silence that ensued, old man Ferhat had gone into the hall. The man, who knew how to aim, shot him in the lung and in the stomach, leaving him to die in agony, suffocating on the prunes he stuffed in his mouth.

Grandfather Garabet shrugged, but the others looked over his shrugging shoulders and, seeing the names written on the unvarnished wood of the cross, they received an answer from Anton Ferhat as to the times that were on the way.

The second answer came from Eshek Simon, or Simon the Mule. This was another Simon, not my uncle Simon, who at the time was getting ready to be repatriated, beguiled by the brass bands, restaurants, free houses, and tax exemptions that the Communists dangled as bait in their slogans aimed at Armenians on every shore of the Black Sea. Eshek Simon was short and had wiry hair, which he combed upward so that it looked like a shoe brush. Although it looked comical, that hairstyle was intended to add a little to his height, or rather to the height he lacked, as were his thick-heeled shoes, cobbled specially by Krikor Minasian. He had dark piercing eyes, which were handsome if you took each eye separately, but unfortunately he was so cross-eyed that the focus of his gaze was a point on the bridge of his nose. In the description of himself that he sent to Father Ignadios in Galați, in the hope of being included in the priest's marriage eligibility list, even Eshek Simon acknowledged it: "I've got beautiful eyes; each looks crosswise."

Before the war, Eshek Simon opened a teashop on Main Street, where, to attract customers, he put on little shows featuring the even shorter Rupen the *kemancheh* player, who had come from Constanța especially. Perched on a high stool, his legs dangling in the air, strands of hair slicked over his bald scalp, Rupen would play his *kemancheh*, a kind of mandolin, and moan grievously about his love, eliciting sighs from my grandmothers and aunts, as well as other ladies of those days, dressed in their tight-fitting tailored jackets and skirts, clutching their handbags in their laps, crossing their ankle-strap shoes, since it was not nice to cross your legs, even if it was a tearoom and not a café, and shedding an occasional tear before dabbing it with their hankies. Our grandmothers and aunts were plump; they had dimples in their cheeks and their elbows. Sweating in their starchy suits and throttled by their tight bowties, the men in the tearoom liked their plumpness. Chubby cheeks flushing, the ladies coquettishly dipped their sponge biscuits in their tea and then brushed the crumbs from the corners of their mouths with their fingertips, tittering or laughing out loud since Rupen's laments—punctuated by shrill sighs of *vah! vah!* from ladies in the audience or, in deeper voices, *aman! aman!*—would be followed by Eshek Simon's comedy sketches. Since he was too young to have attended school in Erzerum before the massacres and too old to start now, never having begun, Eshek Simon spoke a mixed language that could be understood by anybody, no matter where he might come from. His sketches, delivered in tilted words, sounded funny, and combined with his grave mien; with his shock of hair, which rose like a pharaoh's headgear above his puny body; and with his crossed eyes, he garnered roars of laughter. Even after Eshek Simon died, people still used to recite his little poems. We children learned them by heart and repeated them at parties, and the old Armenians would laugh all over again, like they used to do in Eshek Simon's tearoom. Here is the most famous of all, the fable of "The Grasshopper and the Ant," terse in form and couched in flawless Romanian-Turkish-Armenian:

Kreyer și pornik
—Madam pornik, madam pornik
Dai la mine un bukatzik!
—Toată vara djukat, kantat;
Siktir, nu dai nimic!

[Grasshopper and Ant
"Madam Ant, Madam Ant
Give me a little bit!"
"Singing, dancing all summer long;
Bugger off, naught for you!"]

But the nickname "Eshek," "mule," was not from the times when Simon was the merry, prosperous proprietor of a teashop. In those days, the only shadow of sadness was cast by the fact that on the eligible matches list kept by Father Ignadios in Galați there was a blank space next to Simon's name. In the very best case, Father Ignadios might have inserted the name of some hideous old widow with a moustache, who would have been unsightly even to Simon's cross-eyed gaze. Rather, "Eshek" was the name that stuck to him as a result of something that happened after the war, and it provided the second convincing answer to the question about the times.

If he had had a café, the times might have spared him for a year or two. But tearooms were rare, and from Czernowitz and Jassy all the way to Focșani, the Russians had not come across any other. The officers therefore came to sit at the tables in Simon's tearoom. That was the good part since the lower ranks avoided the place for that reason. The bad part was that the officers could not have liked it there more. They sat cross-legged, with their pistols on the table, in full view, and ordered Russian tea. Simon did not know what Russian tea was like; he asked them in the beginning, but after that he realized that any tea was Russian as long as it was piping hot, and this the officers confirmed. The officers were served a tot of cognac or rum, which they straightaway knocked back, asking for another to go with their tea. They were also each served a sugar cube, which they held under their tongues as they noisily slurped their tea.

But since the new customers began to drive away the old, Simon's evening shows became more sporadic, and in the end Rupen the *kemancheh* player vanished, abruptly and without trace. The new customers were wont to add a drop of tea to their cognac rather than the other way around and often neglected to pay, not to mention that they turned up at all hours of the day and night and sat for however long they liked, without caring. Simon grew tired of it and sent a complaint to their superiors, who carefully read it. But having to choose between satisfying Simon's demands and letting the officers behave as they pleased, they concluded that Simon was incapable of understanding what an honor the glorious Red Army was doing him and that he was therefore unworthy of keeping the tearoom. The tearoom was requisitioned and, after Dik Bedrosian's watch, this proved to be the second tribute that the Armenian community of Focşani paid to the Soviet liberator. "What mean this?" asked Simon. To him, the word "requisition" was hard to understand and sounded unpleasant, given the determined look on the face of the officer sent to do the requisitioning, accompanied by two armed bumpkins, who had already set to work on Simon's sweet jars. "It means we're taking your tearoom," translated the officer and jabbed his finger in Simon's chest in a manner that suggested that he might also do the jabbing with the barrel of a gun or a bayonet if that failed to persuade him. "You take, you take," said Simon bitterly, "but what you give in exchange?" "That's a good one!" came the reply. "We don't give anything in exchange. The army has requisitioned it." Simon was hard put to understand such a bargain. He scratched his bristly shock of hair, rising on tiptoes. "You know what I dream?" he asked, after pondering the matter. The officer stared at him wide-eyed, taken aback by the novelty of the approach. Simon then explained, gesticulating illustratively: "I dream this: my arse, he cabbage; you goat, and the goat, he eat my arse." Despite the mangled language, it was all too plain what Simon was insinuating. The officer turned bright red. His first impulse was to reach for his pistol, but he said to himself that a bullet in the brow of such a freak would have been too great an honor, so he grabbed him by the scruff of the neck and tried to shove him through the door, yelling, "Mule!" But Simon would not be ejected; he planted his feet and with surprising strength braced himself against the officer. Without loosening his grip on the scruff of Simon's neck, the officer pushed harder. The officer then brutally translated Simon's dream, kicking him up the backside, or "that fucking cabbage of yours," as he put it. Punching and kicking, the officer finally hurled Simon into the street before delivering the following ultimatum: "Don't let me catch you around here again, mule!" No matter how downcast Simon might have been, when, over coffee in the churchyard, they urged Eshek to tell the story of the goat and the cabbage, it would provoke roars of laughter. But the dream remained a dream, and the tearoom remained lost. Without Simon's touch, the tearoom first lost its charm, then the aroma of the English, Chinese, and Indian teas; the colored teacups became chipped, suitable only for vodka and brandy, and in the end the place turned into a dive. Eshek Simon would hang around until late into the night, until after the stomping feet and raucous voices died down; he would peer yearningly through the torn curtains, breathing on the greasy windowpane and rubbing it with his sleeve. Then he would huddle on the steps, rocking back and forth until daybreak. They found him there one morning and kicked him in the ribs to make him clear off. When they saw Eshek Simon slump to one side, without flinching in pain or surprise, they realized he was dead. They summoned Grandfather to take the body away, lest it put off the customers. They were not put off but merely stepped over the dead man, who did not alarm them but did them good since the sight of death whets a Russian soldier's thirst. After a lifetime of trying to find a cure for being cross-eyed—placing a candle to his left and his right and straining to look at them both at the same time until his head throbbed with pain, rolling his eyes up and down and back and forth, wearing lenses of every possible thickness—Eshek Simon finally discovered that the cure was death. Before Minas the blind man came to close his eyelids—they always called him to do that since his touch was the lightest—they saw that Eshek Simon's eyes no longer crossed. With that impediment having been removed, it would have finally been the moment to include Eshek Simon on Father Ignadios's list of suitable matches. Unfortunately, however, in acquiring a straight gaze, he lost another quality demanded by the list: that of being alive. But anyway, Father Ignadios himself had died long before, and the list, which in its time had matched many couples, including Grandmother Arshaluis and Grandfather Garabet, lay forgotten in the vestry of the Armenian church in Galați.

What was going to happen? Such was the answer provided by Eshek Simon, and the others, when they remembered, burst out laughing. And Eshek Simon was aggrieved that the others did not take even his death seriously.

"My store was just a humble cobbler's workshop," said Krikor Minasian, looking at Anton Merzian out of the corner of his eye, resigned to the thought that his sad words would elicit a smile of satisfaction from the other man. "I can't understand what they wanted it for. Factories I can understand, although if you think about it, what state takes away your property instead of protecting it? But my humble workshop and two apprentices? It wasn't enough for them that I had to repair Russian boots free of charge for two years. Or maybe that was precisely the reason, because they'd got used to not paying for anything. I'm still doing the same work, but is it better this way, with a secret workshop in my kitchen,

without any apprentices, because they resent you if you make them go to the
bother of denouncing you to the fisc for not giving out receipts? You'd have to
be out of your mind to pay 90 percent tax on profits, or benefits, as they call
them nowadays. They say that when you earn, it's a profit, but when the state
earns, it's a benefit because the state doesn't profit; it benefits. I can't believe
they don't know I still run a cobbler's workshop when otherwise they know every
last thing you're hiding in your woodshed. I think that what annoyed them the
most was the shop sign. I was stupid enough"—and here he cast Anton Merzian
a meaningful look, to show he ought not to agree so wholeheartedly with the
word "stupid"—"to make myself a big, colorful sign, bright enough so that you
could see it from the end of the road. Now it's sitting in the storeroom, behind
the tool cupboard. I take it out every now and then, prop it against a stool, and
look at it. I decided to keep it because who knows? Maybe I'll need it some day.
But in the meantime, the paint has started peeling, the rest has faded, and it
sits in the dark, poor thing. Shop signs feed on light, like the leaves on the trees.
What could be sadder for a trader than to see his shop sign perishing before his
eyes . . . ? How do that lot think we can make a living in a country where the
shop signs are dying? When they took it away from me, the only thing I was able
to salvage from the shop was the bell above the door. It hasn't grown old; it's still
a child and tinkles merrily. It's still happy when the door opens, but how can it
know it's not the same door?"

Another question that nobody needed to answer. In those days, the Armenian cemetery was surrounded by a rough wooden fence. In the meantime, the
cover of *The Book of Whispers* has been painted silver, but back then the cover
was the color of wood. They were surrounded by *The Book of Whispers*, and like
everything within it, their voices were so low as barely to be audible. That's why
they signaled for Anton Merzian to be more cautious; because he spoke in questions, the ends of his sentences were shriller, and that made them easier to hear.

"Don't we have to go on living?" asked Anton Merzian by way of an answer.
"We have to, don't we? Isn't that why we left home? Isn't it because we were
afraid of the yataghans? Isn't that why we came here, because some said Romania was a blessed land where you just needed to squat to take a shit and you'd
still make money? Isn't that why we made huge efforts to get permits, with our
hearts in our mouths at the beginning of every year, when we had to renew
them, like the wretched Nansenians we were, because what else could we do?
Weren't we afraid of the authorities because we were stateless? Without documents weren't we at their mercy? They received us here, but where else could
stateless people like us go, even if we crossed the Romanian border clandestinely? Who else would take us, except maybe in the middle of the sea, if there's

still some uninhabited island somewhere? But there aren't any such places left, and even if there were, how would you make a living as a cobbler all on your own on an island? But we're not going anywhere; our homes are here; this is where we drink coffee, where we have our cemetery plots; it's been forty years since I stole my wife Zaruhi from her father Panciu; she's old now and so deaf that she wouldn't even hear me close the door behind me if I left; can I leave her? I for one am sick of leaving all the time, traveling to far horizons, and can't you see that wherever we go, there's always someone who will catch up with us, whether they're Spahis, Kurds, Bedouins, or Bolsheviks? And so, what do I say? Shall we do what they tell us if that's what they want?"

"And what do they want?" asked Sahag, who had his suspicions.

"Let's do the sums, shall we?" asked Anton Merzian, becoming animated, rounding off his sentences with a shrill rhetorical flourish. "How much do you earn, Dik, as a vendor of watches, you who once were the biggest watchmaker on Main Street?" And since Dik Bedrosian was silent, rubbing his bare wrist in embarrassment, Anton Merzian went on: "If you make three hundred lei a month, you're grateful, aren't you? What about you, Ştefănucă, big lawyer that you are?" Ştefănucă Ibrăileanu, with his shaggy mane of hair and shadowy eyes, the spitting image of Grandfather Garabet, less the beard and hypochondria, was unable to answer the question straightaway because he would have first had to remove the half-lit cigarette he kept clenched between his lips. "Need I say that you earn more or less the same amount? And what do you do with that money, which is barely enough to pay for your bread ration, not to mention that you eat dry crusts, like a hermit, and still wear the same clothes you've had since before the war? Wouldn't you be glad if there was another war and we got rid of this lot as easily as they got rid of the other lot so that you'd be able to get new clothes? Doesn't war come down on us when we're doing well, not when we're poor, like we are now? Don't they say that the cannons don't fire at the poor man, and when we're not as poor as we are now, won't it be only because we'll be even poorer? Look around you; if it goes on like this for much longer, we'll end up dividing the crumbs of bread and fish between us, like our Lord Jesus Christ did, won't we, Father?" And the priest, sitting in a corner, with his hands joined together inside the wide sleeves of his cassock, as if inside a muff, nodded, deeming the mention of the Savior's name as something positive, even if the context was so depressing. The priest may have been old Father Dajad Aslanian, who died shortly after the war; or it may have been Father Mampre Berberian, who, when the Armenians began to emigrate from Romania in the 1960s, was among the first to apply for an exit visa; or it may have been his replacement, old Father Varjabedian, with his rounded beard and the fine web of red veins that covered his face, through which flowed the remnants of the bottle of communion wine from one Sunday to the next; or it may have been young Archimandrite Zareh Baronian, who was as handsome as a Byzantine icon. But whichever it was, the priest nodded. "But we who are afraid, what are we going to do?" Anton Merzian went on, emboldened. "We're going to do what the state wants, what else? The state doesn't give us enough to make a decent living, but we still have to live because we're human, even if we are stateless, and there are plenty of people without states, but who's ever heard of a state without people? So in order to live, when they don't even let us work as much as we'd like, what can we do except pilfer, which is another way of saying, what can we do except steal? Don't you see that the state wants us to steal so that it won't have to look after us and so that it will be relieved when it sees how well we understand what it wants us to do? And so that's why we understand what that man with the long head"—here he referred to Krikor Minasian, as you can imagine—"doesn't understand— namely, those of us with a normal head on our shoulders—because if we all understood, it wouldn't be a good thing since then we wouldn't have anybody else to steal from, so isn't it the cleverest of us who steal? But you have to have a keen eye and an agile hand, which is why we're not able, but our children are, and so I told my sons: 'Lads! What are you waiting for? Where's the best place to steal? Where is there no owner to keep watch and no tax inspector to keep a check on you? In the cooperative! Then let's join the cooperative!' The lads work at the cooperative during the day and in the workshop at home in the evening. The lads bring us everything we need: leather, rubber soles, hobnails, glue. Has your hammer broken or your pliers or your boot tree? Here's your hammer, your pliers, your boot tree! The only thing is that my lads have started bringing home the bad habits they pick up at the cooperative. I have to keep an eye on them, and I shout, 'Cut that leather straight; don't waste it; where do you think you are, at the cooperative?' And so let me tell you what's going to happen: you learn something for everything you unlearn; otherwise why would the state take our shops away and then give us the cooperative in return?"

There may have been some truth in that. Grandfather Garabet rummaged through some boxes and found a pair of shoes. Yervant Hovnanian had died in the Lubyanka by then, and so had Zaven Saruni and old man Harutiunian; the shoes had been left without owners forever. "And if you'd managed to give them to him," said Anton Merzian—unhappy that the others had not thought his answer sufficient, all the more so given that his speech had been a hotchpotch of questions and that two well-aimed questions are more enlightening than a hesitant answer—"wouldn't we have made fools of ourselves? Rather than shoes like that, you're better off wrapping your feet in rags to keep out the Siberian frost, like our dead did at Deir-ez-Zor, isn't that right, Sahag?" Sahag Sheitanian made no reply, nor did his younger brother Yusuf.

Vrej Papazian spoke up. He was younger than the others, and he had a handsome face with almond-shaped eyes and a warm smile. His sister Virginica had the same smile, as well as long, wavy hair and a slender waist. But since Virginica was a woman, she attended such discussions only in passing and in silence, staying long enough only to place a little fragrant requiem halva on the plates on the table. Vrej Papazian spoke on her behalf.

"What a hard-working, beautiful girl Virginica was," said Vrej, combining Armenian and Romanian words, as was his habit. "But she fell in love with the wrong man. Like so many good girls, she had no luck. Of all the men who came knocking on our door, she couldn't choose one who was decently dressed, who brought flowers and champagne, flowers and bonbons, or just flowers, if he wasn't so rich; she went and chose one in a shabby overcoat, without gaiters, a prisoner of war who, when he wasn't emptying the shit buckets and clearing dead leaves from the gutters, was sitting in solitary confinement. That I cannot understand. And the icing on the cake was that the man had a wife and children at home in Nakhichevan; he kept photographs of them in his pocket. At the crack of dawn my sister Virginica would go to wait for him at the garrison gate, in her best clothes, in a black two-piece, with her hair in a mesh, like a girl at finishing school, on the off chance that he might come out with his broom or his toilet-cleaning brush, her prince in light brown long johns and scuffed boots without laces." "Horrible, isn't it?" said Anton Merzian, picturing the worn-out boots. "At the crack of dawn, when there wasn't even a cabman to take her to the station, she would walk all the way to the garrison, after sitting up all night to knit him socks and darn his undershirts by lamplight—the undershirts that kept warm the photographs of his wife and children. True, the lad wasn't ugly, but in fact, who knows what he looked like, unshaven and stooped after all those years in prison? I ask her, 'What do you see in him, girl?' She says, 'He knows how to listen.' 'What do you mean by that: he knows how to listen? We all know how to listen if we've got ears to hear with.' 'Yes,' she says, 'but he knows how to listen nicely, and he never gets bored.' If you looked at him from a distance, like I did once, it was true."

Virginica and her soldier would set off from the garrison gate, taking short steps, the way people do when they are happy at being able to walk together, with the guard following them a few yards behind. They would head to the public park. For an hour or two he would sweep the leaves from the lanes with his broom, and then they would sit down on a bench. The guard would sit at the other end of the bench, having been bribed with food or sometimes a fistful of cigarettes. Virginica would open the food parcel. In summer she would slice tomatoes and peppers for the soldier; in winter, pickled cucumbers; she would spread soft cheese on his bread; she would unwrap the other food items and arrange them in order and prop the thermos of tea or warm milk against the backrest of the bench. The soldier ate slowly, with lowered eyes. From time to time he looked up at her, meeting her eyes; he smiled, and then sank back into his thoughts. He carefully chewed every mouthful, to please her; they both knew that the guard would leave them in peace as long as he had not finished eating. She would then quickly tidy up because the part she liked best came next: he would turn to her, smiling gently, and, as he clasped her fingers in his cupped palms, she would talk. He did not interrupt her and never had anything to add. That was first of all because what Virginica told him about her life was clear and simple, and as she described every event down to the last detail, there was nothing to clarify. Second, it was because he had nothing to say about his life in prison, and he spared her the story of his previous life, no matter how much she questioned him about it. She, on the other hand, was highly attentive to all the things that went on around her, anything that might provide her with something new to say: a fragment of dream, a letter from far away, a community gala, a piece of cloth she was going to use to sew a new dress, a new shoot put forth by the lemon tree on the veranda. The lemon tree grew between them. Virginica picked a lemon and brought it to him on the days when she was happier than ever. She arranged the subjects she was to talk to him about with the same care as she arranged the food in her bag, and if she had still not finished when the guard started to show signs of boredom, she would plead, "Be kind; let us have a little longer!" And she could not be persuaded to stop talking until the afternoon passed because if he returned after nightfall, the man would have received three days in solitary confinement, which for Virginica would have meant three days of waiting in vain by the garrison gate. When the garrison gates remained barred to that prisoner of war, forgotten in a foreign country, Virginica returned home downcast; she opened the food parcels and ate a little from each, with tears in her eyes, imagining how the meal would have unfolded on the bench as she recounted to him the thoughts she had carefully collected the night before. The rest of the now pointless morning she spent in front of the lampshade, mending the stockings brought by her sister-in-law Arusyag, who had a repairs counter that did a good trade in a period when silk stockings were hard to find and ladies were obliged to repair the ones they already had. Given that she had to keep her mornings free, in the afternoons Virginica worked as a shopgirl, selling trinkets and cheap geegaws, as well as thin gold chains and silver jewelry, some of it coated in fine golden powder. In the evening, she made up the parcels for the next day, stowing them in the cellar to keep them cool. She kept the tea or soup by the gas stove, ready to heat it before pouring it into the thermos flask first thing in the morning. Then Virginica would lock herself up in her room and pour boiling water into her washbasin, scenting it with salts or blue crystals that she had bought from some Turkish Gypsy women in Balcic. She would wet a towel and rub herself until the salty hotness dilated her pores. With freshened skin, in naked splendor, she would sit down in front of the mirror and comb her hair. Motionless, she would close her eyes, although seated in front of the mirror, and stroke her shoulders and then her nipples, which were the violet color of a woman with coppery skin. She would slowly run her hand down her body to her parted knees, to the recesses between her thighs, slowly caressing, sighing, until her womb gave a spasm. Then she would clench her thighs around the now motionless finger and sit like that for a few minutes, waiting for the quiver in her belly to ripple throughout her body. She would look in the mirror and then, glassy-eyed, flushed with shame, crawl into bed, hiding from her fantasies and returning to the things that she would tell him the next day, which never included the quiver at her womanly core.

Every word spoken by those around, whether scolding or flattering, every day-to-day event and its circumstances—the queues for rationed bread; the clothes bartered for bread; the workers' meetings at which they read passages from the party newspaper, *The Spark*, and which she listened to standing by the wall, keeping herself apart—all these took on unusual dimensions in Virginica's stories, first of all because of the power of the detail, and then because of the passion she put into the telling as she searched for various interpretations, put forward alternative solutions, and pointed to undeclared guilty intentions.

We cannot gauge with any degree of certainty how long that love lasted, a love that was possible only because the times were becoming more and more oppressive, and the more brutal a regime becomes, the more impotent it is in the face of impossible things. The time went on too long, in the opinion of Vrej Papazian, who, out of pity for his sister, kept praying for it to end; but the time did not go on long enough for Virginica, in whose life nothing worth recounting was ever to happen again, apart from the day when the lemon tree died, having waited three full years to give up the ghost in her arms. We cannot know how the time seemed to that man because he enters *The Book of Whispers* only fleetingly, softly closing the door behind him, never to return. The life of every person elapses in parallel biographies, one of which is recorded in the official documents. These are scantier or more numerous, more succinct or more intrusive, depending on the times. Somebody happened to leaf through a file that mentioned the Armenian prisoner forgotten in the prison of the Focșani garrison, and thus it was that the Red Army remembered him. One autumn morning, as Virginica waited for him outside the garrison on the Bucharest Chaussée, her smile dissolved on seeing him emerge in a new overcoat and holding a wooden suitcase instead of his usual brush or broom. Virginica experienced the journey to the railway station as if in a dream or a hallucination. She would have liked to pull him aside so that they might run away together. "But you're free now, aren't you?" But he was not free. He was to be taken by train to another garrison, under Russian military escort, along with other prisoners who had been forgotten until then in other garrisons. Back in the Soviet Union, he was to be interrogated endlessly. He would have to answer for the sin of having fallen prisoner. He would have to confess to all the Soviet strategic secrets he had revealed to the enemies of the people while he was held prisoner, which is to say to the German Army and to the Romanian Army in the period when the king was its supreme commander. "What is going to happen now?" Virginica kept asking, for the first time clinging to his arm, heedless that he clenched his arm to his body, walking slightly to one side in embarrassment. "What is going to happen?" asked Vrej Papazian, repeating the question, to justify why, under the present circumstances, he was telling the story of Virginica. Misak Torlakian was right: train stations are for lovebirds. Amid the turmoil of the platform, enveloped in whirling clouds of smoke from the locomotives, beneath the big Garnier clock, Virginica dared for the first time to press herself to his chest and throw her arms around his neck. For a few moments he stood frozen in surprise, still holding his suitcase, and then he placed his other hand on the top of her head and slowly drew it toward him. Such scenes had been frequent during the war; they were unusual now that the war had been over for three years. But even so, in peacetime the war could still bring back together people flung apart in forgotten corners. He stroked her hair, unsettled, not knowing what to do, after so many years, when a woman fell into his arms. "Come back," she whispered; "look for me . . ." "If they let me go, I'll come," he said. "Do you promise?" she insisted, not because she did not want to believe him but to hear him say the words again. He bent down, opened the suitcase, in which he had stuffed the bag of food—"Mind you don't spill the tea," she had warned—and took out the mandolin he had made in prison. "You keep it till then," he said, and handed her the instrument. As she took it, her slender fingers brushed the strings, striking a long, tuneless chord. Without taking his eyes off him, the guard handed a Soviet officer the documents. The officer looked at both sides of the pages and gave an order to the soldiers waiting two paces behind him. The soldiers seized the man by both arms and barked something in Russian. Virginica was left on the platform, watching with quailing heart as her lover was violently shoved up the steps of the carriage without even having time to look back at her. She stood motionless for a long time, clutching the mandolin in her arms and waiting in vain for him to appear at the window and wave to her. After the train left, she went to the edge of the platform, tears streaming down her face, and did not flinch until she heard the whistle of another train approaching down the same track. For an instant, the crossties held her in fascinated thrall, promising salvation. But in the end Virginica resisted the temptation; the fact that she did not commit suicide helps this story not to remain in the shadow of other more famous stories. Virginica thus saved her story from a predictable outcome; she also saved the mandolin, which, after she devoutly preserved it till her dying day, is now exhibited in the Armenian Museum of the Bucharest House of Culture, with a label that explains it was crafted by an Armenian soldier of the Red Army while he was held as a prisoner of war in Romania. In this way, Virginica's story returns to the pages of The Book of Whispers, almost having left them. But her strength to resist the temptation of suicide did not spare her the suffering that was to come.

"I thought it was over," said Vrej Papazian. "We all thought it was over, even if we would find her at night by the window overlooking the street, sitting up in bed, wrapped in a sheet, like a ghost, and during the day she would sit frozen, next to her lamp. If we didn't shake her to remind her it was time to go to work, she would have darned away whole fishing nets of silk thread. We were waiting for the time to pass and with it the passion that was draining the life out of her, the way all things finally pass in this world. But then the other disaster happened, which caught us completely unprepared, and there was nothing else we could do because after they confronted her with the accounts, Virginica confessed to everything, with a kind of joy at all her troubles being over. We always used to say we're honest Armenians, we make coffee from chickpeas, but even so you'll never see a dead devil or an Armenian in prison. But we saw an Armenian in prison, and someone from our family to boot. Virginica got three years, and it was as if she was overjoyed to escape from the Sunday visits and having to walk up and down with the tray of rose preserves and the sherbet spoons in glasses of water, serving the suitors who, on discovering that Virginica no longer had a lover, all beat a path to our door. I hired a lawyer, but there was nothing else he could do since the damage was done and Virginica had taken full responsibility. What with one thing and another, it was three and a half ounces of gold and I don't know how much silver that she took from the shop and sold for next to nothing to Weissmann at his secondhand shop in the market so that she could buy food and woolens for that jailbird. She should have come to us, to save us from the shame and her from prison, but if I stop to think about it, I doubt I would have given her so much money, had she asked. It was utter madness; when we were eating lentil soup mixed with scorched onions to give it a bit of a fried flavor, he was eating grilled filet and crème à la Focșani. You couldn't even ask her anything because she'd snarl at you like a wild animal." "What about the man, the prisoner, I mean?" asked Ștefănucă Ibrăileanu, who knew the story up to that point since he had been the lawyer the family hired. "Next you'll say he came back right when the girl was in prison!" "How could he come back?" replied Vrej, extracting a walnut from the fried semolina. "Nobody heard from him again. We think he must have perished in some labor camp in Siberia, which is where they sent them, the prisoners of war they found in the garrison prisons around Europe. Virginica, the poor girl, says he probably went back to his wife and children in Nakhichevan—in other words, better that than his being dead." "But how did you know about the photograph of his wife and children?" asked Minas the blind man, who had an obsession with photographs. He read them with his fingers. During the war, women used to queue up for him to run his fingers over photographs of their husbands who were at the front so that he could say whether they were still alive. Sometimes, if a woman saw Minas run his fingers back and forth over a photograph of her absent soldier husband without feeling a sign, she would come back the next day with a different one, in the belief that the photograph had been to blame. Minas would smile sadly, but he never lied. "Can you imagine?" said Vrej. "It was he who showed it to her, instead of hiding it. And she would look at the children in the photograph and pretend to be enchanted." "Then she deserved it, didn't she?" concluded Anton Merzian, casting a glance at where the women were sitting, with Virginica puffing on a cigarette, a bad habit she had picked up in prison, blowing smoke rings and watching them dissolve. "She was stupid," he went on, "but has she at least learned some sense?" "Theft is a serious matter," added Mgrditch Tcheslov; "it's no good botching the job. Anyway, when you steal, you steal for yourself. Who steals to give to somebody else? That's why they caught her, because somebody who steals for himself is careful; he cares about his own life; that's why he's stealing, for his own good, but if somebody steals for another, then little does he care about himself; he doesn't care two bits about his own life." He raised his forefinger and went on: "When you steal from the state, you can't be careless; you have to keep your ears pricked up at all times; you never know when the state will come down on you." "And so I can't tell you the story to the end," concluded Vrej Papazian, "because it hasn't ended. Nobody knows what became of him; he's never given any sign of life, and she's been waiting for him to this day. The only thing that happened was that the lemon tree died. It waited until Virginica came back, with a single lemon hanging from its last green branch, and when she sat down next to it and put her arms around it, it gave up the ghost." "How can a tree give up the ghost?" asked the priest, who had never been summoned to administer the last rites in such a case. "Like a man, first it goes limp, then rigid; it closes its eyes and no longer absorbs the light." The story was back to front: the man and woman were not banished; they remained in the world where they had fallen, but the tree that gave them its fruit had become mortal.

Grandfather then pushed the box in front of Arshag the bell ringer. "People were downcast," said Arshag. "Many came to church; they sat on the pews; some remained standing, by the wall. But nobody was sitting in the choir stall since there was no service that day. The box had been placed in front of the doors to the altar. They heard the bell tolling, and that was why they came. Those who knew already brought shoes wrapped in newspaper; others brought whatever they could. I saw them from the belfry as they came. I've always seen what's going to happen earlier than the rest of you do because I can see farther from the belfry. That's why God took away my hearing, because he gave me sharper eyesight. Where I am, the birds often come and sit on the roof. At night the bats flutter, and the spider webs glitter. When the bell tolls, the flocks rise into the air and wheel above the belfry. I envy the birds for how high they can soar and how far they can see. I've laid snares, but I've never been able to catch one. When they see me, they know I am going to ring the bell again. And because I can see far into the distance, I ask myself the question more often than you. You might think since I know a minute in advance what is going to happen that I'm clearer about it, but it isn't like that. They've yet to build a belfry so tall that you can find the whole answer by looking out of its windows. I might even say that I'm unsettled by the things I see where your eyes can't reach and that to you look more like a streak of mist. That's why I'm uneasier than you. That's why I chose to ring the bell, because it seems unnatural and unjust to me that it should be so calm and at peace while we're unsettled because we don't know what is going to happen. And that's why the birds fly away, why they avoid perching on my shoulders; they feel the unease, and they don't like uneasy people. As you can very well see for yourselves, the birds and our eyes betray our unease. And in this story of ours, which is made up of lots of other stories, like a rope of knotted handkerchiefs, people die with their eyes open. You know this best, Minas, because you place your palm on their cold brows and slowly move it down their face, closing their eyelids. Remember Harutiun Frenkian, with his hands clasped together on top of his will, in his little room, where it smelled of walnuts that had turned to ash on the stove. Remember poor Eshek Simon, whose eyes suddenly uncrossed. And Ohannes Krikorian, in the soccer stadium, when he remained sitting in the stands after all the others had left, looking at the middle of the pitch, cold and as yellow as wax, waiting for the kickoff in some match known only to him and to God. Even you, Minas, when you die, even you will have wide-open eyes; Garabet is my witness since he'll close the eyelids of the dead from then on. Remember Anton Ferhat, covered in blood, his mouth flecked with white foam, but with bulging eyes. And you, Garabet, you told us about others who are not of our people but who in their own way answer our questions and who died with their eyes cast like anchors into the world they left behind: the ones who died at Vadu Roșca, starting with Aurică Dimofte, the milkwoman's husband, and even Mantu the Gypsy, who's waiting for us in the churchyard even now, not knowing which of us he is about to play his tuba for. Probably even our dead in Siberia had their eyes open; they had even more reasons than we others do, except that probably nobody bothered to close their eyelids, and since you haven't received any news of them, you're probably not wrong to go on waiting for them because if their eyes aren't closed, they're not fully dead. The one who tells our story will have to write that in this book people die with their eyes open since what they lived wasn't enough to help them find the answer. And with that, Garabet, my good friend, all that needed saying has been said. In the box you placed by the doors to the altar, some placed pairs of shoes that no man will ever wear. When my turn comes, instead of an answer to the question 'What is to be done?,' in eternal remembrance of the weary, barefoot people in convoys everywhere I will place the sight in my eyes after I take my final breath."

There were now more people in the church. Some of them, with glinting eyes, were ready to give their answers; others were pale, with chalky white faces.

In the silence, the first who ventured to approach the box was my grandfather Garabet Vosganian. One by one, making sure that they took up as little space as possible, he laid down all the shoes, even the unpaired boots that some present had brought, placing them in a row, one next to the other, as if on the threshold of a sanctified chamber or on a meadow of new grass, from whence the people may be supposed to have continued barefoot on their journey.

Then Mikael Noradungian came with one of his maps, the one whose edges had faded the least, in the bottom right-hand corner of which was a series of black dots; next to one of the dots it said, "Deir-ez-Zor," after which the edge of the earth sheered away, suggesting that thence began either the desert of Mesopotamia or the Garden of Eden, but only he who had traveled that road to its very end could know for sure. Mikael Noradungian placed the map in the box, but as is plain, it could not provide a satisfactory answer since the answer began beyond the edge of the map.

Then Harutiun Khntirian came. He made the sign of the cross before them and held aloft his rubber stamp. He pressed it to his inkpad, in the hope that one day it might be of further use. He then laid it to one side so that it would not smudge Mikael Noradungian's map.

Arshag Svagian came and took from his breast pocket a photograph that had faded from the sweat of his body. The photograph had a black fleck, a droplet of blood that had dripped from the old man's head in Strejnicu Forest. From the photograph he brushed dead leaves visible only to him. He then released it from his hand, and it fluttered down like a leaf.

Harutiun Frenkian came. He took out his will and on a blank page patiently wrote down the names of all those present. When he did not know a name, my grandfather whispered it over the old man's shoulder. He blew on the page to dry the ink, smoothed it, placed a handful of toasted walnuts in the middle, and then carefully wrapped them in it.

Onik Tokatlian came. In the box he placed his eye, which had trickled down his shattered face. He pondered, and with his fingertip he added the reflection the eye had cast in the mirror.

Minas the blind man came, treading heavily, and above his head he held the lamp with which he guided lonely travelers by night. He blew out the flame before putting the lamp in the box since in the world beyond the edge of the box he could see, but the others were as blind as he had been.

Then my grandfather Setrak Melikian came. He smiled that smile of his, which was appropriate in moments both happy and sad. From his pocket he drew his string of prayer beads, made from threaded olive pits; he slowly counted them between his fingers and laid them in a ring on top of the other objects.

Levon Zohrab came, and at first he caused bewilderment because his hands were empty. But since all he had left was his word, this was what he brought. He stood beneath the image of Christ Pantokrator in the cupola, which for an instant he imagined wore his father's face. He cupped his palms until they warmed and filled, and then in the box he placed a pallid ray, a sliver of light, which was invisible, although the others believed in it.

Khoren Melikian came, my grandfather's older cousin, and he brought fine brown coffee powder, which he sprinkled like earth over all the other things.

My grandmother Arshaluis was among the first of the women who ventured to approach. She had gained courage because what she displayed as an answer was not in fact her answer. She had brought Mrs. Spiegel's flowery dress, carefully folded. It was one of those dresses that Mrs. Spiegel and other women like her, now dressed in black, would never wear again.

They looked at him, but Sahag Sheitanian, the man who had asked the question, with the disquiet native to a man in whose breast dwelled two creatures, thought it more appropriate to remain where he was. Through him passed his father Rupen, with tattered clothes, tied with string so that the wind would not seep through the torn edges, and with feet bound in rags. Since Rupen Sheitanian wore two bits of wood tied to his rags to protect the soles of his feet from the frozen earth and since the wood did not bend to his tread, he approached with the shuffling gait of the newly dead. He held the crow by its legs. Since he stood before the altar and since none before him had spoken, he refrained from saying once more that God was dead. But before he folded the crow's spread wings so that it would fit inside the box, he held up its twisted head, with its gaping beak, thereby suggesting that even if we do not dare to proclaim that God is dead, we may at least say the same thing about those who bring the news.

Levon Harutiunian came, old before his time. He swept his eyes over those seated on the wooden pews and looked up at the balcony, from where a small organ could be heard playing *Amen yev ënt hogwuyt k'um* (And with all thy spirit). He then turned his eyes to those standing along the wall. He pointed at Hagop Djololian Siruni and Vahan Gemijian, who had gone to the choir stall, this being the only place in the church where they could talk. "Only we three will return," said Siruni. "In the place where we are, we think of you and of your box of gifts that you, our brothers from Focșani, brought us many years ago, on Christmas Day. We could not guess what was inside, but I have to tell you that here nothing is of any further use since each of us is alone in the face of death. Our eyes have begun to turn white, scorched by the resin we have to collect drop by drop from the tree trunks. After such long labor, high up in the branches, in search of pockets of resin, our arms fall down, powerless, drained of blood. Often the kasha we eat tastes of meat because it is mixed with the blood of our receding gums. I have forgotten the names of the women I loved. We have been given new names, made up of numbers, which say everything needful to know about each of us. The first numbers refer to the article in the Penal Code and the last two numbers to how many years of imprisonment. We cannot be told apart from our sentences, and we are no longer anything else." Levon Harutiunian nodded and took out the certificate he had received on his release from the camp and put it in the box, as an eventual answer for whoever might ask. Siruni gave up his single most precious thing: his thick magnifying glass, the only means by which he could read after his vision turned white, since all the other precious things he had once possessed—the manuscripts, the old documents, the letters—had been packed in crates and hidden in the basement of the Securitate archive. Then, all three, Levon Harutiunian, Siruni, and Vahan Gemijian, went out, returning to the endless white expanses where they were unable to flee from anything inside or outside of them; this was the twentieth century's great discovery: a carceral space in which there is penance without atonement.

Virginica Papazian came. Even in the yellowish smoke of the incense, the lemon in her hand shone. It was a fruit larger than they had ever seen, but they remembered that Virginica watered the roots of the lemon tree with the blood that had flowed since then, in keeping with the times, and then they understood whence came that unearthly shine.

For a few moments nobody else came, but nonetheless they watched, for it was as if somebody approached the box and slipped inside, heedless that he might take somebody else's place, and they knew that the person who had just come was the all too genial Mr. Stayputian, who, precisely because he did not exist, was familiar to all.

Arshavir Acterian elicited cries of wonder since he came holding an answer in each hand; nobody had done so thitherto. But Arshavir did not wish to break the rules and give multiple answers, taking up more space in the box than he was allotted. He had not yet decided which of the two was to be his answer. In one hand he held a dog-eared book, from the shelves of the used bookstore where he worked, and in his other hand he held a pair of handcuffs. He pondered for a few moments, tempted to leave the book. However, the question had not been asked that he might give the answer that pleased him but that he might give the answer he deemed to be true, even if he feared it. Arshavir slowly put the book in the large pocket of his coat and placed the handcuffs in the box.

Behind him came Simon Sheitanian. He took a handful of earth, moistened it with the steam of his breath, and kneaded it into a ball. He bit it like an apple; he slowly chewed, shifting the bolus from one side of his mouth to the other, and then placed in the box that fruit picked from another tree, which, having been banished from the Garden of Eden, may or may not be the tree of the knowledge of good and evil.

Mariam, the priest's widow, came, and over the toasted halva she sprinkled cinnamon and fried walnuts and hazelnuts, in remembrance of all the others.

Misak Torlakian did not come since he was not yet ready with his answer.

The small organ fell silent, and the plasterwork of the wall closed up, leaving behind a fine, alkaline powder. The people waited in silence. When it became clear that nobody else had an answer, the first to have come, my grandfather Garabet Vosganian, stepped in front of the altar doors once again. It was time since the box was full. He carefully closed the lid, and then, with difficulty, he hoisted it up on his shoulder. He walked out slowly, feeling his way with the tips of his toes, lest he trip. Then the others went out. Some believed that it would be like on Good Friday and that they would circumambulate the church, that they would hold the box above their heads so that each could walk beneath it before reentering the church. But Grandfather made a sign for them to go on ahead, across the broad churchyard, down the lane through the old graveyard, past the stand of chestnut trees and the buildings of the old Armenian school, and out into the street. The procession followed him in silence. Mantu and his brass band were waiting by the church fence. Before they took up their positions at the head of the procession, Mantu cast Grandfather Garabet a questioning look. "I hope you have not forgotten," said Grandfather. "Beethoven's Ninth Symphony. Third movement. *Andante*." Mantu nodded and then turned self-importantly to the others. Little Mantu, Budișteanu, Frunză, the Cîlțea brothers, and Fofoc raised their trumpets, horns, and trombones. Mantu gave the order: "Strike it up, lads! Softly . . ." Grandfather Garabet handed him the score, but the Gypsy did not need it. A good few years had elapsed since the day when the books had burned and they had stopped the smoke from dispersing, so they had had plenty of time to understand what it was about. They set off down Station Road, and then they turned down Tanners Street, the long road to the cemeteries. Mantu's tuba held the smoke in place, stopping the smoke on the ground from rising and the smoke in the sky from lowering. They now advanced through that sea of parted smoke. Setting the rhythm of the march by the sound of his tuba, Mantu shortened his steps to allow the bringers of gifts to move ahead, with their tokens clasped between their hands. Mercan had brought his most precious jar, in which he kept the air beaten by the wings of a passing archangel, who, to judge by the greenish color inside, seemed to have been Raphael. From his cupped palms, Angheluță blew glittering white flour, which illumined the smoke above, and Bobîrcă scattered olives and coffee beans, which darkened the smoke below. And up ahead was Taor, the halva vendor, pushing his cart, walking slowly; one second he might be two paces away, and the next he might be at the far end of the road, and it was impossible to discern the interval he crossed between near and far and back again. When you came out of the yard of the Armenian church, Station Road led to all the town's cemeteries, so many people came and swelled the procession. Nițu Stan came, holding his old and useless gun by the barrel, and he mingled with the others, along with the men from Suraia and Vadu Roșca. Next to him was Cristea Paragină, his chest lacerated by the barbed wire.

In front of the St. Spiridon Church, the convoy paused for a few moments. The brass band stopped playing. The powder blown from cupped palms settled. The parted smoke merged. They turned to all four points of the compass, making the sign of the cross. My grandfather had wearied, but not for one moment could he entrust the box with the gifts of answers to anybody else. For a

few moments, one of those named Simon—Simon Sheitanian, Simon Pilibbosian, or Eshek Simon—came and helped him, carrying the box for a few
paces until Grandfather, who increasingly resembled Archimandrite Komitas,
caught his breath, barely able to carry the load on his shoulders any longer.
The convoy went on its way, Grandfather rested as he walked, and they did not
stop, even though some were exhausted by now; even if the road had begun to
scorch and crumble into sand; even if the swirling smoke was as ruddy as the
steam that lifted from the waters of the Euphrates at noon; even if they now
staggered, leaning against each other so as not to collapse, tying their tattered
clothes with string; even if they looked more and more like sights they wished
to forget. Mantu, who was struggling to keep the beat with his tuba and made
signs to the rest of the band when they had to come in or to pause, turned to my
grandfather, whose face was now elongated, bristly, and the hem of whose black
overcoat fluttered like a surplice. Grandfather looked at the score and shouted
over the others' heads that everything was perfect, that they were playing it flaw-
lessly for the first time. Since he could not pause from his playing, Mantu heard
nothing of what Grandfather said, but when he saw his hand waving the score,
he sensed that all was well, and because the funeral march was flawless, he was
the only one in the cortege who was happy.

When they crossed the railway tracks, Grandfather, who was best able to
answer any question that might have been asked at that boundary, took back
the box, blessing Simon, whichever Simon it might have been. The convoy had
become endless. People were coming out of their yards, or else they suddenly
appeared in the midst of the others. Some asked the name of the deceased but
received no answer. When they saw not the usual funeral banner but the halva
seller's stall and the sparks flying from the cupped hands of the other three
mages, they joined the procession out of curiosity. Others, on seeing my grandfather carrying the box behind the brass band, believed that somebody had
been cremated and that the procession was for the ashes. Since they were not
completely mistaken, they too joined the convoy. Others, who had been peeping from behind their fences, saw familiar faces, who called to them when the
convoy came past their yards. Others joined the convoy so that they might not
feel alone. Some found themselves suddenly in its midst or were pushed off the
sidewalk into its path. There were a few who, recognizing the Ninth Symphony,
even in that pared-down version for brass band, joined in the hope that the fune-
real *Andante* would soon come to an end and then the Ode to Joy would begin,
but the *Andante* was never-ending, and the banks to either side grew steeper and
steeper, like walls, and once they had joined the convoy, they could not leave.

The convoy narrowed to pass through the cemetery gate. Viewed from above, it was like an hourglass: the cortege flowed like a slender stream of sand from one hemisphere to the other, from one world to another, between town and cemetery. Once all the sand has emptied, the hourglass will be turned upside down, and the world of the dead will arise. The cortege will form once more, will pour through the narrow gates, filling the streets, yards, and houses left abandoned and empty, their doors and windows banging in the wind.

When they entered the cemetery, Mantu's brass band fell silent. Grandfather, who knew the way best, went on ahead. Now cradling the box in his arms, he passed the chapel on the central path, where the gravestones were mainly of marble, black or white, but never both colors. He came to a stop in front of the empty Seferian vault. He placed the box on the ground, careful lest the lid fly open and the answers escape, swarming over the world. Tightly shut, having been borne in front of the crowd, with the mages' powder clearing a path for it, the box was transformed into what it had been from the very beginning: an ark for answers to the question.

They then waited for the whole of the convoy to assemble, that motley crowd that went barefoot, their soles swollen from treading on thorns and wrapped in bloody rags, their clothes tattered and caked with dust and sweat, their heads shaggy and lowered or else lifted as they looked unseeing at the sky, feeling their way with their staffs, clutching their children to their breasts, leaning on each other, sleeping as they walked since in the convoy the walking was endless.

Arshag the bell ringer, unable to pick his way through the assembled multitude, swayed, clinging to his rope and deafeningly tolling the bell, which was as loud as the belfries of all seven churches, and the rope swung, lofting him to the side of Grandfather and the others who had formed a silent circle around the ark. Letting go of the rope, Arshag descended; in his right hand he grasped the censer and swung it all around. The priest, who might have been Father Dajad, Father Mampre, Father Varjabedian, Archimandrite Zareh, the servants at the altar of our church of St. Mary in Focșani, or any other of the line of priests that descended from St. Gregory the Illuminator or came before him, sang *I veri Jerusalem*, and in that way they suggested whence the ark had come and whither it would return. After that, the ark, the box of answers not fully spoken, was given to the masons. They removed the slab and placed the ark in the tomb a man had made but in which no man would ever be buried.

Arshag the bell ringer did not have the list that is normally drawn up for such occasions, and the priest did not read out any names in eternal remembrance. Since the answers of so many people had been interred together promiscuously, indiscriminately, the people prayed as if before a mass grave, taking upon themselves the guilt of not having prayed at the other graves, those scattered amid the sands and sealed in haste. And that place, for people who had not died in the same soil from which they had been born or who had not been buried in the tombs they had made for themselves, was therefore reckoned to be a mass grave. The masons dressed the stones that would entomb all the silences, the lights, the confessions; they laid the slab; and they carved the inscriptions, smoothing plaster over them with the skill that only they possessed. After which the convoys dispersed, more quickly than they had formed. Some returned by the cemetery gate, heading toward the railway tracks, which was anyway the only way back. Others leaned against the stone crosses and waited. Still others sank into the earth, like rainwater in May.

Once the ark had been buried, it turned out that answers die too, like people, making way for life to go on.

12.

The history of mankind is also to a large extent the history of horses. Except that the chronicles for the most part mention only the men, which makes history not only unjust but also, quite often, unfathomable.

After the chronicles finish recounting the wars, each army arrives to collect its dead. On the battlefield only the dead horses remain. When you look at them like that, as they stiffen, their muzzles agape, blood foaming over their bits, their bellies split asunder, their ankles broken, you would think that a war had been waged among horses, not men.

The chronicles tell of wars among armies, they tell of slain men, since these are things that can be explained. And, with a good degree of accuracy, for every battle it is possible to determine who was victorious. The same cannot be said of the slain horses. No justification can be found for their deaths, except that in their cruelty men are often not sufficient unto themselves. From the way abandoned battlefields look, wars among horses have no justification. Nobody bothers to glorify the slain horses. The unknown hero has never been a horse. Even if by fighting and dying for another's cause, the horse would be entitled to heroism, nobody lights a candle for him. For the horse, only the hungry battlefield lights its black candles of croaking birds.

Much more could be understood about the world if the history of mankind and the history of horses were written side by side: the history of horses pulling the cannons with all their might; crossing the passes in exhausting marches; guarding the convoys of refugees; carrying on their backs entire nations and mingling with them; galloping madly over the battlefields with dead riders on their backs; pulling the bedizened chariots of the victors or walking without a halter; carrying the wounded and the baggage of the vanquished; forever running in the vanguard of the armies, without wearing a breastplate, without even being allowed to suffer a wound, since a wounded horse is a dead horse. Horses are counted among the vanquished, never among the victors. Not that they want to be victorious over anybody. For history's gladiator, the horse, the only way of being victorious in a battle is to stay alive. The chronicles tell of the victors; the vanquished get a mention as a way of making the victory look more glorious, but the vanquished horses augment nobody's glory; it is more glorious to be a killer of men than a killer of horses because men can fight back.

Not having been written for any imperial court, *The Book of Whispers* tells mainly of the vanquished, who either were among the weak or chose to be among the weak, because what they wished to conquer could not be found in this world. In such a story it is natural that people and horses cannot be explained one without the other.

Perhaps I was fated to be the storyteller of *The Book of Whispers* because of the little wooden horse. It was not a comely toy. In my childhood they had not yet invented toys with little motors and lights that roar and flash and move around by themselves. The toys of my childhood were motionless and silent. I had a few rag dolls stuffed with oakum. They were from the time after the war, when, forced to close their hat shop, Grandmother Arshaluis and her sister Armenuhi made dolls, which they sold for a pittance. I also had a big elephant, soft to the touch, and a plastic lion, on whose paws I liked to gnaw with my first milk teeth. And there was also the little wooden horse, which survived precisely because it could not be torn or bitten or bent. Nobody gave it to me as a gift. I found it one day on the shelf by the stove, next to a thick folder bound with string and inscribed "Nemesis." But in those days I did not know how to read, and even if I had known, I would not have been able to make any connection between the goddess of revenge, whose name was inscribed in sepia ink, and the little horse, which was no more than six inches long, whittled rather clumsily and painted a nondescript color. It was the toy I loved most, first because it was a gift from nobody; I found it, and it became mine. And then I loved it because they wanted to take it away from me. The little wooden horse was the object of my first act of defiance. "You're not allowed to play with that!" said Sahag Sheitanian. And what else could I do except climb up a tree, where the adults could not come up after me? They spoke in a whisper, but it is well to know that children can hear whispers clearly. "Leave him be," said Grandfather; "he doesn't know, and he didn't do anything wrong. In the end, he's right; the wooden horse is just a toy . . ." "What kind of toy is that?" snapped Sahag Sheitanian, who was unused to toys and did not have children through whom to live his unlived childhood. "Why play with something like that?" "You just do . . . ," replied Grandfather, with the calmness of unassailable truths. Then he waved at me to come down from the tree with my horse, and just to make sure, I hid it under the blanket and fell asleep clutching it.

The first wooden horse arrived at our house in the spring of 1951. At first, when they told him it was a parcel from America, Grandfather thought, "It means my sister in Argentina is doing well and she was able to send me something." However, the parcel was not from Argentina but from the United States. In those days, you couldn't just go to the post office, sign for a parcel, and take it away. First you had to say who you thought might have sent it and why. Then, after they informed you who the sender was, you had to provide information about him, saying whether he was a relative and, if not, where you had met him. You had to say what you thought was in the parcel and whether you had asked for it or whether the sender had mailed it on his own initiative. You had to say whether you corresponded with the sender and whether he had promised to send you an invitation to go to the United States. You had to say what you thought about it all in general. "Misak Torlakian," said Grandfather. "I know him. We're not relatives. We were friends here in Romania. He vanished during the war. I didn't even know he was in America," he added, realizing from the look on the post office functionary's face that it was a bad thing to be in America. "So you don't know what he sent." "I've no idea," said Grandfather, with a pang of the heart, knowing Misak's passion for guns and knowing he was capable of almost anything. "Then let's open it." With a pair of pliers, the functionary started ripping the nails out of the wooden box. He moved aside the scrunched-up paper and rummaged inside. "There's something hard here," he said, causing my grandfather's heart to leap into his throat. But when he pulled out the wooden horse, both were surprised, each for his own reasons. The functionary was dissatisfied at that being all there was since it meant there was nothing for him to take; Grandfather was relieved for the same reason. After signing for the box and taking it away, Grandfather fell to thinking. And so did his brother-in-law Sahag Sheitanian. Sitting on the bench, among the soft pillows, with colored *fincanlar* of coffee in front of them, they looked at the wooden horse in the middle of the table. Sahag remained silent, with the same question as ever on his lips: "What is going to happen now?" What happened showed that the ark of answers had been sealed too soon. It was only now that Misak had arrived at his answer, and it was different from all the others. Grandfather Garabet remembered what had happened many years before, in the yard of the Armenian church in Focşani. "It is the sign of revenge, Sahag," he sighed, since he would rather not have spoken those words. He went inside the house, rummaged in the cupboards, and found the cardboard folder tied with string. Once again they read through the names of the avengers and those killed. Then, in ink the color of sepia photographic plates, he added to the list of avengers: "A wooden horse." Next to it he left a blank space and added only the month and the year: May 1951. He picked up the wooden horse and examined it closely. "This is not the horse Misak showed me," he said. "He's made one the same and still has the other one . . ." "But why?" asked Sahag, so that he would not have to be the one to provide an answer. Grandfather opened the folder again, crossed out "a wooden horse," and wrote above it "the first wooden horse."

The second wooden horse arrived a year later, also in May. Since the parcel did not have a *par avion* label, it meant it had come by sea, which, reckoned Grandfather Garabet, would have taken two or three weeks. The parcel must have been sent in late April, when the Armenians commemorate those who died in the massacres. "Oh Lord, Garabet," said Sahag, "what is to be done?" He said it to himself since Yusuf was by then very old and no longer recalcitrant, merely waiting for the other man finally to die so that he would not have to stalk him any more, so that he could finally find peace. He gazed with melancholy at the little horse, which reminded him of a world in which the two of them had been turned inside out, like a glove, and where Sahag had been the one struggling inside Yusuf's rib cage. Grandfather Garabet, who otherwise always had an answer ready, did not know what to say. "Who can it have been this time?" asked Sahag. It was a day of hard questions for Grandfather. "There were eighteen names on the list Misak showed me. It might be any one of them." "He ought to give it a rest. Let's write a letter to him or to General Dro." He would have liked to add, "If they've got such a thirst for killing people, maybe they should try the Bolsheviks," but he refrained. "You're mad," said Grandfather. "We don't have an address. The box only gives his name and the State of California. Where would you find him? And anyway, what would you write? They open all the letters. They'd start all that madness to do with the general's arms again." "All right, but we don't know where Dro's guns are . . ." "Who would care? They just like to torture you; they don't care about finding out." Sahag held the wooden horse in his cupped palm. "We can't even tell anybody," he sighed. Grandfather examined the horse on every side. "I think there is somebody I can tell, somebody who'll give us advice . . ." "Don't get carried away," whispered Sahag. "That would be the last thing we needed, for them to find out about Nemesis." They were talking in whispers, in the middle of the yard, as far away from the fence as possible, in the shade of the old apricot tree. "Who could you tell such a thing? Who could you trust so much?" "It's the inviolability of the confessional," said Grandfather. "Father Mampre?" snorted Sahag. "Is there anything the old man finds out without his telling his wife and daughter straightaway?" "I'm not talking about Father Mampre. I mean Vazken Baljian, our bishop."

At the crack of dawn, Sahag Sheitanian opened his sweetshop by the station, and on the primus stove he made coffee, over which both men lingered. Grandfather then took the train to Bucharest, to confess the secret, a secret all the more onerous in those times when secrets were so hard to keep.

Like any other book, *The Book of Whispers* is a chronicle not of things lived or imagined but of things confessed. But for this part of our story, it remains wholly unknown to us since not only do we not have any confession, but we do not have any inkling as to how things later turned out, as was also the case with the meeting between Onik Tokatlian and Mesia Khacherian. We know that Grandfather traveled to Bucharest, and when he got there, he went straight to the bishopric on Strada Armenească. But rather than Asadur, the building caretaker, he found a policeman, who brusquely told him to be on his way. Grandfather looked over his shoulder, but the windows were closed, and the only explanation the policeman gave him before telling him to make himself scarce was that there wasn't going to be any dance that evening. Bewildered, Grandfather went to the yard of the cathedral next door and looked for Partogh, the bell ringer with the broken nose, and it was only then that he discovered what had happened. In the middle of the night, men from the Armenian Front, together with the police, had gone around to the back and knocked on the windows of Bishop Vazken and Diramayr, his aged mother, demanding that they vacate the premises within two hours. Bishop Vazken and his mother threw what they could into two jute sacks and found themselves out on the street. "I found them on the church steps at daybreak. They were lying on the sacks, half asleep, trembling with cold," said Partogh. "For a time they stayed in the bishopric offices in the churchyard, until we made up two rooms for them upstairs. Neither the bishop nor his mother complained, but it's an outrage what they've put them through." "Why is there a policeman at the door of the bishop's residence?" "Why wouldn't there be? It's so that nobody will go in without permission, the bishop in particular. For a while, they used it as a storeroom for all kinds of stuff taken away from the churches: books, archives, vestments. In the end, they took everything away and burned it, starting with the books. They gave the building to the Armenian Front for its headquarters, but it didn't do it any good because in the end, the Communists, who created the front so that they could destroy the rest of us Armenians, abolished that too. Now it's a kind of club. Young folk come to dance. If they weren't dancing on the floors of the bishop's residence, it would be nice. Romanians come too." Grandfather had not been to Bucharest for two years. The last time had been when he was summoned to the Ministry of the Interior to apply in writing for Romanian citizenship. Now he was bewildered. But smiling and gentle, Vazken Baljian welcomed him with the same joy as ever, and before Grandfather could say anything, the bishop made a sign for him to be silent. He then invited him for a walk around the churchyard, where, although not shielded from prying eyes, they were at least protected from prying ears. In the evening, Grandfather returned to Focșani. He was troubled, not so much by the circumstances surrounding the bishopric, since such things were common in those days, as by his conversation with the bishop as they walked around outside the cathedral. "Did you tell him?" asked Uncle Sahag Sheitanian in a whisper. Grandfather nodded. Sahag sought a further answer but in vain. "Let us wait," said Grandfather. "We've been waiting ever since the Russians came. What else can we do?" "Let us wait," repeated Grandfather. "If another sign like this one arrives, I'll inform him. Until then, we do nothing. He'll tell us what is to be done." "Is it so complicated?" probed Sahag Sheitanian. Grandfather, perhaps because he had promised not to divulge anything of what he had discussed with the bishop, perhaps because of Yusuf, who, old and enfeebled as he was, still stood between them, like a stranger, could only repeat, "Let us wait," and there was no chance of his changing his mind.

The third wooden horse, which was the same as the others, appeared two years later. Grandfather opened the folder and recorded the date of its arrival, leaving a blank space against the column of those killed. He waited for further news that might help him to fill in the blank space, but it did not come. In a postscript to a letter from his sister, he discovered that General Dro had died in Boston. It was clear that the letter, which had come all the way from Buenos Aires, had been read in some dusky office in Bucharest, given the state it was in: crinkled from being steamed open and hastily glued back. But Sahag Sheitanian was amazed that they had allowed it to reach its destination. Grandfather was of the opinion that as far as they were concerned, any news that depressed the recipient and killed a hope was fit to be let through. As for the journey he should have made to Bucharest with the new sign that the wooden horse announced, Grandfather was unable to keep his promise. A few months previously, Bishop Vazken Baljian had been elected Catholicos, or supreme patriarch of all Armenians, and had gone to Yerevan. Grandfather therefore never found out what action he should have taken, and Sahag even less so. A few years after my grandfather Garabet died, in 1975, Vazken Baljian, wearing a white cloak and a shining white hood, returned to Bucharest for a few days. I was in the courtyard of the cathedral with my father. The times had grown less harsh, and the bishop's residence had been returned to the Church. The deserted courtyard where Bishop Vazken Baljian and Grandfather had walked, conferring with each other, was crowded with people. Among them were Sahag Sheitanian, my father, and myself, a tallish young man with a moustache. The Catholicos emerged from the cathedral and blessed the people. As he walked to the gate, he saw Sahag and Father among the crowd—he had never met me— and he called over the other people's heads, "Where is Garabet?" but Sahag's reply was drowned out. My uncle and my father tried to move closer, but the crowd swallowed them up, and the Patriarch's hood moved away. My final attempt to find out about that conversation came many years later, in 1994, when I myself met Catholicos Vazken, this time in Armenia, at the see of the Armenian patriarchs in Etchmiadzin, where the Only-Begotten descended, as the name translates in Armenian. I presented to the Patriarch the gifts I had brought with me: a few books in Romanian and a bag of maize flour; he missed the *mămăligă* he used to eat in Bucharest, and he missed the people he knew there, too. He knew who I was, but he did not know I was Garabet's grandson; I told him and waited for the Catholicos to say what was to be said. But the Catholicos was ailing; he rested his hand on his chin, and he smiled, at peace. As for what I wished to discover, he said only this: "Garabet, yes, yes . . ." The world had changed in the meantime; the borders had begun to resemble Noradungian's maps, but not the dreams of General Dro, since Armenia was now an independent republic but had been reduced to barely eighteen thousand square miles and was isolated and poor. Probably the answer my grandfather expected after he received the third wooden horse, the answer I now tacitly asked for on his behalf, was no longer relevant.

Born in Bucharest, Vazken Baljian had not passed through the circles of death, but he had served as confessor to many of those who underwent the ordeal. From them he had received power over death, so when, at peace with the world, he called death to him, it came, and he died shortly after our meeting. Perhaps what he wanted to suggest to me, when he nodded on hearing my grandfather's name, was that there was no need to tell me what was to be said since the two of them were to meet again very soon.

The fourth wooden horse arrived not long after the third. "This is because of General Dro," said Grandfather. "Misak acted swiftly, lest they believe it is all over now the general is dead. In other words, we shouldn't lose hope." "What hope are you talking about, Garbis?" sighed Sahag. "Look around us . . . Nothing but absurdities." "All the more so, in that case . . ." said Grandfather. And they sat for a while in the yard, looking at the wooden horse. After Grandfather marked its arrival by adding another row to the Nemesis folder, he said to Sahag, "Let's go." He thrust the wooden horse in his pocket, and they set off down March 6, 1945, Street, formerly Cupboards Street; they turned the corner onto Snowdrops Street and then walked down Tanners Street, the road to the cemeteries. They found a secluded spot in the Armenian cemetery—each time a different spot. They turned over two spadefuls of earth and buried the wooden horse, patting down the mound of soil. And then Grandfather, out of respect for the cool, enveloping earth, said the Lord's Prayer: *Hayr mer* (Our Father), and made a broad sign of the cross. "It's strange," said Sahag. "We don't even know whom we're burying. And whoever it might be, he can't be a Christian." "It doesn't do any harm," said Grandfather. "If his God doesn't receive him, that's His business. The cross and the prayer still are up to us." The ark was thus endowed with further answers, which, since the people did not understand them, kept repeating themselves. And at night in the cemetery, fires flickered, fed by the exhalations of decay.

The fifth wooden horse arrived at our house a few years later, just when Grandfather Garabet and Sahag Sheitanian thought things had settled down once and for all. This is why the two old Armenians were caught even more unprepared than they had been when the first horse arrived. Perhaps this is also why they were careless. Forgotten on a shelf, the horse set eyes on me and, thinking I was the little boy parted from another horse just like that one almost seventy years before, it agreed to become my plaything.

A few days after the arrival of the fifth horse, which became one of my toys, President Kennedy was shot. The old Armenians met for the last time in the Seferian vault. The wooden horse slipped inside my pocket and lay there quietly while I played with the windfall chestnuts and walnuts on the cemetery path. Sahag gave him a searching look, but Grandfather was sternly resolved not to say another word about those strange messages from Misak Torlakian, even when my uncle Sahag brought up the question of General Dro's arms.

The sixth horse was not long in coming. By then I had lost mine. More than likely unable to bear seeing me play with that harbinger of death, Sahag had hidden it, and then, along with the sixth, he must have taken it to the cemetery, where Grandfather said the Lord's Prayer twice. But the deed was done: the little horse had chosen me, and I had no choice but to tell the story.

In the meantime, things seemed to be getting better. In 1964, the political prisoners began to return home. I was two when my great-grandmother and Uncle Simon died, so I don't remember it. The third death among those I knew was that of Carol Spiegel. I remember his death as the black dress that Mrs. Spiegel started wearing. The grown-ups had many habits. They drank coffee. Some, like Ștefănucă Ibrăileanu, smoked. Others, like Ohannes Krikorian, were prone to lose their tempers, and then their faces would turn bright red. They played backgammon or *gyulbahar*, shaking the dice in a *fincan*. They had all kinds of habits that we children were not allowed to indulge in. And death seemed to be one of them. I wasn't allowed to drink coffee, but sometimes, on the sly, I would lick the saucers in which a little coffee had spilled because my grandparents' hands trembled with old age when they carried the tray of *fincanlar* out into the yard. Likewise, we weren't allowed to die, although by then a tiny amount of death, as much as the spilled coffee in a saucer, had seeped into the mind of the child I was.

Grandfather sometimes locked himself up in his room, playing the violin and humming heart-rending laments. Death came to him, and it spoke of the unending chain of those who had died. Death told him of them, the old dead, the only dead whose story it was allowed to tell, since only the old dead truly belong to death, while the new dead loomed in the window, with pale faces and glittering eyes, trickling down the pane, as thick as olive oil. Grandfather told death about me; about our walks in the park, down paths of red flowers and thick foliage; about our games of conkers; about "Moby Dick," the whale brought to Obor Square on a trailer, which we children beheld in terror; about how we played Schubert's *Serenade* and Boccherini's *Minuet* together on violin and piano; and about how, when the light was not paying attention, we tried to photograph the mirrors. On hearing all this, death understood that my grandfather still had things to do in this world; it made its excuses and left. Where death had been, even if only for a short time, something was left behind: a sense of melancholy, a mist on the surface of a mirror, an overexposed photographic plate in which Grandfather's eyes looked sunken in their sockets. If we spoke to him, he would not answer, sitting under the apricot tree in the yard. The new dead descended from the fruit trees; they slid down the trunks like wild honey; they emerged from the grass, hissing like slow worms; they alighted with folded wings, after wheeling in ever decreasing circles; and they sat all around him, listening, as Grandfather read to them from *The Book of Whispers*, which wrote itself as I grew, and they nodded in agreement because unlike the old dead, the new dead found greater peace the more that was said about them.

Grandfather closed the book and put it aside. He looked at the seventh horse, placed on the table. The circle of the new dead rippled outward until it vanished, and each returned by the road he had come. They left behind them a cool wind; it was the beginning of November. "Let me bring the folder," said Sahag Sheitanian. "There may be no need," said Grandfather Garabet. "There's something strange about this horse." It was the same as the others, made of whittled wood; the notches made by the knife were plainly visible. Slanting edges made the muzzle pointed. "It's white," said Grandfather. "The others were made of unpainted walnut wood; this one is painted." "What can it mean?" "It's a different kind of horse; it's the horse from the dream. The horse in Misak's dream was white, remember? It was saddled but ran alone, streaming with blood." "But this horse is just white . . ." "Then you might say that the white horse has found its rider at last." "And who might that rider be?" asked Sahag, he himself riding slantwise through his dreams one fine day. "Misak, of course . . ."

After the political prisoners were released and the missile crisis was defused, long- and short-wave radios appeared in Focșani's electrical shops, which meant that you could listen to Free Europe, Radio Freedom, and the BBC at home, albeit taking the necessary precautions. With the sound barely turned up, its needle creeping fractions of an inch across the crackling dial, the radio became a character in *The Book of Whispers*. That was probably why the members of the parochial committee no longer met in the Seferian vault since the Telefunken was no longer the only path across the airwaves to the free world.

The radio sat in Sahag's room, covered by a piece of embroidery depicting troubadour Sayat-Nova. Tuning the radio into the free world was a ritual. We children weren't allowed to listen, nor were the women, but for different reasons; at school, we children might be questioned about what went on at home, whereas the women kept interrupting, asking questions when they didn't understand. Uncle Sahag would remove the embroidery, fold it, and place it on the bedside table. He would seat himself and tell Grandfather to come, calling for sherbet to be brought. First, he had to find the station because after listening to the free world, Sahag would always tune in to Radio Bucharest on the long waves: "Who knows? They're everywhere. Let's not give ourselves away like fools." "Who are they?" asked Aunt Armenuhi, bringing the tray of sherbet. "Them," replied Uncle Sahag, "meaning the ones who aren't us." Made from the petals of the roses in the yard, the sherbet was pink and sticky, wrapped around a teaspoon dipped in a crystal glass of cold water. The sherbet was never served in cups but only in glasses, which had to be crystal so that their translucence would allow the pink paste to gleam like a fruit in the water. After they finished the sherbet, slowly licking it like a lollipop and rolling it around their mouths with the tips of their tongues, the old Armenians of my childhood drank the water in their glasses, taking small sips. For my old folks, for my godfather Sahag and my grandfather Setrak, this custom probably derived from the desert wanderings of their childhood, when water was sparse and was savored rather than drunk.

Not yet having touched the tray of sherbet, the two men sat down in the armchairs and leaned toward the radio, as if all three were whispering together. Sahag tuned in to the short waves and with extreme slowness began to turn the dial. The slow movement of the needle was accompanied by a series of crackles, whistles, and snatches of speech in all kinds of different languages. "Faster," said Grandfather; "we'll miss the first news items." Sahag was in no hurry; he would turn the needle too far along the dial and then come back too far in the other direction; he would hover over the spot, as if sniffing out his prey, and finally he would plant the needle in the best place, listen for a few moments, make another careful adjustment of the knob, give a nod of satisfaction, and, taking his glass of sherbet, finally settle down to listen, his head bowed. However tempting it might have been to make comments, they both remained silent until the end of the bulletin. They would cast each other meaningful glances, as if to say, "Exactly what I told you" (Grandfather) or "That's what the Bolsheviks deserve" (Sahag), saving their commentaries until the end, when they finished their sherbet and took small sips of the rosewater.

That afternoon the ritual was suddenly interrupted just as Sahag Sheitanian, having turned the knob with slow, voluptuous deliberation, and Grandfather Garabet were lifting their teaspoons of sherbet to run them over the tips of their tongues. From the spot where they had hastily buried it, the white horse had burst out of the soil; it had circled the world and then reared up on two legs, neighing, summoning its rider, whose blood matched the blood on its saddle and bridle. On Radio Freedom, at the beginning of the Armenian-language broadcast, the newsreader announced that Misak Torlakian had died in Montebello that morning. He was to be buried two days later in the Evergreen Cemetery, and many members of California's large Armenian community were expected to be in attendance. "Misak Torlakian, the comrade in arms of General Dro," they called him. Of course, there was no mention of Operation Nemesis, nor the dream of the white horse, now packed away, as if in a trunk.

It was the evening of November 12, 1968. Undoubtedly, the exact date is of no importance. Although full of dates, like a history book, *The Book of Whispers* is not bound to any of those dates. The real history, the history worth telling, is the one that can turn to legend at any time if there are enough people to tell it and others to remember it; in other words, it is the least exact story of all. I have included dates not because I needed to provide additional details for our stories told in a whisper but because it was the only way in which I could present the sequence of events with any clarity. Whereas in its externals, the story might fit any time and any place, once inside the narrative it is important to know who gives birth to whom, who inherits from whom, who curses whom, and who can go on being a character in the story even after his death. In this last respect, *The Book of Whispers* is rather unusual since unlike in other histories, here death is merely a detail, and what is more important than death and therefore life is memory.

As for the sequence of events, we know that my grandfather Garabet Vosganian did not wait for the end of the afternoon news on Radio Freedom. He rose to his feet; stood staring into space for a few moments; turned around slowly, awkwardly; and went to the door. In fact, he first moved in the opposite direction to the radio, to distance himself from the source of the sound, and then he went to the door, planting one foot in front of the other and moving his arms stiffly. He moved in an exaggeratedly jointed way, which was why, for a normal person, and all the more so for an old man, it looked disjointed, the way the new dead would look if they allowed us to watch them. Sahag followed him, and Yusuf suddenly rejoiced, hopping and tumbling around, like an old monkey.

With his slow walk and empty eyes, Garabet reminded Sahag of the old folk shuffling along in the convoys between Meskene and Deir-ez-Zor; hence Yusuf's joy. Sahag was frightened not so much by this memory as by the fact that it was still possible for him to remember after so long. "What's wrong, Garbis?"

he asked, smoothing his way—in other words, opening the door for him and removing obstacles from his path: flower pots and gardening tools, which Grandfather would have tripped over, given his eyes were fixed on some point overhead. He sat down on the bench beneath the apricot tree. Sahag plumped up the soft pillows for him, and the only thing he could think of doing was rushing inside to make two cups of coffee. One cup he placed in front of Grandfather, and he sipped from the other, slurping noisily, to whet his appetite. "What's wrong, Garbis?" Sahag asked once again when he saw that even the aroma of the coffee had failed to bring him to his senses. When Grandfather finally picked up the cup to take a sip, Sahag was about to point out that the coffee was very hot, but Grandfather did not seem to burn himself. As was plain from his distractedness, his nerves had retracted from his fingertips and bunched up inside his heart. It was then that Grandfather uttered his final words, not with the solemnity of endmost things but in a whisper, which, as we shall see, was to have a dramatic outcome: "It is finished . . . Finally, it is finished . . ."

He sat motionless, struggling to keep his eyes open. He sat with his back straight, his hands resting on his knees, exactly the same as the patresfamilias of his relatives in Afion Karahisar must have sat, surrounded by their women and children in the photographs taken around the year 1915, when Armenians throughout Anatolia, as if with a presentiment of what was going to happen, decided to have their photographs taken while they were all still alive. If, by some magic, the faces in the photographs had vanished as each person died, then just a year or two after they were taken, those photographs would have shown a strange sight: empty chairs, walking sticks standing suspended without any support, children hovering in the laps of invisible mothers, mothers wrapping their arms around empty space; they would have looked like the fictions of exorcists in search of a nation of ghosts. My grandmother Arshaluis and her sister Armenuhi, Sahag's wife, looked through the curtains of the kitchen window in fright. Not understanding what was going on and thinking it was all a game, we children peeped from behind the apple trees at the bottom of the garden. Grandfather Garabet did not take any notice of us and looked fixedly ahead of him, as if waiting for a photographer visible only to him to signal him to step inside or outside the frame. With the bewildered Uncle Sahag sitting in front of him, Grandfather waited for the others, the new dead, to take their seats to his right and left. In our yard, they gathered for the group portrait, the rows of their heads receding into the distance. When they were all assembled, the photographer raised his arm, and as he abruptly lowered it, the powder flashed in the pan. In that instant the preparation for my grandfather Garabet's death began. He rose to his feet unsteadily, or at least so it seemed to us, but perhaps he moved steadily, forgetting to sway to the pitching of the world. The women breathed a sigh of relief, believing it was still one of his bouts of solitude and waiting patiently for him to recover as night fell. But when night fell, they were still waiting; they even forgot to send us off to bed, and we all stood in front of Grandfather's door, which he had closed on us but which we were too timid to open. Behind the door could be heard a kind of droning lament, like the murmur of the camps at Deir-ez-Zor, the uninterrupted whisper of someone who does not pause even to draw breath, as if eager to pour out all the life in him. It was a lament without sadness, like a medieval *sharakan* or a Buddhist mantra, a polyphonic chant rising from all the ventricles of the chest, which summoned death, the same death that had all too often come unexpectedly to my grandparents' people; he now called for it to bring its gift, which is to say, to come when it was called. In the morning, the lament that welled from his chest fell silent, and all of a sudden a host of birds appeared in our yard.

Uncle Sahag was the first to venture to open the door and step inside. Grandfather was lying on the bed; he was still alive, and he turned his head to look at him. His brow was beaded with sweat, and Grandmother mopped his temples with the hem of her long dress. He did not answer their questions. "It is finished," said Sahag Sheitanian in his stead; "finally, it is finished." But he was unable to tell the others about the wooden horses or about the last one in particular, the white horse that signaled that the blood streaming from beneath the saddle and dripping from the bridle had ceased to be foreign blood and that those whose crimes the will of the Lord had tolerated on this earth had nonetheless not been able to escape the judgment of men, who had made up for the will of a God who had proven inattentive in the twentieth century. After more than half a century, Armen Garo's list had been exhausted. "It is finished," Grandfather had whispered to the goddess Nemesis as she danced with glittering eyes, barefoot, with bells around her ankles. "It is finished," he had whispered, but perhaps because of the din of the bells and drums, the goddess seems not to have heard.

Grandmother sent for Dr. Zilbermann, who had long since changed his name to Argintaru. He examined Grandfather, listened to his heart, took his blood pressure, laid his palm on his damp brow, but could not find anything wrong. He prescribed a few medicaments to fortify him. Uncle Sahag saw the doctor to the gate. The doctor looked at the birds in puzzlement and remarked that it was probably going to snow. He refused to accept any money for the consultation, and this was an alarming sign. Dr. Zilbermann now told Sahag, man to man, that he could not find evidence of any illness, but what alarmed him most was the moaning lament. "It's a new illness," he said, "I've encountered in our old Jewish folk who came back from the camps. There's no name for it in the medical textbooks, and no cure has been found."

Grandfather Garabet languished for another two weeks. He refused to eat and drank only tea. They took turns to sit by his bedside and mop his brow. He did not have a temperature, but the sweat poured from his brow as if he had a high fever. Since he refused food and took water only with pills, whose only effect was to reassure those who administered them since they had no effect on him, his body withered; his muscles shriveled, coiling around his bones like thick ropes, tying him down; the skin on his face retracted; his cheekbones protruded, leaving his hooked nose to jut awkwardly; and even when half closed, his eyes bulged, set in fleshless sockets.

As his beard grew, bristly and gray at first, then turning soft and pellucid, hanging like bunches of seaweed on either side of his face, Grandfather began more and more to resemble Father Komitas. When they covered his bald pate with the towel to mop his sweat, he resembled the death mask of General Andranik. When they pulled the blanket up to his chin or when he opened his eyes, which illumined the pallor of his cheeks, drily, unnaturally, then his face was transformed once more. Before he arrived at his own death, he passed through a series of other deaths. In the mother's womb, the fetus resembles a series of other, completely different things: an euglena, a larva, a fish, then a crossopterygian learning to crawl on dry land, all of which might easily be reckoned to be misshapen if their purpose had not been scientifically discovered. Ontogeny repeats phylogeny, as I was to learn at school a few years later. Before it is born and becomes itself, the baby repeats the faces of all the other babies before it. Lying peacefully in his bed, his arms next to his body and his eyes half closed, almost motionless but occasionally writhing and groaning in the womb of death, my grandfather repeated the faces of all the dead before him. When death gave birth to him, a man aged, hollow-cheeked, swathed in his soft, atrophied muscles like a mummy, his brow cold and translucent, he became himself once more, death's newly born babe.

My father decided that the moment had come for us to bid Grandfather farewell. He took me and my brother Melik by the hand; he kissed us, telling us to be brave; and he led us into Grandfather's room, which Grandmother had taken care to tidy up, sprinkling a little perfume, which rather than freshening the air only made it thicker. She had drawn the curtain to let in enough light for us to see. I looked at the mirror that we had not been able to photograph. For an instant I thought that the angle of Grandfather's eyes to the mirror was the one we had sought for so long.

The smell was new to me: the stuffy air around a creature that only exhale without inhaling. We sat down on the chairs that had been placed there in readiness for us; we were told to keep quiet, and we did so, sitting with our ankles pressed together and our hands on our knees. Grandfather Garabet slowly turned his head toward us and opened his eyes. They were now dark; the pupils had dilated, trying to see as much as they could, but relying on as little light as they could. This is the last memory I have of my grandfather alive, although it is not very clear from which side of the gates of death his eyes were peering. But he would have wanted it like that since, as the living Grandfather Garabet used to say, each people is defined by something that comes neither from names, nor from places, nor from the dead, nor from cities but that belongs to that people alone, and the Armenians can best be understood by their eyes, which are large, elongated, with turned-up eyelashes and thick eyebrows, eyes dusky and melancholy, even when, on rare occasions, they are light colored. After he entrusted to me the look in his eyes, my grandfather Garabet unexpectedly spoke.

He had a new voice, which came from deep inside him but which I could hear as if it were whispering in my ear. He moved his lips very slowly; he exhaled the words rather than speaking them, and that is why they thrummed. What he said to me seemed to have a definite meaning; I thought I could understand it, and I strained to listen, not to miss a single syllable. But in fact I did not understand a jot of it. I turned toward my brother, who was looking at the floor in embarrassment. Then I turned to my father, who was standing with his back to us. He sensed my eyes on him, like a cry for help, and he patted me on the head. I would have liked to know if they understood anything of what Grandfather had said, but they did merely what they had to do. I was the only one who struggled to understand, whereas for everybody else things were clear. Grandfather was talking in that unusual voice, which seemed to come from the whole of his body, from the pit of his stomach; it was guttural; it was nasal; it was staccato; it was slurred. But I could not understand the words. They were reassuring, uttered in a tone devoid of sadness; they revealed a secret that—of this I am sure—he would have liked me alone to understand but in a way that I would not be able to pass on further, and that is why he fixed me with those dark eyes. Much later, when I ventured to ask my father, Berj Vosganian, what Grandfather had said, he confessed that he had not understood very much of it either. The words were jumbled, coming from every language Grandfather spoke, particularly those of his childhood: Turkish, Russian, Arabic, Persian. They were hidden memories, unswallowed mouthfuls, quelled fears, words heard at other deathbeds and repeated to me, things that I ought to have known or merely intuited because they had to be discovered gradually. Child that I was, I ought to have looked aside; it was more than I was capable of understanding, but I could not tear my eyes away from his. My grandfather was imparting something to me, and I received it until he fell silent, as unexpectedly as he had started speaking.

As I grew up and began to think not only in joys and fears, but also in words, I observed to my surprise that the voice that sounded in my ears, now speaking my words, was that unusual voice of my grandfather's, a voice consisting of vibrations; it was the way Arshag the bell ringer, overwhelmed among the ever-descending birds, would have liked people to speak in an ideal world. My grandfather's voice had become my inner voice.

The chrism is refreshed every seven years. The new chrism, consisting of the essential oil of more than a hundred different herbs, is poured over the old, and the Catholicos mixes it using the golden arm that encases the relics of St. Gregory the Illuminator. The renewed chrism is sent to Armenian communities throughout the world, and on the Feast of the Epiphany it is poured into a silver bird. From the beak of the bird a few drops of chrism are poured into the water that is to be consecrated. When I was baptized in the silver-plated font of the Armenian church of St. Mary in Focşani, on my forehead I received the sign of the cross, anointed with that chrism, which, if we think of how it is mixed by the Catholicos, might be said still to contain a few drops of the first chrism, mixed not with the golden arm, but by the arm of Gregory the Illuminator himself. The chrism is one of the gifts given us by the old dead that still remains fresh. I received the inner voice from my grandfather in a similar way; the old words were poured into the new. This inner voice, passed down from generation to generation, is perhaps still a living gift received from the old dead. This is a hypothesis, of course. It will be borne out only in the moment when I, in my own turn, impart the voice, but as to this, somebody else will have to tell the story.

I did not enter the room again until a week later, when Grandmother Arshaluis, with the practicality that women maintain even in tragic situations, changed the bed sheets, drew the curtains, and opened the windows wide. The large mirror remained covered until the fortieth-day memorial service, but I can confess that during that interval I entered the room many times and drew the black veil slightly aside, looking into the gleam of the mirror as if through a half-open door. It rejoiced to receive the light, like when you bring a tethered animal food.

Arshag the bell ringer sat among the birds in the yard. The more they thronged the branches and the more the larger, blacker ones sat with folded wings on the paths and flowerbeds, the more he felt they had come for him, and with outstretched arms he begged the birds' forgiveness. And when the first bird landed on his shoulder, ignoring that he was the hunter of birds or mistaking him for a tree as he kept vigil, Arshag felt that there was nothing more to be done; he knocked on the kitchen window and made a sign for Grandmother to go for the priest and the other members of the parochial council. Since Grandmother Arshaluis was sitting huddled on a chair, holding the corner of a handkerchief to her eyes, Arshag did not wait for her permission but walked to the gate, moving the birds aside, like a curtain.

They entered the kitchen and sat around the table in silence. Grandmother put a plate of small, dry cakes in the middle of the table and poured them each a cup of coffee. They drank without speaking. The young archimandrite Zareh Baronian was sitting at the head of the table. He made the sign of the cross, and the others received it. They then took the cakes and either dipped them in the coffee or nibbled them, rolling them around their mouths to crumble them between their gums. They tried to drink without making a sound, which was a new trial for them when sipping coffee. They kept their eyes lowered, each fearful that the others would silently urge him to enter first and with the awkwardness a man feels when another's destiny forces him to confront his own.

Mgrditch Tcheslov understood that as he was the youngest, it was easier for him to pluck up courage, so he entered first. A black light enveloped him, and the door closed behind him. The others waited, craning their necks.

"He thinks he is in the Seferian vault," said Mgrditch Tcheslov, sitting back down in the kitchen.

Perhaps the world as they knew it had narrowed to the width of the Seferian vault, and the vault had expanded as wide as the new world. Then Arshag the bell ringer entered. Because he was unable to hear Grandfather Garabet and since he understood nothing from the movement of his lips, either because it was too dark or because Grandfather spoke without moving his lips, Arshag laid his palms on his chest to read the vibrations.

"He thinks he is a bell," said Arshag, lifting his palms for the others to see.

"He thinks I am Anton Merzian," said Krikor Minasian, the other cobbler on Main Street, in bewilderment.

"He thinks I am Krikor Minasian," said Anton Merzian, when he came out. "Which, from death's point of view, is the same thing, isn't it?"

As Ohannes Krikorian was about to enter, Father Baronian stopped him, raising his right hand, with his forefinger pointing upward and his middle finger touching his thumb, the sign of the Archangel Michael.

"Let the others enter," said Archimandrite Baronian. "You are already dead. What do you care what he says?"

"But I don't want to hear what he says," whispered Ohannes Krikorian. "I want to talk to him. I long to see him."

338

"For that, have a little more patience. For the other things, may God forgive
you!"

Then it was Ştefănucă Ibrăileanu's turn. Before he stood up, he took another
puff on his cigarette, to make it plain he was alive.

"He thinks I'm his father, old man Kevork, whom I never even met," he said,
and nobody asked him how he had understood that; if Grandfather Garabet had
thought him his father, he would have spoken to him in Armenian or Turkish.

Vrej Papazian stayed inside the room a long time. Because he had stored up
courage as he waited, or perhaps because he had a good heart, he listened with
greater patience. When he came out, they looked at him curiously.

"He thinks he has understood," he said.

Being the son of Father Dajad, Agop Aslanian was troubled when he came
out.

"He thinks I am he," he said, with a look that pleaded for help.

Then Sahag Sheitanian went inside.

"He thinks he is himself!"

"Then the time has come," said the young archimandrite Zareh Baronian.

The priest went inside, administered the last rites, and freed him.

On the night of November 27–28, 1968, my grandfather Garabet Vosganian
thus died prepared.

We children were not allowed inside our grandparents' house in the days
before the funeral. We stayed with Aunt Armenuhi in the row of houses at the
front. I know only that Grandfather's brow inexplicably continued to bead with
sweat, which, until the signs of death became obvious, made Dr. Zilbermann
believe that it was a case of clinical death. But such a thing was not in my grandfather's nature.

Because of that sweat, which at first was scalding and then not as cold as it
should have been, a large part of his body quite simply evaporated, like water in
the sun. Later, helping to place my other grandfather, Setrak Melikian, in his
coffin, I remembered what had happened during Grandfather Garabet's death;
he was as light as a bird; his bones had become porous and friable. And the birds
kept vigil. They dispersed only much later, to the trees in the cemetery and then
to the station depot, where there was a train of grain wagons.

The cortege set off from the Armenian church and followed the route of the
ark, down Tanners Street and across the railway tracks. As Mantu was dead and
his brass band had been scattered, there was nobody to part the smoke, to stop
the steam rising from the earth or the clouds descending from the sky, so on the
last day of autumn 1968, the city was shrouded in a fine mist. Walking behind
the truck, in which the coffin rested on a carpet rather too colorful for such an

occasion, I thought I was taking part in something out of the ordinary, a huge cortege, which the whole world watched with bated breath. I was grief-stricken, but like a child, I was proud of my grief and the fact that people stopped to watch us from the sidewalk, taking their hats off and making the sign of the cross. Now, if I think about it, I remember there were only a few dozen people, a disparate group rather than a cortege in the full sense of the word; never will there be as many as there were when they interred the ark, when they amassed all the questions about what was going to happen.

Now, writing *The Book of Whispers*, I realize that my walk behind the truck slowly carrying the coffin did not stop at the Cîmpineanca crossing, where the Armenian cemetery began down a road to the right; that walk is still going on. I walked with slow steps, wearing my checked overcoat, handed down from my older brother; my arms and legs had grown longer in the meantime; the overcoat was too small for me; I could barely button it across my chest; I was growing up; I was an adolescent; I had inherited the elongated, dusky eyes of my people. When Grandmother Arshaluis, Aunt Armenuhi, Uncle Sahag Sheitanian, Grandfather Setrak Melikian, and Grandmother Sofia tired, they climbed onto the truck, to rest on the flowery carpet. Ever since then my life has in large part been that walk behind someone who is too tired, and I have come to understand that no matter how alone I might feel, the loneliness of the funeral cortege is the loneliest of all. I did not break the ranks of the procession; I was too close to the coffin; nor could I walk faster because you cannot overtake the dead.

Nor could they go faster. We came to a stop, some of us in embarrassment, others startled out of their thoughts, in front of the lowering railway barrier. Grandfather had been a patient man; I had never seen him in a hurry. The only time my grandfather is known to have run is on Christmas Day 1944, holding the box of shoes and hearing behind him, from next to the truck with the tarpaulin taking my uncles Hovnanian and the others to Siberia, the rifle aimed at him click as it was cocked. I often saw him motionless but never wasting his time or pointlessly hanging around. Perhaps the wait in front of the lowered railway barrier had its purpose; everything came to a stop in front of its red and white stripes, with the lantern swinging in the middle: the truck, the mists that caused earth and heaven to merge, the birds, and us. The Bucharest train came slowly from the station and paused for a moment by the road. It was the same train that had carried so many characters in our stories. They now appeared at the windows: my uncle Sahag Sheitanian on his way to Bucharest carrying empty jute sacks to fill with grain in Craiova during the famine or on his way back with Mikael Noradungian's maps; Harutiun Frenkian, with his threadbare overcoat wrapped over his sweat-thickened smoking jacket, carrying sacks of walnuts; Misak Torlakian, with his wooden horse in his pocket; Uncle Simon on his way to the port and thence across the sea; and so many others, setting out on their journeys, waving farewell, or stopping to call Grandfather to climb aboard. It may well be that this actually happened. The locomotive suddenly gave a hearty whistle and pulled away, pulling its carriages behind it. The mists mingled with the steam from the locomotives, and so too the birds. The cortege set in motion, the truck rumbled over the railway tracks, the coffin bumped up and down, alive, and everything else took its normal course. The young archimandrite Zareh Baronian recited the prayers in his beautiful voice, accompanied by Arshag the bell ringer, who looked at the birds in fright, not knowing whether they had come for him or for Grandfather Garabet, although in the end it proved to be both the one and the other.

The family stood around the open grave. My father held my hand and my brother's, and the two of us looked at our shoes, frightened by the curiosity that impelled us to look up at the face of the deceased. From time to time, Grandmother Arshaluis approached the coffin to wipe away the sweat that still beaded Grandfather's brow. Aunt Armenuhi and Uncle Sahag were there too. On Sahag's shoulder perched a black bird that had the face of Yusuf. It was one of those birds from the raven family that live long, and it stubbornly reminded us that memories outlive us. Then came the next circle—the members of the parochial council, neighbors, and others whom we did not know but who had joined the cortege, wishing to be witnesses to the event that was death because nothing otherwise happened in their lives. The fine mist had settled behind us but not as low as the blades of grass frozen in the November chill. It came as low as the height of a man since unlike our eyes, which could not see them, the mist could distinguish the new dead, standing in the outermost circle, and it descended only as far as their shoulders. What we did see, however, at eye level, was another kind of mist, which was reddish because we could see only the wounds of the new dead, wounds that had not yet closed.

Then we each approached the coffin before it closed so that we might kiss the brow of the deceased. I did so with my eyes closed, guided by Father. Since Grandmother had not wiped away the beads of sweat, the forehead was as cold and damp as a tree trunk, and the salty taste remained on my lips. What is for sure is that in a way death wanted my grandfather Garabet alive. Before the coffin was closed, Sahag Sheitanian took out the folder whose thick covers enclosed the story of Operation Nemesis and the galloping wooden horses, and he laid it on the deceased's chest next to the icon placed between his joined hands to ward off the devil now that the body was helpless to defend itself. And as the archimandrite recited *Hayr mer*, Sahag repeated the whispers that had freed Grandfather: "It is finished; finally, it is finished . . ."

But since *The Book of Whispers* will never come to an end as long as fear exists in the world, the words spoken by Grandfather in a whisper did not have the power of finality. This time, my wise grandfather had been mistaken. It was not yet finished. Five years later, at the Baltimore Hotel in Los Angeles, an Armenian of almost eighty, who was therefore born at the same time as *The Book of Whispers*, Gourgen Yanikian by name, shot dead the Turkish consul and his secretary. And that the twentieth century after Christ might not remain merely a century of bewilderment and aberrations but also of absurdity, as *The Book of Whispers* comes to a close, the century too forms a perfect circle, like the serpent swallowing its tail, and returns to Trebizond. There, exactly a hundred years after the birth of Misak Torlakian, a boy was born into a Turkish family, and, raised in hatred, while still a young man he murdered Armenian journalist Hrant Dink on February 14, 2007.

After the coffin was lowered into the grave and the clods of earth were cast, we left the cemetery, we in our way, Grandfather in his, and the birds in theirs. All that remained were the mists, entire convoys of translucent beings, walking slowly, unnaturally, like a dream unreeling backward, so many unlived lives, giving birth to the children and grandchildren that never lived and enveloping their companions on this earth, the protagonists of this book and of others yet to be written, in a fine mist of the new and not fully named dead, a bittersweet-tasting melancholy, like air through which no bird has passed.

ACKNOWLEDGMENTS

First of all, I thank all those who, through their writings, through their study and research, through the public stances they have taken, and through their convictions have brought to light the subject matter explored in this book, have kept it in the public eye, and have made it a part of history, albeit one still not reconciled.

I thank those who read the manuscript, providing useful suggestions: Madeleine Karacasian, Eduard Jeamgocian, Sergiu Selian, Arptar Sahagian, Bedros Horasangian, and Mihai Stepan-Cazazian.

For his meticulous work in reading and preparing the manuscript for publication, I thank Ştefan Agopian, and also Magdalena Bedrosian and Bianca Cernat.

For the freshness of the details they provided about the Focşani of yesteryear, I thank Teodora Fântânaru, head of the Duiliu Zamfirescu County Library; Horia Dumitrescu, head of the Museum of Vrancea; and Teodor Passan, head of the Focşani Philatelic Association.

I thank Silviu Lupescu and his young team of professionals at the Polirom publishing house.

I thank brothers Anoush and Agop Kirmizian, Berj Margarian, Arakel Musayan, Antranig Pilosian, Vartan Arakelian, Vramshabuh Derderian, Sharam Hazarian, Harutiun Bartumian, Simon Tavitian, Levon Harutiunian, Bogdan Arşag Căuş, and so many others who, by bringing together their memories and nostalgias, created this book together with me.

I thank my parents for guiding me with their recollections toward the past generations and for being alive.

Armenian

The Armenian alphabet was invented by Saint Mesrop Mashtots at the beginning of the fifth century and is unique to the Armenian language. Each letter of the Armenian alphabet, or *Hayots' aybuben*, stands for a distinct vowel or consonant, some of which have no real equivalent in English—for example, the aspirated velar stop (*k'*), the voiceless postalveolar affricate (*č*), and the voiced velar/uvular fricative (*ġ*). There are various systems for transliterating Armenian, but in the English translation of *The Book of Whispers*, Armenian proper names are spelled in such a way as to allow approximate pronunciation on the part of readers unfamiliar with the language; spellings also reflect those current among Americans of Armenian ancestry. Thus, for example, the common Armenian forename meaning "Baptist" may be transliterated "Mkrtič'" but in keeping with usage among Armenian Americans is spelled "Mgrditch" (pronounced *Muh-gurr-deech*) in the translation. It should be noted that the pronunciation of Armenian names differs according to the two standard forms of the language, Eastern (Classical) and Western. A number of Eastern Armenian voiced consonants (*b, g, d*) are pronounced as unvoiced in Western Armenian (*p, k, t*), and a series of Eastern Armenian unvoiced consonants (*ts, p, k, t*) are pronounced as voiced (*dz, b, g, d*) in Western Armenian. Thus, the Eastern Armenian names Grigor, Gevorg, Petros, Ruben, Tigran, Hakob, Mkrtitch (*Muh-kurr-teech*) are pronounced Krikor, Kevork, Bedros, Rupen, Dikran, Hagop, Mgrditch in Western Armenian. In *The Book of Whispers*, the old Armenians of the author's childhood, who before the genocide had been natives of Anatolia, spoke Western Armenian, and this is reflected in their names. On the other hand, the names of the Armenian historical figures who appear in the novel are spelled in accordance with Classical Armenian, since this is how the figures in question are generally referred to in the history books: for example Father Komitas rather than Gomidas, General Andranik rather than Antranig.

Romanian

Romanian proper names are reproduced according to the original Romanian orthography. The Romanian characters ş and ţ are pronounced *sh* and *ts*, respectively. Most Romanian names have multiple diminutives: for example,

Ana gives Anca, Ancuța, Anuța, Anişoara etc.; Ion (= John; pronounced Yon) gives Ionuț, Ionel. In the translation, when a character is also referred to by a diminutive, the diminutive is given in brackets after the first mention of his or her name. It should also be noted that a particular name may have a number of variants: for example, three different characters appear in *The Book of Whispers*, called, respectively, Nicolae, Niculae, and Neculai, all of which are Romanian for Nicholas.

VARUJAN VOSGANIAN is a Romanian author and Prime-Vice President of the Union of Writers in Romania. He has been a member of Parliament since 1990 and was Minister of Economy and Finance. *The Book of Whispers* has been translated into more than twenty languages; it is his first translation into English.

ALISTAIR IAN BLYTH was born in 1970 in Sunderland, England. He studied at the universities of Cambridge and Durham. He moved to Romania in 1999 and now resides in Bucharest. He has translated numerous works of fiction and philosophy from the Romanian.